STAR KIN

by

Brian Toups

This book is a work of fiction. Any references to historical or literary
figures, living or dead, are used fictitiously. All characters, cities, and
adventures bearing any resemblance to actual people, places, or
incidents are entirely coincidental.

Star Kin: First Edition

ISBN: 9781095589397

To my mother, who introduced me to elves, dragons, angels

and talking lions.

And to my father, who taught me when to close the books

and make some human friends.

✒ CONTENTS ✒

CHAPTER 1
Pearl of the Stars

IT'S BEEN THREE WINTERS since I fell from the sky. I have no memory of the descent or the faraway place I came from. Only that it was dark, a starless void haunted by lost echoes.

My first clear memory is of an invisible weight smothering me, lining my skin like burial cloth. Then the metallic shriek of landfall, my first breath of living air, the way the fear drained out of me at the cautious touch of a stranger. Most of what I know about this world and my place in it I learned from my father, Lux.

He was in the vale planting seeds of barley when he saw me from afar. I came like a shooting star, passing through the emptiness of heaven, all fire and silver dust. My impact tore a hole in the nearest pasture a hundred yards long, and the dust rose and swept across the sky.

"Like an earthquake, it was!" Father would say. "The land in labor and a great ringing bell!"

A band of horseman followed the trail of fire and vapor tints. They came carrying the king's banner, a hunting falcon embroidered in blue thread. Their hoofbeats were like distant thunder, mowing down fields of marigolds until a cloak of severed petals encircled them, soft and violent in the wind.

Lux arrived first, climbed down into the crater, and found to his amazement—me—a girl-child alive amid the scorched wheat.

I could not speak, so he crawled through the glowing

wreckage that smelled of planets and galaxies, metal and fire. The space-dust clung to his boots. The heat of my cocoon glazed his face with sweat, but the inner shell was cool with frost, yawning like a cracked oyster.

Stooping, he lifted me from my bed of mercury, my body small and weightless in his arms, my skin like chased silver. My eyes fluttered, but I did not cry out as he bore me to safety. The new wheat, green as grass, was not yet tall enough to hide in, so he crossed the shallow troughs of black soil to the waterhole where he had left his plow that morning.

Cradling me in one arm, he refastened his bag of seeds to his hip, wishing he had not left such large footprints inside the crater. He knelt behind the rusted plow and wrapped me in his dirty cloak to conceal my glow.

"What a pathetic concealment it was!" he'd say when recounting the story to me by the fireplace. "An angel in rags is still an angel."

I blush, even now, thinking about it.

Hastily, he brushed the phosphorescent dust from his boots and wondered what he, a free man tending the acres he'd earned during the wars, would tell the royal knights and gilded riders. He knew as well as anyone how the sky divided his world from the worlds beyond and how, at certain times, in certain places, the boundary would wear thin, fray, even tear open.

"The king," he'd explain in his rough, fatherly tones, "like any good megalomaniac, had announced his claim on anything that came from the sky. I knew the risk of hiding you from him, but . . ." And his eyes would turn to green mist. "If only you had seen yourself as I saw you, Ava."

The horsemen arrived from the north, twelve armed

soldiers from the kingdom Vanfell over the mountains. And at their head, flanked by six knights and six squires, the High King Sol. The mounted men stopped in a cloud of drifting dust and formed a wide circle around the crater, examining it with fearful curiosity.

The king, circling the outer rim at a canter, spotted Lux from his tall steed. He called out from a distance. "You there! What is your name?"

"I am Lux," he replied, kneeling as best he could with a child in his arms.

"Do you tend these fields?"

"I do." Lux rose stiffly, head bowed. "I saw an object fall from heaven, so I came to see what it was."

One of the squires dismounted but was unable to approach the wreckage. "It's too hot!" he called in a voice cracked with youth.

"I went to it," Lux admitted, knowing the king would find his bootprints. "But the heat drove me away."

"You're a brave man," said the king in a voice both respectful and threatening. He urged his mount closer and stopped an arm's length away. "And who is this?"

"This . . . is my daughter." A name descended from far away, and Lux knew it was not of his own making. "My daughter, Ava."

I can almost hear him say it, though I was little more than an infant at the time. "Father," I whisper into the desert wind, keeping him close by the memory of his stories and his laughter. *Where are you now? Do you hate me for what I did to you?*

It is my third week in the Star Hunters' watchtower, both prisoner and prize. Once a day, when the questions are over, they let me out onto a circular iron balcony where I can smell the desert valley smells and taste the cactus warmth and breathe deep of the lizard sounds and the shilling-glint of butterflies.

Standing there leaning against the railing, I can just make out the lights of Vanfell to the north where the mountains never thaw. Behind me the sun sets red and heatless. But my eyes are only for the pulsar fields, a haze of violet and silver dust far across the dunes.

The fields appeared gradually, nothing like my sudden fall, though we are surely connected. No one was allowed to enter, on pain of death, though some did—those with hearts for adventure or rebellion. I had my own reasons, and ever since I could crawl I was drawn to the fields like a caged bird to the sky. The wreckage of my cocoon had long been cleared away, but I would often go to the spot in the secret hours of the night to be alone with my joy and longing.

Lux worried about me. But he would not stop me from visiting the crash site, the only piece of home I knew. Now I wish he had. I wish he'd chained me up until dawn when the longing passed. Did I know what I was doing? I'd like to think I was innocent, a daring girl with stardust in her eyes. But perhaps not.

"That's enough." A stern voice catches me from behind, startling me. "Come inside."

I obey, saying nothing, not even looking at the inquisitor's face.

"The Lord of the Citadel is not pleased," he says. "We know who you are, witch, and where you came from. You can't hide the truth behind your unnatural age. He sent us looking for a child of four years, he did. And here you are, a girl grown." He removes his glove and slides his fingers across my cheek and neck, then tilts my chin up to look at him, watching my eyes. "You're something else, aren't you? The question is, what?"

I try to twist away, but he grips my jaw hard, his thumbnail digging into my skin. I grit my teeth, clutching at his wrist with both hands. He stoops closer and holds out his torch as if to burn me. "What is the secret of the pulsar fields?"

"I don't know," I plead, shutting my eyes from the heat.

"Where does its power come from?" He lifts me by my mouth until I am standing on my tiptoes.

"Tell me where my father is!" I hiss painfully. "One answer for another."

He grunts through an amused half-smile and shoves me away. "I'll have more questions in the morning." He shuts the iron door to the balcony and turns the key. "I've been patient with you, little witch. Gentle even. Tomorrow I hurt you."

He withdraws by a different door and locks me in. I sit huddled on my cushion hugging myself as the light goes out. I curl up and lie down and wait until tomorrow. My slim white gown is not much against the night cold, but I have never been troubled by the climate of Alta. Hot and cold never bothered Father, so they never bothered me. I lie unmoving, listening to the wind and pressing my fingers against a crack in the wall, the tower's icy vein.

I close my eyes for a long time.

A torch flares to life in the hallway, startling me out of a dream. Orange light flickers through the bars in my door, chasing away the moonlight. The lock turns and a small figure slips through the opening, closes the door behind him. It's a boy, hardly more than a child. I hop to my feet and we stare at each other for a long moment as if expecting recognition. He sets his torch on the floor and sits down beside it, legs crossed.

"Hi, little one," I say in what I hope is a voice of welcome.

He stares up at me, unblinking. He must be terrified. But he doesn't look it. Part of me wants to go to him, hug him, cradle his curly dark head and hold his soft hands and tell him everything will be all right. But I hesitate, wondering if this is some new trick of my captors. How did he get here? Why isn't there a guard to escort him? I try to smile. "Are you a prisoner?"

He blinks once, but no more, studying me. The torchlight flickers in his ocean gray eyes. I inch closer and sit across from him, brushing my hair behind one ear. "I'm Ava. What's your name?"

"Ava." His voice is strange, neither young nor old, soft as petals falling. "I have come for you. Are you ready to go?"

I stare back, astonished. "Go where? Who are you?"

"I am Oberon."

"How did you get here, Oberon?"

"Through the fields."

"You've been to the fields!"

He nods pleasantly and I can't help but be distracted by his many tattoos, the patterns of blue ink deep in his skin, covering his arms, legs, chest, and face. At this point, I'm not sure which is winning, skin or ink. Even the backs of his hands and his long fingers are covered in runes. Aside from brown trousers torn off at the knees, he is naked as a painting.

"Are you ready to leave?" he asks again.

"I am," I whisper, my voice faltering. "I mean, of course I am! I'm just a little scared is all."

"Don't be afraid."

"I can't help it. The way you walked in here out of nowhere, it's unsettling."

"I'm sorry, Ava."

"I shouldn't scare so easy," I say, breathing long and deep, trying to still my heart. "I wish I knew what these men want with me. They were hesitant at first, like they were afraid of me. But they grew bolder. Started examining my eyes and mouth, taking samples of . . . everything. They asked who I was, where I came from, and why I dared to walk the pulsar fields. They think I know something about the fields, that I can do things when I'm there, powerful things. I don't know how to answer. I just hope they'll realize they're wrong, that I'm really nobody."

"Do you believe that?" he asks.

"I don't know," I sob suddenly. "They haven't hurt me, not badly, but they mean to."

"You should follow me, Ava," the boy says, rising and turning his back, which is as tattooed as the rest of him. A fierce lion leaps out at me, its face as wide as his shoulders, its mane glowing. The jaws twitch, smiling and snarling, and the eyes blaze. Or is it only a trick of the firelight?

Oberon exits my cell and follows the corridor left. I hurry after, glancing from side to side. He moves at a quiet, confident pace, seeming unafraid and sure of the way. He did not bring the torch, but I see well in the dark, better than in daytime, better even than my father, who can see a lizard hatchling skimming the dunes a quarter mile off.

Locks click open at his touch. Stairs spiral underfoot. He

holds his finger to his lips, melting into the shadows as a torch flickers past in the next hall. I hold my breath, dreading discovery, but it never comes. We descend multiple stories, swiftly, with a few strategic pauses along the way, finally stopping before a triple-locked door of hewn stone.

He glances back at me, winks and touches the door. It opens with no more than a nudge, the bolts, chains, and other mechanisms sliding aside.

I follow, speechless. This boy must have a knack of some kind. I've read stories about mages who talk to the wind and hold fire in their hands, who speak to animals or become them—men and women who can reshape the *stuff* of the world just by imagining it. Could this boy be one of those?

We pass unhindered through the tower gate and into the cool night. Oberon pauses near the base of the tower as a sentry circles high above. "When I say, you need to run," he says, tapping his finger rhythmically against his knee. "Ready . . . now!"

We scamper across the dunes like hunted things. Down is easiest if you can stop from falling on your face. Then the climb—muscles burning, sand spraying everywhere, the air silky close. Part of me wants to cry out with exhilaration, but I restrain myself, at least while in earshot of the tower.

Oberon does not stop until we are several dunes away and deep in a recess, invisible to any searching eyes. Glancing back, all I can see of the tower is a long metallic cylinder pointing at the sky, a telescope.

"It is fifty miles more from here," he says, sitting in the sand and burying his toes and fingers. "The forest."

I sit beside him, panting, trying to slow my hummingbird heart. "You know where I live?"

He smiles, perhaps unsure of what to say. Then, as if reading the appropriate response from an index of body motions, he shrugs. "Are you hungry?"

I shake my head. "They feed me before bed."

"I see." He nods gratefully. "You may ask your questions now."

Stunned by his manner, I hesitate. He looks at me, smiling privately as if examining something pretty, a rock maybe, with no plans to ever look away. Unlike me, he seems totally unaffected by the escape. His chest rises evenly, his breaths soft despite the steep dunes we climbed. There are so many questions spinning in my head I can hardly think. Finally, I snatch one. "Why did you come to the tower tonight?"

"To set you free."

"But why risk it? I'm nobody to you."

"Because it was a wrongness to keep you there," he says meaningfully.

"Who were they, those men who captured me?"

"Star Hunters," he answers. "Astronomers, archeologists, soldiers: those who seek out fallen things to study and dissect. They serve Agon, a sworn lord to King Sol, and the protector of the outlands. He was ordered to find you and take you to the king."

"Why didn't he, then?"

"Agon thinks you are the key to mastering the pulsar fields."

"So he would betray his king and use me for his own?"

"Humans are capable of tremendous evil," Oberon says sadly. "We both know this, Ava."

"You speak as if they are something *other* than us."

"Are they not?"

"I don't know. All I know is I'm not the one they're looking for. I don't have powers. I can't control the pulsar fields, can't give them what they want."

"Perhaps," Oberon says, watching the night clouds.

"It's my fault," I say. "I was selfish to go so often into the fields. It's my fault they took my father away. I just couldn't stay away. I felt a connection when walking the silver sands. It was fleeting, sometimes present, sometimes as distant as my true home. But many nights, gazing up, I saw glimpses of where I came from in the light of falling stars."

Oberon looks at me sadly, but it might be better to say he looks *into* me. "I see your heart and it is not cruel, Ava. Only lost and full of yearning."

"How old are you?" I ask.

"I am three years in the world."

"You don't act like it," I say, trying to understand how youth and wisdom can coexist so seamlessly. "You speak to me like an elder, know things you shouldn't. Are you from the stars?"

"No," he says simply. "My home lies elsewhere."

I sit for a while longer and look at him looking at me. The air is cooling quickly with the night. The life that seems scorched to death during the day is coming out, and I close my eyes to enjoy the chirping of insects and the soft scurrying of burrowing mammals over moonlit sand. When I open them, Oberon is still watching me.

"My father . . ." I breathe, unable to repress my shudders. "He told me how I fell from the sky, how he found me in the silver ship. He would never keep a secret from me. He called me his pearl of the stars and made it clear it wasn't just a metaphor. He meant it. But somehow I always thought I was still . . . human. Do you know what happened to him?"

"He is beyond my sight. They took him to Vanfell."

"To be executed?" My heart throbs helplessly in my chest.

Oberon says nothing. He does not know.

"Can you rescue him like you did me?"

Again, he is silent, thinking. His face is that of a nine-year-old boy, but his eyes tell of depths and distances beyond imagining. "Your father's spirit is shrouded from my sight. He may no longer be in the city."

"Did he escape? Is he alive?"

"I don't know, Ava."

I nod tearfully. I want to help my father and can't. The city is so far. Oberon could take me there, couldn't he? But what then? The journey would take days, and we'd have to hide from every passing troop and caravan. What good could I do if Father is already gone? "What do we do now?" I ask, looking to this child for guidance.

He remains sad, as if escape for my father would mean something worse than death. "If you're rested, we will walk," he says. "Will you walk with me, Ava?"

I get up, standing a little taller than Oberon, resisting the urge to hold his hand as a mother might. It would be strange, holding a young boy's hand and knowing that he is not what he seems to be. That he, perhaps, is older than the moon and all the stars in the night sky, older than darkness or light.

I hold his hand anyway, comforted by it. It's so warm, a little smaller than mine. We walk in the moonlight, two lost children barefoot in the desert, not sure who we are.

CHAPTER II
Ashes

WE RIDE THE DUNES deep into the night and rest in a hollow in a cluster of rocks at dawn. Oberon does not sleep, but instead keeps watch while I dream in the shade. When it is evening, I scavenge chunks of cactus flesh to suck on, offering some to Oberon.

"Not for me," he says, smiling shyly.

"Come on, just a taste. Look, I've already plucked the spines for you."

"You need it more," he insists.

"If you say so."

We set out again, speaking little, the setting sun at our backs. The new night is clear as a dish of summer rain, a crescent moon rising. I catch glimpses of the pulsar fields as we walk, and something warms inside me at the sight of the swirling vapor and dust. We reach the outskirts and my heart is near to bursting with excitement. Oberon stops on a rocky ledge, peering down from a crouch. He waits, stiff as jackal with its hackles up. "They are watching," he says. "Star Hunters patrol the fields."

"By now they know I've escaped. It won't be safe to go home."

"You're safe with me, wherever you choose to go. I will protect you until we find your father."

I cannot argue with him. His presence makes me feel too young to have any opinion worth voicing. We pass with care into the valley by a hidden gorge and enter the place where the desert sands turn to silver dust and the winds do not come from any direction in the world, but from beyond it. We are over the edge and inside the pulsar fields.

"Won't the hunters catch us?" I ask, scared, even though it's dark, and the night is our protection.

Oberon's eyes narrow. "They will not."

We keep walking until nothing outside is visible. Only the swirling air, a little softer than desert air and a little warmer. Stars float like sparks in the air, and portals to other worlds gather and scatter on the verge of my perception. I feel weightless in some places and heavier in others. My gown clings to my skin, but I cannot feel it. I smell the icy maze of space and the distant blush of fading flowers in bloom.

Oberon looks around, his curly hair wild in the ethereal wind, his eyes like knife tips, the ink in his skin gleaming. He is remembering. Then he turns to me and asks, "What do you remember from your life before your vessel created the pulsar fields?"

I close my eyes. "Nothing, really. Silence. The dark."

"The fields only formed after you came here," Oberon says thoughtfully, smiling like a philosopher who has just proved God. "That's when I came into the world, sent forth by the Great Spirit to complete a focus. I do not know to what purpose I was created, but only that when I'm with you I no longer feel the need to travel, to move, to leave and forget. I can be still and close my eyes and not feel idle. I do right to be here."

"I'm glad you're here, Oberon."

"It all aligns in my mind. The geometry of chance—you falling into the world, me thrust into it, all in the same moment. It must mean our fates are intertwined."

"It must," I say, trusting him, but thinking other thoughts. "Do you think Sol still has my cocoon? If only we could see it and study it! Maybe I could learn from it."

"It is in Vanfell. I can take you there."

My face lights up for an instant, then falls. "Not until we find Father."

"I do not know where he is."

"The last thing he said to me was to run to the forest and find his sister. I hardly know her, and I didn't want to leave him. He meant to fight them off. But I never made it, and that means he didn't either. Maybe, if he escaped Vanfell, he would go to the forest looking for me."

"It would be a desperate hope. I suspect he knows you were captured."

I swallow painfully. "That would only make him suffer more."

"You know him best, Ava. I will help you along whatever path you choose."

I close my eyes, stilling the storm inside. "Please take me home. I have to see it . . . to say goodbye."

"As you wish." Oberon looks thoughtfully around. "The fields could hasten our travel. Come, I will teach you." He offers me his hand.

I reach out—and suddenly the whole landscape vanishes, and it is just him and me, lost in a gulf of stars. *Don't let go.* I hear his voice in my head. The air seems smoky, the violet so deep it's almost black. The stars flutter and spark like pieces of burning paper. They swirl around us as we sidestep through a fold in the fabric of space.

Somehow, without words, Oberon shows me his art— how he manipulates the energy in the fields. Could I do the same one day?

How far across the fields? I ask his spirit. *A day's journeying?*

There is no distance anymore, he responds, and I can almost see his quiet smile.

The horizon blurs, and we appear perfectly whole on the edge of the forest, the fields behind us. "That was amazing!" I gasp, staggering dizzily. "We traveled!"

"We did." He smiles proudly, looking back at the fields we just passed through.

I check to make sure my arms and legs still fit right. Then I remember where I am and sniff the air, wrinkling my nose. Oberon, noticing the soot-stained ground, puts a hand on my shoulder.

The forest stands silvery-fertile in the moonlight. The sounds are all familiar. Crickets, fireflies, and falling leaves. There's the stream where Father and I used to go for water. Here's the old wood-cutting stump, scored again and again by the axe. The rest is just . . . gone.

I stare blankly for a while, trying to cope, my bare toes crunching against the blackened spine of a book. I reach down to pick it up, and as I do, ashes, trapped between the folds of unburned paper, spill out and flutter downwind. The air makes them look alive, the ashes. But it's a mockery of real life. They move like bad actors in a burned down theater, and do not speak, having forgotten all their lines.

I walk amid them, touching the remains of a table leg, stumbling on a pot, putting my hands into the burnt-out fireplace. The rest is unrecognizable. I stoop to examine a blackened lump, half buried by sand. One of the goats, has to be. I kneel beside what's left of her, unable to resist the tears. They come, not in a flow, or in violent sobs, but in soft lines down my cheeks. Nothing stops their fall.

"Could you take me away from here, Oberon?" I ask, trembling. "Are there other worlds better and brighter than this one? Worlds where girls do not lose their fathers? Where nobody kills anyone, or burns things?"

He nods hesitantly. "There are such worlds."

"Could we live there together?" I whisper desperately, foolishly, knowing it is my own childishness speaking. "Could we run and run until everything is new?"

"I can take you anywhere, Ava."

I wipe my eyes, beautiful with grief, not for the house, or for the things in it, but for the memory of my father, who touched the things, and fixed them when they broke, and dusted them, and loved the walls he built, and the books on the walls, and who taught me to read and to sing and to love the stars.

I miss the father who cursed at the goats when they were noisy and sang to them when they were sick, who terrified strangers, who sheltered me, smothered me, hoarded me like a dragon's only treasure until my one wish was to get away, far away, and make my own life like the heroines in stories.

It is not that, now that he's gone, I do not see his faults. It's that now they've never looked so precious.

"You could really take me away?" I ask, unbelieving.

"Yes," he says. "But I cannot abide in the realms beyond. I cannot leave this world permanently until my time in it is finished."

Overwhelmed, I slump against the broken fireplace and put my head in my hands until the ash seeps into my dress, staining the white fabric an inky black. I do not care. Oberon stands not far off, thinking, waiting, listening to my soft sorrow. Then, as if feeling my feelings, he too begins to cry. The tattoos on his cheeks glisten.

After midnight, celestial fire lights up the sky, the same colors I used to watch with my father. I imagine a chorus of airless voices and a winter-light symphony, lending beauty to the darkness while the music lasts. Blue and gold, green and violet—when did I fall asleep?

Before dawn, amid my semi-articulate yawning, Oberon picks me up as if I am no more a burden than the moonlight reflecting off my skin. Silent as a prayer, he carries me to the outskirts of the forest and spreads a bed of leaves for us. There I sleep—Oberon lying on his back very near, eyes closed in an expression that looks like dreaming, though it is not.

CHAPTER III
The Sunless Vale

I AM DREAMING again, always of home. I dream of herbs and cactus broth in the morning. Of ripe peppers and sunberries growing by the stream. Of ornery goats and an old cow we never named.

"Where does the stream come from?" I ask my father, cupping cold water in my hands.

"The forest heart," he replies, washing the dirt from his face. "Your aunt sent it to us."

"Is it magic?"

"I reckon so. One of a kind. Better than a gold mine in this dry land."

"If only we had neighbors to share it with."

He laughs and wrings the water from his beard. "Oh Ava, you know I saved all my kindness for you."

Sometime later, in the way of dreams, we climb to the roof and watch the midnight fire, the lights that dance in the heavens when the night is darkest. Blue and gold, green and violet. We stay up all night watching the rainbow tints drift like curtains in a celestial breeze.

Father tells me stories of when he fought in the wars, of the maidens he saved and lost. He looks up and holds the moon in his eyes and strokes my black hair and tells me how beautiful I am and how fast his little girl is growing up. I fall asleep in his arms.

Afterwards, he helps me down and puts me to bed, humming an old heroic ballad, shielding me from nightmares with the deep tremors of his voice, even as the first light of dawn comes slanting through our kitchen window. Then he goes out to tend the garden and milk the goats.

Ava! A distant voice mingles with the bleating and the bells. *Ava, wake up now!*

I rise quickly, still wet from crying, and cling to Oberon's hand as he hurries me into the hollow of a tree. Men argue nearby—herds of them, thumping and crashing and blundering up the slope toward us. Torchlight gouges through the foliage, making everything naked.

"There on the ridge!" a man growls, rushing past. "Bring a torch!" Several more follow him, adjusting their helmet straps and muttering curses as they trip over roots and each other. When it seems the last has gone by, we dart from our hiding place, slipping and skittering in a flurry of leaves. Too soon.

"There!" A straggler charges after us, tossing his torch aside. "I've got her!" He reaches for me, but never makes it.

Something brushes my cheek, a puff of air maybe. With my back half turned, my breath hissing and heart pounding, I barely notice the soldier's grunt as something invisible knocks him hard into the dirt. "Gurgh!" he croaks, flailing on the ground, fumbling with the buckle of his dented breastplate.

More soldiers rush down from the ridge, but each is struck senseless by the same invisible hand, armor clinking, arms flopping and clutching. Their torches go out one by one like fireflies at dawn.

"Oberon, is that you?"

"Keep with me," he says, still holding my hand firmly. "A little farther."

A tall soldier emerges from the thorn-hedge in front of

us and levels his sword, a slimy grin on his face. We skid to a stop, inches from the glinting blade. Oberon holds one arm in front of me protectively. The other he levels toward his foe.

"There's a kid with her!" The soldier takes a swing at Oberon. "Another desert rat!" He lunges in, so close I can smell the liquor on his beard—but no farther. Just as with the others, an invisible force seizes him, lifts him like a rag doll, and hurls him through the thickest, longest thorns. He grinds away, screaming faintly, and thumps against a distant acacia trunk.

Speechless, I focus on Oberon's fingers, focus on not letting go and not looking back as I stumble out to the clearing where my house used to be. Ignoring the cries of pursuit, we charge headlong into the pulsar fields.

"Do you feel the portals?" Oberon asks.

"I think so!" I pant, flinging up moon dust with my toes. Portals, gates, momentary flaws in reality—I wonder if I've always felt them, doorways, just beyond the touchable. It's part of why I used to spend so much time here. I love these fields for the peace they bring, for the way they take me to the edge of what is. But there is nothing peaceful about being chased by a dozen armed men who hate you and mean to capture and abuse you.

"Here's one," Oberon says, reaching for a shimmer in the void.

The warp happens fast. The traveling, if there is any, takes no time at all. Oberon's whisper-hushed voice echoes in my thoughts as we emerge, hands clasped, in a sweeping, indigo valley with no sun, no clouds, nothing in the sky—only hills and rivers that run uphill and huge, shimmering rocks, and other features too strange for comparison.

"We are safe now." He sits down cross-legged, looking pleased with himself.

I collapse beside him on my back, heaving my relief and stretching my arms over my head. The purple grass is hard and cold, but I like the way it prickles my skin through my sooty, mud-stained dress. "Where are we?" I catch myself and say quickly, "I mean, thank you, Oberon, for saving me . . . again."

He gives one of his thoughtful, loving, mirthless smiles. "This is the Sunless Vale. It is the land between the worlds."

I look around, wondering at everything I see. What looked like shiny rocks before are actually animals, huge lumbering turtle-like creatures grazing on the purple grass. Something moves in the opaline sky like a bright ribbon drifting underwater. The air tastes thin and smells like green ivy and dry wood. A soundless breeze tousles my hair. "The land between . . . what does that mean?"

"It means we can go anywhere, Ava. Walk only a few miles in this valley, and you could turn up in Vanfell, or the Firstborn Lands, or on an island in the sea!"

"Take me to Vanfell!" I exclaim. "Father is there, I feel it. We have to save him! He would do the same for me."

"As you wish. Walk with me."

We walk. I follow behind, a bit unsteady at first, because the sharp grass tickles and hurts a little to walk on. I get used to it, distracting myself from the stinging by looking at things.

The ribbon in the sky moves a lot like the aurora lights of Alta, but it seems closer to the ground, more touchable. The trees here are silver-gray and mostly naked. They stand like scarecrows, always perfectly vertical, upraised branches nearly devoid of leaves. Passing close to one, I notice it has no bark, only a smooth, dull skin wrapping. Something with fur and two round, many-ringed eyes stares at me from inside a knothole.

"Oberon," I say hesitantly. "What do you know of the prophecy?"

"You mean *your* prophecy?" he says. "It's the reason King Sol studies the skies and dispatches Star Hunters every time something comes down."

"Father spoke of it like it was something everyone in the valley could recite. But he would never tell me what it was. He said it would only bewilder me. He liked to use funny words like *bewilder* to make me laugh and forget about the question I'd asked."

"It is not my place to speak of things your father withheld," Oberon says, sounding far too grown up for his body.

"I see whose side you're on!" I narrow my eyes teasingly, but he has not been with people long enough to be properly teased.

"Please don't be angry. You are what you are, Ava. What good is a prophecy to you?"

"That's the same thing Father would say!" I exclaim, imitating my father's rumble as best I can. "Make your own life, my daughter, and it will be the truer for it."

Oberon's gray eyes smile for a moment, shining like the sea. "I understand," he says with a note of conquest.

"Understand what?"

"Laughter."

We walk along an upwards-flowing stream, climbing

steadily. There are many such streams, all swiftly flowing toward the peaks of various hills. The rock-like animals I saw grazing earlier ignore us for the most part, but some raise their mammoth heads from drinking and turn bored, hairy faces with droopy ears and kaleidoscope eyes.

"Look at how they drink through their noses!" I exclaim, thirsty all of a sudden.

"Do not touch the water!" Oberon warns as we pass close.

"Is it poisoned?"

"It is not what you call water," he continues seriously. "These streams carry life and death, energy and substance. They flow because they are alive. Think of them as the silvery veins of the universe. Enter one in the wrong place, and you might end up swept away, or destroyed. But, flowing as they do, together composing all the fathomless energies of the multiverse, these streams are the key to traveling between worlds."

"This must be some special valley," I say.

"In my world the streams have a source, and that source has a Name. No one has glimpsed every part of the Name, for to do so would require an infinite mind. But each of us, through contemplation, experience pieces of the essence that is the Name, the Great Spirit."

"The one who sent you," I recall.

"Yes, the very same! I remember my first impression of your world." He breathes a light sigh and slows his pace long enough for me to come beside him and listen. "It was terrifying. Days passed in a cutting cycle of dark and light, sun and moon slicing gold and silver gashes through the sky. I had no idea how to begin living."

"What changed?" I ask, seeing him shudder at the memory. "How did you slow it all down?"

"I learned to control my perception of time and to interact with the creatures that call Alta home. I have found humans, with their soul-body unions, the most interesting of all."

"Thank you, I think," I giggle nervously. "I get the feeling that you're studying us."

"Oh certainly. I must not fail the Great Spirit."

"What happened after that?"

"I spent nearly three years traveling Alta, learning how to be human, preparing for the next step: to take physical form and do the will of the Spirit in a new way." He reaches down, running his fingers through the tall grass. "I can still remember touching things for the first time. It was like . . . a new birth. In my world, there are some who do not believe in material things, saying there is no evidence to support the existence of trees, colors, people, or any external world. But the Great Spirit showed me the truth."

"Who is the Spirit?"

"He is the maker of all," Oberon says reverently, and he seems to shiver with unutterable love. "His presence gives life and substance. It is in everything that is created. What do they call him in your world?"

"I don't know. Many things."

"He is *one*."

"I only know what I've read in books," I say, embarrassed. "My whole life is in books. Father had so many, though I never caught him reading them. I think he did once, a long time ago. I read them all."

"As have I." Oberon smiles gently, and I marvel at the

library of his mind. "What have you seen of the world outside?" he asks.

"I walked the fields at night," I say, touching the tall, bendy flowers that grow near the streams. At first they're soft as words of love—until the petals retract, and the stems sprout tiny silver thorns. "Ouch!" I stop touching them.

"Don't pay them any mind." Oberon swats one as it strikes at him. "They're tricky plants, but mostly harmless." He leads me away from the writhing, snaky things. "Tell me more about your life."

"Well," I say, sucking on my cut. "I never went far. In autumn, I'd spend quiet afternoons in the forest with the animals, listening to them. They liked me. Once, to repair an old plow and to buy another goat, we traveled to our neighbor village. I learned so much there that I couldn't find in books, like the sound of a group of people laughing, or the way it feels to make friends for no reason. But I've never been to a city."

"You are in for a surprise." Oberon looks at me as if fearing for my safety.

"It can't be that bad, can it?"

"Vanfell is not a kind place, Ava."

"I can handle it. There are dark places in stories, you know. Cities and things. Some of them feel real enough."

"Stories are real, and that's a fact," he agrees. "But you can always close the book. When unpleasant things surround you, touch you, breathe on you, sweat against your skin . . . then you will know what I'm talking about."

"We'll see." I swallow hard, hoping he is exaggerating.

While we talk, the stream narrows, terminating at the top of the hill in a circular pool, quite the opposite of a spring.

Instead of bubbling up, it sucks thirstily into its own depths, swirling like a stirred pot. I study my reflection in the water. "Somebody needs a bath." I rub my dirty cheeks and brush a few leaves from my hair.

"This will take us where you want to go," Oberon says, not listening.

"Could it take us somewhere else?"

"It could. The magic places of the worlds are all connected. But don't worry. I will guide us."

The closer I get to the pool, the more my skin tingles. I'm hot and cold and tickled and pinched all over. "What is that?"

"The flow of energy." He seems pleased. "You're sensitive to it. In your world, it is called magic, anima, or Art, but it exists in all worlds—a fathomless depth of energy for those who can sense it."

"Could I be a wizard one day?"

Oberon seems puzzled. He looks me up and down. "Normally, I can sense inherent power. But with you, I'm confused. Your spirit bears traces of your old home."

"But Alta is my home," I protest, suddenly defensive.

"Is it?"

"It is now. Everything I know and love is here."

"But you've only just left the place where you grew up. You've seen so little, and you know there's more out there. You've felt the call of the pulsar fields."

I don't know what to say. Then, shyly, I ask, "Could this pool take us to the stars? The stars of Alta, I mean. Wherever I came from, whatever I am."

"Not this one." Oberon looks far into the horizon as if searching for a single stream among distant mountains. "But another could. It is a long journey."

"Another time, then." I follow his gaze longingly, seeing only the haze of indistinct shapes. "We need to get to Vanfell."

"Take my hand," he says.

I hesitate. "Oberon, what if we could separate all the worlds like tangled hair. What if we could lay them all out, how many would there be?"

"Only the Great Spirit knows that, Ava. He fashioned them all."

"You can guess though, can't you?"

"All I know is this. Each world has a purpose, none was made without reason. And you would be better off trying to count how many blues make a red. Now take my hand."

I take it and close my eyes, trying not to think. One world is big enough for a girl. Too big even. The more I learn about the others, the more I'd like to hide in my bedroom, crawl under the warm, clean covers, close my eyes, and wish it all away. But I don't have a bedroom anymore, and now is no time to be soft, as Father would say.

We step together into the pool. The moment my foot touches it, seized by a sudden fear of annihilation, I nearly panic and spring away. Instead, I wrap my arms and legs around Oberon and cling to him, pressing my cheek against his. He inhales sharply, surprised and off balance, struggling to salvage his delicate spell. But the damage is already done.

CHAPTER IV
Beneath the Wine Trees

"THIS IS ALL MY fault, isn't it?" I ask, my nose flat against an earthy wall. "Are we underground? Smells like it." I tilt my head slightly to one side, wriggling to free my trapped arm.

Thank goodness Oberon is with me, wedged just above me in the cramped space. He looks around with his young-seeming eyes. "Good news," he says. "There's a light up above!"

We crawl single file through something like a giant rabbit hole, following the light, and emerge from a large tree knot into a bed of wine-red grass. I sprawl among the brittle spines, glad to be free of the tunnel. *Was that tree trying to eat us?* Then I notice my surroundings and gasp. "We're not on Alta anymore."

"Not even close," Oberon agrees.

We stand together in what feels like sunlight, though there is nothing but yellow-orange tints in the sky. The trees around us are cocoa-dark, intricately curved and hollow to the touch, with leaves like waving flags.

Oberon sniffs at the sparse forest of odd-shaped trees and listens as if trying to make out the lyrics in a distant song. "Aha," he mutters like a schoolboy finding a flaw in his addition. "I definitely took a wrong turn."

"It's comforting," I say, "knowing you're not perfect."

"*Something* must have distracted me when we entered the pool," he says seriously.

If he were a normal boy I would think he was teasing me.

I look away, blushing, wiping my hands on my sooty dress. "I'm sorry for jumping on you like that. The water . . . I looked into it and saw a million destinations and a million nothings. I was afraid of the space *between* spaces. I didn't know what to do, so I just held you."

"It's all right, Ava," he says, rubbing the back of his neck under his thick black curls.

"Do you know where we are, then?" I ask, hoping my foolishness does not cost us too much time.

Oberon catches a falling leaf in his hand and stares at it, thinking, perhaps searching for the right words to explain something complicated. He hands me the golden leaf. "There are many universes and many worlds in each," he begins slowly, as if instructing a child. "Creation is like a sand castle with many rooms, and each room is a universe, and within each room the stars and planets of smaller worlds spin and whirl."

"So, when you take a wrong turn and end up in a random world . . . how do you get back to the Sunless Vale?"

"It's a trick that's never the same twice," he says. "Every world has its magic. Places like the pulsar fields, where the film between the worlds is thinnest. All we have to do is find one."

"So anyone we meet will be aliens like me," I say happily.

"One could call them that." He seems unsatisfied with the term. "There are really no aliens, Ava. Only people from different homes. You are Ava. I am Oberon. We are all lost in someone else's sand castle in the end." He pauses, his face tattoos creasing with concentration. "Come. I think I've found another door."

We set out into the forest. It isn't long before the first

animals begin to appear, sniffing curiously at us. The friend-
liest ones are small, squirrel-like, with big ears and short red
fur to blend in with the leaves and grass. Though hesitant at
first, eventually they begin to cluster about our feet and crawl
on us and let us pet them, chattering sweetly in a secret
language.

"They have never once been hunted or tormented by
men," Oberon says. "That's why they are not afraid." He
whispers something to one and it leads us out of the forest.

"Goodbye squirrels!" I say as we reach a field of soft red
stuff like an endless fuzzy blanket. Violets, or something
similar, grow everywhere, swaying in unison. Oberon admires
the grapes in the low-branched trees and the berries on
bushes and the fruits that grow from the ground. All I want
to do is eat them, but he doesn't touch them.

"I'm so thirsty!" I say at last. "Is there something wrong
with eating in another world? Will it upset the balance of the
universe?"

He laughs. "Goodness no, Ava. Please, help yourself."

"You weren't eating, so I thought—"

"If you have been fasting on my account, I advise you to
put an end to that habit before you starve."

We pause and I drink my fill from a stream and eat a
snack of berries, trying to get Oberon to try one. He shrugs
and does so, nodding like a refined judge at the taste. Then he
hands the rest back to me. I do not gorge myself and only
take enough fruit to satisfy my cramping stomach.

"If you want to learn to be human you have to eat," I tell
him.

"Who says I want to be human?" He chews one more
berry to humor me. Afterward, we wander down into a valley,

following the drinking stream to a series of bathing pools. It's here that we find the most extraordinary creatures of all—people.

Oberon sees them first from afar and stops, observing, not wanting to scare them. The people are gathered near the pools, water sparkling on their golden skin. Some mingle in the shade of fruit trees or lounge by the banks. Others watch the dancing violets, moving their heads contentedly to the rhythmic sway. There is no wind, and yet the whole field is dancing.

Oberon watches those in the light with particular interest. "Look, by the wine tree," he says. "They are photosynthesizing."

"Doing what?"

"They are taking in the light of the sun. It's all they need to live—that and to absorb the rain like plants. All this food grows naturally for their pleasure."

"I don't see any sun," I say.

"The sky *is* the sun."

I look up and see that he is right. What I took before to be only a dusky yellow sky is actually the body of an enormous cold star, so close I can almost taste its boundless age and smell the fire bubbling from its surface, keeping it alive. How did I not notice it before? "Hello, star." I stretch my arms out as if to hug it.

"Look, a new sun rises." Oberon points to the horizon where I can now, with some effort, see a space where the huge sun ends and there is only sky. At the brink, a second, smaller sun has begun to rise.

"It's so hard to know what to look at when seeing a new world," I say. "The small differences distract from the great ones." I turn again to the people bathing and lounging in the suns. "They look so happy. They have everything they need, and nature gives it to them. It would be nice if it were like that on Alta, if nature gave us everything. There would be no wars and no reason to steal from each other."

"Would that it were so." Oberon looks at me sadly. "We are born. And the good earth is rich, and it gives us an abundance of food. And the skies give rain and the trees bear fruit, and yet we want more. Humans always want more."

"You confuse me, Oberon. One minute you're talking as if we're not human, and now listen to yourself."

"I am making a point," he mutters, and I imagine a testiness to his voice. "Now, come. Are you ready to open a door?"

Without waiting for an answer, he leads me to a grove of slender-dark trees with fan-shaped branches and clusters of shady auburn leaves. We sit together on the top of a small hill under the largest tree and watch the peaceful people of this world finish sunning, rise, and begin some sort of work.

"They are a young people," Oberon remarks, his back against a mossy rock. "They have not yet built things or explored science, though I suspect they will. They are a thinking race."

Above us, both suns seem to overlap in the sky, folding together like two hands cradling the earth. It is warmer now, but not too hot for comfort. The brightness makes the heavy leaves transparent, illuminating soft red veins.

Down the hill by the water, the golden people seem over-joyed and spread their bright arms to welcome the second sun. Children play games in the river, and their laughter is not words or music, or any sound at all. I feel it in my skin like a shiver, but warmer. When it's over, I instantly want it again.

"Take this." Oberon hands me a fruit from the tree, and I forget about the laughter as one forgets certain beautiful dreams.

We eat together, and it is more than just a snack this time. "You eat well," I say. "It's almost as if you enjoy it."

"It is a delightful activity," he agrees, oblivious to the juice on his chin.

"Just wait until you try sleeping. You might think it's pointless now, but dreaming is one of life's most precious gifts."

"What makes you say that?"

"There's a part of us that wakes up when our eyes close. A certain creative, mystifying, divine part. Just try it. That's all I can say."

"One thing at a time." He laughs through another bite of fruit. He raises his hand and brings a low-hanging branch down to his mouth and begins to suck on it. "These are wine trees," he grins. "I know you're still thirsty. Have some."

"Father would sometimes let me taste his wine," I say, and the memory brings with it a pang of joy a lot like grief. Oberon hands me the stem and I drink, sucking as infants do. The soft, porous bark produces as much wine as I can swallow, and it is sweet and flavorful. "I know a little about wine," I say after. "My father liked to experiment with different kinds of grapes. What kind of wine comes from a tree?"

"Sweet amber wine. The best in the worlds." He begins to chew on a fruit pit the size of an olive, and I let him, giggling to myself until he finally realizes that the pits aren't for eating. "Very funny," he grumbles like a child, tossing the half-eaten pit aside.

"So how does this work?" I ask. "What is the magic that will bring us back to the Sunless Vale?"

"It's happening already," he says. "The wine. And a few spells of my own making."

"I don't feel lightheaded."

"It's not that kind of wine."

I turn to ask him to pass the fruit, but the words catch in my throat. Just like that, we're back in the Sunless Vale, wide-eyed and with a sweetness on our tongues. It is as we left it, a valley of perpetual twilight, always on the cusp of dusk or dawn and never changing. "How?"

"All the worlds are really just the distance of a thought away. It just takes the right thought."

I look around, edging away from a nearby pool. The stream flows upwards as before, but instead of being sucked into the earth, the droplets seem to detach from the stream, falling like rain into the sky. "Will this pool take us to Vanfell?"

Oberon nods. We sit quietly for a while by the pool, our shoulders touching. I try to prepare myself to travel, try to drain the fear from my body. Oberon says nothing, watching the shimmering column of rain. A yellow-golden leaf from the last world is stuck in his curly hair. I reach over and gently pull it out and lay it on the ground beside us. To my astonishment, the purple grass entwines around the leaf, leaving no trace. I stare, horrified. "I liked that leaf."

"That's another feature of the vale," Oberon says, hardly paying attention. "Our clothes and our bodies are acceptable so long as they are on us. But nothing from other worlds is permitted to stay forever in the vale. It balances its own."

I jump up, wary of the grass touching my feet. "Not a great napping place, I take it."

"Are you ready to go now?"

"Yes. Very."

"I promise I won't mess up this time."

"I believe you." I take his hand.

We step together into the pool. My hand tightens slightly on his, and his on mine, and I close my eyes, leaving the seeing to him. A second darkness comes, the darkness of silence, then a third darkness, stillness. Then all that twists apart like needlework unraveling, and I hear an oily splash.

CHAPTER V
Drifting

It is deep in the heart of humankind
to worship what they cannot see.
— Oberon

TO AVA, our *drifting* will only last an instant. Even now, as her atoms mingle with mine, she longs for her father. I will help her find him. Her true home, too, if she wishes it. I think she may be part of why I was sent to this world.

In my younger and less corporeal years, I spent my days wandering, learning everything I could about Alta. My most important learning is that humans are vastly different from my kind. They live as briefly and hungrily as burning paper. They are easily pleased and easily confused. They hate with passion, love with fury. Their bodily lives are both tragic and savory.

What a mystery, the body—this precious lump of flesh and breath. To inhale the universe—it is still my favorite part of being human. And what of Ava? This profoundly naïve, unimaginably kind girl. I hope I can protect her. She is like a flower unfolding. Vanfell is no place for her innocence.

As we travel, I listen to the city—all of it—thousands of conversations. Words whispered through keyholes or proclaimed over drinks. Names spoken in anger or pity or love. I ponder the discordant rhythm of all those broken, yearning, fast-beating hearts—some touching, some unspeakably distant from one another. Most of all, I smell the fear.

Great Spirit, guide me, I pray, longing to fulfill my purpose, though I do not remember it.

Perhaps it is the same for humans, each born with a specific function, a point upon which to focus their whole essence. Men and women long for meaning, and from cradle to grave they search for it. Many fail, having no notion of their function other than *it exists*.

But some live truly, finding meaning, leaving their mark in ideas or sculpture or children, doing what good they can with what they are given. Is this wherein happiness consists? I do not know.

I know only that when I am with Ava, I feel . . . useful. We will retrieve the vessel that carried her through the stars. I must not allow Sol to know of her presence here. His quest for dominance and care for his people will blind his human tenderness. He will use any means to extract knowledge from her. All in vain. She does not know any more than I do of where she came from.

Gathering my soul senses, I extend my spirit toward Vanfell, searching for Ava's father, Lux. Stretching to my limit, I scour the tiers of the city, sliding through windows, sewers, and dungeons, over rooftops, chimneys, and lamp-posts—following the fear.

So much is burned and broken. Sleepless people huddle in root cellars, mourning dead loved ones, praying devotions, or otherwise hiding from the sky. Snow falls faintly on the mountainside, but never enters the city.

Something happened here, not long ago. Something very bad.

I feel the remnants of a mind older than the rest, of a rage nearly as old as the city itself, and not quite human. I withdraw, vastly confused. My time is up.

I open my eyes, feeling the light strike them, sensing the

neural lapse as collisions of atoms seek to make sense of each other. Ava appears beside me an instant later, manifesting in an oily splash.

CHAPTER VI
Vanfell

OBERON AND I appear side by side in a dark alleyway. A foul-smelling puddle, disturbed by our arrival, sloshes over my bare feet. I jump out quickly, expecting to find a monster in the ankle-deep slime.

"We made it!" I exclaim, sucking in air as heavy as smoke. I gag and shut my mouth.

"Nasty, isn't it?" says Oberon. "As one who lived in the free air all your life, this must come as quite a shock to you." Placing a hand on the small of my back, he ushers me out of the alley.

The stench diminishes slightly as we turn a corner, though it is still a presence. "So this is Vanfell," I say, breathing with some effort, tasting the chemical air. "I'll be all right in a minute. I'm tougher than this."

"Of course you are! You were born falling through fire and survived. You lived off the wild land for three years, finding joy in the barest human comforts. You're just not used to the smell is all."

"Pigs smell," I say. "They eat dirt and feces. This is different. It's not a natural smell."

"Humans are not a natural animal."

"You seem unaffected," I say, noting Oberon's relaxed posture and easy breaths.

"Smells fascinate me. All of them." He shrugs and says no more.

I focus on my less delicate senses as we turn onto a larger

street. Lines of clothing hang everywhere. The crooked buildings lean toward and away from each other like uncertain lovers. "Where are the growing things?" I ask, barefoot in the dirt.

"There aren't many of those in Vanfell."

"Where are all the people?"

"Ava . . . this is still an alleyway," he says, obviously worried about me.

"Oh." I shut up and begin counting the cracks in the walls. A man huddled under a blanket near a drain shouts at us, waving an empty bottle in his hand. Oberon forces me to keep walking. When I glance back, the bottle is full of clear liquid and the man is speechless, staring at it.

"We need to change your look," Oberon says after some time. "You are too obviously innocent to blend into this city. And in that skimpy gown? The men here will not leave you alone."

"If you say so. I've heard stories about the bad men in the city who lay hands on girls, and how princess Coraline prowls the night, terrorizing evildoers with her shiny knives."

"Soon you'll find that the world is better and worse by far than your stories."

"Not if the story is good. Not if it's true. Then the world in the story is as real as the world outside."

Oberon shrugs. "Come with me, little poet."

The smell improves when we reach a main street. Here the drains are underground, and the rough, dusty road can accommodate three wagons abreast. A few vendors are setting up shop on the corner, the beginnings of a daily market by the looks of it. I smell chestnuts roasting and coal burning in cast iron heaters. Smoke rises undisturbed into the sky.

Freshly lit torches burn on tall poles over doors or near intersections, casting an unflattering glow on the soot-stained facades. I have never seen buildings so big or so dirty. Narrow, lopsided chimneys poke out from steeply slanted roofs. Blocks of clay and sandstone as far as the eye can reach. The city rises in tiers up the side of a mountain, and we are inside the middle level. Each tier seems to have its own system of walls and gates.

If I could just climb the upper wall and stand amid the clouds, I could look out across the vale. I could taste the distant forests and hear the songbirds bickering at dawn.

Dawn is not far off judging by the bright place where the buildings touch the sky. Even as I watch, a single rusty sunbeam hits me, reflecting orange off the smoke and dust in the air. People begin to filter into the streets, heads bowed, dressed for work. More join their number each minute. On the edges of the streets, hardly noticeable at first, are the scattered bodies of bent people—men and women emerging from bundles and looking around hopelessly, as if dismayed to have survived another night. "Who are they?" I ask, staring.

"Those are the ones with no homes," Oberon says sadly. "He used to work on the walls. That one was an architect. And over there, she tended stables for the king once."

"What happened to them?"

"They fell through the cracks. That's all, really."

We pass on, and the broken faces fade, and a part of my heart with them.

Oberon tries to cheer me up with words. "See those two? Twin sisters. And the best weavers this side of the sands. See the man with the heavy apron? He's a blacksmith, and a famous swordsman in his day! Those three are artisans, dyers by the smell. See the men and women with the nice, nimble hands? They—" He cuts off, distracted by something in the crowd. "Keep your head down!"

A detachment of soldiers marches down the middle of the street, grumbling unprofessionally at one another. The foremost six carry torches. Common folk part like frightened cats before them. I turn my face slightly away as they pass, though no one gives me any notice in the half-light.

"That was strange," Oberon says once the clinking fades. "They shouldn't be here. This is a working district."

People are everywhere now, bumping me, breathing on me, muttering to each other in languages strange and wonderful. So many people talking, haggling, shouting. I've never been in a crowd, breathed the raw sweat and sour spices. I stare in wonder at the factories, the mining towers, this city with so many strangers in it.

In the outlands, strangers were people to be greeted in ones and twos and conversed with. Here are thousands, so many unknown lives and faces, and so few of them friends. In the villages I visited with Father, everyone knew everybody else.

Stalls begin opening up. Fruit carts and wagons full of wine. Carrots in pots and plump tomatoes to be sniffed and squeezed. Tables of coffee and tobacco leaves. Carts full of caged animals and talking birds with wings like rainbows. Markets for old clothes and markets for new clothes. Markets for musicians and artists, astronomers and artificers. All the while, we climb higher into the city, and our surroundings grow richer and more elaborate.

We pass a seemingly closed workplace. The sign is freshly painted and the walls are all washed a pale yellow. I suspect it will be open soon. Oberon uses his magic to unlock the door and ducks inside without warning. I follow him. "What are you doing!" I hiss, glancing over my shoulder. "These things don't belong to us."

He smiles, ruffling through the coats and boots near the back. "They soon will."

"But it's against the law!"

"The only laws I obey, Ava, are the laws of nature. Gravity, time, laws of motion. You are referring to manmade laws. And those have no sway over me."

"But not stealing? That's one of the basic laws."

"Let's see if the universe stops when I do this. . . ." He removes a shirt, coat, and a pair of trousers and proceeds to try them on. It is winter now—but desert winter—warm and dry during the day and snowy cold at night. Not that either of us care. "We'll attract less attention if we dress like everyone else."

"We're going to get caught," I say, brushing aside one of the dark dresses.

"What do you think?" Oberon presents his newly clothed self.

"You look like a thief." Even the meager light coming in through the back window is enough. He looks ridiculous, with just a hint of charming. The silver-blue ink in his skin glistens, always the same, no matter what color light strikes him. He removes the new clothes and puts on his old, torn brown trousers. "Shall I fetch you something?"

"A bath. Extra soapy."

"No really, pick anything you want."

"No!" I say firmly, looking away. "Father and I make our own."

Oberon shrugs and selects an appropriate shirt, coat, pants, and a knit hat for good measure, and puts them in a burlap sack along with his own clothes. He knows my exact size, which annoys me, though I can't explain why.

"We will put them on after we reach the next tier," he informs me. "They will blend better with the middle class."

I do not give him the pleasure of a response. But once we're back on the street, slipping unnoticed into the fray, I can't hold myself back. "I thought you were good."

"Ava, it's nothing to be angry about."

"Don't kill, don't cheat, don't steal. These are the things that set us apart from people like Sol!"

"You didn't protest when I dismantled those soldiers last night," he says.

"That's not fair! They were trying to kill you . . . and do God-knows-what to me. The only thing I want to take from this city is my father! And then I want to go home and grow things and be happy."

"There's something you have to see," he says, sniffing the air, his expression pensive.

He turns and jogs down a cross street, past a row of burned buildings. I follow resentfully. Glancing into the blackened husks of shops, houses, and garrisons, I imagine the raging fires that sometimes afflict cities. So many wooden buildings so close together. But the destruction continues as we walk uphill. Even the stones are melted in places. Everywhere, people are picking through the wreckage, searching for valuables or loved ones.

"What is all this?" I ask.

"Just come, I'll show you."

The crowd diminishes as soon as we are out of the main street. Even the sounds become muted as we reach a place where the road curves and the buildings give way to sky and a few ragged pines. Walking through the tiny park, we emerge on the edge of a manmade cliff.

From this viewpoint, I can see at least half the city below us—the far larger half, spread out like spilled soup. I stand for some time, staring down at the hundreds of buildings, the thousands of people waking up. It is somehow quiet and impossibly still even with all the tiny motions. The risen sun glows like a burning eye between two jagged mountains.

Oberon draws my attention to an obliterated pile of stones. "That used to be a fort," he says. "There was a dungeon underneath for dangerous prisoners."

"What happened to it?" I ask, noticing a few sections still smoldering. "An earthquake? Was Father in *there*?"

Oberon swallows and lets out a held breath. "They are saying it was a dragon from the depths. It burst out of the prison and took to the skies in wrath, circling like a crow of death. Its roar could make your ribs rattle. Its glance could wither a grown man, break him into bits."

"A dragon!" I exclaim in a choked voice.

"It killed a garrison of soldiers, bathed the high city in flame, and then flew into the east."

"What about Father? Can you sense him?"

"You don't understand." Oberon turns away from the scene of destruction and looks at me closely. "Ava, a dragon wrecked this part of the city two days ago. It came from the dungeon, not the sky."

Myths and fables fill my head with unwelcome feelings. I

lower my eyes, imagining the worst. I can almost smell the dusty pages of old books, feel the flickering heat of an oil lamp, the soft breeze from my open window. "What are you saying?"

Oberon's expression is serious. "It was Lux."

"You're scaring me," I say, seeing no falseness in him. "How do you know my father did this?"

"Did your father have any body markings?"

"A few," I say, faltering. "Not like yours. He had a woman on his shoulder, on his calf a house by the sea. One on his neck, on the side." I close my eyes, picturing it. "It was solid during the day, but at night it would move sometimes. I remember a face, one half human, the other—something else."

"Inari's Kiss," Oberon nods gravely. "He is a dragon-blood."

My breath catches, shallow and weak. "I always thought it was just another tattoo from the wars. People put the strangest things on their bodies."

"Not this time. This is a birthmark, passed down through generations."

"Inari's Kiss is only real in stories!" I protest, my confidence failing. "There must be thousands of people who get that tattoo. It's just ink."

"Do you really believe that?"

"It would sometimes glow silver under the moon." My voice fractures. My eyes fixate on a solitary wildflower growing through a crack in the dusty ground. It has seven blue petals, one slightly larger than the others. Five leaves. Two pairs and one by itself. The leaves are green.

We stand in silence for a full minute before Oberon asks,

"What do you want to do now?"

"I want to say you're a liar." The words spill out of me, and they sound harsh.

"I would not lie to you," he says gently. "You know better than that, Ava."

"He's alive," I whisper, smiling out at nothing, then looking down at the boy before me. "My father is alive. That's what I came here to find out."

Oberon nods, his face creased in concentration. "I cannot sense him, so he must be far away. Do you know where he might have gone?"

I nod, wiping away a tear. "Probably to his sister, deep in the old forest by the pulsar fields. I'm sorry, Oberon." I sit heavily on the ground. "This is a lot all at once. To imagine Lux going there, and his sister, Mira. I've only seen her twice, both times in her forest garden. She never leaves it. It's a long walk from anywhere."

He sits down beside me and puts an arm around me. "Your father is alive, Ava."

"He's alive!" I exclaim, tears filling my eyes and falling into my lap. "He's alive," I tremble. "I don't get to see him. I don't get to tell him I'm alive too and feel his arms around me. But at least I know." I hug my knees tight to my chest, letting my vision blur. "I still can't believe it. Father, a dragon? There are so many legends of changers, the good and the evil, the heroes and the cursed. I never once imagined. . . . He kept it secret."

We sit together for a long time before I say, "Can we leave Vanfell the way we came? Can we go after him?"

"I'm sorry, Ava. There are no magic places here. The pulsar fields are a week's journey. From there we can go anywhere, but only once we make the walk."

"No . . . wait . . . there's something else!" I recall, brushing wet strands of hair behind one ear. "My cocoon! You said it was here in Vanfell."

"I did." Oberon's eyes flash like a thundercloud, realization dawning.

"We need to find it! When it shattered, the pulsar fields came to be. It must contain traces of the same power."

"You're brilliant, Ava!"

Unused to Oberon showing emotion, much less offering compliments, I flush and smile through my tears. "Let's find my cocoon!" I exclaim, standing with fists clenched ever so slightly. "And this time we won't have to steal. Because it already belongs to me."

CHAPTER VII

LUX:

The Madness

NIGHT. COLD. THE RAGE. Should have died in that dungeon, failure that I am. What man calls himself a man, can't save his own daughter? *Ava, my darling. You are the only thing that's right in all I've done.*

My wings flex and glide through scraps of mist and dense cloud tapestries. I can hear my fierce heartbeat. Blood and lava. The hiss of breath as it passes through the hollow cavities inside my chest.

There is a certain, feral delight in letting go of human reason and embracing instinct. Oh how the savages dance and sing with indecent gaiety—while civilized men stand brooding in their graves! Better to live as a dragon, to embrace the madness, to forget the rest.

Far below, the valley seems to go on forever. But I know better. If I fly far enough, I'll reach the pulsar fields, and then the forest near my old home. And then, if the madness doesn't take me, the sea. *Ah, madness, old friend. I feel you building, rising like a river of molten iron. Eroding my skin.*

"Ava! Daughter!" I roar in the dragon speech, no human sound. Blood pounds through my skull like a battle drum as I labor to stay aloft. Can't change back now. No choice but to die. Do I remember how?

I remember the earth in my hands, the numerous seeds, only some of which would survive. The way I was a slave to rain. I remember the constant wood repairs. The desert wind, damaging roof and windows. I remember the animals, always sick, the goats, yielding little. I do not miss it, any of it. I care little for this life. If not for Ava, I would not suffer it again. *Ava, my pearl of the stars. Where are you now?*

She came to me three winters ago, and not in the usual way. When the king came questioning me about her, I lied. "This . . . is my daughter." A name struck me from far away, a name not of my own making. "My daughter, Ava."

"Father, I know of this man!" The king's own son kicked his gelding forward. "They say he plows his fields with no mules or horses."

The King surveyed my fields: symmetrical troughs of black soil, the largest of any farmer in the plains before the mountains. He laughed, the bitter old fool. "Impossible."

"My wife is ill," I lied quickly, wary of his eyes on Ava. "She's . . . resting. I was enjoying the evening air with my daughter when the thing lit the sky."

"Go home to your wife," said the king. "This is my land now."

I knew to nod dutifully, but my heart was heavy as I turned away from the proud men and their winded mounts. Where would we go? How would we live? No matter. At least for now, she was mine. I would give her everything a father could give.

Three years I had with her. She grew up smart and fast— faster than any human child I have known. She adopted a mortal appearance, but the semblance fades if one looks into her eyes. Irises like two golden nebulae in the silk of space. She does not remember her birthplace among the stars, though surely she must be one of their own.

After Sol's men took my land, I moved with Ava to the

outskirts of the forest and built a cabin there. What was once my farm and homestead lay to the west. The once fertile vale became an unreal desert known as the pulsar fields.

The crops fell ill from some interstellar malady, and all the vegetation died. The valley soil cracked with heat, and the sand became like quartz powder. The touch of the dust spread for many acres, driving out hundreds of farming families, and finally halting before the forest, as if held at bay by enchantments.

The center of the fields, several acres nearest where her vessel crashed, had a supernatural aura, veiled in celestial mist that never blew away and seemed to grow with time. Ava loved it there, and I would watch with dread each time she, a tiny thing, barefoot and ever-smiling, vanished into the swirling void.

As I streak past the ruin of my old cabin, I descend, flying low over the misty treetops in search of my sister, my last hope, both for myself and for Ava. Mira is a great healer. If anyone can change me back into a man, it is she.

Could Ava be with her? Could she have possibly slipped the trap? If Ava is not safe in the forest, as I hope, I do not know what I will do. Kill Sol for starters, the maggot. Fire is too clean a death. I'll eat him alive. Then I'll level his city, scrape it like dirt from my nails.

What then? Devour the world? Destroy myself? No . . . not yet. Not while hope lasts. The rage has taken hold of me, true enough, gripped me with its talons. But I have, for the moment, my own mind. Best not waste it.

The night passes. Long hours on the wing, and I'm beginning to tire. *Is this really how I end?* If not for Ava, I'd drown myself in the sea and be done with it. I have lived, like the entire human race, by causing pain to others and suffering it myself. And I have been shown just enough of love and passion to fear losing it, and to cling to it, or to its memory, like a madman. *Is this a worthy life? Do I even have the right to smile?*

"Father," Ava said to me once at the kitchen table before dawn. "Let's pick grapes today."

"It's early for that," I said, gulping down coffee. "They're still ripening."

"Let's walk then. We can walk between the vines and just look at them."

"All right then. Where did you put your shoes?"

Outside, amid the foothills north of our cabin, Ava touched the grapes and squeezed some between her thumb and forefinger like I taught her to. "They're close," she said.

"We will harvest soon," I agreed, picking a handful, examining them in the predawn light, and eating them.

"There are so few of them," she said regretfully.

"That's a good thing," I told her. "They grow on a harsh hillside near a desert, surviving dust, heat, and snow. It is the vines that suffer most that produce the fewest, finest grapes. A bottle of this wine could buy you a pony. You'd like a pony, wouldn't you?"

She grinned. "Only if you have one too! And we can ride together."

"Oh Ava, I'm too big for a pony."

"A horse then! A huge, black destrier like from your stories."

"I'm getting old," I said, staring out over the fields, remembering. "I could use a break from the plow now and again."

"Father?" Ava said, seeing loss cloud my eyes.

"Yes, Ava?"

"Are you happy?"

I paused, a grape between my fingers, hovering near my mouth. I lowered it slowly. "What do you mean?"

"You tell so many stories," she said, shy but determined. "There's so much pain in them. You don't smile a lot."

"I'm happy," I nodded unconvincingly, wrinkling my brow. "I'm happy to have you here, picking grapes, asking silly questions."

"Even if you can't answer them?"

"I just did, didn't I?" I growled, unintentionally crushing the grape between my fingers. "Didn't I?" I said softer.

"I'm happy too!" Ava said suddenly, forcing out the words. "I'm happy too."

She dashed through a gap in the thickest vines and disappeared down another lane. I watch her pale skin flashing through the leaves, even as the moonlit forest flows under my wings.

I reach the sea before dawn and turn south, following the coast until I find what I'm looking for—a flaw in the towering cliffs, like the inclusions of a gemstone. As I approach, the flaw becomes a crack, then a yawning cavern, just large enough for a dragon.

I'm expected, I see. I land heavily near the opening and slither inside. The stones grind close behind me. I pass into the inner chamber, a green place full of vines, herbs, flowers and babbling streams. The roof is open to the sky, though well-hidden by the forest. This is indeed my sister's work.

There I fold my tired wings, gasping and coiling, crushing plants and tilling the soil with my talons. I cry out to her with my broken voice and lie there like a wounded beast. The tame creatures that live inside her garden all flee at the sight of me. Even the flowers turn their faces away, looking to the midnight sky or to the stone walls of the open-roof cavern, all hanging with vines.

I do not know how long I howl and shiver there, tasting the crystal spray of breakers, the brine-wind on my tongue, the darkness and green water. I do not know if my sister will come, or if she does, what she will be able to do to turn me back. I am wretched indeed to have come so far and risked so much only to fail a second time.

Mira, sister, kill me now. Kill me before I burn your beloved forest to ash. Ava, daughter, bless me with your tears. Lift the curse that drives me so far from every living thing.

CHAPTER VIII
Heroes

VANFELL IS A LABYRINTH of dust and cobblestones. New mixed in with old. A hodgepodge of architectural styles —wood, stone, metal, just stuff thrown together. There seems no formula to the neglect, but Oberon knows the way. Part of him is scouring the city for my cocoon. The other part is with me.

"What do you want to be when you grow up?" I ask.

He makes a show of considering it as we approach a tall wall that separates our tier from the next. "I want to be me."

The gate is open during the day and we pass through it into a slightly wider, far less dirty street. "What do you mean?"

"I want to be the best version of myself. The truth of who I am."

I nod agreeably, thinking his answer a bit vague, but deep too. "I want to be a hero. People would feed us and give us places to sleep and congratulate us in the streets. Wouldn't that be nice?"

"Being a hero is a short-lived profession."

"I'm interested in the food, mostly," I say sheepishly. "And the many admirers."

"I prefer to walk incognito," Oberon says, solemn as a church boy, missing my joke. "But you're in luck. I'm ready for food and a bath about now. Then we can find your cocoon."

"I thought you didn't eat," I tease.

"I plan on taking care of this body. Staying fed and clean is important. I haven't found your cocoon yet, but I've stretched my senses far, and I think it's in the royal tiers. If we plan to walk unnoticed on those marble streets, we need to look and smell the part." He opens his palm to reveal two silver pieces.

"Where did you get that?"

"It doesn't matter. You choose the inn."

"You didn't steal it, did you?"

"Not this time. Promise."

I refuse to admit to him how badly I want to clean up after days of sleeping in the wilderness and wandering through multiple worlds. A hot meal would go a long way. Still, he's so sneaky! Where is he getting this money?

My internal conflict ends at the sight of a fine, large inn with shutters the color of honey. We go in, and Oberon speaks briefly with the innkeeper. We sit in a dimly lit corner and have a meal of sausage, eggs, and milk. He eats slowly, savoring his bites as he tastes animal food for the first time. He eats as if it is a great privilege to be fed, as if this is the only milk in the world and these eggs were bought with gold.

"We used to keep hens," I say, watching him delicately cut the white from the yolk. "They'd lay an egg a day if they were happy and fed."

"Marvelous creatures," Oberon says absently, taking his last bite. I finished a while ago.

Afterward, we go upstairs where two baths are being prepared in rolling tubs of polished copper. I stand fascinated for some time as the attendant, working a hand lever, pumps steaming water from huge cauldrons in the basement. Someone has been working on a leaky pipe, and there are tools lying around and a pool of water on the floor.

"Dragon," the attendant says, nodding toward the mess and frowning. "Shook the place to pieces."

Soon we are alone in the small, sparsely decorated room with one window, a newly lit fire, and a sloped floor leading to a drain.

"After you, Ava," Oberon says, adding with a smirk, "You smell worse."

"You're too kind, but you should go first. You're dirtier."

He smiles as if having a private joke with himself, and I wonder how accurate my statement actually is. "I was dead a few days ago," he remarks with no hint of embarrassment. "I *really* need this. Still, go ahead."

"You need to work on your jokes."

He shrugs. "Just hurry up!"

Unable to argue a moment longer while so near the steaming water, I remove my filthy white gown and slip in, sighing softly. Oberon busies himself in the corner. Once I'm settled, he rolls a table of cleaning salts, scented oils, and sand-brushes beside my basin. Then, sorting through the plumber's tools near the patched pipe, he holds out a steel-bristle brush for removing rust and nods encouragingly at me.

"I'm not *that* dirty," I protest, shoving the horrible instrument away.

He laughs, then wheels his tub beside mine. Dispensing with his clothes, he hops in. All I can see from where I am is his curly head as he leans back. Then his dirty feet pop out of the water and touch mine. I giggle at him and look away. "The water tastes funny," I say.

"Why are you drinking it?" He dunks his head and begins

to scrub himself with one of the sponges.

"It smells good," I say, splashing water on my grimy cheeks. "Like jasmine and lavender."

He hums his agreement and we are silent, just enjoying the warmth. Afternoon sunlight streams through the small cross-shaped window, lighting Oberon's feet and turning his nails white. I almost fall asleep.

"Want to see a spell?" he asks.

"Sure I do."

Oberon gestures toward my bath and I feel the warmth in it renewed. Suddenly, conjured from the deepest part, air pockets begin to form, bubbling up around my chest. I look down at them, laughing. "They tickle!" He sets a thousand foamy bubbles popping in his own bath and we both seem to be sitting in buckets of boiling water, though the temperature is still perfect. "I love it!" I exclaim. "How do you do it?"

"Magic," he laughs. "I know the secret threads that make the world."

I lean back and let the water completely soak my hair while the bubbles thunder around my ears. I close my eyes for a long time. Pretty soon my fingers will look like dried fruits.

"I'm sorry your father is a dragon," Oberon says after a while. He added soap to his bath, and is now sitting in an overflowing container of pink foam. Every time he moves, suds spill out, covering the old floor like a fragrant rug.

"You're such a mess," I say to him.

"At least you know he's safe," he adds, poking his head out of the suds.

"Yeah, at least. The blunt old dragon! I can't believe it. But somehow, I can. Things are becoming easier to believe every day. Yesterday, I never would have thought I could travel to a thousand other worlds. Today, I've already been there, done that."

"We went to *two* worlds, Ava. I'd say you're still new at the whole planet-hopping business."

"Still, you know what I mean! It's amazing, isn't it?"

"It is," he agrees, soaping his feet.

"And a dragon isn't the worst thing Father could be. Think of all the changers you've ever heard of. The stories are full of them. Men who turn into wolves when the moon is full, or fish when the tide calls them home. Cats, sharks, snakes, frogs . . . a dragon is way cooler than any of those. Besides, he's still a man, too." *Isn't he?*

I turn away and peer at the rack of soaps, cleaning salts, and essential oils. I've only ever seen two types of soaps. One is made from beeswax, the other from goat fat. Personally, I prefer bees. I select based on color and begin to move the pink and yellow bars all over my body. The water ripples gently, dancing like a real sea.

"You have a merry heart," says Oberon. "I will help you find your family, mortal and immortal."

I look at him, wondering what he means. "I have one family: Father. The rest is just guesswork and longing. Better to stick with what's real."

Feeling a bit overwhelmed, I dunk my head and stay there, feeling the shape of the water around me. I miss him so much. His daily lessons, the sound of his knife as he'd carve wooden figurines for me to play with. The dried maple smell of tobacco when he'd smoke his pipe by the window, the moon outside. The way he'd rescue strangers in the desert, just to bring home a piece of the outside world for me to talk to.

He pretended to hate the company, and maybe he did. He did it all for me. Did I think it would last forever? I emerge from the water and scrub between my toes until the skin turns red.

After the bath, we dry off, clean up the frothy mess Oberon made, and put on our fresh clothes, including my knit hat. We sit down by the fire for a while. I squeeze my wet hair, smelling lavender and the sweetness of burning sap. A slender girl with brown eyes and pigtails brings us tea.

"You're spoiling us," I say, sipping as she slips away with a wordless smile.

The new clothes feel so soft and smooth against my skin. The mud and dirt and dried tears are all washed away. I look into the fire. *Father, I'm glad you're all right,* I think as if speaking to him in my head. *You should have told me you were a dragon. I would have understood. I would have still loved you.*

I look over at Oberon. He turns to me, the tattoos on his neck glowing in the firelight. He's worried about me. Somehow, after the bath, I expected the many patterns of ink in his skin to disappear. But it's all still there, lining his face, his forearms, making him look older and more severe, like some sort of sacrificial symbol or incarnate god. But there's still enough skin to see that he's a kid underneath. And so much kindness in his eyes.

"Tell me about your tattoos. What do they mean?"

He looks at his patterned hands. "I suppose you've guessed that I chose this body for a reason."

"You do everything for a reason."

He stares into the fire for a full minute, one hand on his face. He looks down at the lines of blue on his arms and shoulders, at the mysteries scrawled beneath his threadbare shirt. Then he looks at me and they are all gone. All I can see is the warm brown of his skin and the unquenchable gray light behind eyes, like the coming of dawn. "How is this?"

"You look . . . different." I stare at him. I thought he would appear younger without the markings. But that is not it at all. He seems to have grown years in just a few seconds. Perhaps his physical age is nearer to mine, he being eleven, and I thirteen or fourteen. It's hard to tell how old I am. I am only three years in the world, but Father used to call me his little teenager. "How did you do it?" I ask, wanting to touch the naked skin on his face.

Oberon looks away, and when he glances back all the tattoos have returned. "Magic," he says. "Illusion."

"I'm not asking you to get rid of them," I say quietly. "I was asking what they mean."

He nods self-consciously, his curly hair bouncing. "I just wanted to show you what I look like without them."

"You look nice," I say, adding quickly, "but you look nice with them too."

"The illustrations are the work of magic. That's why they glow. That's why I can make them disappear temporarily. Though they *are* permanent, they aren't ink."

"Amazing," I say, touching the top of his hand and tracing the silver-blue artwork with my finger. It's not quite geometry, though dots, lines, and curves are all used freely. It's as if the artist were inspired by a dream of shapes that only exist in dreams, and look strange when rendered in two dimensions.

In between the shapes are pictures. On the surface, these are familiar—people, animals, miracles, and impossible things. But when I look away for even a moment and glance back, I can never find the same image twice. It's as if the tattoo has already changed. I test my theory several times to be sure.

"Infuriating, aren't they?" Oberon says, noting my confusion.

I nod, stupefied and look away before the visual trickery drives me insane. "Do they tell a story?"

"The story of my life," he says solemnly. "The lion on my back is the god Zintahu, wisest and fiercest of the desert gods. This young body was once the body of a desert boy, the shaman's son. He was meant to be a religious leader from birth. On his tenth name day, as is the custom in that village, he was given the ritual markings of the god.

"But he died young and the markings spread beyond control, beyond death, covering every inch of his body. Many considered this a sign of doom from the gods, revoking the shaman's authority, and the village perished. I chose the boy to show him a better life."

"So you could just as easily have chosen an old man or a woman?" I ask, astonished.

"I chose what I chose. I do not know if it could have been another way. We souls do not have bodies, but we know the meaning of feminine and masculine temperaments. There is more to the sexes than just bodies."

"That's comforting." I smile a little.

"Why?"

"I don't know," I say, a little shy. "So you chose this body. Now it's yours, right? Does it feel like it's yours?"

"I do not know in what sense I own it, Ava."

"If you left it right now, would you miss it?"

Oberon is silent at this. He moves a little closer to the fire, sitting on the edge of the carpet. I follow suit and watch him stir a cube of sugar into his tea. "Curious," he says at last. "You just gave me an inkling of what it feels like to want something."

"To want what?"

"To want to remain a certain way, to remain corporeal. Were I to want that, and to fear its loss, it would be something like the human fear of death."

"It was just a simple question, Oberon. No need to get all philosophical about it."

"Sometimes the simplest things are the hardest to understand. To live, to love, to hope. These are basic. But that doesn't mean they're easy." Oberon looks out the window as if looking past the reaches of light. "I do not know where human souls go when the body dies, for they are far different from the spirits I call brothers and sisters. I know humans live on after death, though to what purpose I am ignorant. Perhaps they live in bliss, perhaps in waiting, perhaps as nothing at all."

"I don't want to be nothing," I say, feeling a chill and reaching my hands toward the fire.

"If I were a human spirit," Oberon says. "I would desire an afterlife where I could pursue everything that made me passionate about being alive in a fresh and glorified way. To love and pursue a woman, to contemplate truth, to write poetry on a mountaintop, to create symphonies and make discoveries, to build things with my two hands—these are the kinds of things I hope humans are able to engage in after the body dies."

"I hope the same is true for stars," I say, not sure why. We are different, Oberon and me, but we share something in common: we are alone of our kind, lonely together, for what it's worth. "It's hard to imagine having hands and feet and building things after you die," I say, closing my eyes to think. "Hard, but not impossible."

"It's worth wondering about," Oberon agrees. "I can tell you this. A human soul, when it passes on, is no longer burdened by the happenings in the world. Their deeds echo into eternity. Their bodies turn to dust. I chose this body because I did not want to see it as dust. I don't know why I felt such tenderness toward it, but I think it has much yet to accomplish. Ava, I am beginning to love this body as if it were a part of my soul-self."

Oberon's words stun me, and I bite my lip to repress a smile. "I think I like you too," I say, turning away from the fire to look at him. "Sometimes people talk about choosing their friends. I don't think it's like that with us. Someone chose us for one another. I think that's beautiful and exciting."

"The Great Spirit," he ventures, eyes softened by flame.

"The Great Spirit," I repeat, having no idea what I'm talking about.

We watch the fire for much of the afternoon and into the evening, and chat more about Vanfell, and about Father, and about where my cocoon might be.

Oberon takes up a meditative pose and begins to scour the city with his soul senses. He says he's extending his spirit, peeking over the walls of his body to see farther. I still don't quite understand what he means.

After my third cup of tea, he returns to his body and shakes himself awake. "No luck yet," he whispers.

"Thank you for helping me." I pat him on the shoulder. "I think it's wonderful that you came to Alta. I've never had a friend before except for Father, and it turns out he was lying to me the whole time."

"He wasn't lying," Oberon corrects. "He just didn't know how to tell you everything. It's hard to tell your adopted daughter that you're a dragon, after all."

"I guess so." I unclench my fists. "He was never scared of anything. Not a thing in the world, or so I thought. I never dreamed he might be scared of me."

"Huh," Oberon murmurs, returning to his meditation. "Imagine that."

CHAPTER IX
The Prince

WE BEGIN OUR SEARCH for my cocoon in the morning. The city is mostly the same as it was yesterday. The streets full, the people working hard, neither smiling nor suffering. The buildings stand in untidy rows, not quite falling apart, like battered dolls that have been loved or neglected beyond recognition.

But something is different today—lots of shouting and chattering in a plaza where two major streets meet, as if some rumor has brought a spark of vitality back to the community. Ahead, men in bright uniforms clap shoulders and exchange news, looking meaningfully southward. The nearest one, an officer of some kind, curses, tears at his beard, and utters an oath so foul that a passing maidservant drops her groceries.

"He's afraid," Oberon says, seeing through the man's bravado.

"Why? Is it to do with Father?"

"There are reports of an army massing south of the desert. The scourge-city Obul, they say."

"Is it another city-state like Vanfell?"

"Yes, but twice as savage. Didn't your father teach you about the wars that shaped this continent?"

"Only that he fought in many, off and on. Long, long ago. That's how he earned his lands. He said any peace with Obul is temporary."

Two dark-headed boys play-fighting with wooden swords burst out into the street, kicking dust and shouting. One bumps my shoulder, nearly knocking me down. Oberon, though he is not much older than they are, leaps do my defense and shoos them away. They scamper off, continuing their game. He looks as if he's about to chase them.

"Don't," I say, tugging on his arm. "It was an accident."

"Much blood has been spilled in skirmishes over recent years," he says, watching as one of the boys takes a chop to the face and starts crying. "Obul has never been content with defeat. This will mean war."

"It might be time for heroes after all," I say. "If Obul attacks Vanfell, it might be just what these people need to unite again, to love their city again."

"Vanfell is fading," Oberon says. "Has been for a long time. The Obulan army is like a coiled adder. If they attack, it will be before Sol can raise the strength to oppose them. I do not want to be here during a siege."

"Then we better hurry up and find my cocoon! Where do you think it might be?"

"I don't know." He watches the smoke-wreathed heads of the tallest buildings as if expecting to see a glimmer of silver-white metal, still hot with starlight. "There's the royal palace, of course. Sol has his usual dungeons, towers, museums and laboratories. I have sent my spirit searching, but I do not sense it. If I could narrow my search to a single building, then maybe."

"That's pretty neat how you can extend your spirit," I say. "Part of you here with me, part of you in every corner of the city."

"I wish it were that easy," he says, wincing. "I feel stretched sometimes, thin and ghostlike. I don't like leaving my body anymore."

"Don't hurt yourself. We'll find my cocoon one way or another."

I lead the way up a wide stone ramp toward the next level of the city. Sol's palace looms closer, its huge, gloomy spires rising up to pierce the sky. The castle surrounding it is enormous and very old, carved out of the mountain itself. I count four bastions, two jutting out like the shoulders of a hunched sphinx, and two more butted against the mountainside.

Some sort of keep stands in the center, the highest place in the city. None of it, I'm sure, has ever been cleaned. Soot and smoke seems stained into everything, from the walls and rusted ironwork to the soaring glass windows.

"Those gardens," I say, pointing to the vines and bright flowers spilling over the sides of the keep. "How do we get there?"

"Not easily," Oberon says, squinting against the glare. "Why?"

I feel my heart flutter, much like it did during my brief childhood when I'd approach the pulsar fields at night. "I can't explain it, but I think there's *life* there. More than just flowers and dirt."

"Your cocoon?"

"Maybe."

"Strange that I can't sense it." Oberon peers up at the keep, his gaze passing through walls like light through an open window. "This building used to be a stronghold, a last defense against enemies. Now it's a place of learning, study, and politics. The lower floors serve many functions of government."

I admire the gardens from a distance, only half listening. "Beautiful," I whisper, my whole heart stretching, reaching—

thunk.

Absorbed as I am, striding jauntily ahead, I plow straight into a broken fruit cart that's blocking the road. I take a moment to catch my breath, cradling my stomach. "Sorry," I gasp, bending down to help the oblivious owner gather his spilled produce.

"Oy!" He lunges at me, seizing my arm. "Stop, thief!" When he sees that I'm only here to help, he releases me and mutters an apology, tugging nervously at his shirt. "Thank ye," he says when we finish.

"You're welcome." I pet his donkey while he feeds her a long dirt-colored carrot. Meanwhile, Oberon crawls under the cart and touches the fractured wheel, making it new again. We scurry off before the old man has time to notice.

"Maybe I should lead," Oberon says, ducking into a side street and gliding through a narrow, neglected path crammed between the backs of buildings. "You just run into things."

"Seems that way," I say, no choice but to laugh at myself. A lane of rough-hewn steps rises twisting into the unknown. We begin to climb. He offers me an apple, pilfered from the broken cart. "You confuse me, Oberon." I wave him off. "You did a good thing mending the wheel, but then you go and ruin it by stealing."

He bites into the tender skin and shrugs. We continue the climb. One hundred, two hundred, three hundred steps. My legs are just starting to burn when we finally emerge onto an elevated footpath that runs along the base of the castle wall.

From this vantage point, I can see clean across the city to the valley below. Gazing down, I notice activity on the roads. Hundreds of wagons and carts snake slowly toward the city, accompanied by thousands of people walking and riding.

"I count caravans of grain, wheat, ore, and firewood," Oberon says. "Other supplies, too, all from the outlands. It seems these whispers of war are more than rumors."

"This is crazy. How can things get so bad so fast?"

He shakes his head sadly and turns away. "Come on, Ava. This grave has been a long time in the digging. Best keep our feet out of it."

We turn our backs to the valley and begin making our slow way around the colossal bastion, toward the front of the castle. I hear them before I see them. Faint at first, but growing steadily louder. The unmistakable sounds of human beings in great numbers.

"What's all this?" I ask, rounding a corner to find the castle gates open and a buzzing swarm of people already pressing its way inside. I've never seen so many people gathered together in my life.

Oberon hesitates for half an instant, his facial features going slack as he taps into his uncanny sixth sense—probably sifting through a hundred conversations at once. "You won't believe it," he says. "The king is to give a speech."

"You can't mean—"

"Sol."

"Should we come back later?" I ask, horrified at the idea of having to face the man who spent the last three years hunting me.

"Don't be afraid of an old scarecrow. Come on, we'll slip in with the crowd!"

Before I can say a word, we are already mixing with the people. Oberon grins at everyone, amused and captivated by realities deeper than the skin. I wish I shared his optimism. To me, it's just hot and cramped. A hot, sticky cauldron of stale beer and old sandals. Before long, I'm drenched in other people's sweat, perfume, and sour breath. Oberon, still grinning, dives right into the heart of the crowd, leading me by the hand while I hold on for dear life.

Pressed on all sides, we pass through the gates into what seems to be a city of its own. We move like leaves in a river, ushered forward by those behind. I keep an eye on the gardens far above, trying to find a path, a way out of the throng as it makes its way irresistibly toward the palace.

"That's where we need to be!" I point up toward the gardens, bumped and jostled, trying to make myself as small a target as possible. Grim-faced soldiers are stationed at every gate and crossroads, confining the flooding multitude into a single stream, like wine being funneled into a bowl. "How do we get past the guards?" I ask, looking to Oberon.

He seems to consider it, chewing persistently on the core of his apple. "I've taught myself a few tricks since the tower."

"Magic tricks?"

"Something like that. Care to try one?"

"You know I trust you."

Suddenly, where before there were only bodies, a gap opens. I slide inside, Oberon pressed close behind.

"Jimbo? That you?" A peasant next to me bellows, apparently noticing some relation in the crowd. "By me beard it is! Come here, ya ugly bastard!" The two men embrace warmly, leaving just enough room for me to slip in behind.

A thin man shoulders past, trying to fight his way to the front. He trips on a raised cobble, curses, plows into a tangle of knotted limbs. A fight ensues, but we are already well into the inner courtyard, sneaking and slithering our way toward one of the well-guarded archways along the sides.

For a while, the crowd is our protection. But the moment we break off and sprint for an exit, one of the guards spots us.

"Oy! Stop right there!" He rushes to cut us off, sword clinking at his side, gesturing fiercely with one hand and holding his plumed helmet in the other. His sword is halfway out of its sheath when a vacant expression comes over him. He lurches to a halt, squinting against a shaft of glare, seeming to forget what he was angry about. Oberon swerves close enough to blow in the man's ear as he streaks past.

"That was cheeky," I whisper as we pause under the shadowed archway.

Oberon says something, but his voice is drowned by a sudden, violent cheer. Peering between the latticed brickwork, I catch a glimpse of the palace doors opening and two men striding across the lawn to a raised orator's platform at the edge of the waiting crowd. The peasants cheer and yowl at the sight of their king. But the cheers are short lived, and the silence afterward is stifling—a tense, watchful silence, like the family of a sick person hanging on the doctor's every word.

My silence is far more hostile. I stand in concealment, shaking with anger, resisting the urge to leap onto the stage and kick Sol in his kingly shins.

A handsome, much younger man, dressed in the same finery, stands to the side of the king. He looks out over the crowd with unmistakable sympathy, regal but tense, as if he'd rather be among the people than above them. He takes a deep, settling breath and rests his hand on his scabbard.

"People of Vanfell, my subjects, friends, loyal and otherwise," Sol begins in a voice that must have been stately once, long ago, and is now slightly labored. "I assure you, both by my words and by my presence here, that this is a grave matter."

As he speaks, I study his thin, wilted features, aged beyond his natural years by stress and addictions. Maybe it's contempt I feel, after all the hurt he's caused me, and the harm he still intends. But there is also pity. Though not old, he seems crippled, gaunt, and fading. He wears fine clothes, shieldsilk it's called—strong as steel and artfully woven—though it does nothing to hide his skeletal frame, which fits the material about as well as a hanger would.

"The hordes of Obul are in motion, raiding and burning as they approach our borders. We do not have ample warning to amass an army to meet them or to protect the pulsar fields, which are ours by right. Our garrisons in the south have all been overrun. What strength remains, I will withdraw and consolidate within these walls." A gasp ripples through the crowd, and only Sol's increased volume stops the whispering. "It will be our duty! To prepare our homes for refugees! And to prepare our hearts for war! It is to be a siege. Obul, as always, strikes swiftly and without mercy. But we will not be undone!"

A feeble cheer rises, followed by the drone of many voices, too loud to be overcome by any one man.

"The arrow falls swifter than expected," Oberon says in a flat voice. "What could drive a people to such madness? To leave the warm, volcanic caverns of their home city, and to strike out across a vast desert for the ruin of all?"

I inhale sharply through my nose, eyes wide, my skin crawling with fear. Even in my darkest moments, I would never have wished this on the king or his people. I know nothing first hand of Obul. Only the legends and rumors, such as they are.

Some say they are crude imitations of men, the work of some demented thaumaturge from a time when magic still flowed and did not trickle through the veins. Others say they are barbarians, tamers of monsters from beyond the sea. Pale, hideously scarred, flat-faced and dark-eyed.

"My father just called them the enemy," I say, very softly. "Is it true that they eat spider eggs and drink the poison for spirits?"

Oberon says nothing, his expression flat as death. It seems he too is processing all that has been said. War will come swifter than anyone expected.

Sol raises his withered hands as if to lay a curse and the whispering ebbs. He speaks of the southern watchtowers falling one by one. I imagine them all on fire, the walls crumbling, the desert overrun by fearless men with moon-pale skin and obsidian eyes. The tower they kept me in will soon be abandoned, if it isn't already.

"Can we go now?" Oberon pokes me in the ribs.

I nod numbly and pull myself away. We miss the rest of the speech as we hurry through a maze of hedges, pergolas, and sweeping verandas, keeping to the shadows. "Oberon, who was the man with Sol?" I ask, chewing on a memory.

"That was his son, Hector."

"If only his father wasn't so evil," I say, blinking self-consciously.

Oberon gives a knowing smile. "You look like you've just tasted perfect honey and would rather put the spoon down than go on eating."

It's pointless to deny it, so I say nothing. Picturing the prince is like reading a sentence too pretty to simply pass by.

So I stop reading, but I can't quite close the book. Uncommonly handsome, hardly past his teens, tall and slight, with hair like summer wheat. I want to remember more, but I resist, holding him at bay.

I'm having mixed success at this when we come upon a squad of six soldiers. At first, I expect Oberon to dive headlong into the nearest hedge and wait for them to pass. Instead, he strides ahead with confidence, giving a little wave for good measure. Only one of the soldiers notices us, his eyes straying for an instant. Then he turns away and scratches his ear.

"What did you do?" I ask once we're well clear.

"I made us forgettable."

"That's it?"

"I learn new powers every day. It's part of adapting to a body, to a world."

As we near the keep with the magnificent gardens spilling over, I notice signs of my father's destructive flight. A series of unrecognizable structures lie in ruins, the stones melted and scattered. Men work with chisels and heavy hammers to break the stones into manageable pieces and cart them away. The incessant clinking and cracking echoes off the high walls.

"We'll use the gardeners' path," Oberon says, opening a locked gate with a gesture and leading me down a grassy alley.

"Why would Sol want me so badly?" I wonder aloud, my mind lingering on the image of his withered face. "What good am I? I don't know anything. I have no ancestry, no special powers. If I have any kinship with the stars, they've long disowned me."

Oberon seems about to dispute that point, but merely sighs. "Sol is desperate, and that makes him dangerous. If he thinks you could be of use, any at all, he will not hesitate to take your freedom away."

"Sol would." I hurry to match his increasing pace. "But not Hector."

"Maker help us!" Oberon cries in a rare display of emotion. "A boy flashes his cape at you and you go all dewy-eyed."

We swing around a corner, practically running. The posted guard opens his mouth to reprimand us. Then he frowns, looks puzzled, as if he's forgotten a candle burning. We continue through a wooden gate to a smelly side yard where a man dressed as a servant is dumping a pail of sludge into a hole. He notices us at once.

"Hey!" he says. "You kids . . ." He trails off, staring vacantly at his empty pail. When he comes to, he stands suddenly straight, spits into the hole, and enters the keep by a side door. We follow him in, keeping to the servants' passages. The cooks, stewards, and housemaids ignore us, and we proceed unhindered.

I want to talk to Oberon, but he seems to be concentrating. For someone who just learned human magic, he's not half bad. He locates a hand-driven lift that the gardeners must use to carry soil, mulch, fertilizer, and other materials to the roof. The crank turns on its own and we begin to rise.

"I didn't know Sol had a son," I remark, staring at the crank as it revolves mysteriously. "The way he looked out at the crowd . . . like he was looking at *me*. It made me feel older. Made me feel beautiful. Like I wasn't beneath him."

"He is, perhaps, a good man," Oberon admits. "Still, better steer clear of him. I suspect his duty to his father will outweigh any tenderness he feels toward you. Ah!" The lift begins to rattle slightly, whining in its metal shaft. "We're almost there."

"I have a feeling that something important is here," I say as the lift grinds to a halt.

The door opens onto the rooftop gardens, an intricate maze of green hedges, fountains, and long, cedar-plank flower boxes filled with colorful things. Shades of red and lavender, yellow and dawn rose. Butterflies flit about from flower to flower, sipping nectar. One lands on my shoulder, rests its wings for a moment, and flutters away.

The diversity of life is staggering, but there is no wildness here. Every leaf, stem, and wisp of grass is perfectly pruned and trimmed, shaped and edged, made more beautiful by the care taken for it. Nothing wilted, spotted, or brown, and yet there are no gardeners in sight. Oberon's work, no doubt.

"Looks like we have the place to ourselves," he says with a mischievous grin.

"There's something in the air," I whisper, my hands shaking. I sniff softly, lest the scent vanish. "Something more than pollen or manure, similar to the pulsar fields, but fainter. Can you sense it?"

Oberon nods slowly, eyes glimmering with excitement. "You are more sensitive than I am to relics of your past. But I feel it now. Lead on."

I enter the maze, intent, quiet, listening. The city disappears as I pass under the shade of sculpted trees. White and gold flowers twine their way through arched trellises, washing the cobbles in dappled light. I solve the hedge-maze in seconds, and emerge in a tree-sheltered clearing near the back of the keep. A variety of wind chimes and clay hanging pots decorate the space.

Then I see it, swaying gently on a long cord. Standing on my tiptoes, I unhook the pot and sit down in the grass to examine the solitary flower growing inside. The stem is transparent, needle-shaped, the petals veined with purple light, rigid as slivered glass, as if they would shatter if touched.

"It's from the stars," I breathe, awestruck. "I don't know how I recognize it, but I do, like a long-forgotten memory. It must have been taken from my cocoon."

"It has been tended well." Oberon bends over the flower, curling his tattooed index finger around his chin thoughtfully. He breathes on the petals, which drift readily for a moment, then stiffen again. "This one does not remember the journey through the heavens. It was only a seed then."

Only a seed, lost in the darkness with a sleeping child. Me. I want to admire it for the same reason that I loved to walk the pulsar fields at night. I want to touch the petals and feel the shiver of lightning—and the answering thunder—echoing in the hollow places inside me, finding me out. Gently, I brush the stem with my fingertip. "Oberon?"

"Yes, Ava?"

"This flower . . . it knows where my cocoon is being kept." I stand slowly, moving to where the branches part, and I can see the mountains rising behind. "That one." I point to a black spire, one of the two high towers butted against the rocky slope.

"Are you sure?"

I return to the starflower, touch its spindly roots, address it as I would a long-lost friend. "Yes, quite sure."

Oberon swallows nervously. "Of course. The obsidian tower."

"Didn't you check there already?"

"I tried. The place is filled with so many strange magics. Things too dangerous for museums, or too priceless for auction, things taken from all over the world. I tried to be thorough, but I must have missed something."

"How can we get inside?" I ask, picking up the starflower by its pot and holding it close to my face to thank it.

"Ava, you know I will help you, always," Oberon says seriously. "But the obsidian tower is the heart of Sol's power. It is a school, a fortress, a temple—a place where his magicians live and work and study. We'll be taking a great risk."

"Can't you make them forget? Just like you did the others?"

"It will not be easy. I've tricked commoners and fools. A wizard would see through my illusions."

"You underestimate yourself."

"I have the power to confuse men, to impede them, even to destroy them. But my reach is not unlimited, and I cannot protect you from a host of wizards. We'll have to be careful and tricky-clever."

"I'm willing if you are."

"Remember, Sol wants to capture you. Going to the obsidian tower, even to reclaim your cocoon . . . it is reckless."

"What about Father? I have to find him! You said it yourself. My cocoon is our way out of this city."

He looks hard at me, judging my resolve. Then, knowing nothing he can say will sway me, he nods. "As you wish, Ava." He leans against a tree branch, reaching out with his soul senses. "Give me time to examine their defenses. We'll only get one chance at this. I'd rather not mess it up."

CHAPTER X
Orphan Star

I have spent hours naming raindrops.
— Oberon

I SEARCHED the obsidian tower with my soul senses, which are undetectable to the best of my knowledge by any human magic. The starflower was right. Ava's cocoon is there, locked safely away in one of the upper chambers. Our only chance of reaching it is to enter in secret. The wizards are busy preparing spells and potions for war, and will not expect an invasion at this hour. Surprise is our advantage.

Ava listens intently to my instructions. The day burns away amid our conversation, and we agree to go in at night. We sit face to face in a deep embrasure on the edge of the keep, our backs to the merlons on either side. We watch the evening sun descend over the city.

Ava holds the far-wandering flower between her legs, a look of indescribable longing on her face. It has passed the same galactic clusters as she. It has seen planets and moons rise and fade in the journey through dust and fire, the same journey she took to get here, though she was only a child, and it a silver seed.

"We can do this," she says for the third time, eating a berry and licking her lips. "Tonight we take back what's mine."

I nod, sitting cross-legged on the edge of the wall, looking out. I lean my head out as far as I can, feel the wind ripple and whine through my stubborn curls, the channels of my ears. "You are going to touch a piece of your home world," I say. "That is exciting. I may even be jealous."

"I haven't felt like this since the first time I walked the pulsar fields." Her eyes mist over with memories. She gently strokes a single petal of the solitary flower. "Do you think this one is from my world?"

"It might be."

"Could it wonder about where it came from as much as I do? Or do you think it drinks water and air and is happy?"

"Flowers don't get happy or sad, Ava, not even this kind. They don't have existential angst, or ineffable longings, or a gift for self-destruction. Flowers just live beautifully and die, and their good consists in other things than reason and wonder."

"It makes me joyful just looking at it." Ava wipes a tear from her cheek and shivers. "How are we going to get the whole cocoon out of there? It's so heavy."

"We won't need the whole thing," I remind her. "Only a piece. Remember the magic wine? Power is not governed by size or appearances."

"I remember." Ava leans back against the stone merlon, sighs, extends her legs, nudging my knee with her foot. "This is all so new to me," she says, holding the flower in her hands and wiping away one last tear. "Everything about being in a city is strange. Vanfell is as beautiful as it is broken. Exciting and terrifying at the same time. Sometimes, when I'm surrounded by all those people, I can hardly breathe. It's so strange to be seen."

"To be seen," I repeat, knowing what she means more than she might guess. "To have a body."

She nods and sniffs. A gust tousles her hair and she lets

it. It is surreal, sitting here with her in the light of this near star, sharing the roof with these sun-eaters and rain-drinkers, the most peaceful of living things.

We recline on crafted walls overlooking a city of clay, stone, and machinery. Even as the sun grows red and the stars appear like ashen coals in the winter sky, my eyes focus on the most dramatically dark area of the city. There are no flowers there, nothing even for the rats to eat. The refuse who exist between those shadows do not know of the war or the coming night. Many do not even know if they wake or sleep.

The last sunbeam shafts through the desolation, the smoke and rotten dust. Forges light in every corner of the city, glowing red in the coming night, the hot soot rising. All around us, in the close distance, I hear hammers, shovels, chisels, and saws. Muttered words of respect and encouragement. Here, a father teaches his son how to hold a sword. There, a mother and her daughters sew burial cloth.

The city is in motion, but the people are far from ready. I slide my fingertips along the lines of mortar, enjoying the cold, the nearness of the stars, the intermittent gusts that smell of vapor and frost. What use am I to them?

"It all happened so fast," Ava says during a lull in the wind.

"That's the way of the scourge city. They strike like vipers. If they succeed, they destroy everything they conquer. If they fail, they retreat before a counterstrike can be made. The rumors are coming true. Murdering and burning in the lower fiefdoms, people fleeing north to Vanfell as their villages fall."

Ava looks at me thoughtfully.

"You weren't talking about the war, were you?" I ask.

She shakes her head and sits straighter against the stone. The right side of her face glows with twilight as the rest darkens. "My father used to tell stories about the elder wars against the hordes of Obul. He always spoke as if he pitied his enemies, even when he killed them. Especially then. They weren't all evil, he said, only twisted by ideas or cruel masters —taught hate, not born to it. And yet he had to kill them to live."

"If we don't leave this city soon, you'll have your own tales of war, Ava."

"Yes," she says, smiling a little through a shiver. "I will."

"You're eyes went dark for a moment just then," I say. "Why?"

She wipes her eyes self-consciously. "I'm an orphan, Oberon. I do not know the stars, and I don't know what happened to my mortal father. I'm lost."

"But you're not alone."

She stares at me with softening eyes, absorbing my words. "No, not alone. If it wasn't for you, I'd still be imprisoned, questioned, tortured, maybe even killed. I owe you every-thing."

I look at her as a cherished friend for the first time, not just a girl who the Great Spirit, Archeälis, sent me to protect and guide. I see now that she is a good and loving daughter, devoted and graceful, even as she suffers. Her voice reminds me of something I have been trying to remember all my life. I prefer these minutes in the twilight with her to a thousand lifetimes in the sunless place where I was born. There is light there, and companionship, and even joy, but there is no Ava.

She yawns, squinting until a single tear appears on the

corner of a lash, and I feel something break inside me when she lifts her wrist to wipe it away. Her scent is wild dust and nectar and the smell of the sky before a storm washes in from sea. Her long dark hair falls in layers down her back, across her shoulders and chest. She glances up at the obsidian tower and seems to shrink back from it as if there are a multitude of eyes behind the glassy black, staring out.

"Don't worry about being seen," I say. "I'm shrouding us. It's an easy illusion at this distance, so just relax. We have a big night ahead."

"We do," she agrees. "We're going to take back a piece of me that was stolen. I didn't know how much I wanted it until now." She looks down at the city, hugs her knees to her chest, tiny and compact. "There is good and beauty in the people here, shining like tears under the flaws. It is worth protecting."

"Your eyes are clearer than mine, Ava."

She lifts the starflower and kisses it. "Why does Sol think I'm a weapon?" she asks casually, as if the question has never once kept her awake at night.

"Why indeed," I breathe, sensing the time has come to share my learnings. "Ava, over the past few hours, I've examined my memories, starting with the day your vessel created the pulsar fields, the day my spirit descended to Alta."

She looks at me, silent, receptive, a flower waiting for rain.

"Three years ago, when you were still a child, the fields were not so empty. Sol explored them well, sending scientists, astronomers, and daring mages to gather samples of rocks, dust, and atmosphere. Men with star almanacs tracked meteor showers, hunted lizards, and studied the dust, moisture, portals, and other phenomena. Through these pawns Sol learned many things. He knows about the portals that transport matter from one place to another, a valuable tool in war, no doubt. His mages have even been able to replicate the power in small ways, and some among them now apply teleportation in their techniques."

"I had no idea he was so thorough," Ava says, gaping a little.

"He didn't stop there, though. He kept studying, kept digging . . . and eventually found glimmers of a deeper power, a power to control matter in other ways. But when he tried to master the secrets, the fields became violent, and many Star Hunters perished, taking with them all the knowledge they had gained. The project fell apart. That is, until a lone sage returned from the desert saying he had seen a girl alone, speaking to the sky."

Ava stiffens at that, her brow slightly furrowed. "I thought I was careful. . . . I avoided the few men I found there. It wasn't often they came."

"One glimpse, and your fate was decided. That was two moons ago. The sage's tale reminded Sol of the day your cocoon fell. The memory of your face troubled him. You were fairer than any noble child in the kingdom, and he wondered if perhaps you were more than a farmer's daughter after all. That's why, with his health failing, he sent his sworn lord, Agon, and his soldiers to the fields to look for you. Agon expected a young girl, no more than four years old. But on finding you, despite your appearing as a teenager, he had no doubts: he had found whom the king sent him for."

"But he disobeyed his king," Ava whispers. "Lucky for me, I guess."

"The greed of men served us there."

"How do you know all this?"

"I have been gathering the details for some time, stealing bits and pieces from the minds of men, even Sol, even his son, the prince."

"Earlier today, you mean? What are you, a mind-reader now?"

I am whatever you need me to be. "It's complicated. While part of me was tricking guards and finding paths, the rest was . . . busy."

"You're sneaky," she says. "And powerful. So much so, it scares me."

"Don't be afraid, please. My powers adapt to your needs. Watching you gaze at this flower, I knew it was time to tell you everything."

"Thank you for this, Oberon." She looks at me, perhaps wondering what other secrets I keep. But no, there is no accusation in her eyes. Only more questions. "If I'm a weapon, what kind am I?"

To that, neither of us have the faintest idea.

When it is nearly dark, I stand up to stretch my legs and offer Ava a hand down from the ledge. She hops down without my help, touching my hand with two fingers to be polite. Then, before retrieving her flower, she looks at me curiously, standing as straight as she can. "Oberon, when did you get taller than me?"

"It must be the shoes!" I say, kicking them off hastily. "I didn't like them anyway."

We stare eye to eye. "Now we're the same height." She taps her bare toes on the dirt.

"Strange," I mutter.

She bites her lip and shakes her head in confusion. "Growth spurt, maybe?"

"Maybe." I put my hands in my pockets.

Ava turns toward the obsidian tower and sighs. She lifts her precious flower one last time and whispers something to it. To my astonishment, the tips of the petals begin to glow, then tremble. The stem vibrates like a plucked harp string. Then, like pollen blowing in the wind, the leaves and petals turn to silver dust and drift away, leaving only dirt and clay. Ava watches the sparkles fade.

"Did it want to go home?" I ask, curious as to how she knew what words to say, or how she remembered them from years away.

She nods subtly and smiles as a mountain gust disturbs her hair. "At least some of us know what we want."

CHAPTER XI
Lux:
Dragonblood

I FIND AVA in the storage cave a stone's throw from my fields. She waves me in, grinning royally as if the cave belongs to her. She is the queen of the forest and the desert, the queen of dust and rain. And of course, the queen of the dry grotto where I store my excess grain once the barn is full.

"At your service," I say, stooping to enter.

She sits perched on the tallest of nine granaries, hardly an adequate throne for one so fair. She adjusts her crown of sprigs. "Father, why do you farm so many things?"

"I enjoy it. The grapes, the olives, the grain. Beats raising cattle."

"You used to do that too, didn't you? In the Firstborn Lands, so far away?"

"Seems I've done it all at one time or another."

"No fair! You've done everything and seen everything. I bet you remember the spell that made the world! I bet you know the Seven Words that coaxed the dry land out of the endless deeps!"

"Ha!" I bark. "The Seven Words? Even I am not old enough to remember those, dear one."

"Oh really?" She crosses her arms skeptically. "Tell me about the Firstborn Lands."

"What is there to say? Months of total darkness. Cold that gnaws the bones. Crops only grew in one season, maybe two. In the frozen plains where the wind can bite through wool, leather, and flesh, I kept cattle. During blizzards, they'd clump together and trudge for miles, tails to the wind. In the morning, I'd find some of them alive and break the icicles off their nostrils with a stone so they could breathe."

"Such a harsh place . . ." she says, slumping a little, the wind sucked clean from her sails.

"Is this land any better? You know I hate sand. Nothing grows in the sand, and more blows in every day. Not to mention the wilting summers, the locusts and dust pneumonia. That's why I ask you to put wet sheets over the animals' faces when the sandstorms come."

She nods in her obedient way, slides down from her perch, opens an access lid to check on the grain. "Looks all right. No bugs. Dry too."

"Good girl."

"Were you born a farmer, Father?"

"No, dear, but I would like to die as one."

"Me too!" She turns serious, cupping a handful of threshed grain and letting it trickle through her fingers into the sandstone container.

"You? Baby, you don't want to be a farmer."

"Why not?" she protests, standing suddenly, fidgeting in the only slant of light that ever touches these stones. "It's good enough for you!"

"It's just one way to live. You need to find your own way."

"When?"

"When you're ready."

"How will I know? And who's stopping me from being a farmer anyway?" She reaches into the granary, scoops out a cupful for supper, and gently replaces the lid.

"Just don't do it for me," I say, surprised by my own

insistence.

She sets her hands on her hips, playing the queen once more. "I will do what I please!"

I often recall her in that posture, standing barefoot on the ledge, both regal and childlike. Part of me wants to take back my words and keep her there, forever. I loved her. How I loved her. Sometimes she loved me too. If only I'd loved something else enough to pass on. I gave her dusty shelves and old books and a barn full of oats and a four-walled pin where the goats gnawed growing things into dust. None of it was worthy. And now it's all gone.

Who's there? What's that sound?

"Lux, peace. Peace. You're safe now."

"Who's there?" I growl, scraping off the crust of dreams. "Answer me!"

"Has it really been so long that you don't remember your own sister?"

My eyes flash open, human eyes, and stare up from a bed of grass, petals, and pungent herbs. "Mira? You turned me back?"

"You brought yourself back," she says, kneeling beside me, her hand on my forehead. "I just gave you a little pull."

I breathe in, snort a blast of fumes, my throat dry and sore, my breath catching. I reach up, feel my face with my hands, touch the scars on my cheek, lip, and eyebrow, squeeze the matted beard. I am a man again, for now. Bright sunlight shines down through the canopy, and I raise a hand to block the glare.

"You came a long way, brother. You must be exhausted. Tea?"

"Thank you," I say, sitting up, fighting the soreness in my

bones. I am wearing a plain knee-length tunic fit for travel and a brown cord around my waist. What I took to be purple flowers, growing to either side, are actually soft, fragrant berries, which I've been crushing in my hands. The juice runs through the cracks in my palms. I wipe them on the ground.

Mira brings the tea and pours me out a cup. It's cold as a mountain stream and earthy black. "I do not advise transforming again," she says. "You might remain a dragon forever."

Better that I had, I think, keeping silent.

Mira looks at me sadly, and I at her. She has not aged a day. Her hair falls past her shoulders, black with silver streaks, tied back loose. Her face bears no resemblance to mine, except her eyes, which are gray, almost colorless. Her skin is light brown, lighter than mine, like the rounded dunes that warm to amber in the sun. She favors mother, and I, my father, or so I was told. Judging by the lines on her face, she smiles easily and often, probably to herself, or to the animals, because she rarely does so when I'm around.

"She's not here," I manage to say, my tongue thick and heavy.

"No, Ava is not here." Mira wipes her hands on her dress. "What drove you to this, brother? What good can we make of it?"

"Ruin begets only ruin. I am a foul, selfish dragon in every sense. And I have outstayed my welcome in the world."

"That may be," she says, touching my shoulder gently. "But you are always welcome in my garden."

"I thought she would be here!" I growl, fists clenching, tendons squirming and flexing in my forearms. Sparks gleam on my tongue, in my throat, a terrible burning inside.

Mire shrinks back in fear, but she soon controls it and smiles as if through pain. "Calm yourself, Lux. Have faith in Ava. She has her own magic about her. Now tell me what happened from the beginning."

I feel my face go slack, the anger flowing out of me all at once, turning to defeat. I am in no mood to speak. But Mira has a right to know about Ava's capture, so I share what I remember of the morning they took her: how the soldiers sprang upon Ava as she returned home after a night under the stars.

"They gagged her with saddlecloth, dragged her body through the sand. I went to her, wild with anger, crossing through the desolation, ignoring the lightness of my limbs and the strange taste of the air. I slew her captors with my hands and a spade, anointing myself in their blood. It was not something for a girl so young to see." I let out a strangled breath, glance over at Mira, shame rising like bile in my throat. "They shot me then. Twice in the back with poisoned arrows. I told her to run to you. She made for the forest behind our cabin, nimble as a rabbit. But more soldiers were already riding in from the north to cut her off.

"I reached them first. I do not know how long I fought them or how many I killed. . . . I remember the pain of the third arrow, which pierced my shoulder, and the fourth, and waking in chains days or weeks later to find my wounds healed and my death certain. She needed me, Mira. And I failed her." When I finish, I shudder like a beaten horse.

"I'm surprised you did not transform then," she says gravely. "I've known you to turn dragon over less."

"I was weak and full of apathy. It had been so long." I gulp down the rest of my tea. "Most of all, I didn't want her to see me like that." *To see her face go bloodless, her drowning eyes. To hear her scream and flee from me.*

"You underestimate her love for you, I think. A love like hers will not so easily dissolve."

"After the poison brought me down, their knights and captains all slain, the common soldiers were afraid to kill me, thinking my death would release demons. I listened to scraps of conversation as their self-proclaimed leader, a dull, superstitious man, ordered me sent to Vanfell to await the king's justice. I tore down that dungeon and made it here on my own strength."

"I have been praying for you every day for decades," she says. "You don't think that helped bring you to me?"

"Save your prayers for Ava. At least there you can do some good."

"Prayer is not something to be hoarded, brother. My heart goes often with Ava, especially at night, when she walks the fields."

"I had to let her. Dangerous or not, it was something I could not forbid."

"She might be there now." Mira looks to the west in her far-seeing way. "She might have escaped and returned home."

"There is nothing to return to. They burned our cabin to ash. I saw it from above."

Her face falls. "I'm sorry, Lux." She reaches out to touch me, but retracts her hand at the fierceness in my gaze.

"It doesn't matter now!" I rise with a struggle. "All that matters is finding her. I'll burn that city to ash if I have to!"

"Be sensible, Lux! You'll do Ava no good in that form."

"That bastard Sol, he took her. I'll crush him in my jaws!"

"And then what?" she asks scoldingly. "Are you prepared

for the consequences?"

I feel my chest deflate. *No. If I transform again, it will be for the last time.* "What other choice do I have?"

"It's a long journey on foot," she says. "But at least you'll still be a man at the end of it."

"God's blood, I hate walking. I hate this blasted, good-for-nothing curse! I need to save my daughter, and I have the power to do it, but I can't use it."

"You have other powers too, stronger, more subtle. Your humanity, Lux, a father's love. Listen to me, she is Star Kin. You know this. She has never been bounded by this world. Her fate is beyond it."

"Am I not a part of that fate? Did I not become a part of it when her vessel came burning a gash through the sky? When she landed like an angel in my own back yard? You who always speak of providence and fate, answer me!"

Mira nods in silence, gathering her thoughts. "Remain a man, and I will help you. Here, drink this." She hands me a wooden cup of clear water, no doubt of her own making. She is an adept, and all these streams obey her.

I take it. As predicted, the water eases my spirit and relaxes my flesh without dulling my senses.

"You can't go anywhere until you're well, and the dragon is fully asleep," she says, turning toward a small cook fire in a ring of stones. "Now that you're up, I have a job for you."

I assist Mira in preparing a meal, soothed by the dull, familiar tasks. It has been a long day. Last night I was a dragon, and the morning before, a prisoner condemned to death. No one talks to me like my sister. No one. And though I usually appreciate the candor, patience has never been my strong suit. I should leave soon, before I do or say something

I'll regret.

Her garden looks different during the day. A ravine oasis with a natural spring at the center, from which a dozen streams flow. On the far side, a waterfall cascades down, splashes musically over river-smooth stones, and runs underground. Tinted rays of twilight glint in the white froth. Under the mauve sky, in this place of beginnings where winter never goes, one wonders if the animals ever die or if the flowers ever wither.

I chop things while Mira prepares a stew. When the cooking is done, I set the pot on a flat stone in a clearing and gather my dirty mane of hair, tie it back with a string. Sitting in the grass opposite one another, we begin our meal with a prayer, then eat in silence, sharing a bowl of wine. I drink deep of the wine, and even deeper of the water, renewing my strength with every sip.

"We haven't cooked together in a while," Mira remarks, disturbing the perfect quiet. "Reminds me of when we were kids."

I stop chewing and swallow, pushing food and memories deep in my guts. "Childhood is short and forgetting is so long. I don't remember."

"We are only a few years apart, you and me. I've forgotten who is the elder."

"Huh," I grunt, the shadow of a laugh. "That must have been half a millennium ago."

"You're younger, I think. I've always felt that you are younger." Mira laughs a little to herself. "We would spend rainy afternoons in mother's house. Father was gone by then. Do you remember? You'd read books by the fire while I played the old viola. I can see us now! You, still muddy from playing outside, warming yourself by the coals until the mud heats to clay on your skin. You scratch your chin and turn a page and laugh to yourself at a scene in a story. I'm standing by the mirror, watching myself play. Listening, but mostly watching. Can you hear the music?"

"Your stew is getting cold." I pause between bites. "I don't want to go back there. I don't miss it like you do."

Mira falls silent and sips from the satinwood bowl.

"Have you ever considered leaving this place?" I ask seriously. "I know it's beautiful. I know, when I leave, the animals will return to drink from the spring. I know you love them. But is this everything you wanted for yourself?"

"We were lucky, you know." Mira deflects my question, pulling me back years. "It was a good time. Before the wars. We were wealthy in our own way. The house didn't leak, and mother was a scribe to the king, one of Sol's forefathers, and he'd let her borrow books from the palace library. Do you remember how she'd read to us?"

"Enough!" I stand suddenly, feeling all the vigor and passion and rage return. The warmth of the wine and the spell-rich water passes away like a flavor, like everything that is sweetest and most bitter in life. "I am going now. Thank you for the meal."

"Lux, please. Not yet."

"I have to! Ava is out there. And like you said, it's a long walk." I stalk off like a fool. The sky above is burning out. The stars that are visible seem wrong. I do not even know which direction I'm going.

"Wait!" She rises and follows me through the garden.

I ignore her, but when I reach the entrance, I find the stones closed to me. "Open the cave!" I whirl, furious at the memories she has rekindled, feeling as if I've lost Ava a second time. "The day is nearly gone. You have healed me and fed me, and for that I thank you. Now let me go!"

"As you wish," she says, opening the stones with a wave of her hand. "I'll show you out."

We pass through a damp tunnel, lit in veins of quartz. The passage takes us behind a second, larger waterfall. Water strikes rock in sheets, mist blasting out in a deafening sound. I feel the pressure of the fall on my shoulder, scattering the droplets as I pass. Finally, we emerge in the raw forest on the other side, the air crisp and cold, the trees strangely still.

"Lux, wait!" Mira says, when I move past her.

I hesitate, willing to hear her out, my woven sandals twisting in a patch of crimson leaves. Mira is tall and full-bodied, but she appears small and flimsy under my glare. "Speak, woman."

"What are you going to do when you find her?"

"What sort of a fool question is that?"

"I've spoken to the Maker. This path you make for yourself, it is forever. It only runs one way."

"I do not do well with riddles, sister."

"I can only say what the Maker told me."

"Spare me your talk of the Maker!" I roar, spittle flying, my gestures wild and accusatory. "Do you think you are the only one who serves him? You build this paradise for yourself. You tend these flowers and thorns and pray for others who are far away, suffering. It is the distance that makes them lovable! Bring the diseased and the dying, the killers and the vermin of the city to this garden, and you would hate them as I do."

"I do not hate, Lux."

The sorrow in her voice nearly breaks me, but I endure. "You have seen the blackness in the hearts of men, as I have. You hide from it. That's all this is, your exile. You care from afar and call it love. But it is folly."

"My prayers are anything but. Please, Lux, do not hate me."

"I hate that you are here while Ava is far away. I hate that you have not visited since the day she was born of the stars. You should see her! She's a woman now. Smart, gifted, and thirsty for life."

"I want to see her! You know I do. But I can't leave— those days are done. We both have our secret well of life, Lux. Yours drives you mad. Mine confines me. It's my calling, this forest, these streams, the animals. I cannot go back to the city."

"You *will* not!"

She shakes her head, shutting her heart to my words. "Everything you say is a dagger in me. I pray because I love to pray. I pray because mother taught me to, because she taught me to say *his* name. Archeälis, help us all. I pray because he wills it."

"Always you talk as if the gods speak through you. Are you a prophet, sister?"

She stiffens and sucks in her breath, standing as straight as a torched pine. A cloud covers the moon, the trees around us creak and murmur. Her eyes are not dangerous; she would never harm a living thing. But they are . . . changed somehow.

Eyes as old as mine, but much wiser. Eyes the color of water and foam, a rain to drown the world. The words she speaks are slow and burn like cold iron. "You were her caretaker. If she is in danger, then go, rescue her. But do it without asking something impossible in return. Do not ask her to be your little girl forever."

How dare she? I glare at her, a terrible heat rising, tickling the back of my throat. "Can I do nothing right!" I erupt, jamming my finger into her chest, sprawling her out in the leaves. "Our father *left* us! I will not leave that void in a daughter's life! And yet you criticize me!"

"He left because he had to, Lux," she gasps, curled up on her side, clutching her chest with one hand. "You know why."

"He could have stayed, the coward." I turn my back on her, ashamed at having struck her, even lightly. *One should never strike a woman, not even with a flower.* "We could have carried the burden together. It was from him, after all, that I inherited . . . *this*. . . ." The last word is a hiss of sparks from my tongue. "Like mother, you have a gift for growing things, nothing more. Do not pretend to know what it is like to be more dragon than man."

"I need your word," she says, leaves rustling as she gathers herself. "Go. Help Ava, but do not try to have your old life over again. Those days are done. If you cling to the past, you will only hinder her from doing what she was sent to Alta to do."

"Why do you speak to me as if I'm a villain? As if I wouldn't bleed for her, do anything for her?"

"Do I have your word, Lux? It is a grave matter."

"Stupid woman, weakling! Do you think yourself above me?" I hiss, turning on her, my eyes dark slits, my voice cold and menacing. "Do you think yourself my better, secluded in this chamber of prayer and isolation? Every day I weed the fields for the people of Vanfell. Every autumn and every spring there is harvest. By my toil each seed is planted and watered and picked. And when the wagons come from the villages to cart off my grain and my grapes, I am left with only enough to keep Ava alive another winter.

"Blood is my offering. Sweat is my prayer. By these hands thousands have been fed! Stay here if you will, hate me, pray for me, do nothing, and death take you! But I will not be scolded like an errant child!"

Snorting a blast of fumes, I shoulder aside the nearest tree, its young roots splitting and popping as it falls. Without a backward glance, I blaze a path into the night.

CHAPTER XII
The Shard

WE BEGIN by stealing a sturdy rope from the stables near Sol's palace. It says a lot about my dedication to finding my cocoon that I do not even pause to admire the horses, to pet them, or ask their names.

"What does this say about me as a person?" I ask, carrying the coiled rope over one shoulder, "that I don't feel any remorse for stealing this time?"

Oberon grins. "If I didn't know better, I'd say it means you're human."

I mute my laugh with one hand, shoving him fondly with the other. Might as well own up to it—I love sneaking around at night.

We move under the cover of darkness toward the place where the city ends and the mountain rises into a snow-capped wilderness. Oberon shrouds us, so that even if we are seen, we will be forgotten.

The night is mostly clear, but moonless, and it is very dark under the mountain. Oberon reaches the wall first and stops short, staring up three stories to the frozen slope beyond. The wall is durable enough for war, and well maintained, but its main function seems to be as a barrier to keep tumbling rocks and snowdrifts out of the city.

Oberon presses his fingertips into the wall, testing the mortar, tracing the outlines of stones, getting to know them. Satisfied, he takes the rope from me, slings it across his neck, and climbs straight up the wall like a squirrel up a pine, his fingers finding the chips and cracks, his toes never slipping.

Once he's on top, he throws the rope down and holds it fast while I use my hands to grip and my feet to walk steadily up the wall. No freakish otherworldly agility here, just a good childhood and lots of time in trees. It's a good thing too, or he would have had to hoist me the last ten feet.

"Onward! To adventure!" he says, hopping down into a snowdrift, vanishing up to his neck.

I follow after, landing lightly, the snow barely wetting my ankles.

"How did you do that?" he asks incredulously, kicking and flapping his way out of the snow, finding refuge on a boulder. "You'd have to weigh less than a dove to make such small footprints."

I shrug, staring up at the tower as it plunges like a spear into the heart of the sky. "We'll worry about that later. For now, there's thieving to do."

We follow the snowdrift up the side of the mountain, avoiding the sporadic sheets of ice. It's slippery in places, but not too steep. "Strange," I whisper, my bare feet indifferent to the damp cold. "I've never seen it snow like this. So thick. But back in the city, it's just a flurry."

"Magic," Oberon says. "Wizards' work. Sol has charged them with keeping the ice and snow from the high pass at bay."

"Seems like a lot of work. Snow isn't so bad. Once or twice a winter it collects on the forest floor. I used to gather all that I could find and try to make a tiny snowman before the morning burned it away."

We reach the upper third of the tower in the early hours of morning. The tower itself, as the name suggests, is crafted from obsidian glass taken from the heart of the mountain. But even magic towers need vents and windows, secret passageways and trap doors. The human eye could never find these carefully hidden features, and even the cleverest divination spell would leave a trace. But none of that matters to Oberon. He uses his soul senses to map out the entire building as easily as a child traces shapes.

"Find anything?" I ask.

"We'll see," he says.

From this place on the mountain, Vanfell is a bowl of fireflies far below, flickering and alive. Beyond the walls, campfires glow along the river and in the valley. Refugees from the surrounding farms and villages are out there, gathering, hoping to be let in.

"Huh," Oberon grunts as we approach, shrouded. "There's a network of caves below us, deep in the mountain. Tunnels, chimneys, ventilation shafts, but none large enough for a person." He leads me up a slope until we reach the sharp-edged spine of the tower.

I press my hand to the frosted surface and shiver. "Is this really the resting place of something so precious? This glassy headstone, this tomb?"

"For now," he says, finally reaching a narrow plateau where a hundred years of ice deposits have formed a bridge between the mountain and the tower. Crossing over, Oberon uses his soul senses to locate the hidden door and unlocks it. It slides inward, then to one side, making no sound.

My heart quickens as I tiptoe over the threshold. I expect to feel the suffocating pressure of the arcane, to be awed and haunted all at once, to touch the delicate verge of old magic. Instead, all I feel is my own heartbeat, my noisy, steaming breaths. The stale air smells faintly of gear oil. The pads of my feet press silently against blue marble as we pass under a transparent ceiling into a workshop of strange contraptions.

"These machines . . ." I whisper, turning dizzy circles, "they study the stars?"

"That's right." Oberon pauses to examine one. "Telescopes, both magical and mechanical. There's more math than magic here, though. They're used to study the constellations in an environment nearly free of distracting light."

I realize, as my eyes rove the levers and dials, that Sol must use these cylinders of glass and steel to track falling objects from days away. That's how he was able to find me minutes after I fell. He knew where I'd be. These instruments have a sole purpose—to find a creature born of the stars, someone ancient and powerful to exalt his city. And he got me instead, and not even that.

If not for Father, Oberon, and men's greed, what would I be but a slave? I desperately want to look through the small eye-shaped lenses, but I'm in a bit of a hurry, fear of discovery and all.

Oberon pauses to examine a star chart on the wall. "We're close," he says. "Many of the wizards are awake, preparing healing salves, concoctions for war, or studying spells. But no one is expecting us."

He guides me through another locked door and down an unlit corridor of soft, finely woven carpet. The obsidian walls are set with torches, all unlit. We pass through another set of rooms, meeting no one. The high chambers of the tower are rarely used, it seems. Oberon stops before an elliptical door at the end of a narrow hall. A strange series of locks adorn the front, twisting and curving like the valve levers of a brass instrument. He makes easy work of them, opens the door soundlessly, peeks inside. . . .

And I see it.

As bright and flawless as the day it landed, my cocoon waits for me. Rather than rush in like an idiot, I make a quick scan of the chamber. It's about the size of my father's old barn, full of clutter, broken equipment, and tools, but no people. Satisfied that we are alone, I rush to my cocoon where it lies fastened to a steel workbench. A shiver runs through me as I touch the polished hood. It's colder than the outside air and vibrates slightly wherever my fingertips wander.

At first, I can't think of anything to say. I'm too happy to cry. "I thought I'd never see it again," I say, turning to Oberon.

He nods, sharing in my joy. Then he glances at the door we entered through, wary. "Do what you came for."

The surface of the cocoon seems solid, but it is not. The wizards have tried without success to breach it. The shattered remains of countless tools and strange instruments lie strewn about the chamber.

"They tried everything to breach the shell," Oberon says, glancing through a hand-written inventory and experiment log on the table. "Chisels, cutters, blasting powder, ballistics, torches, flash-gas, smelting stones . . . the project has been cancelled five times this year."

I pity the wizards. They do not know the way of this metal. It cannot be melted down or smashed or cut. It cannot be opened by force, only words. I run my fingers along the hood, feeling the knowledge come, not from me, or even from the cocoon, but from elsewhere.

How do I know all this? Secrets from my infancy, from oblivion . . .

I whisper a phrase, instantly forgotten, and reach inside, aware of the cocoon's inner workings as I am aware of my own thoughts. Another thrill shakes me. Gently, I roll back the surface. The inner chamber is tiny, hardly large enough for a child. Glass-smooth and hard at first, but with the right touch it conforms to my skin, soft as flower petals.

This is where I lay three years ago. This is the chamber that kept me safe during my long journey across the universe, and endured the crash that vaporized the rest of my vessel. What hands formed this tiny cradle? Who sent me to Alta and what were their hopes for me? Did they dare to dream I would live? Were they frightened or proud or glad to watch me go?

It is hard to imagine being that small, and only three winters past. I reach deeper. My fingers brush something altogether solid. The immortal heart, no larger than a plum, dense as a perished star. I clasp it. Not quite spherical, not quite smooth, the texture blends into my hand, conforming to every line, sending tendrils of light inside me, filling me like a prism. . . .

. . . A halo opens in the sky, tearing away the tower, the mountain, the atmosphere of Alta. I look up, or try to, but my body is no longer mine. The halo expands like a drop of oil in a rain barrel. It dilates closer, eating the sky. I hurtle into the dark.

On the far side, I open my eyes, touch the velvet of

space, watch the ripples pulse between bright novas, filling the emptiness with cosmic dust. I admire the symmetry of the stars. This galaxy looks familiar, a mother, many young lives inside her. I see faces in the turning of worlds. Do they remember me, my brothers and sisters? I try to cry out to them, but my voice makes no sound.

I fall past the event horizon of this galaxy's heart, feel the heat of the darkness and know it is something more. I reach too far. My orbit falters. I fall into the night, and it is not empty, but full of hoarded light, too bright to be seen.

I am vaguely aware of being on Alta with Oberon, of holding the crystal heart of my cocoon. But my waking mind is so easily tricked, it is the dreaming mind I trust. I stand on a bluff near a midnight ocean. Waves crash against the shore and pull away, repeating. I see a girl kneeling in the sand. Her hair is as long as time. She looks at me with a face like a sun being born.

Absently, she picks a few blue and red stars from the sky and adds them to a sandcastle she is building, formed from the grains of life. Inside are endless rooms, and each room is a universe. The ocean swells and falls away, taking with it some of the stars. Somewhere in the vast creation of this silent girl is a green and blue speck, lit by a young sun. I see it all now, as if I was helping make it. In a way, I am.

The girl again, this time kneeling on the sky playing marbles with the stars. She makes them collide and explode like glass ornaments. The cosmic fireworks dance in her eyes. I watch her, transfixed. Looking down, I see I am standing on the sun, sinking, howling inside. I cannot break apart the waves of light. My hand reaches out, my voice is silence in the void. The girl with the unseeable face pays no heed.

What is this place? I wonder, pulling myself farther from the vision by the force of my doubt. I can feel the shape of the cocoon's heart in my palm, the piece of my homeworld, the pulsar shard. *How did I know to call it that?*

Then the vision takes me again. Strangely, I am brought back to a day in the woods last spring. My father, Lux, showed me how to set traps and snares in a mess of leaves. He could build traps made of saplings and string that wouldn't kill the foxes or rabbits they snared. I let him teach me, and made one to please him. The moment his back was turned, I dismantled it. I never saw a reason for the traps. Animals always came to me on their own. They wouldn't ever show up when Father was around, maybe because of his dragon blood. Maybe they knew he wanted to eat them.

"Stubborn girl! Don't make me get my bow," he'd growl at me whenever I sabotaged his traps.

I remember how he would stalk into the forest with his longbow. He'd go in like a starving jackal and sometimes return looking worse than when he'd left. Other times he would come back gentler, content. Now it all makes sense. He needed meat, more than I could imagine.

He taught me to eat meat, and I liked it okay, though I liked live animals more. I told stories to the goats even when they spit at me. One time, the billy spit at Father and he knocked it so hard on the head it forgot how to stand up. We kept pigs for a whole summer, but when winter came we didn't have enough to feed them, and the sow ate her babies. I went into the forest and cried all day.

"Don't eat those berries!" Lux said when he found me with my lips stained purple. "I showed you the roots that were safe. I told you where to find wild onions and herbs. I showed you what not to eat, didn't I?" He furrowed his brow doubtfully, perhaps thinking himself a poor father.

I wanted to laugh, but all I could think of were the pigs. "I thought you were joking. I eat them all the time."

"Bless the stars," he said and looked up at the sky, then back at me. "You are full of surprises."

That's when we found out I can't be poisoned, not by plants at least. I've never been sick either. But what does it matter? I'm light on my feet, immune to cold. I see well in the dark. I get all tingly when I walk the pulsar fields or look up at the sky on a clear night.

What does it all mean? Would the universe let me feel special if I'm not? Would it let a stump dream of flying? Are we given wishes that cannot be fulfilled in any world? That can't be so. I will not believe it.

Ava, wake up. Can you hear me? A familiar voice in my head.

I dream. But I am afraid. Afraid to dream with open eyes.

Ava! The voice again, a male voice, hesitant. *You're talking in your sleep. Come back.*

Would a stump dream of flying? I turn stubbornly toward oblivion, but the voice calls me back. I hear it from afar like the dusty memory of a long-forgotten story.

"During the first year of my travels, before I took a body, I saw a tree struck by lightning. It died instantly, cracked and singed down the middle. The groundskeeper came out the next sunny day and cut it down for firewood. But it was a strange tree, very light. The wood had less density than the cork on a wine bottle. A toymaker, knowing the value of the wood, sawed a single slice off the stump, and using a pillow case and the balsa wood for a skeleton, he carved a toy kite."

"What's a kite?" I ask very softly.

"It's a stump," he says simply. "A stump that flies."

Is that you, Oberon? Is that . . .

. . . I return to reality to find Oberon shaking me. I stare vacantly at him, remembering only fragments of my dream. I try to put the memories together, but it's like one of the old puzzles Father kept in his closet: dusty, slightly mildewed, and missing pieces.

"What did you see?" he asks.

"Memory and dust. A goddess. I don't know. I saw myself."

"Do you have it?"

I lift the pulsar shard and show it to him. "Everything I need."

He looks at it, discerning more than I can fathom. Then he nods. "It is an artifact of tremendous power, a sidereal remnant. With it we can walk through worlds."

"We can find Father now!" I say, still breathless from the dream. "We can help with the war. We can fix everything!"

"We could, in theory," Oberon says. "But I don't know how to use it."

"Neither do I," I admit, trying to piece together images from my dream. "I saw darkness. It was like a hole in the universe, squeezing everything inside itself. I fell in. I thought I'd die. But it was bright inside, like all the light from a thousand suns held in the bowl of a thimble."

"You must have seen it for a reason," he says. "Now, we need to hurry."

I freeze. Just over Oberon's shoulder, less than ten strides away, the cloaked form of a wizard stands in the doorway between us and freedom. At least, I assume she's a wizard. Maybe she's only an apprentice, a young woman, not much older than me. Her robe is a little big for her. She seems as startled as I am. "What's going on?" Her voice sounds thin. "I thought this project was shut down."

"We are retrieving a vial of ezepsin for the battle preparations," Oberon answers quickly. He sounds older, his voice deep and sensible.

"As you will," the young woman nods, seemingly satisfied. "Brother, remember your death."

"Sister, remember your death," Oberon echoes the unusual salutation.

Just when I think we might make it out of there with our skin, a second cloaked figure appears, a balding man of advanced age and prodigious anger. He storms into the room like a raving schoolmaster, waving a crooked finger at us. I have the presence of mind to hide the pulsar shard in my pocket.

Oberon tries something, a spell of forgetting maybe, but the wizard only narrows his eyes, barking something in another language. "He knows who we are!" Oberon shouts, standing between me and the wizard. "He'll try to bind us in words!"

"Intruders!" the wizard growls, holding out his hands threateningly, his robes rippling.

The air tremors. Oberon seems locked in concentration against the wizard. I can feel the strength of their wills like swords bound together at the hilt. The space between them shimmers, cracks, explodes.

I sprawl on my back, ears ringing, eyes burning with tears. Oberon crumples and slides across the floor, colliding with a table and upending it. Glass shatters. Toxic chemicals mix in a smoking, reeking, spitting, mess. Oberon curls up instinctively as an entire cupboard full of laboratory materials crashes on top of him.

The old wizard is also on the ground, equally stunned, sweating and flailing under piles of robes. The explosion knocked him through the open door and halfway down the hall. A whirlwind of dust and shredded parchment tears through the chamber, eventually quieting.

I scramble to my feet, snatch up a shard of broken glass, watching the woman to see what she will do. Our eyes meet. She tries to say something, a spell maybe, but with so many fumes in the air, all that comes out is a cough, followed by a high-pitched wheeze. Clutching her throat, she retreats awkwardly and shuts the main door, locking us in.

I drop the chunk of glass, infinitely relieved at not having to use it. I hurry over to Oberon and begin digging, pulling at drawers, boxes, beakers, and metal canisters. "Be still! I'm coming!"

He squirms underneath the wreckage, groaning. I uncover his head and brush the glass from his cheek. There's something like a self-depreciating smile on his face, his bottom lip cut and bleeding.

"Pain is such a mystery," he says thickly, sucking on his lip, touching a gash on his forehead. "My kind know nothing of pain, and yet . . . perhaps we are the lesser for it." He grunts with effort, shoves a dented cabinet aside, and sits up, one shoulder hanging limp. "Wizards," he says crossly, scratching at a red stain on his neck where some concoction spilled. Satisfied that it is non-caustic, he turns to his misshapen shoulder.

"Is it dislocated?" I ask, wishing I could help.

He nods, glaring at the shoulder as if to reprimand it. Miraculously, the torn fabric of his shirt moves and the shoulder slides back into place. He nods, pleased with himself, and tests the rotation.

I gape at him, at the mended shoulder, his perfect lip, his forehead which bears no trace of injury, forgetting for the moment that there are probably a hundred angry wizards converging on us.

He stands up and I follow by reflex. He quickly scans the room, shaking glass and yellow sulfur from his hair. "We need a way out."

"How about the front door?" I ask, hearing noises in the hallway.

He runs over and tries it. "Locked by magic." He sets his will against the enchantments and frowns. "There are binding runes on the door, some sort of security feature. We can't go that way." He looks frantically at the walls and ceiling. "I could clear us a path, but breaking the lattice might bring the central spire down on top of us."

I brandish the pulsar shard. "I have another way!"

"Give it a try," he says.

I focus on the crystal, feeling the solidity of it, the slow smolder of untold power. "Problem is, I have no idea how it works," I say after a long moment.

"Keep trying. In the meantime, I have a backup plan!" Oberon runs his fingers along the frame of the locked door, fusing the material to the metal frame. He sets his own glowing runes in a pattern between the hinges. "There. A crude binding, but it will buy us time."

There are no windows that I can see, and only one door,

spell-locked and welded shut from the inside. There is a fume hood used to ventilate the chamber, but getting up it would require something smaller and braver than me. I look around at what we have to work with. Beakers, scalpels, mirrors, a crank vice, a cold forge, a library of tomes stacked in a corner. The workshop is hopelessly messy. "What is all this junk?"

Oberon passes his trained eyes over the workbench. "Metalloids, lens cutters, diamond saws, vials of acid and glue, prisms, spectrometers, six liters of ezepsin." He shoulders past a contraption, seeming not to notice the shattered glass under his bare feet. "Lead, silver, gold . . ." he trails off and begins to gather components. "Let's go, Ava! Our way out won't build itself." He waves his hand at a closet and the door bangs open, an assortment of strange metal tubes clattering to the floor. "Get me six of those."

Rather than stare at the pulsar shard and hope for a miraculous breakthrough, I set to work. Oberon tears off what's left of his shirt, douses it in clear, pungent liquid, and begins constructing something in the center of the room, using a combination of Art and mechanical genius.

I help him by collecting the items he points to, tiptoeing between piles of broken glass. Oberon sets braziers burning and gear-wheels spinning. My hands begin to sweat, my eyes water. The air is so full of fumes, I can hardly swallow.

We've barely started when I hear the first wizards arrive, cursing, arguing, unbinding the spell-hardened door. How much time? I continue running errands, amazed by the secrets lodged in every shelf and corner. Star charts on walls, jars of dust, space rocks, roots. Vials of black and silver seeds. All sorts of things taken from my fields. Even a terrarium with one of the rock-eating lizards inside.

It stares at me, looking cold and underfed. Then, in a flash of phosphorescent dust, it teleports, appearing on the opposite side of the cage, its claws scraping at the glass. "Never seen that trick before," I whisper, feeling my eyebrows rise. "Think you could teach me?" I pry open the lid and free the poor creature, not sure where he will go. He crawls to the edge of the glass prison, bobs his head twice, and disappears.

I rush back to Oberon just as he finishes arranging a series of crystals, each paired with a chemical light emitter. With the ezepsin, some kind of liquid explosive, he prepares an array of dangerous looking tubes. "Don't let it spill on you," he warns as we arrange the tubes in a neat circle on the floor. "Now, you might want to take cover."

Outside, I sense the disturbance of spells being cast. The door vibrates like a gong, creaking and ringing with stress. It won't be long now.

I find a hiding place and clutch the shard to my chest, feel it responding to me, growing hotter, more awake. Or is it my imagination? I examine it carefully. It looks different than it feels. The texture is that of a gemstone, hard, symmetrical, and cut with many ridges. But to the eyes it has taken a smooth, slightly oblong shape like a river-stone.

As I hold it, spellbound, heart thumping and breath hissing, the shape and clarity seem to fluctuate, all the colors of the universe shifting in its depths. "Teach me to be like the lizard," I breathe.

Here I am, staring at a pretty rock that has the power to save us. Meanwhile, Oberon slaves away, the resourceful hero, piecing together a workshop full of junk just to buy us a few more seconds. It isn't right for him to do all the work, to save me again and again while I stand by, useless. It's the same thing Father did the day we were separated. He sacrificed himself for me when he could have easily gotten away. I won't let it happen again.

I clutch the shard and close my eyes, searching it for sparks of anima, alchemy, or Art. Machines and magic, I don't understand either. But I understand friendship. If this all goes wrong, I want to be there for Oberon. And I'm holding the answer in my hands.

CHAPTER XIII
Sol:
The Prophecy

WIN OR LOSE, I will not survive this war. The throne goes to Hector. He is a good son to me, loyal, as a son should be. But he is young. Were it not for the blood that clogs my lungs, were it not for the fluid in them, for the shaking in my hands, I would rule another forty years.

My people do not know of my illness. Only the doctors —and Hector—know how I sit on a throne of gold while my insides rot like old cabbage. It is better that I die in battle, as a king should, than in my shame, in bed, suffering.

Hector will rule well; he is strong. And he is kind, all things considered, with his mother dying in childbirth and my temper and ways with women. It is a wonder, really, that he has the heart he does, a heart for the people, for others. I have hurt him. I see that now, as I suppose fathers do when nearing death.

He spends his days in the lower tiers helping the poor and sick and dying. Gives away all he can, so I don't give him too much. The people love him. He's a bit of a hero among them. He'll make a good king, better than I did, at least until our treasury runs empty and our grain supplies diminish and he can no longer give out free money, food, and medicine.

I sometimes worry that he does not take a woman. Why does he wait? He is of age, and there is no shortage of noble blood in the archipelago. My secret hope is he will take a queen from the strongest of our neighbor islands, from

Lerais or Cov. But it's too late for that now. War is upon us.

The armies of Obul have taken the pulsar fields, barely a week from our walls. Vanfell needs a leader now, and I am he. And Hector will lead after me until he is dead, and then his children, and so on, until all the bones of all the kings come to dust and the world ends. *Vanfell, do you think yourself immortal?*

A knock echoes through the door of my study. An attendant hurries over, opens a slot in the wood. "Your highness! Your son is here."

"See him in," I say, sitting up in my chair, adjusting my back painfully, shuffling papers and maps on the desk.

Hector enters, clothed in his usual nondescript uniform, flecks of snow melting on his shoulders. His cloak is like a shadow, storm gray, cast iron black, bearing no trace of a royal standard. He is wearing his sword. "Father, thank you for seeing me." He covers the room in three strides. He is taller than his old man, now. That is good.

"I would be a poor father to refuse," I say, remaining seated.

Hector sets his hands on my desk, dismissing with formalities. "Dad, you look like hell."

I chuckle, a sound that has been known to make newborns cry. "You're just trying to make me feel better. What brings you here in the middle of the night?"

"I couldn't sleep. I see you can't either. The generals are restless. They're sectioning off the city. Rogues and thieves are taking advantage of the confusion, preying on the people." Hector frowns, clenching his jaw. I half expect him to storm out, sword in hand, and put an end to the opportunistic scum himself.

"What would you have me do about it?" I ask, crossing one leg, wincing as a familiar pain shoots through my spine to my teeth.

Hector is about to reply when the attendant interrupts us. "Lord, Sol—"

"See them in!" I bark. "Be quick."

An apprentice mage whom I do not recognize shuffles in, an envoy from the obsidian tower. "Your highness!" she cries, throwing back her hood. "Intruders in the black tower. We've captured two intruders."

"How is this possible? I was told the tower is impenetrable."

"Until tonight, it was, my lord." Her voice is dry, slightly raspy. "There's one boy, a duster, and a girl with him. We found them in the Sidereatrix."

"A girl, you say?" I don my gloves and rise stiffly.

"Yes, my lord."

"How young?"

"Perhaps fourteen."

"Describe her."

"Um . . . pale skin, like moonlight. Black hair past her shoulders. I didn't get a good look. The duster attacked us. He used the Art!"

"Bring them here, now."

"It would be better." The mage stumbles at my gaze, her voice a nervous squeak. "It would be better, forgive me your majesty, if you came to the tower. We do not know what they are capable of, and we have our warders there to protect you."

My mind races. I tremble for a moment. One might ask

why I am afraid, what could be so dangerous about two children? But only a fool would ask such questions. Not all things in this false and mirthless world are as they appear. The most ancient and formidable powers in existence often disguise themselves in innocuous forms. Farmers with the strength of dragons in their blood. Blind sages, living alone, who could break the world with a word. Faceless horrors that never die and remember the day the dry land was raised up from the primordial sea.

Could this teenager be Lux's daughter, the one I have been searching for? The one the oracle spoke of? She could be the weapon I need to win this war before I die.

"Sire?"

"I will heed your council," I say. "Use your arts to bind the girl against every form of escape, magical and otherwise. Alert me when she is . . . safe."

"What of the other?"

"Take him captive, but do not harm him. He might know something."

"As you wish." She bows and hurries out, her cloak flapping behind.

"Is this why you came to see me, Hector?" I ask, turning on my silent son.

He shakes his head, but does not lower his gaze or flinch when I look at him. Yes, he will be a good king. "Then why are you here?"

"It might sound strange. I know I should be cleaning my new armor and getting used to the feel of it. But I wanted to be with you, here. Now."

"I know I'm dying! I don't need you here sniveling to tell me that."

"Not sniveling, not mourning," he says firmly. "I just want to be with you. To talk, maybe."

"To plan the war?"

"We could do that."

"What do you want, boy?" A bout of coughing racks me, and I use my handkerchief to dab the blood from my lips. "Brandy," I croak, gesturing toward the bar behind me. There's a hot coal lodged in my throat, a searing dryness that never goes away.

After tending to my needs, Hector slides into the chair across from me. "I thought we might just talk," he says. "Maybe about how good the fishing is this time of year, or how the city is alive again, united in a common cause. Or maybe about what it means to be king, the kinds of things old kings teach and young ones learn."

I sip my liquor, considering the man across from me, his confident manner, his unwavering gaze, his beard thickening as winter sets in. *Could this really be my son, a man grown?*

"Pipe," I grunt, and an attendant furnishes me with one, already lit. "Listen, young man. I know you. I was you, once upon a time. Handsome, noble, enamored with danger, with a need to do things and do them well. I knew deep in my heart, as you do, that I was young and could not die. Look at me, son. I'm old now. And I feel my mortality like a noose around my neck." I pull steadily from the pipe, spitting, coughing, savoring the taste, until the room is wreathed in smoke.

Hector listens as if, deep beneath the melodrama and self-pity, he might extract something useful from my babbling. Not likely.

I rattle on, "Fools may tell you, from time to time, that old age is serenity. That's horse shit. I'm angry, my boy, angry all the time. Age has not lessened my need to do things and do them well—to dig my nails into the rich soil of life, deep as I can, until the cities and rivers of Alta are washed in my sweat! But it's too late, see? Too late."

"Too late for what, Father? Your body is weak, but functioning. And you still have your mind. This self-imposed despair seems a bit premature."

A fair point, damn him. "Forgive me, Hector. All I have is this war and the words of that bitch of an oracle. Would you rob a man of his last hope—that something good will come from the stars? Did you not hear the envoy? Intruders in the Sidereatrix! A girl with skin as pale as the daytime moon. She came back for it, don't you see? Came back to claim the vessel that carried her to our world! It must be Lux's daughter."

"Father, you've been fixated on this thing that crashed in the desert for years. We have it. We've learned next to nothing from it. Do you really think it could have carried a person inside?"

"You do not lie well, Hector," I growl, seeing his confidence flicker in the torchlight. "You know there was a girl. You were there the day I came upon her and the dragonblood, Lux. The day I claimed the pulsar fields. Of course, I did not know what she was at the time."

"Nor what *he* was for that matter," Hector says. "Otherwise you never would have brought one of the accursed dragon-race to our city alive."

An unfortunate oversight, to be sure. To this moment, I can still hear that awful roar, feel the ground quake, the dungeon break, old stone splitting, men's screams and the hissing, spitting flames, the demon voice shaking my bones. It was less than a week ago that the beast escaped and wreaked havoc on the high city. Had I known what Lux was, I never would have allowed him to live. I wonder if Agon, clever and treacherous, sent him as a gift just to spite me.

"Damn, fool wizards. Hard-headed. Unreliable." I glance at the door, anxious to see the girl for myself. "What's taking them so long? Surely she must be tamed by now!"

Hector's jaw works silently. "What will you do with her?"

I scratch my thin scrap of beard. "She is Star Kin, a creature born from above. If the fields are hers, as the oracle foretold, she must know how they work."

"Not necessarily. But for the sake of argument, let's say your faulty line of reasoning proves true. Do you think she'll share her secrets willingly?"

"Willingly? Perhaps not, but given the right incentive . . ."

"You mean to force her, to hurt her if necessary?" Hector's voice is hard, his eyes narrow, dangerous.

"Whatever it takes to protect my people. My Star Hunters have already unlocked certain features of the pulsar fields: illusion, teleportation, and other forms of energy manipulation. They've proven the power is real, controlled it even, but not with impunity. So many have died. . . . I will not have their years of study wasted!"

"It's only a waste if you refuse to move past it! Let go of the ghosts, the visions, the what-ifs. Focus on the tangible. The walls need fixing, badly. The moat has not been properly dredged. The men are willing, though most are underfed, undertrained, and lacking responsible leadership. It is in overcoming these small, daily challenges that we will have victory, not in dreams and visions!"

"Do you remember the words of the oracle?" I ask, only

half listening. "When the Light Eater rises to devour all, and Obul sends forth her hosts. When hopes are dust and darkness falls, and all that's good seems lost. Despair not, ye mighty, but look to the stars, a falling gift to claim. Despair not, ye bold—"

"I know the damn prophecy!" Hector snaps, finally losing his temper. "You have a lot of faith for an atheist, Father. Strands of a plan, nothing more!"

"Enough!" I hiss, my voice hoarse and ragged. "As we sit here, argue, and debate, the vermin of Obul swarm across my lands, burning my towns, my fields, slaughtering my people. With my supply lines compromised, my political enemies at my throat, my soldiers deserting in droves—I dare to hope in something! And yet you criticize me, think me a fool, grasping at strands and nothings!" Breath rasping, fists shaking, I struggle to calm myself, lest my heart give out. "No, my son. In this dark hour, strands will have to suffice."

Hector merely shakes his head, keeping silent until he has regained his composure. "It is, as you say, a desperate time. And I admit, your intentions are good. But the ends do not justify the means, Father. This star creature, this girl, this other being—she is not to be tortured or abused! Question her if you must, but do not use her as the Obulans use their battle slaves."

"Ah, the soldier philosopher," I sneer, rising and gesturing for my coat. "How romantic. Perhaps you should tell her how you feel. You'll be seeing her soon enough! I'm done waiting. I'm going to the tower, now. If you want any say whatsoever in her fate, I suggest you accompany me!"

CHAPTER XIV
Moonflight

OBERON IS just putting the finishing touches on his invention when the mages break in, blasting the oval door into identical glass-metal fragments and filling the room with smoke. Hiding in a corner, I hold tight to the pulsar shard while Oberon faces them.

The wizards enter in pairs and spread out, weaving enchantments to clear the choked air. These are not healers, diviners, or soothsayers. These are battle mages, those who wield crude, deadly elemental magic and are good at killing things. There is nothing subtle about a battle mage.

I can see Oberon moving in the shadows out of sight. He casts a spell, igniting flammable metals and salt emitters of his own design.

The first flash disorients the wizards, and they raise their hands in defense, casting magical shields. The second flash nearly blinds me through my eyelids. The third sends wizards thumping to the floor, flailing and writhing in their floppy robes. It's like they're drowning in their own clothes.

"Now!" Oberon says.

I spring forward as his handiwork flares into action. It's some sort of alchemic torch, fueled by ezepsin, meant for burning a hole in my cocoon. Where it failed on the adamantine metal, it succeeds in burning through the hard glass-iron floor. In the midst of the smoke and gas, Oberon and I jump through the hole and into a lower room in the tower. I land awkwardly, falling on hands and knees on something soft. Oberon does better, keeping his feet and his wits.

We are in a storage closet full of bags of magical seeds. I climb off the bag that broke my fall and some of the seeds spill out on the floor. Immediately, they begin to grow, sprouting into flowering vines with vivid flame-tipped petals. The green fruit is already ripening on the branches as we charge out of the closet into a much larger room.

"Uh-oh," Oberon mutters, skidding to a halt. What was supposed to be an empty sparring chamber is quickly filling with wizards. Six bodies block the only exit. Another dozen stand facing us with spells at the ready. They must have anticipated we would try to go through the floor.

"You are well trained, duster." A sharp-eyed man with short, graying hair steps forward with an air of command, addressing Oberon. His black robes seem better tailored, more distinguished than the others. He wears the eclipsed-moon insignia of a Star Hunter on his chest. "A valiant effort, to be sure, but as you can see, it's over. Come quietly, and you and the girl will be shown mercy."

Oberon says nothing, his eyes glistening with power, smoke leaking from his clenched fists.

I notice a young woman standing just behind the Star Hunter, the same woman who first discovered us. He whispers something to her and she scampers off. "What are you, thieves or assassins?" he asks.

I hold my tongue, Oberon does the same.

The Star Hunter gestures irritably toward his sub-ordinates. "Take them!"

"No!" Oberon springs forward, shielding me with his body, holding our attackers at bay with a lattice of conjured light. His tattoos blaze and smolder, dripping sparks from his skin.

It is a noble gesture, he is always noble. But I've never seen him tested like this. I have no idea if he's reached the end of his strength—or—if pushed a little farther, he could turn all these hostile wizards to ash.

Even as he strives against them, more drop in from behind, hacking their way through the closet full of vines to ambush us. "Look out!" I cry, pointing. Oberon retreats, shuffling sideways, keeping all our enemies in sight. Soon we'll be cornered, and then what? *Teach me to be like the lizard!* I beg, still holding tight to the pulsar shard.

"I can't fight them all!" Oberon cries, grasping for my hand. His eyes flicker toward the heavens and he mouths a silent prayer.

"I feel the door," I say, my back to the wall, tracing the outline of the pulsar shard with my fingernail. "The door to everywhere."

The foremost wizards cast spells. Most deflect harmlessly off the invisible barrier of Oberon's will. Some break through. My arms feel heavy, my movements sluggish, my mind clouded. I grit my teeth and squeeze the pulsar shard with all my strength, wishing desperately to be far away.

But there's something holding me here. A terrible pressure in my skull. Tubes of iron, rising from the floor, snaking up my leg, binding my hands and feet in ever-tightening cords. The same thing is happening to Oberon. He cries out in a secret tongue, his tattoos burning like rivers of fire in his skin, melting holes in the iron even as it encircles him. One arm breaks free, skin dripping molten metal, fingers weaving a spell.

Two wizards freeze in place, topple like statues. More move in to seize us. Though I can't move my arm or even my fingers, I can still feel Oberon's hand on my right, the pulsar shard in my left, pulsing, burning hotter than ever. *Anywhere!* I plead. *Anywhere but here.* I imagine the night sky. I imagine . . .

A blinding flash.

And suddenly the obsidian tower is gone. The sky rushes in. The hot, chemical-smoke air is replaced by an icy mountain wind. I stagger on an uneven slope, fall to my hands and knees, crushed under the weight of my bonds. Someone touches me, and the metal cracks and flakes like cooled wax. I crawl free, shivering with joy and wonder. "We traveled!" I exclaim, standing on a rooftop in an obscure part of the city.

Oberon looks around, sucks a deep breath through his teeth, lets it out, hands on hips, gripping the cold roof tiles with his toes. "You amaze me," he says, smiling halfway, his face slightly drawn, as if he's just run miles in the sand. His tattoos slowly return to normal, the red light fading to blue, then pale gray.

"Where are we?" I ask.

"In one of the lower tiers, somewhere near the outer walls. Be ready. They may give chase."

"How could they follow us?" I hold the shard tighter and look up through the obscurity to where the obsidian tower should be, far above us, miles of rooftops between.

"You really don't know anything about the arcane arts, do you?" Even as Oberon speaks, the air cracks and three cloaked figures appear, tall and dark in the moonlight, their cloaks billowing in the wind. "Warpers," he says.

I recognize the Star Hunter among them. "Get the

duster!" he growls, using the derogatory name for the desert people, Oberon's race. "He is an adept!"

The nearest wizard, a woman, rushes at us, wind in each fist. The other conjures ice and fog. The Star Hunter remains by a blackened chimney, muttering old words, crouching to keep his balance on the fragile roof caps.

The moment the wizards unleash their spells, Oberon explodes into motion, devouring their magics in his own. His spells are soundless, colorless, nothing at all like the wizards' elemental magic. Their spells are breath, heat, and biting winter. His are like a hole with no bottom, eating them up. When the last spell is extinguished, he turns to me, looking weary. "Run," he mouths, giving me a hurried push.

I flee across the rooftops without a second thought. He scrambles after me. Shingles explode under our feet, but we are already gone, sprinting barefoot to the next rooftop. I hurdle a gap and land running, weaving past chimneys, over dormers, feet skipping and pattering, eyes watching for obstacles.

Two wizards follow closely, a man and a woman, casting wind and ice at us. The Star Hunter, the fire wielder, follows behind, unwilling to use his element at the risk of destroying the city.

The shingles are brittle and sharp, but my feet hardly brush them as I run. I do not dislodge a single piece of clay. Oberon is nearly as fast, even as he fends off spells with counter-spells of his own. I wonder fondly if there is anything he can't do.

Our pursuers stumble often, swearing. The shingles give way under their heavy boots. Leading the chase, I work my way into a slum, where roof repairs are common, and thatched sections appear amid the clay. Seconds later, I hear a shout as one of the wizards falls through a badly mended roof and disappears with a crash. The others abandon the rooftops and follow below on foot, weaving through alleys, using some mysterious Art to speed their strides.

They split up, probably meaning to head us off and trap us. I lose track of them and focus on running, rabbit-like, my heart beating uncontrollably. I've heard of frightened animals fleeing until their lungs and hearts give out. I might not be at risk for that, but right now I feel a deep kinship with all hunted things.

Oberon is always beside me, or just behind, my only comfort. He also is having a hard time with the straw thatching, but he manages. Sprinting over the rooftops in the predawn hours is every bit as thrilling as it is terrifying. The houses flash under us, chimneys breathing warmth into a sky of frost and starlight, the moon to one side, perfectly still.

Most everyone is asleep at this hour, and I imagine them waking from time to time as their rafters creak. Others wander the narrow streets—thieves, drifters, insomniacs, looking up as we pass over, shadows in the night. I hold the pulsar shard in one hand, trying to tap its power. I don't know where it will take me, but I don't care. Anywhere but here.

Suddenly, as I leap the gap between two shacks, something lodges under my shoulder blade—paralyzing cold. The force of it jolts my body forward, and I land awkwardly, twist into a painful roll, scramble for a hold, miss, and tumble off the roof. Oberon follows, calling my name, but I barely hear him.

My body careens through two lines of drying laundry

into the dirt alley below, and finally crumples next to a pile of rotting filth. The pulsar shard slips from my icy hand.

I lie for a moment, unable to breathe, stunned by the fall, but also by the sudden stillness. The open sky, the wind in my ears and in my hair—all gone—replaced by throbbing pain and the smell of beef broth and rotten fruit. My right arm is as hard and immobile as marble, like it belongs on a statue. I turn over and begin to crawl toward the pulsar shard.

My cheek drags across the winter-hardened dirt, one eye open and bleary, neck stiff and painful sore. From my sideways angle on the ground, I see the boots of the Star Hunter approach, puffs of dust disturbed by his sweeping cloak. I hear words of power. Then Oberon's bare feet appear between us. "Go no further!" he says.

"Out of my way, duster!" the Star Hunter growls, an inferno in his clasped hands.

Oberon remains poised, hands level and relaxed. I reach for the pulsar shard as it lies glistening in the filth, and clasp it just as the wizard unleashes his spell. I feel its energy fill me, thawing my dead arm instantly. Fingers still tingling and numb, I grab hold of Oberon's ankle. . . .

The sky falls to pieces.

The cold air is sucked away. I taste earth and singed hair.

"Maker, bless me," Oberon whispers, swooning with wonder, my hand latched tight to his ankle. Recovering quickly, he helps me to my feet. "How do you feel?"

I stretch my neck and back, wincing. "I'd be better if I knew what I did."

"You took us across the universe." He says, still in awe. "We didn't even go through the vale."

I wipe the mud from my face with my sleeve, staring

around at the bare, hilly landscape. When I look up, the first things I notice are the many moons of this world, some full, some only slivers. Twin moons burn brightest, crescent shaped, almost touching, a slice of space between them. Even as I watch, they clasp each other like mother and child, casting double shadows. The brightness is incredible, yet it is still night.

I marvel at my two shadows, then Oberon's, amazed by how tall we've become, and how heavy. Above our heads is a sphere of darkness, incredibly dense. "The galaxy's heart," Oberon whispers with just a hint of fear. "A light eater. The lord of these stars."

It looks like a black globe in the depthless sky, rings of fire surrounding it. It sparks a memory from my dream, but this time I know what I'm seeing is real. "I've seen one like it before," I hiss, my voice strange and distant. I can hardly see Oberon. It's like the color is being ripped from his skin.

"Ava, get us out of here!" he cries.

I hold his hand and grip the pulsar shard. I pour my desire into it as I did the other times. Nothing happens.

"Ava!" The light eater is far too close. It's taking in everything. I sense the presence of a landscape, but I can no longer see. There's no light to see by. Even the embracing moons have gone out, leaving only the void.

"It's not an evil thing!" I scream, not sure if Oberon can hear me. Is it eating my voice too? "It's just too full of light. Too bright to see!"

A pulse of energy rises from the heart of the darkness— a ring of fire, rotating, reaching out. I can feel it scorching distant worlds. The quasar fire burns like the heart of a scorned lover, pouring out into the universe. It is the single brightest, saddest thing I have ever seen.

Ava, now! I can feel his skin on my palm, slipping. If I let go, will I lose him forever? The thought brings tears to my eyes. I squeeze his hand, delve into the pulsar shard, and wish us far away. . . .

We manifest, not on Alta, but somewhere.

"Alive! Still alive!" Oberon exclaims, collapsing into stillness.

I lie on my back for a full minute, eyes closed, letting my breaths slow. When I open them, Oberon is lying next to me in the grass, looking spent. I study the horizon. The new world is warm and green. The sky is ocean pink, full of clouds. I could not feel safer. I roll onto my side and lay a hand on his shoulder. "We made it."

"We . . . sorry . . ." he murmurs, folding his hands over his bare chest. "I need a moment."

"Was it the wizards?" I ask, still short of breath.

"It was a little bit of everything. I'm sorry for losing my composure back there."

"No need to apologize." We rest in silence for a while. I close my eyes and try not to think about the light eater or the wizards. I've read myths about the strain of working magic, how it drains body and soul.

Oberon certainly looks drained, his eyes clouded, far away. I hate seeing him like this. I will never know what it cost him to give up his immortal life, to save me again and again, to ward off killing spells. It doesn't seem right that he'd risk himself for me when I've only caused him hardship. I watch his chest rise and fall and wish I had something to give. "Oberon?" I touch his shoulder gently. "You okay?"

He looks at me, startled, and his eyes come back into

focus. "When I saw what was happening," he breathes. "I saw our lives. I saw your soul and mine and the quasar fire. I was afraid. I did not want to discorporate."

"I was scared too," I say. "And I didn't even know what was happening. You understood."

Oberon closes his eyes and leans his head against the tall, fragrant grass. He looks up at the daytime stars and at the huge, glowing dandelions that float in the breeze. He catches one and holds it out to me. "It is not good for a soul to fear the death of its body," he says. "I am immortal. I know I am. . . ." he trails off. "Most of all I feared for you."

More dandelions fall from the quiet sky, alighting on the drifting grass. I touch one and a needle-like petal sticks to my finger. I blow on it and it floats away. The wind is warm in my hair. Between the peaks of distant mountains, the sky lights up in streaks of silver and white. The heat lightning is soft as aurora tints, but there is no sun or moon.

"We should get back to Alta," Oberon says, rising stiffly. "Now that you know how to control the shard, we can find your father. We can fix everything."

"It's just a stone," I say, trying to be realistic. "It's from another world, my world maybe, and it gives us access to the manifold. But it won't stop a war, or bring my old life back."

"It's not our war to stop," he says. "Besides, maybe your new life will be better."

"Maybe." I stand up, surprised at how easy it is. I wobble my arms in front of me, bounce up and down on my toes, floating a little higher each time. I giggle with delight, can't help it. My body feels as light as flower petals.

Leaping high into the air, I gaze out from the cliff where we materialized. Rivers and trees appear tiny in the spring-green valley below. Golden salamanders dart between the brown stones of an adjacent cliff. Some are at play, warm and full of energy. Others bask on the rocky slopes. They remind me of the desert salamanders that I would sometimes find in the pulsar fields. Of all animals, they were the only ones that could thrive in the liminal space between worlds, feeding on mist and mineral dust.

I land lightly and hop around the clearing, trying not to fall. "This is tricky!" I cry, eventually losing my balance and sprawling in the soft grass. I lie still, giggling at my clumsiness. "This feels so weird." I get up and try again.

"It's always evening here," Oberon remarks when I finally come down. "But it is not the vale. It is somewhere else, somewhere safe."

"Are you sure you don't want to stay?" I ask. "Rest a while?"

He shakes his head. "I have rested all my life."

"Even so, you look tired," I say, holding out the pulsar shard. "Also, I have no idea how to use this."

"How did you do it before?"

"There's no formula. No command word. It's like making a wish."

"Then wish."

"Why are you in such a hurry to go back to Alta?"

Oberon looks shy and traces the tattoos on his forearm with his index finger. "It's where we belong for now," he says, his eyes flickering toward me. "Anywhere else and we're simply running away."

He's right, as usual. I polish the shard with my thumb and nod. "You ready?"

We hold hands like we have so many times before. I am

beginning to like the feel of it. It means we are about to travel someplace new. I look at Oberon and smile. His eyes are full of this place. I wish I knew where we were. I try to remember every detail, the way the air smells, the softness of the grass, the painted sky.

Maybe one day, when the world we love is at peace again, we can find our way back and walk amid the dandelions.

I feel the hardness of the shard, the prismatic sharpness, the intrinsic warmth. Where did it come from? Is my time on Alta only a sojourn? An interlude between my dawn and my destiny? The shard vibrates faintly in my hand. When I learn its secrets, will it lead me to where I belong?

Guide me, I beg, feeling my palm heat up. I conjure a mental image of Alta, the familiar sky, the fragrant seasons, the colors of the night. I think of it in all its precious flaws. I was not born there. I will not end there. It is not safe or peaceful. But at least for now, it is home.

CHAPTER XV
Refuge Dreams

WE APPEAR with flower petals still in our hair. I smell the alien pollen of the breathtaking world, the honeydew air, the many-colored sky. I panic for a moment, wanting it back, wanting to feel safe.

Our supernatural arrival into a small space disturbs the sparse decorations on the walls and blows open a window, letting in an icy draft. I swing the window shut and latch it while Oberon searches the area with his senses.

This place is familiar even in the dark. It's the same four-cornered room in the sleepy inn where we had a bath two days ago. It is unoccupied and the hearth where we shared tea and stories is vacant and cold.

"They'll be melting through the walls any minute," I whisper.

"I don't think so," he says. "You teleported beyond the world of Alta and back this time. You used the shard to take us to other galaxies, therefore making us untraceable."

"Are you sure?"

Oberon kneels in a thin layer of frost, wiping the floorboards clean with his hands. He pauses for a moment, taking the pulse of the world and listening for a heartbeat. "I know a place where they'll never find us," he says.

Unlocking a supply closet, Oberon pulls down an access hatch and we climb a folding ladder, fighting our way through the spiderwebs to a forgotten attic. Lying around, empty and overturned, are various half-barrels, all smelling faintly of fermented honey. A few sacks of used clothes are strewn about collecting dust, along with holiday decorations, a ratty old mop, two whiskey kegs, heaps of tarnished silverware, and a dozen empty fruit crates. The straw packing is sticky and smells of apples.

Oberon sits on the floor beside one of the two dormer windows, out of the light, and rests his head on an evergreen wreath, fingers interlocked over his chest.

Exhausted, I sit down on the aged wood and look out a cracked windowpane at the waning moon as it sets over the rooftops. It is below freezing outside. The chimneys across the street smoke pitifully, distorting the air a little. A few dormant ones gleam with sparks of frost.

We are alone in the loft, but the soft light and the comfort of our presence make it cozy, almost peaceful. I look down at a deserted plaza framed by four mature jacaranda trees. This variety blooms year-round. The flowers are a ghostly shade of violet, petals littering the courtyard. Seeing blooms in this harsh time somehow gives me hope.

I watch the thinning branches for almost an hour. Sometime before dawn, clouds cover the moon. Darkness rolls in and it begins to rain. The sound of the rain on the roof calms me. I turn to Oberon as water streaks down the windowpanes. He is still breathing easily, his expression soft and thoughtful.

The far corner begins to leak, dripping from the rafters, and I set an empty barrel under it. Another leak, directly above me, strikes me on the nose. "We haven't had rain in a long time," I say. "I'm happy to see it."

Oberon sits up and nods as another raindrop splatters on my shoulder. "You don't mind the cold," he says, watching me brush off the rain. "I see why now. You have a human appearance. But there is warmth and light in you that cannot be put out." Without explanation, he clears a space on the floor and sets a tiny crystal flame in the air between us. Its light cannot be seen from the window. Outside, the rain continues.

"Do you think the wizards are still looking for us?" I ask, wondering how something that looks like an ice sculpture can produce light.

Oberon shrugs, unconcerned. "The city is vast. We are safe."

"I just can't stop worrying."

"Ava, how did you bring us here to this exact place?"

"I don't know what I did exactly. I just imagined a safe place, and the shard did the rest. It's strange, I could have taken us anywhere on Alta, and I brought us back to Vanfell. Do you think it's a sign?"

"A sign of what?"

"That we have something to accomplish here?"

"I suspect there is a simpler explanation," he says. "Maybe it's just one of your most recent good memories?" He holds his hands over his slow-dancing flame. I feel its warmth and move closer, sitting across from him.

"I guess we should feel accomplished," I say. "We outsmarted a tower full of wizards."

Oberon chuckles. "Not all wizards are so dim. Not all charge high tuitions and wear flamboyant robes. I hope one day you will meet someone who uses their Art for the good of others, not for riches or acclaim. Someone you can look up to."

"Aren't you a wizard, Oberon?"

"Of a sort."

"How do you work magic?"

He sighs, winter fire reflected in his eyes. "I was born knowing some things. I guess you could say we souls are given certain privileges that human wizards have to learn the hard way—like the true speech, the tongue of what is."

"Sounds like something out of a fairy story," I say.

"Hah! That's how you know there's truth to it." He grins, showing the first sign of true mirth since his fight with the wizards. "I don't know everything about magic, but I know a few names, the forms of truth. The act of naming gives me power over things."

"What sort of language is it? Can it be spoken?"

"Of course. It's the language of the real, and nothing said in it can be a lie."

"So if you know the names of things you can summon them? What if there's no fire around to talk to? Can you still make fire?"

"I can," he replies. "All I need to know is where the fire is. The imperishable flame."

"Where?"

"Just a thought away." He reaches up and coaxes another fire from the air, gently, but with deft accuracy, as if grabbing a butterfly. "The same goes for all the elements." He blows softly on his hands and the two fires merge into something warm and bright as molten glass—no longer erratic, but moving as if in a slow stretching ritual. I've never seen fire behave that way.

"Is this how you get money?" I ask, entranced by the crystal flames.

"Exactly. I go to the horde." He pulls a silver coin from

the air and hands it to me. Then a gold one.

"It's heavy," I say, weighing the gold against the silver. "I'll have you know I intend to give these to someone who really needs them."

Oberon tries to show me how he grabs coins from the air. He says you just have to know where they are. The invisible realities are the fuel for every spell. I don't know what he means. I guess it would be silly to ask where the imperishable flame is—the place where all fire comes from. But it must exist. How else could he hold it in his hands?

"So that's magic," I say quietly. "Art, adepts, wizardry. It's all just knowing the true names of things."

"Not all," Oberon says with an eager smile. He loves teaching me things. "Controlling the elements is only a piece of what magic is—just as names are only pieces of truth. If you want to do real magic, you have to know the source behind the names, the Namer."

"Is it a person?"

Oberon smiles in a way I've only seen him smile when he's looking at me. But now he's looking out the window at the rain. I watch him carefully as his spirit reaches toward something indescribable. Something that not even the pulsar shard, with all its power, could touch.

After a time, he blinks away the far-off look in his eyes and turns to me. "Do you ever wonder why you were born, Ava? Is there some higher purpose for your life?"

"I can't say I've never wondered," I reply. "But it's not something that keeps me up at night."

"Never?" He detects my insincerity.

My mouth hangs open, but no sounds come out. I swallow and try again. "I mean, sometimes I can go weeks without thinking about it, but the longing is like a heartbeat. Most of the time you don't notice it because it's so quiet. But it's always there, just beneath the surface. Every night that I walked the pulsar fields, I asked the sky why I felt so restless, why I couldn't sleep. I guess the times I sleep are the forgetting times—between one longing and another. I do feel like there's something more, Oberon, like it's written in my heart."

"Our purpose is to serve the Creator," Oberon says softly, almost lovingly. "One cannot have purpose otherwise."

"None at all?" I ask skeptically.

"Only the illusion of purpose, quickly fading, leading nowhere."

"Huh," I say, still not so sure. "I knew nothing of eternity when I met you, Oberon. I'm still a fool when it comes to the supernatural. All I know is I want to be a light in the world. I want to spread kindness, cultivate joy. I want to learn the names of things, to visit far off places. I want to fall in love."

"These are beautiful yearnings, Ava."

"And I want to find my true home."

"We all want that."

"Why do you believe in the Creator?" I ask. "This Great Spirit?"

"I have seen him . . . felt him. At least, I think I have. The longer I am in your world, the easier it is to forget immortal things."

"What is his name?"

"It is seldom spoken. He is called Archeälis."

The air seems to resonate with the name, and I have a glimpse of what Oberon meant when he spoke of the power of names. Every syllable of that divine name remains inside me, as if it was always there, underneath everything. "Do you miss being near him?" I ask.

"He is always near," Oberon breathes. "What I miss is knowing it, knowing beyond any doubt that he is with me. I must constantly remind myself that I am surrounded on all sides by immortals. Humans are beloved by Archeälis, far above the animals, and even my kind. And I cannot feel him!"

"Now you need faith like the rest of us."

"Do you have faith, Ava?"

"A little. Not enough. I feel so broken."

A silence falls between us, a silence of breath and falling rain. Sometimes I feel like a raindrop falling—a lonely, plunging thing surrounded by others like me, but forever detached, rushing toward something unknown with no going back. "Oberon," I say, holding my palm under the leak to catch the drops. "Is there a way to travel through time?"

"Why do you ask?" He seems surprised.

"Now that I have the shard, the multiverse is opening up like a rose. Soon, not a single fold of it will be hidden from me."

He dissolves my grand words with the angle of his smile. "What does that have to do with time?"

"I don't know. I feel so limitless. I'm thinking of all the things I could fix if I could just go back a few weeks."

"Your intuition serves you, Ava. Time is a lot like space. But once inside it, we are powerless against it. It cannot be turned back even one instant."

I feel my shoulders fall. "Is there anything we *can* do?"

"If you were a timeless being, a goddess or a world-maker, maybe you could step beyond time into the realm of prayers and dreams. But I can't say for sure. I forgot so many things when I left my old life behind." He taps his chin thoughtfully. "I do know this. The passage of time will always feel the same to you. But it varies from world to world. Usually the difference is small, hardly noticeable. Sometimes a day in one world might equate to years on Alta. In rare cases, the difference is even more extreme. Have you heard the tale of San-Silas the Traveler?"

I shake my head, eyes wide, eager for a story.

"There was once a man known as Silas, who used his Art to explore the multiverse. He traveled to countless worlds, documenting everything he saw and returning with gifts for his family. He traveled often, and he was the best at his craft, and his family prospered from the rare and marvelous things he found. But there was also a woman. . . . And it was for her that he saved his most precious gifts, pouring out all the splendor of his labors. But for all that, he could not win her love.

"He tried and he tried. For years without success. But one day, near to giving up, Silas met a trickster who told him about a green and silver moon covered in the most exquisite flowers, flowers that could win for a man any heart he desired. But it was said that to pick one would mean certain ruin.

"Silas, desperate and eager to win beauty's heart, decided to risk everything. So he traveled to the far-off moon, entered it for only a moment, and picked the smallest and most humble flower he could find. With the flower in one hand, and a ring in the other, he returned home to kneel at the feet of his love and ask for her hand." Oberon pauses dramatically. I bite my lip, waiting, knowing the tale will not end well. "But when he returned to Alta, ruin had preceded him. Everyone he had known, the woman he had loved—and her husband—and all of their children were many years dead. He was left alone with a wilting flower and a broken heart."

When Oberon doesn't continue I frown. "Is that it? There has to be more."

"Not the happy ending you were hoping for?" he asks sheepishly.

"No, not really. You need to work on your stories!" I tease, poking him in the ribs.

"Sorry," he says, flinching away, a bit crestfallen. "I suppose it does lack a certain gratifying quality. Perhaps the story of San-Silas is merely meant for instruction."

I nod thoughtfully. "If the flower-moon is real, I hope I never go there. Ever. I have to be more careful about using the shard."

"Time is a tricky thing," he says. "It always moves forward and will never make you younger. This journey, this adventure we are all on together. Life. That is irreversible."

"It's better this way," I say after careful thought. "I wouldn't want to have anything over again. I want to keep moving forward. Honestly, if I could go back, I don't know what I'd change. I could try and warn Father and flee into the forest with him. But then I never would have met you! That would be a tragedy."

Oberon says nothing, but I can tell he's holding a joy in his chest like a song. We lie back together, and I contemplate the roof joists. The workmanship is excellent, but someone did a bad job with the shingles.

"Father would be proud of whoever built this place," I say absently. I can see him now, gliding his huge, gentle hands along the varnish. Tapping walls with his knuckles. Staring appraisingly at the molding. Who puts molding in an attic? "This must have been an apartment once," I remark. "See where the stove used to be?" But Oberon is thinking other thoughts.

"Thank you, Ava, for teaching me to love the little things," he says, a deep sincerity in his voice. "Thank you for taking my mind off seeking meaning long enough for me to taste it. I think it's like that. The seeking is the having, in a sense."

I shift slightly, moving nearer to the fire. Without thinking, I rest my head on Oberon's chest, making sure to keep my hair out of his face. His chest rises gently and he is so still. I almost fall asleep. Like a curious boy he reaches out and strokes my hair, almost reverently. "I have never touched hair like yours," he says meaningfully.

I smile, my eyes closed. His fingers are gentle and soft and they move for me. We remain like this, his hand on my hair, until the moon sets and only the crystal flame remains. His arm falls idle, his fingertips brushing my neck.

I rise as if from a trance, the spell of his touch lifted. I sit up slowly, rubbing my eyes. Oberon is quiet. I watch him, full of a joy I can't explain. He's sleeping for the first time. I wonder if he dreams.

CHAPTER XVI
Heart of a Hero

SLOWLY, THE CRYSTAL fire hovering between us darkens like a sunset and goes out. For the first time since we met, Oberon seems vulnerable.

Shuffling through fraying bundles, I pick out an old coat and drape it over him, pausing to admire the tattoos on his chest. Then I fold a black and green scarf into a square and slip it under his head as a pillow. He does not stir. I know it's silly to look after someone who's immune to cold. But I do it anyway.

Filled with a sudden restlessness, I go to the window, the pulsar shard flashing silver in my hand. I miss Father, and I want to see him. I think of him all the time. Even though my control over the shard is spotty at best, now I have a way to escape, to put Vanfell behind me and fall into my father's arms. *And then?*

My hand trembles slightly. What would Father have me do? Could the shard change him back into a man? What would he think of Oberon? Would he take him as a son, as a farmhand? What would our lives look like? And what of the war, the people who are about to die? Here are thousands in need. And I hold a tool that could help them, maybe, if I could master it. What else is it capable of?

Still, I want to find Father most of all. I want to know that he is safe. There are reasons to stay, some of them noble. But I would be a poor daughter to stay. I squeeze the shard, the primordial jewel that patterns the multiverse together. I press it into my pocket and sigh. This will be my last night in Vanfell.

"Father comes first," I whisper, "before Oberon, before Vanfell, before me."

Looking out the window, I consider the stars. The rain has stopped. Clouds are scattered over the city. I catch a glimpse of something moving in deep heaven. The sight of it sends shivers through me, a knocking of the sky, the same tingling I felt when I first touched my cocoon. Images from my vision recur—the stars dancing in circles, the faceless girl crying into the ocean until it swells and drowns her.

Compelled beyond resistance, I press my cheek against the frosted window, trying to track a shooting star, impossibly bright and close. I dare not open the window, but I want to see the star before it disappears. In my dream, I could see all the colors of light, every ray and wave. But now, in waking, all that is hidden from me.

If only Oberon were awake. He could use his soul senses to pierce the clouds, describe to me what lies beyond. I try to calm myself. I will let him sleep and dream. He deserves it after who knows how many lifetimes of being awake. I turn my whole attention upwards, mouth open, a parched traveler waiting for rain.

The star flickers through nimbus wisps, calling through the void. I can almost hear it speak. It reminds me of home, what it used to be. Then it is gone. . . .

A sudden gust strikes me from behind and I stumble forward with a shriek. The smells of the attic, the smoky city and puddles of black ice—all gone—replaced by sand and wind and desert sky.

I stand alone in a waste of ash and memory, the remains

of my old cabin. A grain barrel lies half-buried in sand. Beside it, a crumbling chimney. A ways off, our faithful plow, the blade dulled by dust storms. Seeing the place where I was raised evokes a mixture of sorrow and fondness that makes me sway. Hot tears stream down my cheeks.

I did not ask to be here. It seems the shard needs only the consent of my heart, not my mind to work its magic. That scares me, reminds me how little control I have over this new power. Gently, I remove the shard from my pocket. Even sheltered by my hand, it glows with the spinning suns of a thousand worlds, each the distance of a thought away. If I only knew where on Alta my father was, I would hug him this instant!

My father . . . I can still feel his hand on mine as we swing on the glider he built for us. I hear his voice in the wind like a leaf crackling from across a dell, or a butterfly resting its wings, or the sound rain makes before it is absorbed by the dust. I hear the past ushered back in the call of the storm, in memories and ghosts.

But I can't leave Oberon sleeping alone in that attic room. Tomorrow, when he is rested, I will return here with him, and we will use the fields to find my father together. I crouch behind my chimney, close my eyes, hear my father's voice across time, and the press of the wind is his hand ushering me to flee. "To the forest! To my sister. I will meet you there!"

Men die around me, their cries intimate and final. I try to envision the tiny room where Oberon sleeps—the crates, the silence, the smell of apples. But other images flood my thoughts, the smoking chimneys across the street, the jacaranda trees, the shadows on broken stones.

I materialize with a jolt of fear, exposed in the middle of the empty plaza. On instinct I warp again, and again, each warp becoming less controlled as my fear and delirium grow.

A bright world appears—sunlight and shining water. I fall tumbling through the sky as if dropped from a cloud. The ocean is ten thousand feet below with waves as tall and slow as mountains.

The next few warps happen faster than blinking. I try to hold the attic room and Oberon in my memory, but our peaceful time together fractures, as do most treasures when held too close to the heart. After what seems like an eternity of drifting, I finally crash down . . . somewhere.

The dizziness hits me all at once, a crippling, gut-wrenching nausea. I lurch forward, fall to my knees, vomit pitifully into the slush. Fighting through dry heaves, I fumble the shard into my pocket, using my sleeve as a glove so as not to warp again accidentally. *Oh Oberon, we'll laugh about this tomorrow when you wake!*

Sometime later, blinking away tears, my heart rate finally slowing, I'm relieved to find myself on the outskirts of a familiar plaza of jacaranda trees. Crouched under a café awning, I scan the various inns, looking for some sign of Oberon. Candlelight flickers through curtains and frosted windows, but the dormers are all dark. *Is that our attic hideout? Or that one?*

I set out along the darkened storefronts, but only make it two blocks when a nearby sound catches my attention. I freeze, listening. A girl's voice, no more than a whimper. Straining my ears, I hear a man's rough, clucking laughter. Then the whimpering again.

My better judgment screams to run, but I ignore it. No

matter how badly I want to feel safe, there's no way I'm going to skulk by and let someone else be hurt. Without a second thought, I slip into the nearest alley to investigate. I see them before they see me—two men clad in rags and standing over a lone girl.

She's young, hardly a teenager, her brown hair done in pigtails, though one has fallen out. She's dripping wet from running in the rain, her clothes torn and unsettled as if handled by rough hands. Unaccustomed to playing the hero, I find I have nothing to say. I simply stand there, fists clenched, and glare at the two men.

The one holding the girl notices me and jerks around. "Devil's breath, what have we here?" he says, his initial shock replaced by curiosity. The second man, cloaked and hooded, says nothing.

I steady myself and prepare to say something fierce and brave, a command worthy of a war poet's song. All I manage is a pathetic squeak. "Let her go!"

The first man passes the girl off to his partner and steps closer, a crooked smile forming on his thin, peeling lips. He is not a wizard, or a soldier, or even a thief. To all appearances he is a beggar, skinny and poorly clad, with mean eyes and scarred knuckles, his beard torn from fighting. He removes a chipped knife from his belt and twirls it gleefully.

The girl screams for help, and the hooded man shakes her roughly by the neck, choking her cries. Scraggle-beard lunges for me, but I spring out of reach and scramble up an ice-slick drainpipe to a second-story balcony.

Seizing her opportunity, the girl begins to struggle and kick, distracting her hooded captor. Before he can subdue her, I leap from the balcony onto his shoulders, shoving his cowl hard over his face. He grunts, stumbles, fumbling with the hood while Scraggle-beard charges in from behind. Both men catch only air as I leap off the shoulders of one and over the clutching hand of the other. When I look back, the girl is gone and two furious thieves are puffing and clattering after me.

Now I've done it. Whatever satisfaction I feel at rescuing her is quickly replaced by sheer animal terror. I run.

Feeling them gaining on me, I leap for a window ledge, catch it, and scramble up just as a hand grasps the air where my legs had been. Fingers and toes finding shallow mortar lines, I manage to climb to the next window.

Scraggle-beard tries to follow, but his fingers are too big for the cracks. Standing in an empty flower box, I kick repeatedly at the soot-blackened window until it breaks, then slip inside, careful not to snag my sleeve on the broken glass.

The room smells of damp and mold. This might have been an inn once. But it is long abandoned, with dormant chimneys and dirty, wet rooms. Icicles hang from the leaky ceilings and tarnished chandeliers. Rats and critters worse than rats huddle for warmth in the sagging walls.

I need a way out.

I find a spiral staircase, but I can already hear footsteps pounding up from below. I run the other way, up several flights to the top story where the old, buckling roof is open to the sky in several places. Leaping to catch the exposed joists, I hoist myself through one of the rotten gaps and into the open air.

I run deftly across the roof, past cold chimneys, over broken tiles, scanning the inns across the street, trying to locate the loft where Oberon sleeps. Scraggle-beard, a dagger between his rotten teeth, emerges from a different hole in the roof and creeps toward me.

Feeling trapped, I disappear behind a dormer, mind racing, eyes flicking in every direction, desperate for a way down. My hand strays to my pocket and the primordial jewel hidden there. Out of options, I clasp it and summon its power. . . .

Nothing happens.

I'm about to run when the dormer window explodes outward in a shower of glass and strong hands seize me by the wrist and shoulder. "Got yer!"

I yelp with surprise, try to twist free. A gloved hand crimps down on my mouth, shoves my head against the clay tiles. My vision blurs in and out of focus, hot blood in my hair. "You don't look right," growls the hooded man, peering unsteadily at me. "You one of them fancy whores?" I wriggle and writhe, but it's no use. My arms are pinned, my legs useless. "By God's own beard, you see that? I'm tellin' ya, her eyes ain't right!"

"That's them new drugs," Scraggle-beard ventures, licking his knife as he approaches. "Makes the pupils funny."

"Maybe," my attacker replies, far from convinced. "Damn unsettling." He tilts my neck back for a better look. As he does, I manage to free one arm and rake my nails across his cheek, drawing thin lines of blood. "None of that!" he bellows, slapping me roughly across the face.

The pain about wipes me out, my body goes limp. I imagine what Oberon would do if he were here. He'd probably be merciful, use his imperishable magic to turn these men into pigeons or something. My father . . . he would make a terrible mess. I try to reach for Oberon with my mind, as he's done before for me, but I don't know how.

I blink fully awake, feeling my cheek swell. The blood from my split scalp soaks through my knotted hair, begins to run down my neck. The two men are still over me, shaking out my coat, arguing over the gold and silver coins they found in one of the pockets.

"I'll have the gold. I'm the one what caught 'er!"

"Got lucky is all, ya worthless scabshyte!"

What was I thinking going into that alley? I don't know a word of magic. I'm worth next to nothing in a fight. Desperately, I probe my right pants-pocket with one hand. The shard is there. I feel the edge of it, the untapped potential. *Come on, come on. Don't let me down.* My heart is beating so fast it might explode. *Just a little farther . . .*

"Silver's good enough for me, I reckon," Scraggle-beard mutters. "What you hiding in those drawers, girlie?" He shoulders his partner aside, leans in, pawing at my chest, my inner thigh, whispering whiskey breath into my ear. My skin crawls, but his movement shifts my arm just enough. . . .

It happens as quickly as a warp, but it is something else. I feel a heat fill me, an unstoppable outward pressure pulsing in my veins, throbbing in my skull like a second heart.

Scraggle-beard, feeling the same heat, jerks back in surprise. As he does, I bring up my free hand and push against his chest as if to throw him off. He's not as heavy as I thought. In fact, he feels as light as a straw pillow. A crimson light ignites his chest. He doesn't even have time to scream.

My anger washes over me, my fear and pain, breaking wood and stone. Roof joists crack, tiles melt and shatter. My head throbs harder, bleeding down my back. There is nothing left of Scraggle-beard but ash, drifting like the remains of torched paper. The hooded man turns to run and trips on a buckled shingle. He screams, loses his balance, and plummets several stories to the ground.

Another flash, fire and lightning. I try to let go of the shard and can't—it won't let go of me. So I clutch it tight to my chest and close my eyes.

The tiles underneath me crack from heat and stress, and I try to hold still. I can hardly see. My eyes still burn from the first flash. My throat feels swollen, choked with smoke. I curl up into a ball, feel everything shift under me. Then the tiles supporting me flake away and I crash through the roof. . . .

. . . My eyes flicker open. Darkness. I survived the fall. My whole body aches. How long have I been lying here? I wiggle my arms, then my legs. One leg's gone numb, trapped under a crushing weight. Most of me is bleeding. I curl up, whimpering amid the stench of mold and melted varnish. Dust particles drift between sheets of splintered wood. I close my eyes for a long time.

I hear a man's voice, deep and urgent. Then a second voice, a woman's, giving orders. Men grunting and puffing, rubble shifting. I try to focus, feel myself being gathered like a sack of flower and slung over someone's shoulder. I groan incoherently, thinking my ribs must be broken. I hope I've stopped bleeding. The world lurches and I feel dizzy.

My eyes open for a moment. Stone cobbles, voices, the jolt of someone walking. A woman with hair like flame walks behind, a belt of daggers from her shoulder to her hip. A tall dark-cloaked man follows last, looking about warily and cradling a package under one arm.

Who's carrying me? I try to bend my neck to see and fall back asleep.

CHAPTER XVI
Dustfall

Who am I to be born deathless while so many others fade?
— Oberon

CRYSTAL DUST from the high mountains floats in the air like snow. It is a rare sight—falling diamonds, powder-fine and sparkling in the sunrise.

In ancient times the dust was thought to be crumbs falling from the table of feasting gods. In Vanfell, a city ruled by materialists, the phenomenon is traced to precious mineral deposits in the high peaks. For the minority with a sense for spiritual things, the dustfall remains a symbol of hope.

I open my eyes, blinking away flecks of blue, silver, and pink crystal. The double-window, poorly latched, has blown open, and my skin is covered in particle-infused frost. I let it melt, waking slowly as if from a drugged sleep.

"I dreamed, Ava," I whisper. "In my dream I saw a girl, a world maker. She looked like you. Her eyes—I remember—like emerald nebula rings splintered with starlight. She saw right through me, to the very essence of who I am. She saw what I still can't see. Ava?" I turn my head to look at her, but she's gone.

I stand abruptly, scanning the room like I've lost a part of myself. The cuffs of my trousers fall well above my ankles, the fabric stretching nearly to tearing as I traverse the room, ducking my head to avoid the low rafters. I do not remember it being my intention to age this body, but the result is undeniable. I am a hand taller and years older, overnight.

Glancing around the room, I notice my reflection in the frosted windowpane. The same brown skin, curly hair, gray eyes. The cheeks are sharper, less rounded, the jaw too. My tattoos also have changed, the patterns less dense than before, the coloring pale silver. There's no time to wonder why. Perhaps my sleeping mind knows better than I what I want.

"Ava, are you hiding from me?" I reach out with my soul senses to find her—or try to. I try again. My senses do not obey. My mind is an island in a storm with no mainland in sight. I try to break apart the waves, but it's too painful. Huge swells of emptiness crash over me, numbing my mind. I cannot lengthen my spirit beyond the confines of this room. My repose has dulled my immortal powers.

The wise ones warned me about this *spiritual disintegration*, the effects of being corporeal, the effects of food, air, sunlight on skin, and most importantly—sleep. I am forgetting who I am, what I am. But I remember why I came to this world: Ava. Where is she?

I go to the window and examine it, using the powers I have retained. I notice strange markings on the inner glass, arches and whorls—fingerprints in the ice. Pulling the window open all the way, I edge out onto the roof for a better look.

Across the street, an entire building has burned to the foundation, splinters and ash clogging the street below. I was told by those who sent me that a soul's first sleep is a sleep like death. Still, how could I have possibly slept through that?

My heart quickens for Ava. I call her name and it is taken by the wind. Eager to examine the wreckage, I leap from the roof, falling four stories to the ground. The landing shatters the bones of my legs, but I'm walking again in moments.

The street is not as deserted as I had hoped, and several onlookers gasp in horror and fascination. I make them forget and begin clearing the street, pulling aside clay and timber, brick and mangled ironwork, lifting a joist as if discarding a rotten walking stick. I burrow into the debris, cutting my hands on broken glass until my palms are slick with blood. My wounds heal instantly. I keep digging.

My spells of concealment are best served by subtlety, and the disturbance soon draws attention. "You!" an authoritative voice calls. "Get down from there 'fore you hurt yourself!"

More voices join in. "You addled, boy? You lost somebody?"

If Ava is in this wreck, I will find her. I tear at charred beams and splintered furniture. I find one corpse, a man's, crushed under a chimney damper. *Great Spirit, please . . . not Ava.* I don't have much time. A sizable crowd is already gathering to watch my grief-stricken frenzy. *She's not here. Not here!*

More voices demand that I stop. A constable and his son try and restrain me. Easier to stop a falling oak. I move a final rafter aside, shoving it with the force of ten men. Underneath, amid scatterings of rubble, I see something that stops me dead—the pulsar shard.

I pick it delicately from the dirt, stare at it for a moment before placing it in my pocket. *Ava, wherever you are, I promise —I will find you and return to you what is yours.* A half-burned scrap of fabric catches my eye. I rub it between my thumb and forefinger, wondering whose blood that is as it crumbles to ash.

It took magic to extinguish such hungry fires. The obsidian tower must have had a hand in stopping the blaze last night. I can only hope they did not find Ava, but it's no use staying here when she is obviously gone. Soldiers will be around to investigate before long, wizards too, and the crowd is growing bolder.

"Peace, young one." A woman holds out her hand, praying over me, begging me to calm down. A man grasps my arm from behind, but I dance away, moving like a cat across the debris. I retreat into an alley and disappear amid the garbage, sneaking along until I'm sure no one is pursuing.

I need a place to think. I move through the city like morning mist, clinging to shadows, avoiding faces, unable to sense Ava or anything else. I still have some powers: my strength, my healing, my Art. I make myself invisible, forgettable, wandering as I did before I was corporeal.

But my soul senses are gone. I have not felt so naked since leaving the Harmony, my home realm. Confined to the senses of this body—I feel as if I'm somehow dying, but I refuse to despair. My powers of naming, at least, have not diminished. If I knew Ava's true name then perhaps I could find her, but it is a name far more complex than the names of gold or fire. It is beyond me.

Overwhelmed, I begin to weep.

Perhaps I have failed. Perhaps I let myself become too attached to this world, to this body, to Ava. I suspect she is alive somewhere. A light like hers is not easily put out. But I cannot know for sure, and it is a painful ignorance. This is, I suppose, how her father must feel, wondering, hoping, but never knowing she is alive.

Is it time for me to return to my origin? Is my time on Alta complete? I do not feel accomplished. And worst of all, I no longer feel the Great Spirit, Archeälis. Is this a test?

I think of Archeälis, of his hidden ways. The voice that sang the worlds into motion. The hand that set the wheel of time turning.

Is it his will that I lose Ava? To what purpose? I know so little of the mind of the Great Spirit. I am a raindrop. He is the storm. I am a thinking soul. He is thought itself. In so many things I am ignorant, but I do know this: whatever he asks, it's worth it.

CHAPTER XVII
Iridium Sky

IT'S STORMING AGAIN. Dust swirls in the obscurity outside the kitchen window, trying to get in. I help Father press sheets into the cracks under doors in an effort to stop the entire desert from squeezing into our home. In the dining nook, dishes clink and quiver on wooden shelves.

"Unusual storm tonight," Father says after we finish. "Unnatural."

"Is it the pulsar fields?" I ask, kneeling backwards on a chair, my arms draped over the high back.

He runs his finger through the dust accumulating on the windowsill, holds it close to his face and sniffs it. He grunts, brushing his hands together dismissively. "Silver powder. Very fine. Nickel. Iridium. Iron." The wind outside intensifies and he pauses, listening. "Ava, it's time for bed."

"But it's early!" I protest. "And I like listening to the storm."

"You can listen in your room. It's safer there."

"Yes, Father," I say, rising obediently.

Outside, the wind roars. The whole house quakes. As I hug Father goodnight, one of the windows shatters inward, spraying glass everywhere. The wind howls in, stinging my face with metal dust. I press my knuckles against my eyes and clench my jaw, trying not to breathe. Before I can think to curl up into a ball, Father has already wrapped me in his cloak. He carries me to my bedroom and shuts the door.

Coughing, I strip the comforter off my bed and stuff it

under the door to stop the dust from invading while the storm ravages our dining room. I hear the sound of a stone water jar cracking, a bookshelf toppling, wood splintering, the wind wailing in a vortex of shredded paper.

Father curses, hammering on something. He must be boarding up the broken window. Gradually, the howl of the wind increases in pitch, then ceases. But the rumble remains.

I can't sleep. The sounds of the storm are too fascinating. I feel it in my chest, in my bones. Where did it come from? The wind, the shiny metals, the night with no moon. I peek out through a crack in my shutters, but all I can see is the churning desert, the air full of sand.

There is a sound like the sky inhaling suddenly, and the pressure changes. I see the stars clearly for a moment, but they are strangers. The sky I am seeing is not the sky of Alta. The constellations are all wrong. I retreat from the window, breathless, and draw the curtain.

Eventually the hammering stops and the storm calms. Poking my head out the window, I see the scarlet forest, the windblown desert landscape, and beyond—the pulsar fields, an opaque, weatherless cloud. The air smells like rust and fire and space, and I breathe deeply through my nose and mouth, sensing traces of moisture.

It's nearly dawn, and the remaining stars are faint and familiar. I hear Father outside unbarring the heavy barn gate where he confined the animals for the night. Dusty and grunting, two goats plod past my window into a pen.

Father returns to the house, swearing under his breath. "You can come out now." I hear his voice from the living room. "I know you're not sleeping."

I open my door timidly and step onto a layer of dust.

The entire house is covered with a thin blanket. The living room saw the worst of it, dust drifting through doorways and under furniture, filling cracks in floorboards and settling on the upholstery. Even the closets and cupboards have a silvery sheen. Father's clothes, most of all, are thick with it, all glittery and reflective. He sneezes loudly and the dust scatters, floating in the air. We both laugh.

"Hell and ashes," he says, in unusually good spirits. "Might as well knock it down and start over."

"Now I know why we don't have any neighbors," I say, investigating the extent of the mess, leaving small footprints everywhere I go.

The table is torn in half, the top removed and repurposed to board up the imploded window. A hammer leans against the wall, all dusty except for the handle. It looks as if the world's worst juggler had a go at everything in the room, furniture included.

I pick up an unrecognizable book and wipe the cover with my hand. *Of Happiness and Other Dreams*—a philosophy book I've been trying to read. It's not as exciting as myths or fairy tales, but I like the way the author thinks about life.

I go into the kitchen and start sneezing uncontrollably. To my relief, my favorite flowers are dusty but un-wilted over the washbasin. I breathe carefully through my sleeve and open a window. "I'll start in here," I offer.

"I've got the house," Father says. "Look to the animals. We've got ourselves three asthmatic goats and they like you better."

I nod dutifully, blow gently on my flowers to remove the powder, and go out. But the moment I open the front door a dim light hits me and I squint painfully. I hear a voice, not

Father's. The scent of the fields and the animals and the familiar house vanishes.

My eyes flutter open.

I hear the crackle of a fireplace and smell hot pinesap. My body aches in several places, and I remember my fall from the roof. I want to slip back into the dream, into the storm, and study the unfamiliar stars. Back to happier times with Father when the worst of my problems was a sandy breakfast.

How can my body hurt so badly? I feel feverish, my head is on fire. My swollen ribs throb and stretch with every breath.

I am lying on a soft bed in a dimly lit room. The curtains are drawn, though a sliver of cool light tells me it's nighttime. How many days did I sleep? Someone tries to give me water. I blink for a long time. Maybe I sleep again. When I open my eyes, it is morning.

"Sorry," the nurse says, noticing me groan. "I didn't mean to wake you."

I glance around the richly decorated room, blinking to clear my vision. "It's nothing," I whisper, trying to sit up. A fresh wave of pain reminds me why I am lying down. I feel a cool hand on my forehead and tilt my head to one side, enjoying the touch. "Thank you," I say to my caretaker, seeing her for the first time.

The woman is not dressed like a nurse at all. She is young, tall and stately, somewhere between twenty and thirty. Her fancy clothes fit perfectly, accentuating curves. Her auburn hair is made up into curls which kindle to flame near the tips. She has a kind voice, freckles, and the look of someone who goes where she wants and does what she pleases.

"To whom do I owe the honor?" I ask, my voice weak and scratched.

"I'm called Cora," she says easily.

"I'm Ava," I offer, trying to smile. "Thank you for taking care of me."

"It's no trouble to me." Cora waves a hand dismissively. "Raul did the carrying."

The night. I remember killing those men, falling and hitting my head, whimpering on a bed of cinders. Then warm arms around me. The young woman with the sash of knives. The nervous dark-haired man. Suddenly, I realize the pulsar shard is not with me.

"What is it?" Cora seems startled by the look in my eyes.

I manage to control my breathing. "Nothing. Do you, by chance, still have the clothes I was wearing?"

Cora wrinkles her nose. "They were so torn and dirty. Nothing in them. I didn't think you'd want them."

I swallow slowly and nod, my mind settling down. I know the pulsar shard is far away, maybe on the other side of the city. I feel it calling to me, distant, urgent, waiting. I must have lost it when I fell. But there is another absence, a deeper one, which I keep to myself. "Where am I?" I ask.

"You're at my home in Westfell."

"Forgive me." I try to keep my voice casual. "I don't know where that is. I'm from outside the city, a stranger here."

"Stranger or no, you are welcome here," says Cora. "Let me open a window and show you." She moves beside my bed and unlatches the huge double-window, pushing out gently, letting in the light.

I raise my head from the pillow and a shock of nausea

hits me. My body is horribly sore and there's a lump on the back of my head that I can feel through my hair.

"I called for a healer," Cora says, seeing me wince. "But all of the royal healers are with my father in his tower. He's quite sick, you know. He took a turn for the worse two nights ago, the same night my servants and I picked you up."

The complete lack of concern in Cora's voice catches me off guard. I swallow through my growing sense of dread, remembering the woman with hair like flame, the silver knives. "You're princess Coraline," I say numbly.

"And you're the one my father is looking for," she says simply, her eyes dark and knowing.

My breath catches in my throat. Knowing I am at her mercy, I resort to transparency. "What do you want from me?"

"That depends." Cora adjusts one of her silver earrings. "Can you save my city?"

I meet her eyes for an instant, then look down at my hands. "I don't know."

"My father thinks you can. He had a mind to make you, but unfortunately his mind is rotting now. My half-brother is occupied with the war. That leaves you and me."

I shift painfully, sucking air through my teeth.

"I study medicine a little myself," Cora continues sunnily. "Nothing broken. You are healing remarkably well. Too well, in fact. You'll be all right."

Not sure how to respond, I glance out the open window. I know the look of Vanfell at dawn. But I have never seen it from this angle. I am high up and far to the west of the city. Peering over the walls of Cora's estate, surveying the surrounding mansions and keeps, I can't help but feel awed and a little jealous. *So this is where the rich people live.*

Her property sits above the rest on a vast plateau, completely walled in, the northern section adjoining the mountainside. From what I can see of the various mansions of Westfell, hers seems modest by comparison, a historic castle carved into the mountain itself, its towers, barbicans, and crumbling battlements renovated over the years until it is more eclectic manor than forbidding fortress.

The inner walls are tall, decorative and veined with green ivy. Beyond the perimeter, along the slope of the mountain, is a protruding cliff large enough to divide this district from the rest of Vanfell. Squinting, I can just make out Sol's castle and the obsidian tower far in the distance.

"Oberon," I say softly, not realizing I am leaning out of my bed toward the light.

"What was that?" Cora asks. "Can I get you something for pain?"

"No, thank you, I'm all right." I swallow. "I don't suppose I'm at liberty to go?"

Cora smiles pityingly and shakes her head.

I edge out of bed, test my muscles and joints, and make my way carefully to the window. Cora makes no move to stop me. "What are you going to do with me?" I ask, looking out over the city.

"I only ask this one favor—that you have dinner with me tonight. I like you, Ava. You have a light in you that I can't quite explain. I would sooner trust your own words than my father's oracles. Speak with me, explain yourself, and then I will decide if you go free, or to my father."

I think on what I know of princess Coraline—scatterings, nothings. Rumors about her being disowned by the royal line.

One tale makes her out to be a mythical hero who fights thieves and killers by night. She is untamable and wild and connected to Sol by blood only. I would do well to earn her trust. "I will have dinner with you," I say, bowing my head slightly.

"Good girl. You should rest now."

I ease my way to the edge of the bed and sit down, keeping my back straight. I know if I lie back I'll fall asleep.

A flash of brown and white fur passes through the open door. It's a cat with a luxurious coat and fierce, golden eyes, dulled somewhat by a long domestic life. It pauses by the foot of the bed, leaps up on the comforter, and settles itself possessively on my lap.

Cora raises her perfect eyebrows, somewhat bemused. "Look at you," she says. "Guinevere hates people. She won't even let *me* touch her."

"She's heavy," I say, smiling in spite of everything.

I look down at the tiny lion in my lap. I'm used to skinny, malnourished tabbies, the ones that lounge in alleys or sun themselves on peddler's carts. Just like their wild cousins, they all let me pet them. City animals need love as much as wild ones, maybe more so, and they have good hearts. I've never held one this fat before.

I stroke her behind the ears and wonder if she has a wild heart like mine, if she sometimes yearns to leave the confines of her safe little world and chase the ever-moving moon.

"The night you found me . . ." I pause invitingly.

"Two nights ago," Cora volunteers.

"Did you know then that the wizards were after me?"

"I did." As if bored by our conversation, Guinevere hops down lazily from the bed, stretches, and meanders out of the room.

"So why take me here?" I ask. "Why not hand me over to your father?"

"Dinner is at six." Cora smiles with her lips, but her eyes are sharp as knives. "One of my servants will bring you an appropriate dress." She leaves without another word, closing the door behind her.

I breathe a heavy sigh and lie back in bed, alone finally. Two whole days in this place. Where is Oberon? With his powers, I'm surprised he hasn't shown up by now—maybe even a little worried. Closing my eyes, I imagine him striding in and taking my hand, just like the night we met, the night he rescued me from the watchtower.

I reluctantly pull myself away from the pillow to sit in the sun. It streams through the window in rays of dusty light. I want to cry, but I know it's no use. If I want to see Oberon again, to recover the pulsar shard, I need to get out of here. But not until I'm strong enough.

Ignoring my body's protests, I go to the window and open the curtains as wide as they go. The courtyard below is deserted. A woman appears from a separate building with a rag and a bucket of water. She kneels down on the rectangular pavers near the whipping post and begins to wipe up the blood. She moves slowly, not missing a single drop. I watch her for minutes without thinking, as if under an enchantment. She pauses for a moment to wipe her eyes with the back of her hand, and the spell is broken.

Who was whipped? I wonder. Perhaps there's something more sinister going on than I originally thought.

Closing the curtains, I go and stand in front of the tall mirror on the far side of the room. My body is slender under the nightgown, a girl's body, but rapidly changing. I hardly recognize the pale, green-eyed stranger staring back at me.

Is this what I really look like? This battered, underfed, elfin creature? I feel my face and touch a bruise that is well on its way to healing. I've never stayed hurt for long. Last summer, sleeping in a tree as I'd often do, I fell out in the middle of the night and broke my wrist. It healed in six days.

I smooth my hair between my fingertips. Dark as a moonless night, it falls past my shoulders and waves slightly at the tips, signaling the coming of spring and the precious moisture it brings. I feel my chest and hips, surprised by the gentle curves. I am getting older. Barely three years since I fell from the sky, and my body seems to have aged at five times the normal rate. It's hard to believe I'm even the same person Father rescued from that fiery pit.

After inspecting my injuries, I slide back into bed and stare up at the ceiling, wondering what kind of dinner the princess has planned for me. I think of Coraline and try to piece together the vague rumors I've heard about her. Part of me wants to believe she is honest and will listen to my story, that she would not harm me, would not hand me over to Sol to be his slave.

But part of me does not want to rely on hopes, on the chance, small or great, that another person will be reasonable or kind. Part of me wants to slip quietly away in the night, alone, as if I was never here at all.

CHAPTER XIX
Lux:
The First Changers

THE DUST BOWL swarms with Obulan savages. The pulsar fields are taken. My crops are pulp and ash, trampled by ten thousand booted feet. The hordes spread like wildfire, burning villages, livestock, and people until the smoke seems to erase the valley sky, leaving only ash-wrack nothingness and the stench of corpses.

Witnessing the desolation, I am reminded of ancient wars—row after row of enemies, their long hair, red and black and gold, shining like oil in the sun. Their painted skin and scarred faces, masks shrouding humanity—as if they want to appear as something other, something more than human, something fierce and unkillable.

But I know differently. Obulans bleed red. They scream and writhe when torn open. Some do not enjoy war, yet they are taught as babes to hate Vanfell and all who live there.

One of my first missions as a soldier was to scout the motions of a nomadic raft people newly washed up on the southern beaches. They built a city and named it Obul, which means *mother-root* in their clicking tongue. I warned the old king of the danger they posed to him. The fool did not listen and focused on quelling rebellions among his own people, reacting to threats rather than anticipating them.

Then the wars came, and though Obul could not conquer the island of Halcyon, neither would it be stamped out.

Centuries of life have taught me to read the doings of

kings, to analyze the motions of armies with the mind of a tactician, but my heart is not in it. I do not care what happens to this island or its people. I was born here, but I do not owe these stones my loyalty. I do not answer to peasants or kings. Make no mistake, if I could only find Ava and bring her to safety, then the rest can burn.

I sit in the cold dark, watching the fires of the enemy from my mountain lookout. I feel the ground quake to the rhythm of war drums, hear the distant chants of ecstasy, and smell, despite a fresh mountain wind, the fleshy insectoid reek of mutated beasts.

It is time to move again, but I cannot take the southerly way. I would be spotted by Obulan sentries and forced to fight. I do not want to turn dragon again, not after my sister's warnings. If I were to change, it would take a healer stronger than Mira to turn me back, and I am not sure such a person exists.

Mira's words echo in my mind, tormenting me. *What will I do if I find Ava? If she is alive, what will I tell her? The truth? She deserves to know. Only then can she freely choose to accept or reject me as I am. Will she still call me father?*

I am gambling everything that she has made it to Vanfell, either as a prisoner or as a free person. All the outer villages are evacuated, all watchtowers are empty. All roads lead to Vanfell. Perhaps the onset of Obul is a blessing. Now, at least, I know where Ava should be.

After leaving my sister in her garden, I skirted along the foothills near the blood elm forest and marched three days north. Finding the southerly route blocked, I had to kill an Obulan sentry who spotted me near the outskirts of a camp. Then, as it became too dangerous to travel in the hills, I entered the mountains east of Vanfell.

It will take several more days, perhaps a week, to reach the city. This blood in my veins has some advantages at least, physical prowess among them. I will exploit the dragon, make it serve me. After all, without my dragon blood I would be five hundred years dead and no good to Ava.

No army could traverse these peaks. But sentries are sparse, and a single man with enough determination and stealth could make it. A dragon-man, even better. I travel by night under the cover of mist and snowfall. My stolen clothes are torn and brittle, my beard and hair white with frost. But my skin burns with an inner fire, and I do not tire.

Most of my time is spent climbing. The stones are slick and break easily, but I know well the consequences of failure, and my hands have the strength of dragons in them. All manner of animals flee from me, even the mountain lions that rule these peaks.

Yesterday, I killed a wild ram with a stone and ate it in a cave while a blizzard raged outside. Its flesh was hot and lean and it renewed me considerably. I wasted nothing. I've been in the habit of cooking my meat, mostly for Ava's sake. The meal was savory, but I regretted it almost immediately. It is said of my kind that eating raw flesh only hastens the onset of the madness.

There was an age, remote and shrouded in myth, when my kind were leaders of men, respected and admired for our gifts. But joy and serenity, like beauty, do not last.

In some histories, the first dragonbloods arise in the elder days, in the first pairing—a dragon goddess who took the form of a woman and bedded down with a mortal man. Whether it was out of love, need, or desire, the stories differ.

Some versions say she seduced him and left him, and that in wrath he killed her offspring, or cursed them. Not that it matters much which version is true. As for me, I am only an old dragon, soon to die. The last one, maybe. More's the pity.

Some say the first changers were not gods, but mortals, men and women who could take any natural form they pleased. These changers lived as dolphins and eagles, orcas and white tigers. They brought peace to any land they inhabited, sowing harmony between human and animal kind, but at a cost. The more they experimented with their power, the shorter and more brutish their lives became.

The very wise lived in seclusion and rarely changed. Others sought darker avenues of power, spirits and prophesies left over from the fashioning of matter, and gave up a piece of themselves. Gradually their powers grew corrupt and their changes grew increasingly more violent. Soon they lost the ability to change at will and retained only two opposite forms, man and dragon, reason and instinct. The longer a changer lived, the more his powers deteriorated, until eventually he became a dragon forever.

There are many tales that seek to explain what went wrong, why changers lose their sanity with age, why everything becomes corrupt and disordered. *Entropy, chaos, the death of the universe begins in man.*

I remember growing up in the city, back when Vanfell was little more than a dozen buildings propped against the mountain. Back when kings were kind and worthy of a boy's love, and the wars had not yet ravaged the land. My mother was a scribe, an adept, a brilliant woman. She gave me life. As for my father—my only inheritance is his madness. To him I owe my curse. To him I owe my loneliness.

I am a cruel man, selfish and full of desire. But I am not such a monster that I would seek relations with a woman. I will not bring a child into this world. This cursed bloodline ends with me.

And yet that yearning cannot die, the yearning to live on through a single seed and a woman's love. I have been with many over the years, but there was not love. A man can satiate his carnal desires easily enough. But without love, without honesty, something inside him withers and dies like his seed upon the ground.

I wonder at times if my memories are true. My father was a dragonblood, and that's a fact. Beyond that, what do I really know? His power passed to me. Power, madness, and something else, ancestral memory perhaps—visions of the past, snatches of feelings from other bodies, shattered and remote. Dreams where I am neither man nor dragon. *Was I always human? Is this even my true form?*

Ava asked me the same thing, once.

God's tears, how I miss her. The thought of her fortifies my soul—Ava, yawning into my neck as I carry her up to bed. Ava, sitting cross-legged by the hearth reading. Ava, dancing in the kitchen, a toy doll clutched tight to her chest.

I will see you again. I climb, foot against stone, fingers searching for cracks in the mountain. The cold invigorates me. The challenge makes me bold. Reaching a high precipice, I look to the west, Vanfell invisible in the distance. If I am lucky, I will reach it before it falls.

CHAPTER XX
Coraline

I RESTED all afternoon, and I feel strong enough to escape, even though my wounds still throb from time to time. I've heard that it's foolish to try and run the first night of captivity, or even the second, but risks are meant to be taken. And besides, this will be my third night in Cora's keeping. I'll leave tonight once everyone is asleep.

On my way to the dining chamber, I pass groups of refugees in various wings of the house. There are more in the lush gardens outside, wandering in twos and threes between hedges and antique pillars. I can see them through the window with twilight in their eyes. They hold hands and don't talk much. Some look to the sky, sipping cups of soup, knowing their whole world is out there in the dust bowl, burned to the ground.

Part of me wants to go outside and sit cross-legged amid the flowerbeds and talk with them, comfort them, make a plan for the future. But I dare not. I can't insult Cora while so much hangs in the balance—my life, Oberon's, my father's. Not while Sol is out to get me.

Cora, like Sol, must believe I am a weapon to end the war. I think back on what I did that night with the pulsar shard. I taste the heat of folded stars, the metallic dust, and the fleshy reek in the air. I recall the way my hand opened up like an origami flower, how space was torn in two, how something bright and massive reached out and killed a man, brought the whole building down. *Could Sol be right?*

I know the pulsar shard is far away. I long to hold it again. And Oberon . . . where is he now?

I try to clear my head as I swish down the final steps in the dress Cora gave me, my bare feet making no sound. I dispensed with the shoes first thing. They were pointy, fragile and too clumsy for walking, let alone running. I suspect I am terribly unprepared for this new world of courtly etiquette. How should I stand? Where do my hands go? I try to put them into my pockets, but the dress doesn't have any.

Arriving in the dining room, I find the table is just as fancy as I feared, long enough for a family of twelve to dine comfortably even if all the kids brought a guest. Thankfully, this is the wrong room.

A servant leads me down a hall to a smaller dining nook. The room is cozy, sparsely decorated, a small fire flickering in the corner. The table is a simple rectangular slab of ancient wood, large enough for four people to sit around comfortably. Cora sits at the head, a lean, dark-haired man to her right. The man stands the moment I enter the room. A servant pulls a chair out for me across from Cora, and the dark-haired man does not sit until I do.

"I'm glad you could join us, Ava," Cora says brightly. "I think introductions are in order. Ava, this is Viktor."

"With honor, I greet thee," Viktor says, his accent thick and strange. When I reach out to shake his hand, he bows to me with the slowest head movement possible, then turns back to his wine.

I soon learn that Viktor is Cora's foreign cousin, a steward of sorts. He is only partially fluent in the common tongue and seldom speaks. Everything he does is exaggerated, theatrical—even the way he removes his scarf and gloves, or the way he adjusts his napkin in his lap, smoothing it repeatedly with grand motions.

The first two courses pass in idleness, the kind of useless talk that makes slow circles around the real reason for the evening—my provisional incarceration. I try not to let my impatience and anxiety show. Sometime during our salads, the real conversation starts.

"You are taking in refugees," I say, sipping a delightful strawberry wine. "On behalf of all who live in the valley, thank you."

"I only wish I could do more," Cora says. "Thousands have abandoned their farms and homesteads to come here. Others seek refuge among the mountain tribes or float the river until it spills into the ocean. Some are even selling themselves as slaves to foreign masters to secure passage to the Firstborn Lands."

I listen in silence, wondering what uncommon fear could drive people to abandon their families, their way of life, to flee to unknown shores as slaves rather than face the possibility of death.

"My own brother made such a bargain," Viktor says, shaking his head regretfully. When not speaking or drinking, he fidgets in his chair, constantly touching his flop of black hair to perfect it. When the main course arrives, he picks at his food like an ungainly bird, wrinkling his nose at every bite.

Cora reaches across the table and touches my hand. "Ava," she says. "You aren't eating."

"It's delicious," I say, raising my fork. "Much better than the lizard broth we make in the desert this time of year. I just haven't eaten this much in so long."

In truth, I am too nervous about tonight, about my plans. I dare not eat more, but I keep this to myself.

"What are you not saying?" Cora asks, her voice losing some of its pleasantness.

"I think I'm quiet because I'm afraid." I reach for the wine glass and find that my hand is shaking. "I'm wondering what you have planned for me."

"Don't be afraid," Cora says, biting her freckled lip. "I'm not like my father."

That remains to be seen. "How did you find me?"

Cora ignores my question, seasoning her fish in silence. "What do you know about me, Ava?"

I consider my words, not wanting to offend her by saying the wrong thing. "I am not much for gossip. But a few stories filter down to the outlands. I heard that prince Hector is your half-brother and that you are second in line to the throne."

She purses her lips. "Give me more."

"There is talk of you prowling the city at night and terrorizing evil men." I blush a little. "You're a bit of a hero, you know, for girls like me. I heard you can bring down a hawk in flight with a single thrown knife."

Cora frowns. "That's a little dark for me, don't you think? Killing birds for no reason."

"It's just an odd story I heard once. I also heard that you help people when no one else will."

The princess nods, seemingly satisfied, then sets her elbows on the table. "To answer your question, I was out in the city terrorizing evil men. My servants were nearby on other errands, and I summoned them when I saw what you did to those thieves who attacked you. We got you out before the whole building collapsed."

"I know what I did," I whisper, pushing my food away, my appetite dissolved. "But I don't know how. I've never done anything like that before."

Cora's eyes flash, hard and intent. "Ava, I know a weapon when I see one. Do not pretend you are harmless."

"If I'm so dangerous then why would you try and threaten me?" I say quietly, rising stiffly from my seat.

Viktor stands as well, on reflex, and Cora gives him a withering look. Then she turns to me. "What are you? Help me understand."

"Why does everyone keep asking that? I don't know! Okay?" My voice is shrill but deadly earnest. I glance to the stained-glass window as if expecting some hero to burst in, covered in gems of glass, a sword in one hand, the other outstretched to take me away. "I fell from the sky three years ago," I say. "My father took me in and raised me on his farm. A few weeks ago I lost him to Sol's greed, and all I want is to see him again. Please let me go."

"Why were my father's wizards looking for you?"

I hesitate, tasting the edges of a lie, then think better of it. The truth has gotten me this far. "I reclaimed something that is mine from their tower," I say.

Cora looks at me expectantly. "Which was?"

"The heart of the vessel that brought me to your world. I only had it a short time and lost it in the fire."

"If you found it again, would it give you power?"

"Yes. Some power. Not enough for what Sol intends for me."

"What would you do with it?"

"I would find my father," I say without hesitation. "And then . . . I would do what I can to save the people of

Vanfell."

Standing, Cora reaches out and brushes my cheek with the back of her hand. She touches my chin, my lips, the tips of my ears. Then, leaning closer, she runs her fingers through my hair. I stand like a statue melting in the sun. Her touch is so gentle. She stares into my eyes for a long minute.

"You're telling the truth," she says as if surprised. She withdraws her hand and I can breathe again. "Very well. You are free to go."

I hesitate. "I am?"

Cora motions for her servants to clear the table. "What did you expect?"

"A little more resistance, I suppose. I thought I might have to battle you, your skill with knives against my terrible magic."

Cora laughs a bright, musical laugh. "You have the truth on your side, Ava. And that is a far greater weapon than knives or fire from heaven. If you had lied to me today, I would have known, and I would have bound you in irons. Now go, before I change my mind."

I stare at her. Not sure why, I skitter forward and give her a quick, tight hug. She is too surprised to respond. Then I nod to Viktor and scurry out of the room with as much dignity as I can manage. I return to my chamber and shut the door, amazed by my good fortune. Soon I will be far away, and the days I spent here will be a memory.

Cora's questions got me thinking about what makes me happy, the things that I really love. It's not the dirt or the farm. It's not being alone or wild. It's my father. I miss him so much. It's Oberon, my first real friend. I long to see him, his shy smile, his eyes as deep as time, holding me.

I will find him and the shard, and I will find my father. I can see it all happening like a moving picture in my head. I bite my lip, feeling devious, alone in the darkness. I turn and lock the door behind me.

CHAPTER XXI
Midnight

REGARDLESS OF Cora's good intentions, I would rather leave once it's fully dark. I lie in bed for a while as the candle on my nightstand burns low. Then I go to the window and watch the moon's slow flight, arms crossed against the sill, leaning forward until the glass fogs. Around midnight, when the moon is hidden behind a cloud, I ease the window open. The sky fills my small room with its frosty breath.

A hidden part of me remembers how disastrous my last midnight escapade turned out—the numerous warps, the nameless brown-haired girl and her captors. It all started with a streak of light in the sky. I remember watching it fall. It felt so significant then, like a birth or a death, but it was probably just a piece of dust perishing in the atmosphere.

This time, all my senses are on alert. I sneak out in dark tight-fitting clothes that I found in one of the bottomless dressers in my room. I think they were meant for a boy, maybe a dancer. I feel more like a chimneysweep. My bare feet make no sound, and the wind masks the click of the window closing. The cloud shadows envelop me as I creep to the edge of the roof and peer down into the courtyard.

I hear a pleasant mewing from behind and turn. The cat, Guinevere, has somehow found her way outside. She is sitting on the roof, majestic and startling, meowing at me. I give her a disapproving look. "Shh," I hiss.

She meows louder, rubbing against my thigh.

"You're like me, aren't you?" I whisper. "You love the

night. Nothing could keep you away." I leave her on the roof, her tail twitching, her eyes huge and owl-like, pools of reflected sky.

Slowly, delicately, just as I would climb the thin red-leaved trees in the outer forest, I descend, using a patch of ivy on the wall. The thick-corded vines provide good grip, and I soon reach the courtyard, my wounds aching and stinging under stressed bandages.

I steal through the darkness, past the whipping pillar, moving from shadow to shadow until I reach the outer wall of the estate. I see the proud mansion behind me for the first time as the moon comes out. It is three stories tall, a blending of wood and stone, renovated again and again until it is impossible to tell what the original castle must have looked like.

I stay hidden until a cloud shades it again. Even with Cora's word protecting me, I can't help being cautious. Sol's spies could be anywhere.

After a few minutes, I discover an appropriate section of vines running all the way up the outer wall. I begin to climb, feeling a cut on my side open slightly. I wince and move a little slower, choosing my handholds carefully. These ancient vines seem perfect for climbing, almost too perfect. The thorns are broken away. The leaves part in all the right places. It's as if someone has passed this way before.

Suddenly, hearing the faint rippling of fabric, I press my body deep into the ivy, holding perfectly still. Slowly, I angle my eyes upward, afraid of what I might see. Every foolish, daring part of me hopes it is Oberon, but my more practical side is screaming.

A dark figure looms over me, perched atop the wall,

silhouetted by the moon, cloak billowing in the wind. By some miracle, I stifle my cry of surprise and keep my feet firmly planted on the vines. I hurry back the way I came, quick as I can. The figure takes a different route, a spider moving in for the kill. He reaches the ground before I do, waiting for me.

I drop the last few feet, turning quickly to face him, tense as a rabbit about to flee. On seeing him, some of the tension eases out of me. He is a boy not much older than me, dark-skinned like Oberon, and taller than most. He keeps his distance, not wanting to scare me. He seems hesitant, timid, self-conscious even, as if I was not the only one sneaking. He is dressed more warmly than I am, in some sort of animal skin, lightly lined with fur.

"I know you," he says quietly, wiping his hands on his shirt. "But I can't say we've met." He seems to unconsciously mask his accent by enunciating every syllable. "I am Raul."

"Ava," I say.

"It is good to see you well," he says. "The other night—"

"Cora told me that you're the one who carried me out of the fire," I interject, not meaning to be rude. "Thank you. I owe you a great debt." I wince, feeling blood moisten my side were my wound reopened.

"It was my duty," he says with a shrug.

"Thanks all the same," I say, not sure what to make of him. He is dressed in fine clothes, though his knees are dirty and his hastily rolled sleeves are burnt around the edges. One of his eyebrows is divided in half by a thin, hairless scar.

"So . . . what brings you here in the dark of the night?" he asks.

"I had hoped to slip away unnoticed," I admit.

He nods, having already guessed my answer. "I would help you," he says regretfully. "My mistress already gave the word. But there is a complication."

"What complication?" I ask cautiously.

"Sol knows you're here."

My heart skips a beat and I gape at him, momentarily speechless. "Then it's even more important that I leave now."

"I'm doing a bad job of explaining things," he says. "Last night, Sol's wizards traced you to Westfell and set up a perimeter. The princess was furious, of course. When they asked to search her estate, she told them to piss off."

"Won't that make them even more suspicious?"

"Not really. She and her father may be on unfriendly terms, but she's still royalty. Third in line to the throne. Within these walls, she's in charge. The wizards don't know you're here with us. But as of a few hours ago, they've locked down all of Westfell looking for you. Cora sent me to warn you."

"Is there any way out?"

"Not that I can find. Not yet."

I feel my shoulders slump, let out a measured breath. It seems to take all my courage with it.

"Take heart, Ava," Raul says, his voice softened by pity. "Given enough time, perhaps we could—"

"But I need to leave now!" I say, ashamed at how desperate I sound.

"Even if you somehow make it to the wall surrounding Westfell, there's no way through the gate. The soldiers may be bartered with or tricked. But the wizards see everything. They've even blocked off the sewers. I trust the princess will find a way through, but it will take time."

"I see," I whisper, collapsing into a bench on the garden path. Heart heavy, I stare at my hands. Moonlight glimmers on my palms where the dark form-fitting material ends. I sit there and try not to cry.

Raul merely stands by me, thinking. "You wish I would have left you there," he says suddenly. "You wish I would have left you in the city where you were free. I'm sorry, Ava."

"No," I make a dismissive gesture. "You meant to take me somewhere safe, to heal me, to save me from a fiery death, from scavengers and bandits in the night. You did right. It's the circumstances that wronged us both. Besides, if you and Viktor and Cora hadn't been there, the wizards would have found me."

Raul seems to relax, his shoulders lifting a little. "Ava, look," he says, sensing my indecision. "If you must go, wait a while, a few days at least. Lay low if you can. Then meet me here on the third night. By then the lower city will be under siege, and the most powerful wizards will be repurposed. I will guide you." He looks to the east, heaving a weary sigh. "Even then it will be utter foolishness."

"You don't have to do that for me," I say.

"Deal?" he says, holding out his hand. After a moment's hesitation, I take it. He hauls me to my feet and we shake. "Good."

I give him a long, hard look, seeing no falseness in him. In truth, I'm a bad judge of character. I trust practically everyone. Above, the stars are magnificent, bright as diamond dust. "Not such a bad night to be trapped like a rat in a cage," I say conversationally.

Raul laughs. It is a high, musical sound, though it does not carry far and is soon swept away by the wind. "No, not so bad. How would you like to accompany me on my errands tonight?"

"Might as well." I manage a friendly smile. "No way I'm going back to sleep, not after the fright you gave me on the wall!"

We follow a garden path, shrouded by tall, flowering hedges on either side. Thorns hide behind bouquets of colored leaves, vibrating in the wind. Raul leads me through hidden gardens to an alcove behind the mansion where a dozen odd-smelling, purple-leaved plants are cultivated. He kneels down and begins examining them with uncertain hands. "These leaves can only be harvested at night," he says. "Viktor usually does it, but he's with Cora in the armory."

"The armory?"

"It's her she-cave." Raul gestures vaguely toward the mountain. "It's where she designs her outfits and weapons. Viktor helps. You'd never know it by meeting him, but he's a master swordsman, an arms smuggler, and a bit of an inventor. They spar occasionally."

"Who wins?"

Raul shrugs. "You should go watch sometime. It's a thing of art."

I notice the way he's handling the plants and cringe. "Here, let me help you." I reach in and show him some tricks of harvesting, ways to get the leaves faster without hurting the plant. Ways to fold the dirt and ways to kneel for hours without aching. For my part, I'm glad for a distraction, something to help curb my disappointment. Raul is a quick learner and he seems to appreciate my help.

"How do you know all this?" he asks, picking the leaves much faster now, and cutting them clean, leaving every third one.

"I grew up on a farm."

He nods in a way that reminds me of Oberon. I smile. I consider telling him about Oberon, about why I have to get away. But instead I find a sprig of hyssop to chew on.

After we finish, he helps me up and brushes the dirt off my knees. "That's it," he says. "You should get some sleep. No use worrying. No one can hurt you while you're in Cora's keeping. Eventually the wizards will just give up."

I force a smile and thank him for his company. We say goodnight and I slip back to my room and try to sleep. It's not easy. I keep staring out the window, thinking. Raul is optimistic and kind, but he does not understand Sol or his wizards like I do. They won't stop until they find me.

The thought makes me shiver. Once, near the edge of dreams, I feel Oberon's fingertips brush my hair. I reach to catch his hand, but there is only air. My fist closes and falls, holding on to nothing.

What a fool I was to try and run. I can't escape. I can't evade the wizards. But Oberon can, with his soul senses, his cleverness, his shroud of invisibility. He will come for me, I know it. He will come in the space between breaths, in the whisper of a sleeper's heart, in the darkness of blinking. He will find me like he always does. I'm surprised he hasn't done it already.

CHAPTER XXII
The Wall

Why do so few of us come home?
What temptations await us in the manifold?
— *Oberon*

DESPITE MY BEST EFFORTS, my soul senses have not returned. I cannot will into being that which should come naturally. I cannot find Ava, though I scour the city on foot day and night. She was not captured by the king or his agents, of that I'm sure. I searched every royal estate, castle, dungeon and tower, found nothing. I even visited the king in his fever-dreams and questioned him.

Some nights, my heart raw with yearning, I return to the inn where I lost her, and stand for hours in the snow under the jacaranda trees.

Everywhere there are rumors of the Star Kin. Ever since the seeress spoke her prophecy—that the only hope for Vanfell was born in the stars—this city has been obsessed with building a new legend. Some say she is dead, that the city is doomed. Others claim to have seen her, a pale, elfin waif who leads her own shadow by the hand.

According to the teachings of a popular cult, she fled the island to gather her army of stars and will return only when men are worthy of being saved. The latest rumor holds that she stole into Westfell with a group of refugees and that Sol's Star Hunters will soon have her.

All the conflicting stories are enough to drive me mad. Even if I were to chase down every lead, the city would fall long before I managed it. It is a heavy burden, the loss of my powers, my profound uselessness. But I am not entirely without purpose. What I cannot trust myself to accomplish I leave to providence, which works itself out mysteriously and with its own sense of order.

In the meantime, I will keep her pulsar shard safe with me. I will use what abilities I have retained to resist the armies of Obul, thus keeping her safe indirectly. As long as she lives within these walls, I will protect Vanfell as if I am preserving Ava, until I can no longer breathe, no longer hope, no longer summon lightning in my hands—I will fight until my very last sound, and it will be for her.

Much has changed in the days since I lost her. I am nearing manhood now, a soldier, standing watch on the outer wall, alone on a long span between two battlements. Absently, I adjust the sword at my hip, scratch the black stubble on my chin. It hasn't been easy. Most of the men ignore me, though others are not so kind. They call me duster, curse and spit at me, mock me for the color of my skin.

"It is an insult," they say, "to die beside one such as you. The dust outranks you, desert rat!"

The first day it was so bad, I considered casting an illusion to make my skin lighter, to erase the tattoos on my face and hands. But I will not. I chose this body for a reason, and I cannot mend the depravity of men by ignoring the faults I see in them. I cannot undo evil by letting it change me. I must change it. *Archeälis preserve me! Perhaps I was not sent merely to learn, but to teach as well.*

Despite my race, the marshal needs men, men of any color or age. I have already proven my worth fighting off the first few waves of Obulans, driving them from the walls.

There will be another attack soon, I fear.

I can see our enemy now as they huddle around fires in the dim mist of early morning. I hear their abrupt, throaty speech, smell the ash and blood-dye on their skin. The war-beasts they keep are hidden in tents as large as pole-barns. All the real barns have been demolished and used to fuel their forges.

It is surprising that the clans chose to march during winter. Obulan warriors are known to dislike the cold. It is said they sleep beside magma streams and feed on embers to stay warm—that they were born inside a dying volcano and raised by demons to kill men. I do not believe these irrational whisperings, but the truth is perhaps worse. Hate and human wickedness abound on both sides of this war, and I see no immediate solution to it.

So I stand and I watch, trying to find my place in all this. I have not slept since the night I lost Ava, and I have not taken quarters with the men. When I am not searching the city for her, I return to the wall and stand here without motion, my hands resting on the ice-slick ledge.

At times the high wind swirls and whines, whipping at my cloak. Snow collects in my hair and on my shoulders, gathering around my ears and on the bridge of my nose. Sometimes hawks and wild falcons land on my arms and gouge my skin with their talons.

No one bothers me when I am like this. No one except for Dirk.

"I saw you fight yesterday," the boy says, pausing in his patrol. "Some of the men saw too. They're calling you a demon."

"What do you call me?" I ask, turning to look at him.

Dirk takes a deep breath, squaring his shoulders. He is the son of one of the guardsmen, a tall boy with a lean, honest face. "I say you're something else. Not sure what yet."

"What makes you say that?"

"For starters, you don't sleep, don't eat neither. You break things without touching 'em. Yestermorn, when our lines were nearly overrun, you made those siege ladders crumble and burn. How'd you do that?"

"I reached into the constituent atoms of the wood and unmade it," I say honestly. "Most of the material turned to ash. The rest scattered far into the universe."

Dirk blinks at me. "Could you do the same to a man?"

I nod once.

"Whose side are you on?" he asks.

"I am on the side of light."

Dirk seems satisfied. "I'm glad to have you, demon or no," he says. "Some of the men feel the same, though they won't admit it." He gives a brisk nod, turns, and continues his patrol.

I watch him go, admiring his courage. Of all the men and boys on the wall, he is the only one who speaks to me without fear or loathing.

When he is gone out of sight, I slip the pulsar shard from my pocket and gaze into it, thinking of Ava. Infinite combinations of galaxies turn beneath the patterns of my thumb. The shard is almost godlike in its uses, but I cannot unlock its secrets. It was not made for me.

I turn my attention back to the Obulan camp. The grand attack we are all dreading has not come. There have been small skirmishes—groups of a few hundred rushing the walls and quickly being slain. I am always the first to throw a spear or cast a spell, and I have made my share of corpses. But the attacks seem insincere, and that worries me. Obulans are known for ambush, strange tactics, and even stranger magic. Could this horde of men and beasts be merely a distraction? What more are they planning?

As I think and strategize, I ponder the nature of the Obulans, what little I know of them. They are relative newcomers to this continent. Just a few centuries ago, they beached their rafts in a frantic migration, spilled out onto the southern shores of Halcyon, and began to populate it, seeking the comfort of caves and the heat of the island's only volcano. Perhaps it was this heat and power that drew them.

They were a warlike people, accustomed to doing great harm to one another. They did not mix well with the coastal natives and soon drove them out or killed them. Once established, they lit secret forges under the mountain, and traded with Vanfell, biding their time. Needless to say, that peace did not last. Whether the Obulans came to this island as vanquishers or if they were merely running from something worse, no one knows.

And here I am, caught in the chaos, a loner and a killer.

Archeälis forgive me. If I must kill, then I will, to protect that which is dear to me. And each time I kill, I see the souls of my enemies fleeing I know not where. I see that they are human, and that they are not evil at heart. Yet I cannot know why they act the way they do, or what drives them to leave their warm caverns and trek across deserts and valleys only to fight and die for nothing. *Who or what do they follow? Either a higher power, or a basic need.*

Tonight I will learn the truth. I will cloak myself in shadow and forgetfulness and come down from the wall. I will journey into the heart of the enemy camp and sniff out what evil rules them. I will confront that evil, be it a man, a beast, or an idea—and I will destroy it. I will divide it a thousand times and scatter the ashes to the wind.

CHAPTER XXIII
Broken Lives

RAUL WAS RIGHT. The wall that encircles Westfell really is impenetrable. I've tried a dozen means of escape these past few nights, each time nearly getting caught. Raul comes with me as he promised, mostly to make sure I don't do anything stupid.

The first part is easy, just some basic sneaking through the ancient cobblestone pathways of Westfell. But the wall always defeats us. We can't climb it, can't dig under it, can't slip through the gates—not with wizards spaced twenty meters apart on the battlements, and soldiers in pairs at every gate. There are patrols too, each with the express purpose of hunting me.

For all their efforts, none have managed to infiltrate Cora's estate. Last night, one unlucky soldier made it over her wall. He'd hardly reached the courtyard when Cora set the hounds on him. I saw her dark side that night and vowed never to cross her. For all her kind words and sparkling clothes, she is merciless as a fire.

Due to the growing number of refugees, Cora moved me to a new room on the third floor of the mansion. I would have gladly bunked on straw floor pads or in tepees with the rest of the slaves, masons, and field workers. But Cora insisted on me being comfortable. The bed here is even bigger, the mooncrystal window twice as wide, the walls and floors more ornate. There's even a balcony that I can walk on and look at the stars.

A messenger comes to my door around dusk with an invitation from Raul's family for dinner. I realize, reading it, that no one has ever asked me to dinner before. The thought makes me smile, my eyes misting a little. I've enjoyed his company these past nights, and I think he's enjoyed mine. He helped me try and escape, even though he knew it was impossible. Chances are I'd be captured and locked in a dungeon somewhere if not for him.

I slide on a pair of pointy red shoes and promptly wrench them off, flexing my toes. What sort of a sadist invented these things? I am nearly ready when I hear the rhythmic triple-tap of Cora's personal knock. "Come in!" I call from inside the closet.

She enters like a warm breeze, looking me up and down as I emerge to meet her. "What's the occasion?" she asks.

"Raul," I say. "His family invited me over for dinner."

"Lucky you," she says, a hint of jealousy in her eyes. "His mother is my head chef." She glides past me, slides open the glass door, and steps out onto the balcony. The moon lights her white gown and makes her heels sparkle.

"Where are *you* off to?" I ask.

"A dance," she says. "A party of sorts. It's being held at Lord Galvin's next door."

"I've always loved dancing," I say. "Barefoot front-porch dancing mostly . . . not fancy balls. I'd like to try it sometime. I don't think I'd be very good, though."

Cora shrugs, leaning on the balcony railing. She looks out over the refugees assembled in the orchard, then into the vale and sighs. "To tell you the truth, Ava, I prefer my sword belt to this corset."

I giggle at that, but my heart goes out to her. We are

connected in a way, because of the war. The hordes have wrenched our dreams from us, separated us from loved ones, taught us about death. I'm still early for my dinner at Raul's, so I go and stand on the balcony with Cora. "You look beautiful," I say.

"Thank you, Ava." She touches my hand appreciatively, blushing slightly, and I wonder if we are becoming friends.

"I must admit, it's strange seeing you in a dress after all the leather and blade iron. What's the occasion, anyway?"

"We're doing a dance of sorrow tonight on account of the war. The tear dance. It's one of the nine dances in preparation for the Night Song."

"You're wearing white," I remark.

"And the men wear black," she says. "When the fabrics touch they begin a slow fade to gray, to colorlessness."

"I'd like to see that. What is the Night Song?"

"It's an annual festival that recounts the forming of the islands of Agna Marta. It unites us for a single night of music, dancing, poetry and communal prayer." She looks to the south. "But there are some who do not acknowledge the Night Song. And so there is war."

She looks down at me from her sparkling heels, and her smile is sad. I watch the lights of Vanfell, trying to pick out the inn where I left Oberon, using the river as a reference point as it winds through the foothills to the vale. As my eyes wander, I can't help but notice the red lights of enemy fires in the valley's heart. I trace the dim outlines of huge, shadowy crawling things and shiver. We both turn away.

"Why do you do it?" I ask, studying her face. "Why do you go out at night with your knives, protecting urchins and strays?"

Cora breathes softly, staring at her hands which, though delicately shaped, are hard and quick and strong. "Because no one else will. Because they need me."

I nod, finally beginning to understand her.

"Isn't it about time you head to Raul's?" she asks.

"Yes, but I don't know the way."

"Just down there." Cora stands beside me and points to where Raul lives with his mother and his siblings. It is a small house, all on its own in the back quadrant of the courtyard, surrounded by apple trees. It is beautiful, I think. I give Cora a hug. "Enjoy the dance."

She hugs me back, holding tighter than I expected. I can feel her heartbeat. When she lets go, she looks a little nervous. "Does Raul ever speak of me?" she asks.

The question catches me by surprise. "Sometimes. Always highly."

She nods, a subtle woundedness in her eyes. "Go," she says, nudging me gently.

I leave her standing on the balcony like a pillar of moon breath and diamonds. I walk slowly through the courtyard in my warm coat and new leggings, listening to all the sounds, thinking about Cora.

When I arrive at Raul's, I'm so nervous, I stand on the threshold for nearly a minute before knocking. His mother opens the door almost immediately, bathing me in fire warmth.

She is small and dark-skinned and smiles when she sees me, seeming somehow familiar. She introduces herself as Lana and invites me inside. Forgoing my usual shyness, I come straight in and hug her. I feel small arms around me and look down to see an adorable little girl hugging me back.

Another stands shyly behind her mother's leg, smoothing her dress.

"These are my daughters, Lina and Tifa."

The littlest one, Lina, immediately latches on to my leg. I pat her head until her mother pulls her away. I see Raul next, and he greets me with a genuine smile and a shrug that seems to say: *this is all that I have in the world.* The house is small but well built, and it reminds me instantly of home. There is a warm, rich aroma coming from the kitchen.

"Smells amazing," I say.

"An old recipe," Lana says as if speaking of something sacred. "My great grandmother's mother first made it the day our people came from the wandering islands."

"I've heard of those," I say, smelling fresh bread and apricots. "Ninety in all. They say the islands drift the seas like nomads and come near the fixed lands once every hundred years."

"And then they disappear for another hundred," Raul adds. "And no one can find them."

I nod, spurred on by familiar stories. "And they say no one can track the islands because the islands themselves are the hunters, the seekers. And when they find what they are looking for, they will cast anchor and be at peace."

"People say a lot of things," Lana shrugs. "Sometimes my great grandmother would share memories from when she was a girl, of the islanders and their way of life. Some of her stories had threads of magic—wizards, pirates, shapeshifters, and such. But it was so long ago."

"In legend, the people of the wandering islands always possess magical gifts," I say.

"That would be nice," Raul says, holding out his arms,

palms up. "My hands are just hands."

Lana laughs a good-natured laugh and disappears into the kitchen. I ask if I can help cook, but she won't hear of it, so I slip into the dining room and sit down with Raul at a table carved from a single piece of ivory oak. We talk for a while, mostly of small things. He tells me about how he and his brother built the house, but doesn't say where his brother is now. We listen for a while to the music drifting in through the open window. I stand on my tiptoes and look out at the night.

"That music." I close my eyes, breathing in the night smells. "It makes me want to weep."

"The dance is even sadder," Raul says, his face dark and shadowy in the firelight. He looks into the hearth and stokes the flames with a metal poker.

"Cora's there now," I say, sitting down across from him. "She's dancing with the rest of the lords and ladies."

The music seems to fade into the distance, like the slow death of harps and lyres and high flutes. "She's a great dancer," Raul says without looking up. "I saw her once. She was dancing on her balcony while I watched from the court-yard. She knew I was watching, but she kept dancing."

"It's almost ready," Lana calls from the kitchen. "Tifa, be careful!"

I hear something fall and shatter and get up to help. In the kitchen, Lana waves me off and bends down to wipe up the spilled sauce. I realize then where I've seen her before. She's the woman I saw wiping up the blood by the whipping post. I almost weep, remembering the way she knelt there, head bowed with shame, hands stained red. I blink away a tear. What's gotten into me? Maybe it's the music still in my head.

"Are you all right?" Raul asks when I return to the dining room. Lina and Tifa are sitting next to him, tickling each other.

"I'm fine," I say, misty eyed. "It's the music."

Raul stands and helps his mother distribute the food. He smiles, but there is a sadness deep in his eyes that I wish I could wipe away.

"Where were you today?" I ask when Lana returns to the kitchen. "I had to plant tomatoes all by myself."

"Building weapons, among other things," Raul says too softly for his sisters to overhear. "I don't know if Viktor ever plans to use the things he's making, but they kill with poison and sodium fire. His hobbies are endless, especially the deadly ones."

Lana returns with a pitcher of apple juice and five napkins, and we all sit down to pray. This dinner is pleasant. Lana treats me as one of her own family, although she does ask a few polite questions about my life. I respond truthfully, telling her I am from beyond the pulsar fields, and that I lost my father when the troubles began. I listen for the most part, only speaking to compliment the food.

After dinner, I thank Lana, and help her clean up, happy that she's finally allowing me to do something. Raul puts his sisters to bed and sings to them. Afterward, he and I go out back to a fire pit in a circular clearing surrounded by six mature apple trees.

While the trees in Cora's orchard are bare, Raul's are thriving, heavy with fruit despite the season. I sense deep magic in the roots and wonder where they came from.

Raul rolls out several fire logs. He stands the largest one upright, gesturing for me to sit. He starts a small fire inside a ring of blue-white stones, sits down on a rock under the constellations, and watches the flames.

I can see the same fire in his heart, the softness and the violence—the desire to grow. He loves his family, that's certain. But he is as wild as a flame, stretching erratically, and losing parts of himself in the sky. He is not content to be here, and he is guilty of his longings.

"What are you thinking about?" I ask, aware that I'm being overly friendly. But there's something about him, a knowing that I get with some people, like there's no point in hiding who I am or ignoring who he is. How can a yearning that dwarfs heaven and earth fit so easily into a human heart?

"Just listening," he says.

Immediately, I hear the music. It had faded to the back of my consciousness, keeping me on the verge of tears all night. It suddenly resurfaces in explosions of silence and rapture. I become aware of my breathing. Irregular. I try to relax, but the music is in my blood, not warm or soothing, but fading like a sweetness, the last leaf of autumn, the green flash before the dark.

The euphoric melodies turn poignant, opening into an absence as deep as a whale's call, or the wail of a great, lonely dragon, the last of its kind. I try to follow Raul's gaze into the golden heart of the fire. There is something truly hypnotic about the dance of newly kindled flame. I get lost in it.

"I feel . . . torn," Raul says at last, resting his elbows on his knees. "Part of me wants to be out there fighting for my city. But another part wants to be here helping Cora with her work."

"What does she do, other than fight crime I mean?"

Raul looks at me, puzzled. "Cora? She funds half of the

charitable organizations in Vanfell. She has administrative duties in all three orphanages. Owns one of them. She runs the soup kitchen in the churns too."

I gape at him. "That's probably why I never see her during the day."

He nods. "She has more energy than any woman I've ever known."

"How did your families meet?"

Raul leans back on his hands. "It was after my father left, when my older brother was sick and my mom was pregnant and I was small and we had no money. My mother chose to sell our family to Sol rather than starve that winter."

I can't help but gasp, covering my mouth with my hand. Raul, seeing my expression, makes a dismissive gesture. "It's all right, Ava. Our life wasn't so bad, even as slaves. Things got better after Cora purchased us from her father and gave us our freedom. We work for her now."

"Your family seems happy, your little sisters especially."

"They are happy," he says, letting his eyes fall, his mouth forming that same sad smile. "Lina is already starting work in the estate, running errands and washing things."

I gather my courage. "What happened to your brother?"

"He recovered from his illness," Raul says, not looking at me. "But he didn't like it here anymore than he liked being Sol's slave. He left two years ago, maybe to go find our dad and kill him. I don't know."

"And he left you," I say. "The man of the family."

"It's not that." Raul shakes his head. "Lana is a great chef. She makes better money than I do. She can provide and handle the house." He throws a stick into the fire, then picks up another and snaps it between his fingers. "See, my mother told us that our father was conscripted into Sol's militia and slain in battle, and that's why he never came back. But my brother knew the truth. He knew how we were abandoned, and it gnawed at him.

"I grew up hating Sol. He grew up hating our father. He told me the truth the night he disappeared. I guess I'm better for knowing. But I wish sometimes that my dad was only dead, and alive in my heart, instead of the other way around."

I shiver a little at the look in his eyes. I want to say something but can't find the words.

"My mother still tells the same lies," he says. "About how he was a hero. I wish things were different, that's all. And maybe deep down I want to be what I always thought he was, a protector. A hero. Maybe in being that thing I admired I can redeem his memory. But I won't abandon them like he did. So I'm trapped."

He puts more wood on the fire and gazes into the flames for a while. My eyes stray to the stars, not with longing or desire as they usually do, but with a begging, questioning gaze, as if I can find the answer to his pain up there in the spaces between the lights.

"I've never met anyone with so pure a heart as yours," I say to him. For a moment, we do not look at stars or fire, but at each other. "You want only what is good. You want to make things right. You want to serve, to give of yourself, to learn new ways to love your family every day."

"I think my father's sins have followed us," Raul says, his eyes like a drowning animal's. "I pray every night. I sacrifice my soul and body. But I cannot atone for him."

"You don't have to atone for him," I say. "What you're doing is love, and that's all anyone can do. You don't have to

fight and die to make things right." Feeling a sudden incli-
nation, I reach out, leaning from my log to his rock, and
touch his forehead with my thumb, my fingers cradling his
head. I feel the power of making go through me, not the
same power that is in the pulsar shard, but another power,
that is mine. I feel it shimmer and spark through my
fingertips like a kiss. "You who see truth, teach it to others," I
whisper. "And be at peace."

The tone of my voice reminds me of the time I spoke to
the starflower and told it to be free. Remembering the search
for my cocoon brings a stabbing ache to my chest, reminds
me of how much I've lost. I want Oberon here for so many
reasons, not just for the answers he brings, but him, all of
him. *Where are you, my lost friend?*

Raul starts as if shaken awake, his whole body taken by
subtle trembling. He stares at me, his breaths shallow. He
blinks twice and settles back into his seat, and I into mine.
"What did you do?" he asks, and it is not an accusation. He
speaks like one healed, not of his problems, but of his fear
of them.

"I don't know," I breathe.

He sits easily, appearing to relax for the first time since I
met him. "Of course not," he gasps, incredulous, like
someone who has just witnessed a miracle. "You really are a
daughter of the stars."

"Yes," I confess. "I am. I want to go there one day, to the
stars. But first I have to find my friend, and my father,
wherever they are."

"Of course," he says, taking me in, all of me, with his far-
seeing eyes. "You're not alone. Look at this war, the world's
gone mad. People like us turn away from all the evil here and

look up, as if our souls are out there somewhere in the stars."

"I think you're right," I say, marveling at him.

Could wisdom pass through a simple touch, some insight I did not know I possessed? He seems changed, more serene, yet still his same caring, attentive self. I do not know what kind of power is in him, but I feel it now as I feel the moon when the clouds disperse. I help him build the fire again, and it crackles hungrily. Then I join him on his rock.

"I hope you find your friend," he says.

I look down at the mention of Oberon. There's no point in hiding him anymore, not from a friend, not from someone with a heart so pure. "His name is Oberon," I say. "He has done more for me than anyone in my life, except for my father. And now they're both gone."

"But hope is not lost," Raul says perceptively. "You hope to find him again, your father too."

I nod.

"It keeps us alive, hope like that," he says. "I have that hope too. I see it now. Tell me about him, your friend."

I hesitate. "He's kind," I say. "And wise. He's different, like me, but he and I are not the same. For most people, their souls are like sparks, locked away in bodies, easily hidden by layers of personality. He is more divinity than boy. His soul is a sunrise, a wildfire, blazing through the linings of his skin, too bright to hide. He speaks softly and with reverence for the truth. His voice is young and old. He has hands that care for the living, and for me. And when I hold them, I feel like I'm holding on to something eternal. He would die for me."

"Do you love him?" Raul asks.

My words dry up, scattering like autumn leaves. I try to pick them up and only stutter. "He's . . . important to me," I say, and it sounds inadequate. *Yes, of course I love him.*

Raul nods to himself, seeing through me. "It's a good thing to love." He pokes the fire with a stick, rolls a coal over slowly. "To love a friend as a friend or as something more. To love something even if it means having your heart broken. Something inside us needs that kind of love. And it's worth it, no matter the outcome, no matter the cost."

"I guess I didn't realize how I felt until I lost him," I say. "And I still don't know how he feels."

"That's the worst part, not knowing," Raul says meaningfully and looks up at Cora's window on the top floor of the mansion.

I follow his gaze and partially understand it. I wait for him to say more, but he doesn't. Not wanting to pry, I stand up and stretch. As I do so, my knuckle nudges a long tree branch, making it sway, apples glinting red in the firelight. I pick an apple from the tree. "Here," I say, holding it out to Raul.

"Thanks." He bites deeply of the apple and chews thoughtfully. "I like her," he says suddenly. "It's wrong and impossible, but I do. I've liked her for years." He glances over at me, gives a brief, lopsided smile. "It started in a few words, a change of pitch when she'd ask about my family. In glances when I'd help her carry things, or mend her armor.

"A few weeks ago, I accompanied her to a ball, as a servant of course. After rejecting the advances of half a dozen high-bloods and firstborn sons, she called me over from the servants' table and asked me to dance. Right there in front of everyone. As you might guess, the gossipmongers loved it."

Knowing he is talking about Cora, I hesitate. I am a

newcomer to a play years in the making, with characters of vastly different backgrounds all thrust together. Eventually, mulling it over, I work up the courage to speak. "That dance . . . seems proof enough of her feelings, don't you think?"

"I don't know," he says, scratching the side of his face. "She's a bit of a rebel in her social circles, always shaking things up, scandalizing the other nobility. Sure, she danced with me, in public too. But I just don't know how she feels, if she's flirting, playing games . . . or if it's real. It's too risky to ask. I could lose everything."

I know what he sees in her. Cora is vibrant, witty, as kind as she is just. She's wealthy and deadly and wears sparkling clothes, though I don't think that's why Raul would fall for her. I think it's her compassion he admires, the way she devotes her life to the poor, the wretched and abused.

"Please don't tell anyone," he says. "It's not proper. Not proper thinking for a servant." He pauses at the word, and his eyes glisten like copper jewels. "But for a man."

"I think she likes you too," I say. "Maybe she's just scared to say it. I mean, in her position the last thing she would want is to demand your affections. If she asked, wouldn't you be forced to say yes?"

"But if I ask . . ." He says, trailing off. "The risk used to terrify me. Not anymore." He gazes into the future as if picturing the moment. I mutter some encouragement, but he hardly notices. He is hoarding his words now, holding them close to his chest, like love.

"It's late," I whisper.

He nods automatically. "I'll walk you back."

"Oberon and I," I say as we walk, because I have to get it

out. "We're from two different worlds too. I care about him, maybe in the same way. I need to find him." I pause, feeling overwhelmed, remembering my failed attempts to leave Westfell. "What's wrong with him? Why hasn't he come?" I choke up, angry and confused, frightened even.

I know Oberon would sooner die than give up on me, and yet doubt still laps at my heart, trying to drown it like a rising tide.

Raul lays a comforting hand on my arm and is about to say something when I stop him. "I'll go on from here," I say. "Thank you for sharing your fire." I hug him warmly. "I loved meeting your family."

"I'm in your debt, Ava," he says, kissing my cheek. "You gave me something tonight. It was more than friendship. Are you sure you don't want someone to walk with?"

I shake my head. "It's not far."

"As you wish." He looks up at the mansion, at the polished glass windows and smiles. Then he waves goodbye.

I walk home in the dark, feeling the warmth of the fire go out of me, feeling Raul's longing keenly because it is my own. There are so many walls in life, walls that cannot be seen, but that divide us as surely as a gulf of darkened stars. I would knock them all down if I could, but I'm so weak, my arms so heavy. When I tear down that last wall, will Oberon be waiting for me on the other side? Why hasn't he come?

Under the marble figure of a winged goddess, I pause, bow my head, embarrassed by my weakness even though no one is watching. I turn away from the mansion, my eyes burning, and go into the gardens. I weep bitterly for the first time since the day I thought my father was dead. I weep for Raul and for my own pain. I kneel down in the dark of the silent courtyard where no one will see and weep for Oberon who is lost to me.

I smell the dirt, the frosted grass. I remember the way his fingers brushed my hair, the touch of lightning in my soul. Why won't he come? He has the power to save me. What is he waiting for? If I sleep, it is not repose. If I dream, it is of a future that I never want to see in waking.

CHAPTER XXIV
The Light Eater

I have put my lips to the sun,
played hide and seek among the stars.
— *Oberon*

CLOAKED IN SHADOW and forgetfulness, I approach
the enemy camp at dusk. No one sounds an alarm or even
glances twice at my small, shirtless form scurrying like a vole
under a vast, starry sky.

I pass unarmed over hills of grass and along streams,
coming to where the desert encroaches on the fertile land
and the ground begins to crack like a human palm withered
with age. The river narrows as it bends to the east and its
murmur fades along with the incessant buzzing and skittering
of insects and reptiles along its bank.

The forward sentries do not detect me. Most stare fixedly
at Vanfell, sipping from steaming cups of lizard broth. A few
forage for berries, tend fires, or use their daggers to etch
glyphs into the large, reddish boulders near the hillside. Two
captains hold council, pointing often to the stars, confident
that no counterattack will come from the city this night.

I enter the camp, staying clear of the light of unclean
fires. I do not look the men in the eyes, and they do not
acknowledge my presence. I sneak past a faded tent, ducking
under the thick tethers, my ear just brushing the canvas as it
flaps in the wind. From inside I hear the heavy breathing of a
beast at rest, smell the rancid, decaying flesh.

Mammals, rodents, insects—the Obulan sorcerers will

enslave any animal, grow it to unnatural size, and work it to death. In some of their watchdogs I sense no life at all, only crude animation, the dull pulse of magic behind their unblinking eyes.

One undead creature raises its head, tracking my progress with unseeing eyes. Then it snorts a blast of foul air and turns away. My heart, frozen with sudden fear, beats again. Good. Even from these unnatural sentinels I am hidden.

The camp is quiet with sleep. But it is an unsettling silence, the silence of oblivion and death. Keeping to the shadows, I skirt around the remains of a burned down church and into what used to be a village square, now the center of the enemy encampment. Some of the Obulans sleep or lie dreamless under the stars. Others snore in tents with the beasts they breed and enslave.

The units, twenty men strong, are arranged in tidy sleep-circles, ready to rise and fight as one if need demands it. There are bones strewn about, discarded food smoldering amid the embers of dying fires. These soldiers eat well. Some wear rings and other jewelry pilfered from the corpses of slaughtered townsfolk. Near the cistern, the body of a young girl lies face down, her throat slit, her body torn and ravaged.

I feel anger rise like a pressure inside my chest. My heart quickens. Power fluxes through my being, glistening along the lion tattoo on my back. I may have lost my soul senses, but my ability to work magic has not diminished. If anything, like a man's sense of touch and hearing when his sight is lost, it has only grown more keen.

I know the costs of magic, the way the balance must be maintained. If I call a breath of wind here, somewhere in the world goes still. If I call on fire, some part of Alta must shiver. If I unmake a thing, then the universe finds its balance, and there is newness. This is why I use magic sparingly and only when in need.

I hearken to a pair of sentries bickering about something. Reaching into my memories, I recall their language and adapt to it.

"We should attack now while the city sleeps," says the taller one, a skinny man with a scar on his lip.

"You know our orders," his companion snaps, never taking his eyes off the city.

"Our shamans lack spine," the tall man continues. "The One speaks, and they listen. What use is a council ruled by one? By the dead gods, he's not even one of us!"

"Your words are heresy, and that's a fact," growls his companion, tapping the hilt of his sword. "For the sake of your boy and our long friendship, I will ignore them, just this once."

The tall man swallows, much of his anger dissipating. "What do you know, Rikus? Tell me, I beg you."

"Only what I heard from the One's own priests. The prize he seeks is not the city, but something inside it, something hidden. The pulsar fields will not be truly his until he has it."

The sentries fall silent, and I circle toward the back of the camp, seeking the Obulan leader, this One, the dark power at the heart of everything. What is he? A high shaman? A sojourner like me? A fallen god? After eavesdropping, I become keenly aware of the pulsar shard where it lies in a sealed pouch in my pocket. Could the One be after the shard, or Ava, or both? Perhaps it was not wise to bring it with me.

I approach a low stone table of smooth igneous rock,

and stop dead, my face going slack, my breath snatched away. I dare not touch it where it sits alone under the stars, deeply red, forever stained with the lifeblood of countless sacrifices. It did not originate here, but from deep beneath the earth far away.

Nearby, a dead tree stands, its bark stripped, sap oozing from the wounds where hooks have been driven in. Hanging loosely from the hooks are stingray spines, sharks' teeth, needles of bone, and obsidian prismatic blades for sacrificial bloodletting—all neatly arranged, cleaned and polished. My stomach clenches. I feel a keen desire to retch, suppressed only by my acute control of my natural processes.

It is said that the Obulans trade their own blood for power, and that is why they are so scarred. It is also said, mostly in whispers, that they sometimes sacrifice captured slaves, seeking to snare life-energy before it scatters, and preserve it for a time of great need. The hideousness of the custom does not merit imagination. I pass on, disturbed by the ghosts of the dead, the evil that clings to the movable altar like a stench.

Ahead, a tremendous fire burns in the shelter of a dune. Going closer, I notice hundreds of spiders clustered around it, their bodies overlapping as they huddle for warmth. The largest ones I could ride easily. The smallest could fit in the palm of my hand. The alien rasp of their body segments fascinates me.

I am not afraid, but full of pity. These were natural creatures once. But they have been twisted through sorcery and genetic mutations, cursed to serve an unnatural purpose. I stand for an entire minute watching them, listening to their mandibles click and snap, before moving on.

An evil rules here. I can nearly taste it, a sinister presence, permeating everything like smoke. I reach a section of the camp that is active. The workers move like chains of insects, industrious and efficient, building siege engines in the cover of night. The leaders issue commands with complex hand gestures, fingers flashing, eyes scanning the ranks for any sign of laxity. There are women too, clothed like the men, grim-faced and silent, sharpening swords in the firelight.

An Obulan boy, no older than thirteen, emerges from a large tent, a message in his hand. He holds it reverently, laying it at the feet of a shaman praying under the stars. The shaman says nothing, his headdress drifting slightly as the boy scurries away. I sense little power in this elder, only an authority won by fear. The boy, as it happens, is of great power, though it may be latent. Curious, I watch him disappear amid the dunes. If not for my mission, I would have followed him to learn more of Obulan magic, of where they came from and why they can't go back.

But there's no time. The enemy I seek is deeper in the desert.

I pass between a broken ring of fires, drawn inexplicably toward the back of the camp, to some unnamed source of power. I know I am nearing that which I seek. My feet move as if of their own accord, my toes squeezing the sand.

Ahead, between the shadows of two high dunes, is a clearing where no soldiers or beasts venture. It is a frigid, windless desert of black ice, an anomaly amid the otherwise pleasant valley night. I enter the clearing, still cloaked, and shiver, though not from the cold.

A fire slightly taller than a man burns in midair some distance away, fueled by nothing. The sky above is starless and strange, the land veined with cracks of dry ice. I have stepped into another realm. I continue, feeling my power flicker under that flame. I lose confidence, begin to fear what lies in the heart of the unquenchable fire.

But I will not turn back.

The flame narrows and lengthens, making no shadow, making no light. I realize I am seeing with my soul senses, not with my eyes. Though I cannot extend my supernatural perception, it seems it has not abandoned me completely.

In a sudden, terrible flash, my cloak falls from me, my magic exposed by this nameless power from beyond the gates of death. Without my shrouds, I am naked in a wasteland. The fire burns with an eerie slowness, a rusty, tainted blaze. Like a stain in time. A stain on the world that cannot be erased.

As I near it, the flame slows even more, becoming shapeless. There is no heat in it. It twists and contorts, taking the form of a man—no—not a man, but a being the likes of which I have not faced in any life, corporeal or otherwise. I know it without thinking, like light knows the darkness, like beauty its counterpoint. It is an Inferno, a being older than the world, older than the eldest stars, older than light. I do not know its name. Perhaps it has none.

No. Archeälis, who named all things, would know it. But I cannot speak to him. I realize with mounting dread that I am alone. It is all I can do to face this evil, twisted thing and not weep.

The Inferno extends a long-fingered hand as if in greeting. My body feels suddenly bloodless and cold.

"Wanderer," it speaks. "Why have you come?"

I swallow, hoping my frail human voice will not dull my

intent. "I have come seeking the destroyer, the one who would bring so much death to these people."

"You have come far," says the voice, adopting a masculine quality eerily similar to my own. "Stay. Rest awhile."

"I have not come to rest," I say boldly, feeling the isolation of this place, this field of broken dreams and shattered stars. "I have come to avert war."

"You have no place in this war," says the Inferno.

You have no place in this world, Defiler, I think, for nothing about this skyless spit of dead land belongs in the world of the living. "My place is here," I say. "Between you and them."

"Why do you come with fists clenched and teeth bared?" the Inferno asks, his voice a welcoming hearth.

"I come only as I am. A servant of the light."

As we speak, I notice Obulan warriors creeping into the winter-chilled dry land where the Inferno resides. They move like timid ghosts, insubstantial, their human forms not meant to walk the liminal paths between worlds. Some die instantly. Others struggle on, obviously in pain, but compelled by their master. They stalk me as a hunter might stalk a tiger, with fear and awareness, swords glistening in the unnatural light.

I prepare spells to destroy the Inferno, knowing it will not be easy. I try to remain calm and motionless, but the air shimmers around me where my Art, summoned quickly and with desperation, distorts space-time.

The Inferno, sensing my attack, raises a hand which is both shadow and flame. "Oberon!" He speaks my name in tones of power.

At the sound of my name, my last shroud is cast down and I am revealed for all to see. Even I am surprised by the form I take. I do not twist into a spirit, fade away like smoke, or flare with tendrils of silver light.

Instead I remain in my body. Has it really become such a part of me as to inherit my name? My skin flows with runic symbols, my tattoos like rivers of blue flame. I shimmer with an imperishable light, solid, even in the land of my enemy, even naked as the sun.

How does he know my name? What secret power does he serve? I struggle against him, but I am so weak. The azure lion tattoo on my back begins to roar, first in defiance, then in pain, and the roar becomes my own. His mane sparks and shines, flaring, ejecting plasma into the night. His lifeblood flows across my sides and back.

The Inferno laughs, a sound like wind howling across a field of bones. He reaches out, his long fingers grasping, stretching toward my exposed heart.

Great Spirit, strengthen me! Arm me against my enemy! Without my name, I am nothing. Without you, I am already dead. In the instant of my desperate prayer, I see the Inferno clearly, his true form, which is not man or beast, flame or shadow, or anything within the realm of words. Then, in the scorched place between death and undeath I see his name.

"Ra-Anis," I utter. "Be still." As I speak his name, I see the Inferno for all he is. I see his dark intent, his twisted past, his hopeful beginnings. As I witness this unraveling of essence across time, I see something else as well—something terrifying.

"He is coming!" Ra-Anis croaks, smoke leaking from his mouth and eyes. "He sent me with a focus, and I failed him. Do not gloat! By your hand I am ended, but not unmade. My master is coming! He will make ashes of you and everything you love!"

Could this Inferno be merely the shadow of a shadow? As he dies, a portal opens to absorb him. Where does it lead? I peer through the unreal void, trying to trace the outline of a vast darkness—the one who drives the hordes from afar, the one to whom life means nothing, the Light Eater. I see him lurking in the outer dark, and feel my blood run cold.

The Inferno, seeing me distracted, forms himself into an adder and strikes. As he moves, my tattoos move also, forming a protective aura around me, turning his fangs aside. Furious, I prepare to destroy him, though I know he is only a pawn. He coils sullenly, melting into his true form, a foul-smelling substance the color of tar.

He fears my power and fears the one I serve, but he will not die quietly. His darkness reaches out in tendrils, in whips and cords. A few pierce my aura, sending jolts of pain through me. He screams a demented chorus of anger, hate, and the cries of the dead.

"Ra-Anis, I name you. By dust and bone, I bid you be silent!" At my words, his power flickers. The hunters of Obul, seeing they are overmatched, back away. Some fall dead, struck down by the fury of our opposites.

Archeälis, I praise you. Thank you for returning to me in my need. I reach out to break my enemy once and for all. My hand passes through his aura and grasps the strands of life, the shred of purpose and will that remains to this creature under the insubstantial veil of unbeing. Coming into my own power, tattoos blazing in the sight of all, I name the Inferno a third time. I name him and strike his powers to nothing.

He spits and writhes, cursing me in a language that was d before the sun was born from the dust of space. rified, he recoils, injuring himself as his life-essence stretches and nearly breaks. Seeing I will not let go, he sends his hordes against me, spiders mostly, and I fight them for a moment, killing dozens in the blink of an eye. In the chaos, he slips away, retreating into his own desolation.

The undead beasts keep coming—spiders the size of wagons, hairless dogs that do not breathe, and gaunt horses, their gray, decaying flesh flapping as they gallop toward me. I whirl, an untouchable pillar amid a throng of bodies. My tattoos blaze and stretch, searing beasts to ash, freeing them from their misery. Then come the men, women too, rushing in from all sides, each brave and frightened and alive. I raise a hand and shudder as their bodies crumble.

I unmake a dozen warriors, then another score, holding back only because I can see the humanity in them. I could unmake a hundred, a thousand, but what good would it do? What good is my light to the dead? With each body that falls, more surge in to replace it. My powers, though vast, are not infinite. I cannot bear to kill so many.

Overwhelmed, I am forced to flee.

I leave the dry land and reenter Alta, weary and mad-eyed. I cloak myself in silence and forgetting and disappear into the valley night, leaving the Inferno to nurse his wounds for eternity.

My failure weighs heavy on my heart, but it cannot be helped. I now know much more than I intended to learn. Before he fled, Ra-Anis spoke of a terrible purpose. Why would his master come to Alta? It is a long journey for a spirit, full of peril and unspeakable sacrifice. I should know. Could it have something to do with Ava? I have to warn her, but how?

Just the thought of the Light Eater makes my hands

tremble. I clasp them together, consciously suppressing my adrenal glands. When the time comes to face him, will I be able to protect Ava and everything I love? I could not even defeat one of the Light Eater's minions. How could I ever hope to fight a darkness so old and terrible?

With the Great Spirit beside me, perhaps I could win, but I have lost him again. I shudder, thinking back to my time of preparation in the well of souls, before I came to Alta. I remember learning about evil things, wise and old as angels, things that have no face, things with forgotten names. I knew once why Archeälis permits such evil to exist, why it is better that creatures are free, that light has a counterpoint, so that there can be joy and victory and life, but I have forgotten.

Glancing back over my shoulder, I see the camp of Obulan warriors seething and breaking down. They are in full retreat. I cannot help but feel responsible, but I do not dare to hope too much. I have seen death and corruption—the Light Eater. If the legends are true, nine Infernos will serve him. These are the deadliest and most active of his minions. But not all who follow him are evil. If I could only reach the Obulans and pull them out of their pain and emptiness, maybe I could save them.

Perhaps the spell was lifted a little, even tonight, when they saw the lies of the Inferno, Ra-Anis, unveiled. When they saw their master broken. Perhaps that is why they retreat. They caught a glimpse of that which enslaves them and found the will to resist. I hope so.

These are men and women who have lost everything, who have been conditioned to hate, not born to it. The right lie will enslave a man as easily as any enchantment.

Still . . . they are a cruel people, predisposed toward evil acts: slavery, necromancy, and human sacrifice. But even the most savage creature can be healed with the right touch. The strength of the Obulans to fight the evil that has come into them—it is the only hope Vanfell has.

As the first light of dawn touches the eastern peaks, I ponder what I've learned. I cycle through mythology both divine and human, stories true and imagined, dreamed and spoken, recalling what I can of the Light Eater.

He and I are first things, but we were not made equal. He was born, as with the angels and all the lesser gods, before the world was spoken into existence. He rebelled before the first human was formed or the first fistful of land was raised from the primordial sea.

His evil is corrosive, it consumes all. It is inescapable, it forgives nothing. It cannot be satisfied or destroyed. It collapses in upon itself eternally. It is a bottomless hunger, an endless night. And it is falling. . . .

If life were a play, his coming would be like the last curtain of a tragedy. A signal to all who are watching that no more is to come, ever. I sense a portal opening, a door of sorts, a narrow threshold between the unsuspecting world of mortals and the menace outside. And I, a frail, flickering wisp of spirit, am standing on the brink.

CHAPTER XXV
Snake Stories

IT'S BEEN over a week since I woke up in Cora's estate, all cut and bruised from my fall. Last night, there was a terrible fight in the valley, a war of lightning. I could feel the wild magic even from Westfell, and I recognized it. A tenderness with oceans underneath. The trembling power I've felt in Oberon's fingertips. How is it that the same hands that hold mine and brush my hair and keep me safe could tear down the fabric of reality?

After the battle, the Obulans retreated far into the desert. They move under the cover of dunes and dust, perhaps regrouping. No one knows.

Every night, I dream of a faceless girl with skin like pale morning. She always comes to me on a moon-sliver beach, a sandbar amid an ocean of stars. I'm growing used to the light of her presence.

Sometimes, as we walk the beach together, I even detect features on her skin—the shape of a nose, sky black hair, two drowning eyes, and I think I recognize her. Then she opens her mouth as if to speak. She never says anything, but inside her mouth I've seen the twirling lights of a million billion stars.

When I wake, I can feel the pulsar shard, the one connection I have to my origin, painfully close, calling to me. It is still in Vanfell. I could find it, maybe, if the wizards and sentinels turned their backs even for a moment. But for now, it might as well be on the other side of the world.

Still, not all is dark. With each dream, I feel myself changing. New powers are stirring in me even without the pulsar shard. Yesterday I touched a sick woman's chest and throat, pleading for a healing. Today her cough is gone, along with the fluid in her lungs. I don't know what this means for me, but it must have something to do with why I'm here.

This morning I help Raul in the garden. We begin easily, sometimes working side by side, sometimes chatting with the other workers. Every spare patch of ground in the city is being used to grow food while the siege continues. Even the princess feels the pinch, and most of her estate is now devoted to rice and other grains.

Nothing has sprouted yet, though many of the seeds have been imbued with magic. These I'm told will be hardy and fast-growing. The warmth of spring is in the air, and I know there will be a modest harvest. I eat mostly grain nowadays. Some eat flowers, nettles, and bark bread. The coming weeks will not be easy, but we'll make it.

Kneeling beside Raul, I begin to fold the seeds into the damp morning dirt. "Hi," I say.

"Hi, Ava." He plants like I taught him, with considerable dexterity. "I saw you practicing with Viktor's slingshot yesterday. You're really good."

"I used to have one," I reply, remembering how I found the blackened handle in the ruins of my bedroom. "My father made it for me. He wanted me to shoot animals with it, but I never did. I got pretty good at shooting fruit off of trees, though."

"A deadly skill to have," he says. "You should see the ammunition Viktor made for his slingshots. Scary stuff. One of his concoctions will melt bone."

I inhale sharply through my teeth. "Do all of his inventions kill people?"

"He *is* an arms dealer. It's kind of his thing."

I sigh and shake my head. "How are things with Cora? I know you two have been courting, but she's annoyingly secretive about it."

Raul chuckles helplessly. "I told her my truth, the way I feel. We talk more now, but she's hesitant. She knows I love the orphans of this city, but her calling is not mine. I mean to leave Vanfell eventually." He stops planting and looks at me. "What is love in the midst of war, Ava? Whatever I feel for Cora, and she for me, honest as it may be . . . can be easily broken, smashed, dashed to pieces before it has a chance to grow."

"Then let it grow," I urge. "Don't avoid loving someone for the fear of losing her. You would never forgive yourself."

Raul clenches his jaw and nods, absorbing my words. "Even if I give my all, it is up to Cora."

"She'll come around," I say, moving into the shade of an ivy-covered wall and looking back at the row of seeds we planted.

I feel Raul relax beside me, his chest loosening. I try to think of something else to say, something comforting, but can't. Nearby, the door of the outhouse creaks and a hulking farmer steps in. All I see are his broad shoulders disappearing, and I'm surprised he didn't engulf the house rather than the other way around.

"There's something I've been meaning to ask you," I say haltingly. "A week or so ago, when I first woke, I saw your mother from my window. She was by the old whipping post wiping up blood. I didn't know it was her at the time, but it's been bothering me."

Raul nods regretfully. "One of Sol's spies tried to abduct you your first night in the estate. Cora had him whipped and locked away. She has a tender heart for the innocent, but you'd hate to see her angry, Ava."

"A spy," I say slowly, feeling guilty. "Why was it your mother who cleaned up the blood?"

"The man's name was Abel. He worked in the kitchens under her for years. She knew him rather well. He was considered a good man, though dishonest in the end. I expect Cora will have him released once you're long gone from here."

I nod slowly, not really blaming the man. "I think I just realized something important about the world," I say. "Everyone is the hero of their own story."

As I reach into the bag of seeds at my hip, I notice a flash of movement—a snake, white and red patterned, slithering out from the ivy near my feet. I practically leap out of my skin, stumbling backwards with a yelp.

Quick as a snake—actually quicker—Raul snaps his hand down and grabs it by the neck. He whisks it up deftly and looks at it. It squirms angrily, twining around his fingers. After a moment, he lets it go and it slithers on its way.

"It's not a danger to us," he says. "They come around every so often. We call them rose snakes." Seeing my discomfort, the slight tremble in my fingertips, he puts a calming hand on my shoulder. "What's wrong? You're safe, I promise."

"I know. It's just a memory," I say, moving to stand beside him in the shade. "It would be a good story if it wasn't so sad."

"Tell me," he says as we start on the next row.

"It was a year ago, back when I lived with my father," I begin tentatively, gaining confidence as I remember the interesting parts. "I was in the barn. It was early on a summer morning and I had just milked our goat. I was going out to watch the sunrise when a snake approached me in a way I did not understand.

"Animals generally like me, but this one came silently and with hidden intent. It didn't respond to my voice like the other snakes. I was frozen. It was a large snake, several feet long with a huge head like an arrow tip. It rose up, perhaps to strike, when Father came bursting into the barn. He threw open the doors with enough force to break the hinges! Then he lunged forward, grabbed the snake by the tail and cracked it like a whip so hard its head flew off!"

Raul nearly chokes. "You gotta be joking me?"

"You'd have to know my father to understand," I say. "But it's true. He told me that not all animals are good animals. He said, shaking the snake's limp body in his fist, that he knew it and its kind and that it had meant to hurt me. Ever since then, snakes scare me, even if they're nice snakes."

Raul looks thoughtful, his hands falling idle. "I'd like to meet your father one day."

"I'd like that too," I say. "I'll miss you when I go."

"Same," he says.

I hug him unexpectedly, my cheek against his shoulder. He holds me, still kneeling, his hand on my hair. "I feel like I've known you my whole life," I breathe. "Why is it so easy to love someone? So hard to let go?"

"It's how we were made," he says, his voice resonate. "Bright as new-kindled flames. Brief as leaf-fall at autumn's ending."

I pull away, not wanting him to think less of me for being clingy. *Why in life are the most beautiful things so short-lived?* I wonder. Without thinking, I turn my gaze to the mountains, their proud peaks still buried in softly glistening snow. *Well, not everything.*

CHAPTER XXVI
Night Song

I think often of Ava and the humanity she assumed.
If anyone were to open heaven for mortals, it would be she.
— *Oberon*

I AM TIRED. Not the heavy-lidded, bone-weary lethargy of one who goes without sleep. No. This is much, much worse. My spirit is waning and the Art does not readily obey my will. I have at my peril lowered my bucket too deep into the well of power. I am drawing constantly on the limitless energies of the universe. Alas, to drink so deeply of such cosmic forces only to turn around and spill them out—this can only work to wear and age the vessel.

I often think of the Light Eater, my enemy, and see him in waking dreams. He is not here on Alta, at least not totally. Most transcendent beings are hesitant to enter the folds of space-time and submit to the dominion of finitude. But his arm is long and his malice vast. I recognize his approach by instinct, as a bird senses a coming hurricane.

Standing on the wall alone, I listen to the wind and look out over the deserted valley. I am uneasy. The retreat seems halfhearted, and I suspect Obul will try some new evil before long. It is a warm evening. The sun goes down on the last day of winter, and the city is beginning the Night Song—the culmination of an annual festival, signifying the dawn of spring.

Moving to the inner side of the wall, I survey the city, listening for signs that the Night Song has begun. Normally, it is a grand celebration, a time for artists and poets to unveil new works, a time for weddings, feasting, dancing. Bonfires, drinking games, laughter—a coming together of hundreds of villages in the outlands and beyond.

All along the countryside the budding crops are blessed and prayed over. All work in the city stops. Circuses open and vendors arrive in droves. The greatest dancers in the three kingdoms compete in a midnight ballet.

But not all years are plentiful. Not all days are bright.

This year in Vanfell the Night Song is celebrated quietly, with great dignity and attention to small things. A light over a doorway. Flowers in the windows, colored drapes, or new flags. A single small voice singing from a third-story ledge. A lone flutist holding a note. Or a solitary lover waiting for her husband to return from the wall. Each instance of person-hood, every joy and sorrow, forms a stitch in a vast tapestry of story.

"You're not joining in?" The young voice is somewhat accusatory.

I turn to see Dirk the guardsman's boy standing beside me. Absorbed as I was by my musings, I missed his approach. "My place is here on the wall," I say simply. "What about you? If you like dancing, better get down there. They'll be starting soon, and all the pretty girls will be looking for a partner."

"I got duty," the boy grumbles, obviously miffed about it.

"In that case, you're facing the wrong way, soldier. The enemy's *that* way."

His cheeks flush with embarrassment and he turns to look out over the empty valley, past the river to the outlands. "They won't come for us tonight, not never again," he says.

"They're high-tailing it, thanks to you. Must be halfway to the pulsar fields by now!"

I follow his gaze and see that he's right. Still, I'm uneasy. "Appearances can deceive," I say. "Look at those hills, the way the land folds over in waves. A determined tactician could hide an army behind any one of those, or in that ravine there, or between those dunes, or in the trees along the river."

Dirk nods along as I speak, not really listening. Before long, his eyes stray from the valley to the nearest plaza, a popular gathering place for the peasants of this section. In the two-story squats below, a banjo player plucks strings and a woman's voice rises on the wind, carrying with it an old ballad.

"Look," says Dirk. "Prince Hector is leading the dance."

When only yesterday he was leading men into battle. "He thinks it's important that the people keep their spirit," I say.

"Makes sense to me." Dirk nods the all-knowing nod of a boy.

"Have you fought beside him?" I ask.

He shakes his head. "Only the knights have that honor. And maybe you, if you wanted it."

I want nothing to do with Sol or any of his kin, I think, feeling a stab of anger. *That's my own pride talking, my own weakness . . .*

Dirk gives me a long, steady look. "I heard that the prince himself went asking 'bout you, wanted to meet you. I also heard you slipped him—twice. It's a lie, ain't it?"

"No," I admit, feeling guilty, not knowing what more to say. My anger toward Sol is justifiable, but my anger toward his son is not. It's irrational to hate a man for his father's sins.

Hector is brave, but not foolhardy. A good leader. He has taken the lead role in every skirmish near the walls. It is men like him—men with strong arms, bright steel, and lions' hearts who give our enemy pause, who make them hesitate, lower their weapons, and try to starve us out rather than fight. For all that, I resent him.

"I'm the only one you talk to," says Dirk. "How come?"

I glance over at the boy, hoping I don't look as tired as I feel. My reckless battle with Ra-Anis caused a brief pause in the killing, though it came at a cost. Now that it's done, I feel my own weakness as keenly as a blade in my skin. "I don't know," I say at last. "You call me friend. You treat me like a man, not as something more or less than one. I like that."

Dirk seems pleased but tries to hide it. "The men respect me now, thanks to you. They call you the Lion of the Desert, 'cause of those markings." He gestures toward the tattoos on my back. "They also call you the Hunter. Not sure why."

Below us in the dusty square, people gather to dance. Old instruments, taken from attics, are dusted off and tuned. Those who do not dance or play, stop for a moment, set down their work, and sway with the motions of the song.

Hector moves among them, not as a prince among subjects, but as a man among fellows. His clothes are simple, his trousers worn on the inside from years of riding, his mail undershirt recently cleaned so as not to show off the bloodstains. He picks a maiden out of the gathering crowd and dances with her for a song, then chooses another. He laughs with the rest, returns embraces, gives whoever he is with his full attention, making even the lowest born feel like kings and queens for a night.

I try to find Ava among the sea of faces. I scan the rooftops where people sigh and hold each other. I scan the streets where dirt-smeared children hold hands and screech with delight whenever a performer does a flip or blows fire. Finally, I settle on the square where Hector is. There are many women dancing as daylight dies, but not Ava.

If I saw her, I would come down from the wall, embrace her, hold her close until the music and the voices all faded into the background. Then I would ask her to dance.

For a moment, as I watch and imagine, I forget about the Light Eater. I forget about the Inferno, Ra-Anis, and about my failure. I feel the faith of the people moving in my spirit and I believe, just for a moment, that we could survive.

"What are you smiling about?" Dirk asks.

"The future," I say, patting him on the shoulder. "Goodnight, young braveheart. Keep watch for me."

I go to my room, a large closet inside Bastion South where we store anti-siege weapons. I curl up on the stone floor between barrels of tar and close my eyes. I will meditate to regain my strength. I long for Ava. I trust she is alive, but only just. I lie alone in my room, my mind adrift. Have I forgotten the distinction between meditation and sleep? I'm so tired. Perhaps a few minutes won't hurt. No, I dare not, not after what happened last time. . . .

And yet, against my will, I begin to dream.

I want to wake up, to think my way back to reality, but I cannot. I know I am in my square room carved out of solid stone, my few belongings lying around me. I am permitted to be here only because no one else cares to sleep on hewn stone without straw or pad. I rise slowly to a sitting position and use one of the barrels to lift myself.

Something's changed. When I fell asleep I was in total darkness and the iron door was fastened shut. Now the door is open, a flicker of firelight in the hall.

As I step closer to the firelight, the world changes. I am suddenly standing in the burnt and blasted courtyard of a broken castle. I gaze around in awe, turning a slow circle amid six shattered towers. Above me, turning as I turn, a winter-blue sky impossibly full of stars. I've never seen so many stars.

"Hello?" I call, catching a glimpse of the firelight that brought me here. "Wait!" I scramble through the ruins of the castle, passing from a toppled guard tower into a courtyard of bones. Always the flame eludes me, leading me through black gardens, dungeons, and deserted rooms. Everything seems blasted to bits by magic or dragonfire. The stones crumble under my feet. Iron bars flake to rust.

I chase the flame to the sixth and highest tower, climb the spiral steps to the uppermost chamber. This was a lookout once, but now half the wall and roof is gone, open to the sky. Moving to the shattered window, I look down at the wastes below, a dead world where nothing grows.

If this is Alta, then it is not the Alta I know. Perhaps the future or the distant past. "Is anyone there?" I stand shivering in the cold, tortured by the uncaring stars, by the ashes below. There is no life, no smoke, only the shadows of a thousand endings. Something flickers through a trapdoor in the part of the roof that remains—the flame.

I try the ladder, but the rotten rungs fall to pieces in my hands. Carefully, I climb through the narrow window to a ledge, balancing on the few bricks that haven't crumbled away. Gripping the stones with my fingertips, I scale the battlement, drag myself through a narrow crenel, and tumble down onto what's left of the platform. I rise, panting, my eyes dry and itchy with ash. Across from me something is burning.

There at the end of the world I see him. I see him in the silence of shadows, the withering of life, the place where the sun goes down on the horizon. "You!" I hiss. "You did this?"

"I couldn't have done it without you, brother," says a voice like stones grinding to dust over eons.

"Do not call me that."

"What?" the voice taunts. A foul reek emanates from the darkness behind the flame. "Can you not fathom the beauty of this place? The perfection?"

"This is a dream," I say. "You aren't real."

"You would deny my existence?" asks the night. "As you wish. Those who refuse to believe in me are the easiest to destroy."

Suddenly, like the snuffing of a candle, the fire disappears. A shadow steps out of the darkness that replaces it. Then the shadow falls away like a cloak, revealing a man, his eyes smoking pits, his hands like claws. The stones hiss and crack when he touches them. The broken tower trembles under his feet.

"Are you surprised?" he asks, his mouth an infinite void. "Why do we take their form, Oberon? Is it easier to walk among them if we look the same? Why do we live in prisons of flesh when we are so much more?"

"Why do you invade my dreams? My most private moments?"

"You invited me when you revealed yourself to my servant, Ra-Anis. He will not recover from the blow you dealt him. It was fine work, brother, utterly merciless."

"Light Eater," I breathe, backing away from the shadow. "I am not like you. Why do you call me brother?"

The Light Eater merely shrugs and takes a step toward me, wreathed in elemental smoke. "What do you think of my palace?" he asks. "What do you think of the future?"

"You lie," I say calmly, holding my ground with some effort, my hands clinging to the ledge at my back. Why is it so hard to face what I fear? Even in a dream?

"Do I?" the Light Eater asks. "Where is the world heading, Oberon? You know the answer as well as I. It is heading toward this, toward nothingness, toward me."

"No," I say. "Archeälis is guiding the world. He guides time toward a new beginning."

"And here it is." The Light Eater makes a grand gesture. "Chaos will win. Nothingness. A universe in ashes. Final defeat of the light and the death of everything that is. Do you not welcome it?"

"It cannot be."

"The world will have its ending."

"Why are you doing this?" I ask. "Why do you drive the Obulans to their ruin? What pleasure can it possibly bring you?"

"Pleasure," the Light Eater repeats as if trying out a new word. "It is not about pleasure. It is about purpose. I am chaos. I am present in every burning forest, in every collision of the stars. In the smallest erosion, the withering sun, the militant advance of the tides and the eating away of land. In the irreversible aging of people and animals, in the last breath before the close. In loneliness and insanity, I am there."

"So you have no choice?"

"There is only one choice," says the Light Eater. "And I choose it. Every moment of every year for the last billion. And it is all coming to an end."

"I pity you," I say, taking a step forward to more solid footing. "You were not made this way."

"Do not pretend to remember my beginnings, little brother. Your feigned wisdom betrays you."

"There's something broken in you," I say. "I see it. What is it?"

A sudden bolt of lightning streaks across the sky. The clash of thunder rattles my teeth and hurls me forward onto a ledge where the death of the universe is clearly visible. The stars over my head have no names—he has taken them. The Light Eater is there and everything he touches smokes and kindles to flame. The flames spread and begin to devour the ruined castle and then the world. I wish I could leave this dream.

Last of all, I begin to burn, and it is a slow, painless unmaking of flesh and spirit. I watch it for a while, passive, wishing I could die. My essence, the heart of what I am, the genetic code of my soul begins to unravel. "Enslaver," I whisper. "Why? What profit is there in all this pain?"

"Embrace it," says the enemy. "It is the only way."

"Silencer," I speak without words. "As long as I draw breath, you cannot win. There are those who were born to oppose you." I smile for a moment even as my body turns to ash, thinking of Ava, but saying nothing to my immortal foe.

"You think the star-born will save you?" the Light Eater asks, knowing my innermost thoughts. "Do you know nothing of Voth-Baalok?"

I wince at the sound of the evil name. It is not the true name of the Light Eater, but something others call him, a name that gives him power rather than takes it away. In the old speech of angels it means *black void*.

I look to the horizon even as I die. I count the falling stars, searching for Ava, for the light she brings to the world and what it means. But does it really matter? Would the promise of peace mean anything? Would it last? Would the world last? Losing myself, I cling to the fingerprint of my spirit, the fundamental residue completely unique to a celestial, blessed or fallen.

Still his voice torments me. "Do you, Oberon, with all your intellect and philosophy, have any notion that you have already used up what little time you had in the world?"

"It's not true," I gasp, seeing the last star go out.

"You will die." The Light Eater gestures toward a vision of paradise, erasing it stroke by stroke. "Even if you delay me now, it means nothing. All cities will crumble and fall. All music, art, poetry, and life will be destroyed somehow, eventually. Finally, even the names will vanish, cease to exist." He speaks slowly and with finality. "Legacies cannot outlast the dust."

"No!" I cry. "Archeälis will not let it be so."

"Can you be so naive?" Darkness envelops my enemy like a cloak. "The dust will win, that slow and steady attrition that tends toward chaos and annihilation. Dust to dust. Nonentity. The end. Me."

"There is no spell of ending strong enough to overturn the creative will of the Maker," I whisper, my spirit battered but unbroken. "The dust will not win. We have been created for another story that has no ending."

As if in disgust, the Light Eater turns away. Suddenly, a white bird glides across the sky. It is a winter dove, its wings on fire. I think, watching it flicker past, that it may be the last living thing in the universe. The Light Eater laughs and picks it from the air, watching as the flames burn away its feathers and flesh. He holds it, examining it carefully, delighting in each minute suffering. It glows like a torch of untold horror in his hand until its writhing stops and he eats it.

"I will show you terror." As he speaks the sky opens up and swallows me. There is no pain. In fact, even in death, I am still waiting for something to happen. . . .

. . . I scramble to my feet, heaving frantic breaths, fingers scrabbling against sticky steel-bound barrels. The shock of waking from what felt like death is indescribable, and I feel my own body with a desperate, grateful force. How long did I dream? Something terrible has happened, I can feel it. But what?

Wasting no time, I hurl open the metal door of my chamber. I'm about to go out when a faint, singed smell gives me pause. I look down, my skin tingling with terror at the numinous. There on the cold stones, almost unrecognizable in death—a limp, scorched dove. The dove from my dream.

CHAPTER XXVII
Children of the Lost

"AVA, WAKE UP!"

I stir from dreaming and open my eyes. Raul stands over me, a hand on my arm, looking anxiously out the open window. His cloak is like a shadow over his shoulders. There are no stars. "Moon flies ill tonight," he says.

Still half asleep, I look out past the faintly drifting curtains, trying to find even one familiar star. Moving closer to the window, I expect to feel a faint draft. Nothing. Only stillness. I touch the curtains beside my bed as they continue to shift and shimmer without a breeze.

"What's happening?" My eyes focus and I rise at once, hurrying into my clothes.

"I don't know," Raul says. "I was asleep in the garden when a dream woke me—a feeling of danger. I told the guards about it and they're all awake, though confused. Now I'm here."

I reach into the eerie night. Everything about it feels wrong. "Sound the alarm."

Raul nods and darts out the window. I rush out of my room to find Cora and wake her and warn her. Warn her of what? I burst into her room. "Cora!" I cry.

She is already up, sitting on the end of her bed in the candlelight. She waves at me to be quiet. "What is it, Ava?"

"It's not safe!" I blurt. "There's something in the air. I can feel it."

Cora gets dressed in a hurry, pulling supple boots and a

belt of knives from her closet. "Find Viktor, then both of you meet me in the armory," she says. "Go."

I rush out of the room, rousing servants and refugees as I go. My voice sounds shrill and out of place in the cold, silent halls. If I'm wrong about this, I will feel like the greatest fool ever to live. But Raul felt it too, and I trust him.

I hear Cora's butler muttering sleepily to himself and lighting torches. Thanks to Raul, the private guards are all awake, and there are panic-sounds coming from the torchlit orchard where over two hundred refugees are camped. Viktor staggers downstairs at the same time as I do, a half-shod lunatic, his sword slapping at his side.

"Well met, Ava." He bows to me, an odd gesture considering he is shirtless and still holding one of his riding boots.

I motion to him. "Cora said to meet her in the armory."

He tugs on his other boot and we move toward a side door just as a guard bursts into the foyer shouting, "Intruders in the courtyard! Defend the princess!"

Is it Sol? Did he finally send his wizards to abduct me? Or to settle old scores with Cora? I do not stay to listen to the man's frantic cries, but instead slip out into the night with Viktor. He takes a shortcut through the gardens. I follow him between hedges, keeping to the shadows, terrified by the lack of stars. There is dark magic at work here. It's as if the whole of Westfell has fallen under the shade of some other realm.

We pause under an old pergola, panting. Peering through the hanging vines, I catch a glimpse of the action near the gate. The captain of the guard yells commands as his men unsheathe swords and rush to defend the mansion, their heavy boots thumping over the soft grass, their torches casting flickering shadows.

Squinting, brushing leaves from my eyes, I can just make out dark figures in tattered cloaks dropping over the walls onto the lawn. They advance toward the courtyard, curved swords drawn, flashing hand signals. Cora's war hounds snarl and howl in their pen, begging to be unleashed. Viktor pulls me away just as the sound of metal clashing echoes up, a ringing sound, then the choked voices of dying men.

"Obul!" I hear a man cry. "Obul has breached the walls!" More swords ring out, but I do not turn back to watch. I follow Viktor to the edge of the estate where Cora keeps her armory. Once upon a time, it was part of the old castle that stood here. Now it's just a squat stone building separated from the new mansion by a stone walkway and lots of trees.

"How did they manage it?" Viktor mutters to himself, unlocking the door and letting me in. "What kind of twisted magic?"

I look around at the sparring ring, the cold forge and bellows, the rows of weapons on the walls. What good am I against trained warriors? I've never fought anyone, never killed anyone—until that night on the roof. Even then it was an accident.

Viktor moves to a worktable and decants a glowing yellow liquid into a vial. "I have prepared long for this." He pockets the vial and opens a locker full of armaments. "Do not waste my toil."

"This is all I need." I select a slingshot and a pouch full of colorful ammunition of Viktor's design.

The door bangs open and we both jump. I whirl, expecting trouble. But it's just Cora, armed with her sash of bright throwing knives and a sword at her hip. She hands me a dagger. "For if they get in close."

Two servants carrying rucksacks file in after the princess. Moving with practiced efficiency, they open the bags and begin filling each one with dangerous objects. Viktor dons a shirt, a coat of mail, and gathers his own assortment of pointy things.

Everyone is surprisingly calm. My heart is beating out my chest, and my slingshot hand trembles. I hear muffled cries from outside, glass breaking, men grunting and cursing, the harsh barking of war hounds in pursuit of prey. Someone must have released them.

"Are you ready?" Cora asks.

I set my teeth and load my weapon with a tiny glowing sphere.

We go out into the night, into the screams and the chaos of the orchard where the refugees are fighting for their lives. Is it a slaughter? Are we mounting a good defense? It's hard to tell. Out front, Cora's men seem to be holding the court-yard. The back doors, however, are breached and there is fighting inside the mansion. Half a dozen war dogs move in a pack, striking furiously and leaving only bloodied corpses in their wake.

I can tell from the distant screams that this is not the only place in the city that the enemy attacked. I wish I knew how they got in. Viktor and I make a dash for the mansion, aiming for the back terrace where the huge double doors are staved in. The orchard is teeming with bodies, mostly refugees fleeing or fighting with shovels and rakes.

Trying to keep out of sight, I duck between the skeletons of trees and run hunched along a row of flower boxes on the outer edge of the terrace. A wounded Obulan staggers past, not seeing me. Cora shouts a challenge and he turns, his face painted red and silver, his lips twisted in a snarl of pain. One of Cora's knives takes him in the chest. He looks down at it, takes a shaky step toward her, and falls in a tangle on the steps.

"Get inside! Now!" Giving me a firm push, Cora breaks off from the rest of us, knives in both hands, presumably to defend the refugees.

"Go on," Viktor urges. "Do not worry for her. That woman is an iron fist in a velvet glove."

I do as he says, trying not to look down at the corpses clustered around the entrance. Laden with bags of weapons, Viktor and the servants maneuver their way through the chaos and follow me in a moment later.

"Gods of my fatherland!" the man holding the door exclaims. "You bring hope!"

"With death at our heels," says Viktor, pausing to hand out weapons.

We made it inside—a small miracle. But we're far from safe. There's been fighting in here already. Parts of the wall are chipped and hacked apart and the carpet is stained with blood. Several dining chairs are smashed or toppled, corpses lying around.

The survivors gladly drop fire pokers and kitchen knives in favor of shiny hand-and-a-half swords. Two stable boys, wielding the dull ceremonial swords from over the mantelpiece, stand a little taller when Viktor offers them extendable spears instead. After distributing their weapons, Cora's two porters move to close and bar the doors.

"Urg," one of them groans, taking a black-feathered arrow to the shoulder. A moment later he crumples, jamming the door open with his body. The other bends down, struggling to drag his wounded companion back inside.

"They're coming!" someone cries.

Overwhelmed by the sheer numbers in the orchard, a handful of marauding Obulans head for the mansion, leaving scattered groups of women, children, and old men untouched. The dogs take some of them. A few more burst in, shattering glass windowpanes and throwing the double doors wide. Viktor fires a crossbow into the leader's chest and charges the next warrior in line, sword raised. The rest of the Obulans fan out, engaging guards and servants.

One of the stragglers spots me and grins through scarred lips, his tinted sword raised. He's young, red-haired, not much older than me. Nice looking aside from the scars on his face. Why would he want to kill me?

When he charges, I run, scrambling over chairs and toppled furniture. Not knowing where to run to, I make a circle of the room. He swipes at me twice with his saber, smiling crookedly, enjoying the chase. As we pass through the fray, someone shoulders him against a wall, giving me time to put the huge dinner table between us. He lunges forward, his saber slicing the air near my face, but the table holds him back. Snarling and laughing he leaps on top of it and rushes me.

My breath catches in my throat as I raise Viktor's slingshot. It seems so heavy as I pull back the cord, arms shaky, trying to aim. At the last moment, I let it go, refusing to avert my eyes.

Pling.

There's an explosion, a spray of acid. The red-haired boy screams and clutches at his eyes. He steps clean off the table, blind and dying, his skin hissing and sizzling as he falls past me. Crouching behind the table, I reload the slingshot, trying not to think about what I just did.

There's more shouting, everyone locked in separate, bloody fights. Viktor kills a painted warrior, a clean thrust to the heart. Another comes at him from behind, but he shuffles aside, flicking his elbow into her temple as she moves past. She turns on him, spitting venom, slashes high. He ducks and swings, his sword thunking into her knee, folding it the wrong way. Her scream is so human it hurts. I cringe and look away, searching for a better place to hide.

No, I need to fight. But how? I don't see any trees to climb or branches to shoot from. The stairs, maybe? Leaping deftly onto the banister, I walk carefully up it, crouching low and aiming my slingshot at the windows. No one tries to climb through, so I turn my attention to the hallway upstairs. Everything seems quiet up there, too.

A fierce, resonate barking echoes in from the library, followed by grunting, bellowing and more death-sounds. A wounded Obulan limps headlong into the room, dragging his twisted ankle. He seems to be running away rather than charging. As he moves past, I spot two of Cora's silver knives protruding from his back. Another thuds into the back of his neck and he falls twitching and gurgling to the floor.

Cora arrives soon after, stooping to pull her bloody knives from the corpse, wiping them on her victim's sleeve. Raul is with her, a huge war hound beside him. "Raul! Up here!" I call to him.

"Merciful Father!" he says, obviously relieved to see me alive. "You won't believe this, but I saw you in a dream." He moves closer, leaning against the banister. "You told me to wake up and warn the guards. You saved us all."

"In a dream?"

"I just now remembered," he says, eyes distant. "It felt so real. I really saw—" He breaks off mid-sentence, eyes flicking toward a sound from outside. "Will you fight with me, Ava?"

I nod, pointing up toward the landing. "I'll watch your back from up here."

I drag in a deep breath, trying to steady myself. A lot of people are dead or badly wounded, I can feel it. There were so many of them, women and children, many unarmed, cowering, begging for mercy, receiving none. I peer through the high, narrow windows overlooking the orchard. "They're still coming over the walls!" I say, unable to hide my dismay. "Fifteen by my count. Survivors flee before them."

"Ava, shoot them as they come," Cora snaps. "Raul, Viktor, let's see what we can do about these doors."

With everything moving down there, it's hard to tell friend from foe. I choose one of the largest windows to shoot through, doing my best to pick off the Obulans who pass inside the frame. With such deadly ammunition, I'm terrified of hitting one of our own. As a result some of my shots go high, exploding harmlessly on the lawn.

Viktor, Cora, and Raul, along with five war hounds, seven guards, two stable boys, and a few stragglers prepare to defend the mansion. We let in the battered refugees as best we can, covering their retreat with arrows, knives, acid balls, and whatever we can pick up and throw.

Stumbling inside, a few scavenge weapons and join our ranks. Others huddle in corners to pray or disappear into the vast halls, seeking a safer place. I can hardly blame them. Viktor, Raul, and a team of farm hands work together to upend the dining table. Straining and puffing, they manage to slide it a dozen feet, using the flat side to brace the ruined doors.

"Is everyone inside?" Viktor asks, glancing up at me.

"Yes!" I call back, checking every window to be sure.

"Good." He reaches into one of his pockets and removes the vial he brought from the armory. It glows slightly, full of mysterious yellow liquid.

Outside, wary of arrows and silver knives, the Obulans pause for a heartbeat at the foot of the terrace. When nothing is forthcoming, they howl like a beast unchained and charge.

Viktor shouts something obscene and tosses the vial through the nearest window. It shatters against one of the oncoming shields, a yellow cloud rising up, twisting and coiling like mist in pain, filling the air with screams. The first to inhale it die instantly. The others scatter, wheezing and puking, trying to find a better point of entry.

"Does this mean the whole city's overrun?" Raul asks in the quiet that follows. "How in God's name did they get past the walls?"

"Dark magic, boy, and that's a fact," one of the guards replies. "It's a miracle we're still alive."

"No miracle," Cora says, bending over the torn body of a farm girl. "No miracles today."

"The refugees." Raul runs a hand through his hair, wincing at a spot of blood on his forehead. "They saved us with their lives."

"Brave souls, all," says Cora, clasping the dead girl's hand. She strokes the girl's hair gently, head bowed, her body shaking. When she stands, her composure flows over her like invisible armor.

What can I say to comfort her? What use are words when my own eyes are burning? I'm still blinking back tears when I hear a scream from one of the upper bedrooms. Two lights go out in my mind, two more dead. I sway a little, nearly slipping off the banister. Whatever power I have that connects me to others is getting stronger.

Viktor thunders up the stairs to investigate. He returns half a minute later, his face a grim mask. "They are good climbers, I'll give them that. Good fighters too." He smiles a cruel smile. "But not good enough."

There's a sudden crash, the sound of a heavy gate being slammed and bolted. One of Viktor's mercenaries rushes in from another room. "We lost the courtyard!" he shouts, scowling hard. "Damn their blood! We held out as long as we could."

"Why must I do everything myself!" Viktor barks, leveling his sword at the panting, stricken man. Swearing in his own language, he touches the gleaming topaz gem in the pommel of his sword. It cracks under his thumb, brightens like a tiny sun, like magic, but what kind? He grunts and flexes as if to stave off pain, the tendons in his arms squirming, his eyes dark as the bottom of a well. "Mistress, permission to reclaim the courtyard?"

Cora nods once, gesturing with a knife. "I'm right behind you. Raul, the rest of you, hold here!" She orders, disappearing into a corridor, taking two war hounds with her.

The room feels empty without her, our makeshift barricades shabby and inadequate. With our two best fighters gone, we barely have time to feel properly abandoned when the remaining hounds begin to howl. Raul dives into his new role as leader, offering orders and encouragement in equal amounts. "Steady!" he calls as he and a few others move furniture around the room, bolstering our defenses. "The mist is blowing away! They're coming!"

The moment Viktor's death-mist clears, a new wave of Obulans hits us, harder than before. Even with the doors blocked, there are too many windows to cover. One man falls away from his post, gasping, an arrow in his chest. The doors shudder under a terrible blow, the massive table rocking back. Men scramble forward to hold it in place.

Steady, breathe, I tell myself. *Do your part.* I feel the air turn cold, shimmer and crack, much like it did when Oberon tested his magic against the wizards in the obsidian tower. They must have brought a shaman with them. *And just when I thought we might survive . . .*

A chill wind whistles through the cracks in our fortifications. Outside, some unspeakable power is building. "Get away from the door!" I cry, too late.

His spell hits the mansion like a sudden storm. Glass shatters, a dresser tumbles away, the table splinters in half, the two pieces pivoting and crashing, crushing men underneath. A wave of force cuts through the defenders, hurling bodies aside in a spray of blood and frost. Even as far back as I am, the force of it knocks me off the banister onto the landing.

And just like that, Obulans swarm among us.

Everyone moves at once, screaming and hacking at the air and each other. I pick my first target, but one of the hounds takes him by the forearm, snapping both bones.

Using the slats of the banister as cover, aiming between them, I shoot an Obulan as he charges Raul. He goes down in agony, acid splattering the floorboards, hissing as it eats the ancient wood.

A warrior, fresh from decapitating a helpless victim, spots me. She rushes to the base of the stairs, thinking me an easy kill. She snaps her wrist down and up again, hurling an obsidian knife from her belt. But just as her arm is rising to release the blade, a streak of brown fur catches her from the side, clawing at her forearm, throwing her aim. The knife barely nicks my shoulder and imbeds itself in the wooden archway at the top of the stairs.

I catch only a glimpse of my savior—the whiskery face, the fierce, golden eyes. Guinevere. Then the cat is gone, slinking into the ransacked library as if midnight heroics are just a small part of her many household duties.

Taking advantage of the distraction, I raise my slingshot, fire, but the shot goes high. The Obulan bares her teeth at me, charges. Not knowing where to run, I scramble onto the banister, tuck my weapon into my waistband, and leap for the nearest of four twelve-torch chandeliers.

I make it, barely, and almost lose my grip when the massive thing begins to swing, twisting and bucking slightly on its long chains. I hold on for dear life. As the fixture swings back, the warrior swipes at me with her bloodstained scimitar, taking a few inches of my hair. As it swings out again, I make another leap, this time landing on a chandelier near the middle of the room.

One hand slips, jamming my shoulder painfully against the intricate metalwork supporting one of the unlit torches. As the fixture turns slowly, all its crystals tinkling, I set my feet in the gentle curves the arms make, freeing my hands. Finding an opening, I draw, load, and fire my slingshot, imagining I am shooting an apple with a misshapen stone.

I hit the Obulan in her right eye, melting her face clean off. She slumps over the banister, parts of her skull still dissolving, a rancid smoke filling the air. I almost throw up.

Glancing down at the fight, I'm not surprised to find that both sides have lost. I feel each death keenly. Even the fallen hounds are like wounds in my heart. Raul is nowhere to be seen. Everyone, friend and enemy alike, has retreated or been killed. And here I am, alone, hidden in a broken chandelier as it sways imperceptibly in the shadowy rafters.

I'm about to call out for Raul or Cora when approaching voices startle me into silence. Four Obulan warriors enter, then disperse, their leader shouting commands in a speech that sounds chopped up with a sword. Once he is alone, or thinks he's alone, the chieftain scatters a handful of dust onto the floor and barks an incantation—magic.

My whole body quivers like a horse shaking off flies. The chandelier clinks, crystal against metal, and the chieftain shifts his posture as if listening. I hold my breath and press my face against one of the suspension chains, trying not to move.

After a tense moment, he gets back to work. I watch him, intrigued as he begins to form symbols in the dust, chanting and invoking a name. To some, his strange words and gesticulations might seem comical. But every part of me that is sensitive to magic recognizes his words as words of power. He is speaking a name with passion and invocation, again and again.

"Baalok!" he intones. "Om Baalok, om Baalok, om Voth-Baalok!"

He ceases speaking abruptly and slams his fist into the floor. A pulse like a tiny explosion erupts from the point of impact, flashes out, hurling furniture aside and scorching the priceless rugs. Several crystals shatter, disorienting me and sprinkling my enemy with fragments. He does not even pause to wipe the dust from his shoulders, but instead gazes into a hole in the world—the hole his fist made. He shoves the corpse of a stable boy aside with his foot, making room for the portal to grow. Somehow, this casual gesture makes my blood boil.

Something shimmers in the heart of the portal and I smell the interstellar dust. It smells like home. *Could it be?* A forgotten thrill surges through my muscles like lightning. *Could the enemy be using the pulsar fields as Sol feared they would?* This thought only fuels my anger, ushering in a wrath beyond anything I've ever known, as if something precious has been tossed between irreverent hands and spat upon.

Acting on instinct, I drop down from the chandelier, loading my slingshot as I fall. I land three feet from the Obulan and let fly. His look of horror and surprise quickly melts away as he topples in a heap of charred muscle and hissing, spitting fat.

My skin tingles at the touch of the gateway. I reach for it and feel something inside me stir, my body shivering with anticipation. My slingshot slips from my fingers, making no sound as it hits the floor. I take a deep breath and step through.

CHAPTER XXVIII
The Goddess

I MATERIALIZE AMID the pulsar fields. For an instant, all the helplessness and pain, the tragedy of death, and the fear of more sorrow to come—it all drains away as I float suspended in the stardust void. I feel cool sand between my toes and crouch low, touching the origami folds of space. Light plays across my fingers, and I trace each individual photon as it rides the colorless beams.

Sudden, unfamiliar sounds penetrate my perfect moment and the light fades.

I creep through the obscurity, well hidden, thankful for the swirling clouds of dust. I hear Obulans moving outside the fields. I feel the opening and closing of worlds. There are several stable singularities nearby, and I inch toward them. The gateway I used to get here has already closed, but I'm not worried.

Amid the pulsar fields I am myself again. I am as close to home as I've ever been. The light of stars is in me, and it makes my skin tingle under the sheen of dust that has settled on my arms and shoulders. I rub my hands together, expecting lightning to spark between them. I do not fear anymore. I walk to the edge of the fields and stand alone on the folded sands.

My body reacts violently to the scene before me, to the wrongness and presumption. These fields are sacred ground. They are not to be used for evil, for menace, or war. The secret threads that connect the worlds should not be turned inward, should not be used to tear good things apart, to make the world smaller and more broken.

Before me is a vast desert waste, tall dunes gray in the starlight. Eleven columns of Obulan troops have assembled in the flat expanse surrounding the pulsar fields. At the head of each column, high shamans chant the evil name, *Voth-Baalok*, their supplications fueling portals to Vanfell.

Some of the portals are shiny and reflective like tree ornaments. Others burn like globes of blue fire or spin like tiny moons. The Obulans enter in ones and twos. Too many at once and the portals would grow unstable and collapse. There must be thousands here, enough to overrun the city, but only a fraction have gone into the portals.

A sentry spots me and lets out a howl, gathering more men to himself. Whooping and yowling, they rush forward to seize me. Terrified, I try to turn and flee into the fields, but my feet won't budge. I watch them labor up the dune toward me. My lips move, speak a name. My hand rises and the land rises with it, the sand undulating. I peer down at my fingers, only part of me aware what the other half is doing.

"Stop!" I cry, and my voice is the wind, driving the swirling sands into their midst. At first they press on, hands raised to shield their faces. But as the wind intensifies, they kneel down and cower against the gale as it howls past them into the wastes, disrupting the shamans' chant, causing the eleven portals to flicker.

If I can just close those portals, Vanfell will be safe. . . .

But first we must deal with these few, kill them if we have to.

No . . . what's wrong with me? These aren't my thoughts. These are the thoughts of an intruder.

Call me what you will, Star Child, says a voice, like mine, except colder. *I am no intruder.*

At last, bested by the wind, the leader stops, swaying unsteadily as sand flows around his feet. Using mostly hand gestures, he gives a new command. The nine with bows nock arrows, aim as best they can, and fire away.

Now can we kill them? Laughing at my own discomfort, I brush the shafts aside and fade into the sands. *How could they dream to harm us while I'm with you, here amid the pulsar fields? Why would they even try?*

So many lives inside me, all around me, touching me, whispering words of power. I reach to one side as if to clasp the hand of a loved one, but clutch only dust.

"This is not your power to command!" I say to the shamans, in control again. One by one, the portals wink out like candles extinguished by a wish. The Obulans are left speechless, stranded, with only me and my inner voice as company.

Not knowing any better, their fury roused, they attack. All I want is to spare them, to vanish into the fields now that my work here is done.

But we don't always get what we want, do we, Ava?

The power inside me swells like the sea in storm. The sands begin to churn and whirl, the stinging grains whipping about my face and eyes, pelting my skin, tearing at my clothes until the leather begins to shred. I cry out in helpless pain, but the other me does not care. More arrows fly and splinter into the sky. Tendrils of lightning lance out from my body, and a multitude of souls pass out of the world, their eyes empty, their bodies crumbling to ash.

A minute they last against me, maybe less.

Before long the rest are retreating, their leaders all

broken, their voices lost in the tempest. I let some of them escape, sensing the fear in their hearts and the shame. Others are consumed by the sands, buried and brought to peace. But the eleven shamans I capture, using the sands to draw them toward me as a rip current draws unwary swimmers out to sea. They stare vacantly up at me, and I see through their tortured masks to the evil that drives them—*Voth-Baalok*.

His is a power that has devoured countless worlds. It should strike me to nothing, but I do not fear it, not while I walk amid the fields. "Who are you?" I ask. "A star like me?" *No, silly girl. This is what a star becomes.* "What do you want of my world? What is your purpose in coming here?"

The darkness says nothing. I am not surprised. While I am like this and my true nature enfolds me, not even the great darkness will dare approach. Disappointed, I turn to the shamans.

"Do not kill them, please," I beg of myself.

These men are evil.

"They're just men, their hearts twisted by something worse. Please, don't."

In this I will not be denied. I raise my hands and my fury goes out in a flare, tearing through the desert like a blade of daylight. When it is finished, I lower my arms, close my eyes, and step calmly into the fields, disappearing amid the dust as my sandstorm rages. Serenely, still possessed by some power I know not what, I open a gate, step through. . . .

. . . Adrift on an endless sea, tossed around like a dead thing, each moment becoming more and more myself. The goddess within me diminishes. I increase.

The moment I wake, I begin to sink deeper and deeper into the abyss, the very heart of the ocean. My clothes are ruined, the sturdy material torn and tattered, the shreds dragging through the water as the current takes me. I wriggle free and am left with only my white shift. I kick my way to the surface and splash onto a long beach, soaked and gasping, with seaweed in my hair.

I lay there, dragging in huge lungfuls of air, the sand warm and abrasive on my cheek. It is nighttime and the palms dance gently in the wind. I smell a salty freshness, the smell of movement and life—the ocean. I've seen it only once, the ocean east of Mira's garden. I have never touched it or felt it on my skin. This ocean is like that one, except vaster. It is the ocean of the real, and it contains everything that is.

There, on the far side of the slender beach under a wilderness of stars, I see the goddess. She is looking at me. I can almost see her face this time. She has no expression that I can make out, though her lips are closed.

"Was it you?" I rise hesitantly, dripping on the beach, almost naked, my hair matted and wild. "Was it you who killed the shamans, who closed the portals? Was it you who spoke to me?"

The goddess steps closer, making no prints on the sand. She cups a handful of water and lets it run through her fingers. She is my height exactly. I stare intently into her eyes.

"It *was* you," I say, needing no confirmation. "You closed the portals and drove the hordes away. You saved Vanfell. You invoked the power of the pulsar fields even though I didn't know how."

The goddess pauses next to me, her toes squeezing the

sand. She reaches out. I reach back, a mirror, and touch her hand. A jolt goes through me like I've been struck by lightning.

"You didn't have to kill them, though," I say, my voice falling. "Why?"

I did it to show him who you are. Her voice is an echo of my own.

"Who am I, then? Who are you?"

She turns her head and looks down at the gently lapping waves. The water pushes up across the sand and rushes over our feet, reflecting the starlight. I blink, unbelieving, seeing only my reflection in the water. I stare at myself, mystified, one hand held out as if grasping another, but there is no one else here.

I drift away, guided by a power that is both mine and hers. I walk on the back of time, riding the contours and slipping through the ridges. I ride deeper, taking a breath. The worlds turn without me, and I glide back through a door cracked open. Where will I go?

"Oberon! Can you hear me?" I search for him, but all I feel is silence, blackness, a sorrow and a void. I see a burning dove, its white feathers flaking to ash, and I feel the anguish of a world ending.

Has it been an eternity or only an instant? Finally, after a lifetime of wanting him, I feel him searching for me too. His longing heart nearly draws me in. But he is too far away.

I reach for my father and all I feel is cold. I see the mountains and the gathering snows, the last storm of winter and the dimming sun. I feel his need to move. He wants to find me, but despair gnaws at him. "Father, no! You'll die here!" Is what I'm seeing real? I try to touch his face, to comfort him, but the vision fades.

Cora's gardens appear, wet with dew, and I can tell from the moon that what I'm seeing is in the past. Raul looks tired, overwhelmed even. Going to a weatherworn bench, he kneels down and prays for a while, eventually falling asleep near the roses. I go to him in his dream, feeling the strands of time slip from my shoulders. Was Oberon right? Are dreams really timeless, as prayers are?

"Ava," he says in confusion.

"Raul!" I refrain from touching him, not sure if I even can. "Listen, there is going to be an attack on the mansion. Soon. You have to get up. Wake everyone and tell them to arm themselves."

"Wha—is it Sol?" he asks.

"Worse. Obulan warriors. Warn the soldiers, the guards, your family. Have Viktor rouse his mercenaries. Tell the servants to fortify the doors and windows. Those men who just brought the food shipment, warn them too. They are good fighters and will save many. Oh! And release the war hounds!"

He stares at me as one who is dreaming, with confusion and disbelief. Then he nods once and is gone. . . .

. . . I appear breathless in the devastated mansion. There is not a window or door intact. Most of the furniture is crushed or hacked to pieces. I look around quickly, myself again, tired and in tatters. My clothes are nearly shredded from the sand storm, yet I do not have a single cut on my skin.

How much of that was real? I wonder, trying to judge how much time has passed. Without the pulsar fields I feel weak and small again. As far as weapons go, the slingshot lying on the floor next to me pales in comparison to the companionship of stars. I pick it up, glimpsing my distorted reflection in the polished metal handle. The goddess, I saw her. I saw myself.

Outside I hear the distant thunder of hooves over cobblestones. Curious, I tiptoe through the entrance hall and into the courtyard to investigate. There's still battle raging beyond the hedges and near the gate, but the courtyard seems clear aside from countless dead.

Not knowing what else to do, I check some of the bodies for life signs, wishing I could heal them. No luck. Above, the stars of Alta have returned, each in its place, and I welcome them like old friends. Whatever power came over Westfell is lifted, and the Obulans must know it by now.

I did it. I really broke the spell. I walked the pulsar fields and commanded the fathomless powers that grow there. For the first time in my life I killed men in anger. It seems more like a dream than a memory, but I know it really happened, and the pride I feel at my triumph is tinged with shame.

The sound of galloping horses is getting closer by the second. Closer and much, much louder. A horse's neigh breaks the night and six armored steeds riding abreast strike the main gate, knocking it from its hinges. They enter the courtyard followed by twenty more riders, all clad in black. The riders split into pairs, moving in perfect unity, cutting down the Obulans that try to flee or fight back. I watch awestruck by the cold efficiency. It is all over in seconds.

The captain eases his horse into the courtyard next to the fountain and dismounts. One of the defenders limps forward to meet him. I can tell by her fiery curls that it's Cora. They converse for a moment. Cora shakes her head, gesturing emphatically. She sways, nearly falls, catching herself on the knight's breastplate. She's wounded, badly. Intimidated as I am by the situation, I have to do something. I know I can heal her, just like I healed that woman's cough the other day.

I go to her, feet pattering on the paving stones, not caring who sees me. By the time I arrive, the knight has laid her gently to the ground, his own cloak as a pillow, and is speaking softly to her. I kneel beside him and pass my hand over Cora's wounded thigh, then her ribs. I feel the gaze of a million stars upon me, teaching me. I close my eyes.

The power of the pulsar fields remains inside me, deep down, something I can use or borrow. But this other power is *mine*. I let it flow into Cora, enabling her body to heal. "It's done." I stand wearily, feeling the trials of the night catch up with me.

"So it *is* you," says the knight, a touch of awe in his voice. "You're the Star Kin."

I look up at him, his sword and armor stained with the blood of his enemies, then at myself, noting something odd about my skin, a gentle luminance. "I know you," I whisper. *Whose eyes are those behind the helmet slit?* He looks back at me and sees me clearly in the moonlight. I try to breathe.

"You're under my protection," Cora says stiffly from the ground. "You don't have to speak to him."

"I will," I say. *He's just a man.* After what I did tonight, I refuse to shrink away or cower, no matter how afraid I am. I simply watch him, waiting.

The knight removes his helmet and throws back his chainmail coif, his thick, flaxen hair spilling out from underneath. I can't help but gasp a little. It's Hector, the prince of

Vanfell. "Daughter of light," he says, not knowing my name. "Permit me to—"

"Ambush!" Cora shouts weakly.

An Obulan warrior, seeing Hector as a distracted leader, springs from the garden hedge, a look of pure hatred on his face. As if on instinct, Hector leaps between me and the would-be assassin, sword raised. But there's no need. The assassin hardly makes it three steps when one of Cora's knives spins through the air and spills his throat across the stones.

"Thanks, sis." Hector nods to her, lowering his sword. Still lying on her back, Cora shrugs and closes her eyes. Two of Hector's knights arrive to tend her. "You know who I am?" he asks.

I nod once. "What do you want with me?"

"Just to talk, somewhere safe. Then you go free."

"What about the wizards? Aren't they loyal to your father?"

"They were. Now they answer to me."

"He's dead then?" I ask, trying not to sound too thrilled about it.

Hector gives a noncommittal shrug. "Assassins came for him in his sleep. Very nearly succeeded. His mind was already half-gone. It's only a matter of time now."

I bite back the words *I'm sorry.* "So this makes you king?"

"I don't feel like a king," he says almost to himself. "Well, what say you? Will you ride with me?"

I take a step closer, afraid, but curious. What will happen if I put myself in his power? Hector could be my way out. He could bring me to freedom, to Oberon. He could just as easily bring me to Sol, his cruel, dying father. I turn to ask

Cora's advice, but she is already deep asleep.

"Yes." I give an almost imperceptible nod. "I will go with you."

The prince gestures toward his waiting horse and helps me mount. He slides in behind me, pressed against me. Flicking the reins, he turns and rides out through the smashed gate, leaving his men to finish the cleanup.

We pass through the old, quiet streets. In the chaotic aftermath of so many scattered battles, the wall surrounding Westfell is poorly manned, the gate broken. We pass through unhindered. "See?" says the prince. "Easy as that."

When we reach an open stretch of road connecting Westfell to the rest of the city, Hector brings his horse up to a gallop. Before long I feel my breaths coming in gasps, the horse's muscles shifting under my chest, its sleek mane in my hands. I cling to it, heart pounding. Pieces of my shredded shirt come loose and float away in the wind.

No going back now, I think, feeling invigorated, almost euphoric as the night sweeps past. *Oberon, here I come.*

CHAPTER XXIX
The Dagger and the Rose

AFTER HALF an hour's hard riding, Hector reins in his horse in front of an abandoned drinking house. The sign outside is too weatherworn to read, and all the rooms are dark save one. I dismount and follow him in, my legs a little wobbly.

Inside, I find a fire already lit and crackling merrily. There are no patrons, no bartender, and no servers that I can see. No one. Hector slides a chair in front of the fireplace and gestures for me to sit.

"Where are we?" I ask.

"Oh, this is mine," he says nonchalantly, waving his hand around the empty room. "I've always wanted to own an inn."

I peer around at the mismatched walls. One is brick, the other wood paneling, the other some sort of hewn stone. This place must have burned down at least once over the years.

"It needs a little fixing up," he says, sitting across from me, one side of his face lit by firelight. "It was abandoned for years before I found it. With my official duties and now the war . . . I'm beginning to wonder if I'll ever be open for business."

"So you're an innkeeper on top of everything?"

"An epically bad one," he says. "But I'll get some customers eventually. What I really need is a proper musician. And drinks. And servers. And a bar . . . with stools. The list goes on."

Somehow this casual exchange eases my anxiety somewhat. I let out a slow breath, wiping my mouth on my shoulder. The taproom feels large, mostly because it's so empty. Most of the tables are shoved aside, broken, or leaning against the walls, and all the chairs are stacked up in a corner. There's darts, a stage, a dance floor, and an entire wall full of books.

"Can I get you anything?" Hector asks. Even in the dim light, I notice lines of fatigue on his princely features, his armor chipped and stained with blood.

"I'm fine, thanks," I say. "I'm worried about my friends. I left so quickly, I didn't get to see if Raul and Viktor were okay."

"I wish I had answers for you," he says, rising and disappearing into another room. When he returns, he sets a tankard of water in front of me. "Go ahead, you must be thirsty. You fought well before we came."

I take the drink in both hands and sip it. "I ran mostly."

"The Obulan troops weren't expecting to be cut off from reinforcements." He looks at me knowingly. "Someone followed them to the source and closed the portals. Some think it was the one we call The Lion of the Desert."

"He could have done it," I say, knowing he is referring to Oberon. "But he didn't. It was me. I closed the portals."

Hector nods, pleased by my forthrightness. "Will you answer my questions while time permits?"

I look at him closely, wishing I had Oberon's powers of discernment. I see no evil in him, only the determination to do right. But whether he is noble or cruel, I am at his mercy. "I will try," I say.

"Let's start with your name."

"Ava," I say. "Why isn't there time?"

"I will be called away soon," Hector says. "We are riding out to meet the enemy in a battle to end it. I need answers before that happens."

"I will help," I whisper, hoping that my cooperation will help me see Oberon again.

"Are you the one who was spoken of in the prophecy?" he asks.

"I don't know, maybe. Tell me what it says."

Hector nods, seeing that I am truly ignorant. "There is a relationship between the obsidian tower and the king," he says. "My father has always needed and feared the wizards and their practices. The prophecy came four years ago—when an oracle, the seeress, told my father that his kingdom would come to darkness and Obul would rise again. She told him the only hope for Vanfell was born with the stars."

"Sounds like me," I say, seeing no point in denying it. "What else?"

"Well, naturally, my father was astonished. He asked her how this could be, but the seeress fell into a sleep like death and did not awaken until midsummer of this year. By then she had become old and could hardly speak. She whispered something to him before she died, a name maybe, or a promise. No one knows but him." The prince swallows, gritting his teeth slightly. "Hunting you gave my father a reason to live. Even if it was only an evil reason. He is dying now, and I will be king after he's gone." His eyes flicker. "He would be proud that I found you."

I hold my breath and let it out slowly, fearful that he will turn me in.

"You could heal him, couldn't you?" he asks, a strange,

wistful look in his eyes. "Just like you healed Cora?"

"Maybe," I say hesitantly. "I've never healed a wound of the mind."

Hector gives me a long, calculating look. The feeling of imminent betrayal grows stronger, then passes. He is a good man. I saw that the moment I laid eyes on him during the royal audience. "No," he says at last, almost to himself. "I gave you my word. When we're done here, you go free."

"I could try," I whisper. *Did I just say that?* "I mean, if you bring me to him, I could try."

Hector gives me another look, this one even harder and more curious than before, somewhere between astonishment and respect. "My God. You're telling the truth, aren't you?" he says.

I nod, hardly believing it myself.

"You're something else," he says. "But no. Any cure for old age would go against the natural law. I will not tread those waters. They're too deep for any man."

My sigh of relief is almost audible, but Hector doesn't seem to notice. He takes a deep breath, closes his eyes to refocus, and continues, "There's a second part to the prophecy. After the old one died, my father spoke often with the new seeress, the youngest, highest oracle. She told him that you would return to the city and that you would save it. Never one to put his trust in words alone, he searched for you.

"For months he scoured the lands beyond the valley, cursing the pulsar fields and the desert that hid you. It was not right the way he did it. When he became too old to ride out himself, he gathered stories from travelers, offering obscene sums for desert gossip or even the most tenuous rumors surrounding you. In the end—"

"I was betrayed by a wandering sage," I say almost to myself, remembering Oberon's words on the matter. "All for a little gold."

"Twelve royals to be exact. A king's ransom." The prince bites off the rest of his tale, obviously surprised that I knew the ending.

"Do you believe in the oracles?" I ask.

"Like my father, I fear them," he says. "He was content to use them for their knowledge. But when this war is over, I plan to abolish the order entirely." He makes a sign in the air as if to ward off demons. "The life of a seeress is tragic and brief. She takes her vows at the dawn of womanhood, has four years at most to prophesy. Then she dies, and the next seeress is chosen from the young and promising. It has always been like this."

"So they do know things," I say. "Their power is real."

Hector nods gravely. "They use spirits to gather knowledge, and in return the spirits take their life."

"That's horrible!" I say, shivering at the wrongness of it. "Knowledge may be truth, but it is not good or evil. It is what one does with the truth that defines them. Your father held the truth in his heart and turned it toward evil. It was an evil thing he did, taking my father, taking my home."

"I am sorry, Ava."

I try to calm myself, try to focus on the sincerity in his voice, but words mean nothing to a bleeding heart. "I have not forgiven your father. If it wasn't for his obsession with oracles and prophesies I'd still be with mine. He's still a dragon for all I know. He might come for me and destroy what's left of Vanfell."

"Dragonfire would be a kindness compared to what the Obulans will do to this city," Hector says gravely.

"Then perhaps I should pray he comes soon," I reply, meeting his gaze.

Hector pauses, considering my words. "Perhaps the line of kings is an evil that should be wiped out," he says. "But the people are good. They should not suffer for the deeds of a few arrogant men."

His compassion is undeniable now, and my anger subsides like a flame with no air to breathe, leaving only the sadness. "They captured me," I say, and it feels more like a confession than an accusation. "They tried to kill my father. They put me in a watchtower and meant to use me against Sol, against the whole world, but they didn't know how. And neither do I. If I am a weapon, I am not the sort you want."

Hector nods. "Perhaps the seeress was mistaken and you are only a victim," he says, watching me closely, as if trying to solve a mystery in the linings of my skin. "Perhaps the prophecy has already come true."

I think of how I traveled to the pulsar fields and closed the eleven portals. I'm not even sure it was me who did it. I didn't feel like myself, but I remember it. "How did you find me?" I ask.

"The enemy," he says after a pause, "opened multiple portals within the city. The warriors stepped through rifts in the air and killed on sight, distracting and dividing my men. Some went to Westfell. Others to the palace to kill my father. The rest tried to overwhelm the garrison and open the main gate to the awaiting hordes."

"I thought they'd all fled," I say. "Beyond the valley."

"Not as far as we'd hoped. Not by half. My men reported

a large concentration of Obulans in Westfell. Most assumed they'd come to kill the gentry. So after the business at the palace, that's where need called me."

"So it was chance then, us meeting?"

"Do you think it was random, an entire portal dedicated to Cora's estate?" he asks. "Once inside the city, they were outnumbered ten thousand to one. Their infiltrators could have been better spent at the gate. Why do you think they went after Westfell?"

"For me?" I say, still not sure about his theory.

He nods. "And now they're all dead."

"I killed them," I whisper, wincing at the memory. "It still feels like it happened to someone else."

"So that's it," he says tenderly. "We take your father and your home and in return you save Vanfell. That does not seem fair."

"Either way the prophecy is fulfilled," I say as if it doesn't matter, when in truth I'm screaming inside.

"Either way it was wrong to hurt you."

"It seems so long ago," I say, thinking back to the winter and the tower chamber with no windows where I met Oberon.

"The captain who imprisoned you must have sent your father back to the city as a trophy, reporting that you had not been found," Hector says, realization dawning. "He wanted to keep you for himself, to use your power, for already rumors of you were spreading in Vanfell. A seeress' words move in whispers and glances until everyone knows one form of the story or another."

"If she speaks truth, then I still have a part to play," I whisper. "What I did may have delayed the end. But there's still an army out there."

"You've done enough. A million people owe you their lives, myself included."

"Vanfell isn't saved," I say, trying to maneuver the conversation toward Oberon. "There's still fighting to be done. And I'd like to still be here when it's over. What I did was mostly luck and trickery. There is only one who can end this war."

Prince Hector nods, too humble to think himself worthy. "The Lion of the Desert."

"Maybe that was my role to play," I say. "To bring The Lion to the city."

"What do you know of him?" Hector asks.

"I know he is protecting me."

"But why? Who is he?"

"A friend," I say. "His real name is Oberon."

"I see." Hector seems curious, but unwilling to press me further. "If not for him, Vanfell would have already fallen."

"He found me in the watchtower," I say. "That's where we met. He freed me. Later we were separated. I need to find him. Do you know where he is?"

"I do not, but I have heard much of him. There are rumors on the wall of a duster who fights like a hundred men, though he is only a lad. Each time I seek his council or try to fight beside him he vanishes like smoke, as if he does not wish to meet me. Could this be him?"

"It sounds like him," I say, knowing beyond any doubt. "He's a little . . . shy."

Hector ponders my words for a full minute, his jaw flexing, his eyes roving the burning coals. "I will send you to him," he says at last, rising stiffly.

I hesitate, gripping the seat of my chair. I did not expect this to go so well. "It's strange," I say. "You said you wanted something from me. But it was you answering questions."

Hector smiles. "I just needed to see you," he says, standing tall, turning away from the fire until he is an armored shadow. "I needed to hear you speak and see the truth in you, that you are on the side of light."

"You saw all that in one conversation?" I ask.

"In one moment."

Something softens inside me, and I remember the first time I saw him, how I knew he was different than Sol. I stand slowly.

"I know who you are," he says.

"Is it that obvious?" I approach, feeling very small next to him.

"Not to everyone."

"So you're a wizard then?"

"No," he whispers, feeling me near him but not turning. "You are the one the seeress spoke of. The one who came from the sky."

I bow my head and shut my eyes, remembering nothing of that day or the ones before it. Somehow, hearing the pain in Hector's voice, I feel like I've hurt him and I don't know how.

"I was there," he says, his voice wistful. "I was there with my father on horseback the day the pulsar fields were created. I saw him take your vessel as a trophy. Then I watched for three years as he agonized over it, cursed it, and tore himself apart with seeking you."

"I was just a child," I whisper, wanting him to turn around so I can see his face. "I couldn't have—"

"I know," he says, his hand curling into a fist, not in anger, but to stop the trembling. "It's not your fault. None of it. But this is my life, and you are a part of it now, daughter of light. Goddess made flesh."

"I am not a goddess," I say. "I am not like Oberon . . . immortal. But I'm not like you either. I don't know what I am."

"Perhaps," he says. "But I see the lines that connect all living things. You and me. This Oberon. Even the Obulans. I have seen them all in a dream."

"Hector," I whisper, touching his shoulder. "You are flesh and a beating heart. I am stardust and airless sky. How can you say we are the same?"

"Last I checked you bleed," he says.

"It is just an appearance."

"You're mortal," he says, and I see the mystery of the stars in his eyes. The way they rise and set. The way they sail through Alta's sky, day and night, looking up at us just as we incline our heads toward them. Are we as bright in their eyes?

"How do you see me so clearly?" I ask, gripping his armor until my fingers ache.

"You are a creature from beyond the world," Hector continues, undaunted. "And yet you are one of us. And you, above all, have a part to play in this world. I do not know what it is, but I saw it from afar like a sailor glimpsing the light of his home city after years at sea. It warmed my heart, gave me hope. It is bigger than this city, bigger than this war. And whatever destiny you have, be it tragic or radiant, will not come to be if I keep you here."

Moved by his speech, I can't help but give a slight bow in his direction. "Thank you, Hector. You are a good man. The best."

"Come," he says, adjusting his sword. "I'll send for some-one to arm you properly, and a rider to take you to the one you call Oberon. The final battle is coming. What part you play, if any, is up to you."

CHAPTER XXX
Under Ashen Skies

THE PRINCE INSISTED on sending me into the city prepared for anything. My jerkin is finely cut and dyed, the mesh-armor so beautifully crafted I suspect it may have belonged to the prince himself before he outgrew it.

I have my slingshot, my freedom, a letter bearing Hector's seal, a guide named Delia, and the promise of rejoining Oberon.

It is shortly after dawn and overcast and we are passing quickly through the tiers on horseback. Delia is an excellent rider, and I hold on to her tunic and watch the clouds roll by, feeling the warmth of desert spring in my hair. I cannot hide my expectation, and I feel myself pulled beyond the present moment as I imagine our reunion. What will he say? How will I respond?

"I can't take you to the main gate," Delia says. "Those streets are blocked with men and horses. I know another way, though I doubt you'll like it."

We pass south through the slums. The people of Vanfell, desperate and in need, have ransacked entire neighborhoods in search of wood to burn or iron for the forges. There are no trees. The few that there were have been torn down and burned. They even uprooted the stumps and burned those too.

Worst of all are the animals. Pigs, goats, emaciated dogs, sad and suffering in the muck. Most pets have been eaten, except for those too diseased to touch. I see now, at last, outside of my sheltered interim at Cora's estate, the toll the war has taken.

Delia noses her horse through an alleyway into a street too narrow for carts. "This whole part of the city is dying," she says. "There's no way around it."

"The war did this?" I ask.

Delia snorts. "Goodness no, child. The siege hasn't even lasted a month."

"The winter then?"

"These people have been like this for as long as I've been alive. Some of them might not even know there's a war on."

"Oh," I say, seeing everything in a new light.

At first the crowds part before us, but as we near the wall the streets become congested, and we have to dismount and walk. Delia curses as we enter a particularly derelict neighborhood. "Stay close," she whispers, trying not to touch the lost-looking pedestrians as the street narrows and the air turns foul as a sewer.

Before, when I first came to Vanfell, I would have promptly vomited. But today I walk with my head up and my eyes alert, trying to make sense of the suffering. There are people lying all around as if dead. Young and old, moaning and silent, they lie in their sickness and pain.

My companion holds her sleeve over her nose and mouth. "It's the rats," she says. "They bring the plague. Don't go near that one." She points out a crumpled ruin of a man. "He won't last much longer."

The smell is awful, but I do not shy away from it. I approach the man as he sits propped against the wall of a hut. His armpits are swollen black and blue like he has grapefruits inside them. He coughs weakly, his neck a misshapen bruise, and I feel my heart go out to him, and something more.

"Don't," Delia says, standing at a distance. Her voice trails off as if she is curious to watch what I'll do.

Kneeling in the dirt, I reach out and touch the man's wounds, which are infected and dark with clots. I touch his eyes and mouth. His swelling decreases. His wounds, now mostly scrapes, have no disease in them.

I touch each of the afflicted in turn, walking slowly down the street with my arms wide open. I want nothing more than to see Oberon, but this is important, as important as anything I've ever done. My companion watches as I kneel and touch foreheads, sweeping the alleyways one by one.

One woman clasps my hand and kisses it. Another lays down before me, whispering prayers, her tears falling on my bare feet.

A girl approaches holding her belly, her brown hair done in pigtails. I recognize her as the girl who was being attacked in the alley the night I lost Oberon, though she does not know me. I cradle her head in my hands and kiss her forehead, holding on to her for as long as I can before the press of bodies forces us apart.

"I love you," she mouths as she disappears, and I see a spark of recognition in her green eyes.

Next comes a balding man with ulcers on his face, then his wife and deformed son. I heal them. When it is over, I get up and walk away, eyes following me as if I am light itself.

"It's not right, sickness," I say as we turn a corner. "It's not how life was intended."

Delia leads her horse in stunned silence, eyes intent on the street ahead. We continue on foot, passing eastward through the city until at last we reach the wall, a towering stack of stones a hundred feet tall and many miles wide—the end of Vanfell. "This is it," Delia says, pointing to the upper rampart. "See that flag? That's where he stands most nights. He's not there now. But that's where you'll find him."

I nod and thank her and go on alone, entering the wall by an iron gate. The soldiers on guard duty, seeing that I wear the armor of the prince, let me in without a word. When the quartermaster questions me, I show him the letter bearing Hector's seal. He looks it over, his eyes widening a little. Then he bows to me and opens the inner gate himself.

I find myself inside the wall itself, an underground city complete with its own roads, ramps, forges and living quarters. At first all the commotion is overwhelming, and I shuffle around, vaguely lost, trying not to get stepped on. Soldiers are everywhere, hundreds, maybe thousands— listening to orders, forming lines, marching, and reciting battle songs. The roar and clatter of voices and armor is deafening.

Listening to the scattered conversations, I discover that Hector and his men are preparing to march on the Obulan encampment. A legion has just been dispatched from the mountain barracks, but that is only part of what the excitement is about.

"He went out alone!" a page boy exclaims. "He went out with only those tattoos and his own name. He killed them all! Swept the valley clean!"

So Oberon isn't here. I feel my spirit fall.

The boy gestures wildly to his companion, a knight in armor. "He drove them over the hills, across the second bend!"

The knight nods, his helmet cradled under one arm.

"True enough. We ride out to finish the job."

"He's a god!" the boy exclaims. "Sent to us by Archeälis himself to drive off demons!"

"Pardon me," I say, strolling up to them. "I'm looking for the Lion of the Desert. Prince Hector sent me."

The page blinks at me for a moment, probably thinking me an odd-looking errand girl. "He's out in the valley last I heard, killing like a madman."

"Good luck though," says the knight. "Only one he talks to is Dirk, old Roddick's boy."

"How do I reach the valley?"

"These days, only way out is the south gate."

"Where's that?"

He gives me a strange look, then points to a group of marching soldiers. "Just follow them."

I thank them both and follow the platoon down a long hallway to a vast arched chamber with gates on either side. The inner gate is open, letting troops pass in from the main road in Vanfell. The other is slowly rising, its great gears grinding as they turn, its huge iron chains clanking.

I squeeze my way into the ranks of waiting men, each thinking his own thoughts, coping with fear in his own way. When the gate rises high enough for a mounted knight to ride through, I accompany a platoon of soldiers into the valley.

As I make my way through the torn roadway, I fade toward the back of the line. There is a storm to the north, hovering over the mountains. Lightning strikes the snow-capped peaks, and I hear a distant avalanche. The thunder carries over the city. As we come over a rise and the thunder crashes, I disappear into a ditch and strike out alone across the dead grass.

It is a dark day, the sky choked with dust that blocks out the sun. The dust does not fall, but hovers in the air, the largest pieces tumbling like silvery flecks of ash on the faces of the dead.

The dead . . . they number thousands near the walls, mostly warriors of Obul—the remains of men and monsters. They must have sent a force to attack the main gate from the outside even as the shamans used the pulsar fields to infiltrate the city. Whatever their plan was, it did not work.

I rush through the corpses and the dust, trying not to step on anything that used to be alive. I hold my breath as the air grows nearly opaque, stumbling through the thickness of the reek and rot, through the salty blood scent and the caked ash. The residual sparks of powerful spells linger in the valley, this dry land that used to be beautiful. Most of the dead are so blasted and mangled it is hard to believe they were ever alive.

"Oberon!" I call. "Oberon, where are you?"

I cough, running into a thick cloud of black smoke. I feel the heat on my skin before I see it—three stories tall, a siege engine on fire. I scurry away as the thing crumbles and collapses, shooting up plumes of smoke. It falls, nearly crushing me, but I dive into a trench and crawl free, following deep furrows in the earth. What happened here?

"Oberon!" I call again, venturing farther from the wall into the desert valley until the smoke clears and only the dust remains. I hold my collar to my mouth, breathing through it as I stumble across the scorched earth, the sand burnt to solid glass. I step across it carefully, avoiding jagged edges as I weave through a section of ground that looks like a shattered mirror.

Something massive happened here. I feel a familiar power laced with something strange, an anger and a sadness.

Then, scrambling over a buckled patch of ground, I slide down into a glassy pit. The bottom is layered with ash and dust, and the rest swirls in the air, blocking out the sun. I spot faces, armor, and broken limbs sticking out of the ash and try not to imagine what happened here. There is a presence that is undeniably familiar. My heart beats faster as I scramble across the bottom of the pit.

I find him weeping in the midst of the destruction. He is kneeling amid the corpses of his brothers as well as his enemies, clutching a handful of dirt and staring at it. Here, so far from the wall, I hear the sound of clashing steel in the distance.

"Oberon!" I cry, rushing toward him.

He looks up, and I see his face touched with light at the sight of me. Still his tears fall. I reach him before he even has time to stand, and I embrace him. He is worn out, spent. His body is shaking, practically vibrating with expended power. I kneel beside him and hold him to my heart.

"Ava," he whispers, grasping my hand. "I missed you. I forgot what it was like to touch you."

I rock back on my heels and hold him tightly, scarcely believing this moment is real. I try to say something, but the dust is in my lungs and it comes out sounding like a sob.

He lays his head on my lap, his curly hair falling over my thigh, his tears warm on my skin. I cradle his head, rest my other hand on his chest, and close my eyes. I feel his warmth, his heartbeat, his breathing, and thank Archeälis for bringing us both alive to this moment.

Then, opening my eyes, I am astonished to see his tattoos moving, changing, coming alive. They shimmer and shift, showing images I've never seen before, maybe of the future. I look away.

"I thought you were dead," Oberon whispers. "He showed me a vision. He showed me a lie."

"Who? Who showed you?"

"The one who would unmake the world."

"We're together now," I say, knowing the Enemy that Oberon speaks of. "We can stop him."

Holding my hand gently, he eases himself into a sitting position, leaning back on one arm and looking at me. "How did you know to say that?"

"Say what?"

"He fears us. In my dream, he kept me from waking until after the enemy had entered the city. He kept me from finding you."

"None of that matters now," I say, trying to calm him. "I'm right here. I found you."

"I woke in darkness," Oberon says. "I felt that the enemy had won, that you were dead." He closes his eyes and breathes in through his teeth. "It was all a lie, tricks of dark magic to cloud my thoughts. With you dead, I no longer cared for the city. I went out into the fields. . . ." He trails off, shaking his head as if to clear it. "The Light Eater was right to call me brother. Look at what I've done."

"You can't say that!" I stroke his neck and shoulder. "He's trying to make you forget who you are. But you can't let him."

Oberon squeezes his head in his hands, eyes shut tight with pain. "I can't get him out," he whimpers.

"He's not in there," I say with confidence. "It's just whispers and lies."

"I saw a dead bird in my dream," he says. "I saw a dead world. After that I went out and killed Obulans until there was nothing left but death—and an absence, the silent farewells of souls with no bodies. It breaks my heart to hear them scream."

"They're calling you a hero for leading the charge," I say. "They're mounting a final attack."

"It's begun," he says, pausing and letting the sound of battle cries and clashing steel accentuate his words. "But I have no place in it." He sits cross-legged and leans back, fading away from me. I move closer. I will not let his despair take him.

"You look older," I say, pleased by his appearance, if only he'd smile.

"You too." He looks up shyly.

"Look at us. Like two teenagers."

He says nothing, just stares into the sky.

"But so much more," I say. "Why?"

"I naturally age rapidly," he says. "Even faster than you."

"Is it a choice?" I ask.

He looks down, feeling the concealment in his earlier words. "It seemed right. For the war. For you."

I blush, coaxing his old self out slowly. "I'm alive, Oberon," I say. "Let the pain go."

He closes his eyes and takes slow, deep breaths. Whatever he dreamed, it was enough to cripple his memories, make him forget who he is and why he came to Alta in the first place—a vision designed to unmake him, to hurt him where he is most vulnerable.

"Do you remember the day we met?" I ask. "You told me about the Great Spirit and how he sent you to Alta to complete a focus. You were so mysterious to me, so sure of yourself."

"You captivated me from the beginning," he says. "In all my wandering, I had never met anyone like you."

"You've saved my life so many times, and you've always been a protector," I say. "I needed you, and I need you now. The city needs you."

"I missed you, Ava," he says. "I searched for you so many times. But I lost my soul senses when I dreamed and I could not find you."

"I missed you too," I say, guilty that I almost lost faith in him. "I was trapped by Sol in the high city." My voice falters. "I tried to protect my new friends, but I don't know what happened to them. I hope they're safe."

"We will find them when this is over," Oberon says, regaining a hint of his former enthusiasm. "But it is not finished, not yet." He stands slowly, shakily, then collapses.

"You need more time to rest," I say, coming to his side, inspired by his effort. Once the mental walls fall and his hope is restored, I know he will heal quickly.

He nods, wincing in pain. "When I couldn't find you, I decided to fight to protect you. I even infiltrated the Obulan camp and fought the Inferno, Ra-Anis, and nearly destroyed him. That's when I first encountered the Light Eater, the Black Void, Voth-Baalok."

"Voth-Baalok," I whisper. "It was the name they spoke to manipulate the pulsar fields. They prayed to the darkness and it answered."

"You do not fear his name?" Oberon says. "That is

good."

"Oberon, do you remember the light eater we encountered in the other world, when I first used the pulsar shard? You called it the lord of stars. Is this one the same?"

"Yes and no. He too is a devouring thing. But much stronger."

I think back to something Hector said. "You don't think . . ." I hesitate. "You don't think that maybe he and I are connected somehow? Could his coming here be because of me?"

"It's possible." Oberon frowns, shaking his head. "Perhaps he envies you. Perhaps he wants to break free of the bonds of attraction and gravity and enter the space-time manifold as you did. If he does that . . ." Oberon trails off, his eyes dark and terribly afraid.

I tilt my head back, still holding his hand. "When I'd look up at the stars, I used to see only the lights. But maybe that's not how the world is at all. Maybe there's darkness too, stars and voids, locked in patterns of chaos and harmony. Who am I to break free of that endless strife? The endless turnings of my kin?" I take a deep, steadying breath. "I wish I knew my place in all this."

Oberon looks at me, a spark returning to his eyes. "I wondered the same thing not long ago." His hand slips free of mine, his fingers clenching slowly into a fist. "It is the destiny of the Light Eater to end in nothingness, and he means to take all that is created with him. We can't let that happen."

"We won't." My words fill the space between us like a promise.

Time passes, each of us thinking our own thoughts as the

dust drifts overhead.

"So," he says, smiling slightly. "Where have you been?"

It is my turn to tell him about how I met Cora and Raul and befriended them, about how the enemy invaded the city, and how by luck and powers beyond my understanding I was able to travel to the pulsar fields and cut them off.

"You did well," he says. "You kept your sanity. You kept your compassion." He looks down at his hands, his voice cracking slightly. "I'm sorry, Ava. I'm so broken."

"Yours was the greater burden," I say. "You fought in solitude. I at least had people around me to help me. If I had been alone, I would have never made it."

"I've learned some things," he says. "The Obulans . . . even as I kill them, I regret it. Not all who live there are evil, though they are deceived by an evil master."

"How could the Light Eater win the loyalty of Obul?" I ask. "Twisted magic? Brainwashing?"

"There are other ways," he says. "Tell them they are superior, a race set apart. Weave lies to fuel their pride. Invent tales of northern treachery. Blame any torment on Vanfell and keep them united in shared suffering."

"But there's magic at work, too, isn't there?"

He nods. "The Light Eater dominates and suppresses all he touches."

"And his powers extend to Alta even though he is outside it?" I ask.

"His arm is long." Oberon gives a helpless shrug. "I do not know how many worlds he has touched."

The sounds of battle draw closer and Oberon stands as solidly as he can. I see the glint of power return to his eyes, though it is clouded by his perceived failure. I wish my presence alone could heal him, but I do not know what he has seen, and some wounds go to the marrow.

"Are you ready?" I ask, rising to stand beside him.

He nods solemnly and gazes out across the waves of glass with clear eyes. "Fight with me," he says. "Help me save the people of this city."

"Of course," I reply. "Though I fear my contribution will be small, insignificant. Like a moment in time."

Flashing his secret smile, he gestures toward the universe. "But what is Time but a manifold of moments?"

We climb to the edge of the crater and stand together in the stillness, preparing our hearts for battle, listening to the death sounds. Despite everything, I can't help but smile. A moment ago he was ready to give up and flee, thinking he was a monster. Now he has remembered who he is, what purpose is in him, and the Light Eater's lies have no sway.

"He brought you back to me," Oberon whispers with love.

"The Great Spirit?"

"Yes." He looks up as if describing something in the dust-choked sky, fixing his eyes on a single patch of blue. "You see, he is not merely a god who built toys, played with them for a time, and abandoned them to rust or rot. This is the artist who made the worlds. The uncreated creator. He named all of us, humans, stars, angels. He loves therefore I am."

I listen to Oberon, absorbing his words. "When I first learned about the multiverse," I say. "I felt so small I thought I'd disappear. The way you speak of him makes me feel that way again."

"We are all derived from him," says Oberon. "And yet he

values you, even in your frailty, more than the worlds he has made, more than dusk or dawn, or the voices of oceans, or dancing."

"All that?" I stare at him, awed by his reversal.

"All that," he says, looking as if he's just fit the last piece into an intricate puzzle. He seems so strong and composed, no one seeing him now would ever guess he'd been weeping. His tattoos continue to alter, forming impossible images, meanings in languages I cannot fathom. He is invigorated, as if energy flows into him from beyond.

"I love your words," I whisper as the dust grows thick around us. The sounds of battle are hardly a thousand yards away. The enemy must be winning.

He smiles at me, reaching into his pocket. "Here, I have something for you."

I gasp, feeling the thrill of the cosmos at my fingertips. "You kept it safe all this time?"

He hands me the pulsar shard and I cradle it to my chest, leaning on his shoulder for support, feeling untouchable. I see it all now—the worlds and the power to reach them, a power kindled from my longing.

This is the key to the multiverse. Infinite worlds at the brush of my fingertips. And yet . . . I don't want to be anywhere but here, my world, not the one I was born in, but the one I love. I will protect it from the Light Eater—until the end.

And that's when it hits me. What are the pulsar fields? What constitutes the power to travel between worlds? The power manifests out of wanting. Just as love, the strongest force in the universe, is a power of making, of creation and life—so too, the power of longing manifests in the pulsar fields. To want something so badly it becomes real. A want that you can touch. A yearning that moves you.

I turn to Oberon. "What do you do to stop a puppet with a sword?"

He looks at me curiously.

I give him a wide smile. "Break the strings. Think about it. If we can't kill the Light Eater and he's using men as fodder, all we have to do is sever the connection between the two, the strings."

"I see your point," Oberon says, nodding along. "If we can break the spell that overshadows them and expose the lies of their evil master, we can show them the truth of who they are, the goodness they were born with."

"Your powers can do more than kill, can't they? Could you oppose the will of the Light Eater?"

"I could try," he says. "If I focus on a single individual, maybe. But there's no guarantee it will work on a large scale."

"Not with an attitude like that it won't! Come on. We—" I stop mid-sentence. "Do you hear that?" I ask, trying to peer through the obscurity. "Drums. And not the good kind. We're losing."

"Not for long," Oberon says, his voice like hot iron. "Are you ready?"

"As ever I could be."

He takes a deep breath and blows out across the plain, his breath like a summer storm, driving away the dust. I turn just in time to see Obulan outriders, hundreds of them, sweeping through a nearby ravine. Some of them notice us and break off in a swarm.

My heart darts and leaps like a lioness running down her prey. "If this doesn't work," I say as a fierce light blossoms from my hand, "a lot of people are going to die."

"People will die even if it does work," says Oberon, and there is no laughter in his voice. "Archeälis preserve us!" he cries. "Shield and shelter us! Guide us by swift ways to peace!"

Chapter XXXI
Lux:
To Save a Life

FOOLS OFTEN SPEAK of the end of the world as if it is something momentous and horrible, something to be dreaded. What do the myth-makers know? A man's last days are his own. When I go, so goes the world. What does the rest matter?

I am a coward, afraid of my own power, a waste of flesh and breath. I hide alone in a cave while a storm rages outside, the winter's last-ditch effort, a blizzard driven north to the mountains where it dies slowly in bitterness and fury. I know I am running out of time. I cannot save Ava while I cower here. But if I transform, there's no going back, and I will have already sacrificed her in my heart.

So I sit and freeze and lament my suffering.

All paths lead to death and burning. All paths lead to unworthy ends. I stalk back and forth in the cave, delirious from lack of food and sleep. When I finally collapse, numb and listless, all I can think about is my failure.

I tried, Ava. A sad epitaph for a life as long as mine. *I tried.*

In a dream, I rise and tear down the icy walls of my prison, walking like a blind man through the whiteout. In a sudden lull, I see a figure ahead of me, a young girl in a summer dress.

"You've come a long way," she says in the land of frost and wind. Her voice is strange, distant, even though it is in my head.

I stare at her, ice in her black hair, her dress whipped by the wind. "Are you real?" I ask.

"I am Ava," she says.

"My Ava!" I rush to embrace her, but a wind drives me back. She looks so frail on the icy plateau. It seems the slightest gust could send her plummeting into the abyss. And yet there is a power in her such that no force in the universe could move her.

"Did you love me?" she asks.

My jaw works soundlessly, sleet stinging my skin.

"Did you really love me?"

"Of course I loved you."

"Then why couldn't you love me enough to tell me the truth?"

"I've come for you!" I say in a moment of clarity. "Even now I battle the mountain pass. I dream of you, Ava!"

"You dream only of an end to your suffering."

I glower for a moment at the self-assured creature before me, knowing she is only a thought in my mind, and yet her words sting. "What did you expect of me, daughter? After all I've seen, all the wrong I've done. Did you expect me to be the perfect father?"

"I expected you to try," she says coldly, vanishing for a moment in the snow. "I expected you to teach me tenderness and not hate. I expected you to give me a life."

"I gave you all I had."

"Then let us examine the gift, shall we?" says the girl, reappearing closer than before. "What are you but an unworthy thief? An abomination with no home. All the women you've wronged, the men you've killed—you carry them with you like a slave collar. You are lust and hunger, a devouring flame that gives no warmth. Your only gift is your selfishness."

"I carried you from ash and fire," I plead. "I gave you a home."

"You took my life from me. I would have been happier in any desert household, with any family, but you couldn't allow that could you? You needed me as your own and you expect me to thank you?"

I look away, ashamed and angry. I've torn my life apart with seeking her and now she scorns me. "It's a bad world, Ava," I growl, and as I speak the storm falls away and we are standing on a clear plateau overlooking the valley. "No one knows how we got here or why. None of it makes sense, living, suffering, dying—a life. And you, you were the only thing that made it worth it."

"Father, you can't say that!" she says, losing the ice in her voice.

I do not like this phantom. "Why not?" I ask, deranged, despising my own words. "This world has a way of making us hate the things we love. Death is the great comfort at the end of a life-sentence. The one thing I love, you, makes me afraid to die."

"I think you're afraid of living! But you don't have to be. There's good and beauty here, Father. Can't you see it?" As she speaks, I look down at the fires of life burning in the featureless void. "Where there is evil, forgive it," she says. "Where there is good, praise it. And stop hating yourself."

"Humans are stupid, selfish, and brief," I say as the fires go out one by one. "They thrive on lies which lead to self-destruction. There is evil in this world, Ava. It is moving and alive. It is in every cruel glance and act of malice. In every forgotten child, beaten woman, and broken promise. Part of the evil is in me, and it's in you too. Maybe it was selfish taking you from the wreckage, but I grew to love you, and you taught me something. Do you remember?"

Ava begins to weep and fades away. It seems so real. When speaking to the Ava who was cold as ice, I could be cruel. But now something breaks inside me.

"Wait!" I cry, realizing that often our dreams torture us more than real people do. "You taught me to be a father. I lived, for the first time in my life, for someone else. Maybe I failed, after all. But the moments that were good, however few they were, you gave me."

Ava returns, her face a cold mask. The stars have all gone out. We are standing in a village that exists only in my memory. The desert storms destroyed it decades ago. Ava would have loved this place and its people. With a population of sixty, it would have been the biggest town she'd ever seen.

She walks past me without a word, staring through vacant windows, dragging her hand roughly across a cactus and licking away the blood. I follow her through the deserted skeleton of a town, speechless.

My heart flips again, and I stop. She stops too. "Why do you hate me?" I ask.

"You stole me from my world," she says, her back to me. "I have no mother. I have no father."

"You think you're the only one without a mother and father?" I cry in disbelief. "Half the children in this village grew up fatherless. And now they're all dead. You think you're the only one who's broken? Who wishes things were different?"

"I wish," she pauses, turning around, her eyes on the dirt.

"I wish I'd fallen in someone else's back yard." She locks eyes with me.

It would be easier to put out the sun, I think, losing myself in her gaze, in the purpose, the pure identity.

"I am tired of feeling like a balm," she says. "You can't bandage a broken bone. It doesn't do any good. You need mending and my love can only go so far. You say you loved me, but why couldn't you love me enough to let me go?"

Her words strike me like a blow and I fall back, passing through the ground as if it is mist. The village crumbles and I am falling through the sky. The stars bounce off my skin, spinning and exploding like fireworks through the universe. Is this the madness? Is this what drove my ancestors over the edge of the world—the fear of turning against everything they ever loved?

Forgive me, Ava. You are the teardrop fallen from the cheek of an angel. I am the dust, greedy and thirsty enough to try and keep you.

Did I lead an unworthy life? What do you really think of me? Am I empty? The world rushes closer, and I see all the innumerable islands of Alta floating like rose petals in an overfilled bowl.

Maybe it was an accident, the universe, some cosmic joke. Maybe it's a dream in my mind. Maybe we're all damned. Maybe that's why humans seethe across Alta like rats on a sinking ship, and take what they can, while they can, and give nothing back.

In the moment of my death, I feel something, my soul's last breath, the lifetime that passes in the gasp before the end. I see memories, simple and pure, of Ava.

Afternoon hikes through the forest, her arms around my

neck as she kicks lightly at my back. The scent of earth and clean sweat as we share a bowl of wine after a long harvest. The tap of her footsteps on the threshold as she stretches and catches her breath after a morning run—the sound of her palm against the door when she reaches out to steady herself. I realize that in her three years of life she has redeemed all five hundred of mine.

Not yet, you old bastard. I smile at death as if at an old friend. He doesn't smile back.

I wake gasping on the floor of my cave. It is deadly cold and each breath is needles in my lungs, my limbs slow and sluggish, as if I am cold blooded as well. I try to rise but fail, clumsy hands slipping on the ice. I keep seeing her frostbitten face, pale and evil, over and over again. And the cruel things we said to each other . . . the real Ava would not speak thus. I would never say those things to her.

There is only one choice. I cannot die here in the mountains even as she dies in the valley or the city or anywhere. I know this will mean the end. I know the stories. Dragonbloods who give in to the madness will kill until they are slain. Only then do they return to human form, only in death. I will use this unquenchable fire inside me, this curse I bear, to save them all. I will avert catastrophe by becoming it.

"Ava!" I cry. "Forgive me."

Awake, alive, unafraid, I feel my blood boil and froth inside me. Ice melts, water pours from my skin. I howl until my voice shakes the mountain, dislodging chunks of ice from the roof of the cave. They fall and shatter around me, smashed to bits against the span of my shoulders and back. And still I roar, bones twisting and popping, scales breaking free of flesh. In the darkness, I transform.

CHAPTER XXXII
Wind and Shadow

THERE SEEMS NO END to them. They attack with a madness, slaves to the will of one who walked before the first light shined. Oberon's magic reached some, about two hundred men and women, and they retreated as the shadows fell from their eyes. But there is more than a trickster's magic in the blood of these warriors. There is a lifetime of torture, lies, and spiritual conditioning, a hatred that goes back centuries.

The Obulans keep coming, black-clad shamans leading them, weaving enchantments to control their monsters, war-spiders bred to kill. The spiders do not move like something that is alive, but neither are they dead. Rather than face the wrath of Oberon's magic, the undead beasts turn north to hunt down a contingent from Vanfell, scurrying and killing with frightening agility.

"Come on!" Oberon takes off running. "We have to help them!"

I sprint after him, my feet kicking up puffs of sand. "Take my hand!"

He does so. The pulsar shard flashes, sand and sky blurring past. We appear in the heart of the fight, too late. Most of the soldiers are already slain, their corpses trampled or mutilated by huge fangs. Ranks of rotting beasts surround us, pressing in. A shaman leers at us from the back of the largest one. I focus on him, and his body disintegrates.

Arrows whiz toward me, but I use the shard to render

them harmless. Each time a deadly shaft flies close to me or Oberon, it seems to vanish, the parts that compose it blasted far into the universe. Oberon's tattoos blaze, rings of flame flaring out from his body, consuming the beasts. But for the men he has a different spell, one that burns from his eyes and booms from his voice like a commandment, a string of names meant to break the will of the Light Eater.

Where before it worked to a degree, now it seems to have little effect. The warriors flanking the spiders are painted in shades of red and gold and heavily armored. Seasoned veterans of war, they are deaf to Oberon's magic. Father told me once that some afflictions, like fanaticism and hatred, can only be cured by violence. I never believed him and still don't, but today we have no choice. They rush in, savage and unafraid.

As always, Oberon does most of the work. But every now and then a warrior breaks through his rings of fire. "On your right!" he cries, holding off an onslaught of spears.

I whirl to find a pair of Obulans charging me. I raise the pulsar shard and their bodies vanish in a burst of silver dust. Oberon turns a slow circle, a blinding light radiating from his hands. The great lion-tattoo on his back leaps out in a roar of flame, devouring the rest. When his work is done, the lion-god Zintahu settles back into Oberon's skin, a look of feline satisfaction on his wide, smoldering mouth.

"Where are you sending them?" Oberon asks when it is over, watching the dust of my enemies drift in the wind.

"Home," I say. "I just pictured a lava cave and sent them there."

"Clever." He nods, his curls bobbing. He sniffs the air, angling his gaze to the north, distracted. "We can't stay here.

We need to rejoin the army."

Now that our skirmish is over, I can hear the resonant echoes of distant horns. I nod in the direction of a tall hill about a mile off. "I'll take us there."

He clasps my hand and we vanish in a flash, reappearing just below the hilltop near a bend in the river. One of Hector's scouts, recognizing us, lets out a howl of joy and triumph. I give him a high-five, causing his grin to grow even more. All around us battle horns are sounding. We scramble up a slope of loose stones to the peak of the hill where the encroaching hordes are clearly visible, filling the plain below.

"I thought you drove them off," I say.

Oberon shakes his head. "For a time. But something made them turn back and fight." He focuses his will, trying to undo the spells of the Light Eater. I can see it working in part. A solid portion of the advancing horde seems to hesitate, some of them halting entirely.

"What is it?" I ask, heart pounding.

His face is a mask of concentration and he says nothing. More warriors abandon the assault. Hundreds, maybe thousands. But the vast majority keep on. After several long minutes Oberon's shoulders slump. "He's too strong. I'm wasting my strength."

"You did your best," I murmur, distracted as our cavalry charge across the plain and are met by a surge of undead beasts. It all happens so slowly, a distant violence, yet somehow I feel each death as keenly as a knife to the heart. Well, not a knife, perhaps. But a needle-like stab, like an eyelash being torn out.

Oberon reaches out a hand to steady me. "You all right?"

I nod, wincing as if each death diminishes me. "Secret

threads," I whisper, feeling each one, so gently woven, connecting all of us.

At the base of the hill, I spot Prince Hector riding with the proud knights of Vanfell. A little higher up are several hundred fighting men and even a few dozen battle mages. The mages stand in a line behind a wall of shieldmen, casting deadly spells into the enemy. Ice shards crash and shatter, slicing through flesh and armor like arrows. Fireballs arc down like hurled stones, some exploding, others splashing into thin sheets and burning like oil fires, blurring red and orange through the thick smoke and dust.

The Obulans, faltering only a little, separate into units of twenty or thirty men each and become much harder to hit. The initial clash is quieter than I expected, and most of the sounds blur together, making it impossible to distinguish grating metal from human screams.

"Let's get down there," says Oberon.

I nod numbly and transport us to the front lines. The immediate chaos nearly overwhelms me, but not quite. Not with the shard in my balled fist. Not with the light of a million stars inside me. I fight, subduing more than I kill, hoping foolishly that they will give up and go home alive. Whenever an enemy gets too close, I use the power of the shard to banish him.

It is only when the twisted beasts attack that Oberon and I are driven to use all of our powers. My energy, channeled through the pulsar shard, turns all manner of undead beasts to dust. Oberon, wielding magic even older than mine, unmakes things and returns them to the goodness that first was.

We were not born for fighting, Oberon and I, and we

quickly tire, perhaps more from the emotional toll of the killings than from the energy we expend. To see souls falling into the sky, to see bodies with no life crumpled, torn and smeared in blood—it makes me want to open a gate, slip into a peaceful world, and pretend this was all just a nightmare.

"I can't do this anymore," I say to Oberon, my power flickering.

"A little longer," he pants, his back to mine. "If we fail, Vanfell will burn along with all the good things in it."

"I can barely stand," I say. "Maybe it's the shard draining my life." I raise my hand at an approaching war rhino and wince as its body crumbles, its rider falling in a heap of empty armor. My mind travels back to the first night I used its power to kill, the night on the rooftop where so much went wrong. I stumble, my muscles fatigued, and Oberon catches me.

"You feel weak because you're giving up!" he says. "You can't do that, not at any cost. These people need you, Ava!"

I nod, standing a little straighter, drawing strength from the shard. It is not the sort of thing that has limits—but I am. Oberon casts spells of protection over our archers and wizards as we retreat to a bend in the river where there is a natural rise. Standing on that bluff amid the bent yellow grass, he turns, holding his ground like an ancient cliff as waves of monsters dash themselves to pieces against him. I go to his side.

"He's near," Oberon says during a lull. "The Inferno. I thought I wounded him beyond recovery, but I was wrong. He's . . . changed somehow."

"You're rarely wrong, Oberon," I say, new light burning in my palms.

"The thing that is coming is not the Inferno I fought," he says in a tone that gives me shivers. "He has been remade."

Soon the Obulans swarm the bluff, and we retreat to the lowest part of the valley where the river runs. Trees only grow near the river, and even these are sparse and beaten down by winter. The bushes and drooping reeds provide no cover from our pursuers. Knives hurtle through the air, spears and arrows as well. Oberon swats them aside, seeming to anticipate each missile.

Hector's reserve arrives from the west, bolstered by a detachment from the mountain guard. Rallied together by Hector and his knights, we form ranks and meet the Obulans head on.

I do not know the workings of war. All I can say is what I feel—the madness and chaos of it, the adrenaline forcing me into a state of hyper-alertness. Lost in that state, I see more than a writhing throng, an army of nameless faces and brutal weaponry. I see people, humans who love and breathe and desire to live peaceful lives. Humans who are willing to die to protect what they love.

A clan of warriors tries to ambush me and I raise my arms as if to ward off a blow. When I lower them, the whole field for a hundred yards is scorched clean of life. It's almost too much to bear. There was something sickening and personal about the way Viktor's weapons killed with acid, but at this magnitude the feeling is so much worse.

When did I become the weapon Sol could only dream of? Is this the reason I was sent to Alta three years ago, to protect one people by destroying another?

More come and I send their spirits into the sky. Oberon has taken a sword and is deep in the fray, fighting as if he has trained all his life. Where his sword arc passes, a dozen fall, as if the blade extends ten times its actual length. His tattoos burn like rivers of fire in his skin, leaping out in the shapes of animals and tearing with smoldering claws at anyone who gets too close.

Hector rides with what is left of his cavalry, wearing the silver-blue falcon standard of Vanfell, holding his men together with the sound of his voice and the glint of his sword. He has no cosmic powers, no divine might, but there is another strength in him, the strength to lead, and his men will follow him to the end.

And, in spite of all our efforts, the end comes.

I feel for a moment, as I spin in a sphere of starlight, like a tree caught in a rising tide. As the ground erodes around me and the army of Vanfell crumbles, I feel my roots torn out, my body lifted free. We are losing.

There is no time anymore, only the smell of blood on my lips, only the stacked corpses and the enemy clambering over them to kill me. Even Oberon seems exhausted, falling back to the faltering line. Grim men with shattered shields. Pale wizards muttering to themselves. Wounded horses limping riderless through clouds of dust. I've lost sight of Hector.

"There are too many," Oberon says, hurrying to my side. He is bleeding from a dozen wounds and does not seem to have the strength to heal them.

"You told me not to give up," I say, breathless.

"We are alone," he says, glancing over his shoulder. "And the Inferno is near. We need to give ground."

I see it's true. Most of the army is already in retreat. We follow them, broken and abandoned, the scattered remnants of a once proud legion. Oberon and I take up the rear, trying to protect the stragglers from the now enlivened enemy. The dust is even thicker now, and I trust my feet more than my eyes.

"Oberon!" I call into the obscurity. "I can't—"

Something slices into my ribs, just below the lung.

I gasp sharply—big mistake. Pain blossoms from the wound, made worse by every breath or twist of my torso. I stagger, trip over a corpse, sprawl painfully in the dirt. My fingers fumble for an arrow shaft and find only the short metal hilt of a throwing knife. I can't move with this thing in me. Stifling a scream, I yank it out and immediately feel my blood flowing freely from the wound.

Have to get away. I crawl a few painful yards, the pulsar shard burning white-hot in my palm. I struggle to my feet only to lurch and fall again, this time on my side. I clutch at the wound awkwardly. It's impossible to put pressure on it through the mesh-armor Hector gave me. I take it off, wadding up my underclothes, trying to staunch the flow. My head feels light, my arms leaden. I go limp, my forehead scraping the ground, my vision flickering.

In my semi-consciousness, I see this whole writhing mess of people and creatures as one huge misunderstanding. What could have stopped this slaughter? What spoken kindness or word of love? Could any one person have given enough to change the outcome?

Strong arms gather my crumpled body, lifting me, holding me close. My savior stands tall, taking measured steps to avoid the piles of dead. I feel his heartbeat as I cling weakly to him. He smells like sweat, blood, and oiled metal. I feel the fallen souls around us, men and women, friend and enemy alike, and I know they were not born for death.

Death entered the world as an intruder and is carried like a plague through generations, feeding off the slow dimming of hope, a yearning turned to loneliness. We come into the world alone, and no matter how many mourners we have near us, touching us when we die—we leave this world alone too.

I wish there were a cure for loneliness. I wish I had that power. I see it in every creature, in humans the most. I see it in angels and stars. I feel it inside myself.

Sometimes I think the most abundant ingredient in the universe is loneliness. Other times I know it's love. I know it like I know my own name, my own body. I know it like I know I am. Love is how things are made and have being. Love turns the planets in their arcs and makes the rain fall and the flowers blossom. Love keeps people alive, and it is only when they lose sight of it that they feel alone, and give in to death.

I wish my story were more about love and not the wanting of it. More about the sky after a storm, or rainbows, or forgiveness. Less about fear, uncertainty and wrong turns. I wish I was less hesitant and more decisive. I wish I smiled more.

I feel my savior trip and stumble. He falls and I know I'll crumple underneath him. But he takes the fall on his shoulder, cradling me in his arms. I look up vaguely to see the bloodied face of the prince, his eyes on mine.

"So lovely you are," he whispers. "It isn't right that you should die here."

"Your horse," I stammer, knowing it must be slain. "I'm so sorry."

My breath catches in my throat when I see his wounds.

How could I let him carry me like that? The enemy approaches, but shies away like wolves from a bonfire. Then Oberon is there, standing over us, his tattoos incandescent, his hands overflowing with power, a flaming lion by his side.

As Zintahu prowls a protective circle around us, Oberon reaches down with both hands and lifts us gently from the dirt. Something in his touch gives me the strength to stand. Hector, seeing me blinking like a lost bird, offers me his arm, then nearly collapses, his hamstring partially severed, blood soaking into his boots. I lend him my shoulder and we stagger beside Oberon, retreating with a roaring lion at our back.

For a while, nothing can touch us. The monsters shy away from Zintahu and warriors scream and clutch their eyes at the sight of his mane. It seems for a moment that they are thinning, that Oberon will never falter until the war is won. But it is not to be.

Suddenly, the ranks of Obul part, letting through a shadowy figure, armor with nothing inside. "Go," Oberon says, turning to face the Inferno.

"I won't leave you!" I cry.

He seems about to say something, but a clot of darkness fills the sky, strikes him down, smothering his light. Zintahu roars in defiance, his mane turning to smoke as his essence flows back into the tattoo.

Twice the height of a man, the Inferno looms over us, his followers behind him, expressionless, waiting for his command. He approaches warily, as if he expects Oberon's limp body to rise up and stab him.

I face down the monstrosity, standing between it and Oberon. The pulsar shard burns in my hand, but I'm barely conscious. When I try to unleash its power, the starlight flickers and dies, and I collapse next to Oberon, still bleeding steadily from my knife wound. Holding Oberon's hand and reaching to catch Hector's, I try to take us to another world, but nothing happens.

"All this time I hunted you," the Inferno speaks in a language older than sound, yet somehow I understand it. "And now you give yourself to me."

Hector, ignoring his many wounds, stands in front of me, the only one with the courage to raise his sword. The Inferno laughs, a sound like stone eroding over eons, and extends a hand. Hector staggers to his knees, his back unnaturally arched, tendrils of shadow protruding from his mouth and eyes, wiggling and clutching like fingers. He falls.

No. No, no, no. Around us, the world has become ashen and faded, devoid of sound, as if we are gradually slipping from the land of the living into the Inferno's domain.

"Wait!" I cry, fumbling to my knees and covering the prince's body with my own. I proffer the shard, my upturned palm trembling. "It's this you want. Take it."

"A pretty jewel," says the Inferno, stepping near enough to touch. "But common beyond the veil. I did not overcome a second death to collect rocks, daughter of stars. I am here for you."

To hear it spoken so plainly in this language of gods and devils, it is almost enough to stop my heart—that this loveless creature of ash and undeath, this being of torment and wasted purpose, has come for me.

What if this sudden war is only a pretense, a footnote in a bigger story, and these two armies are really here, all these people dead, because I fell from the sky?

"I serve another," I say, struggling with each syllable, feeling my heart slowly pump blood from my body.

The Inferno seems to hesitate, then raises a hand, not to destroy or enslave me, or to crush Oberon in an armored fist —but to protect himself. From what? I try to look and see, but a burning wind takes hold of me, forcing my head down as the dust rises and rolls.

The Inferno inclines his head to face this new enemy, this demon of wind and shadow, and even he seems to quail a bit. Then I hear it, not so much with my ears as with my bones, a sound to which earthquakes, thunder, and the lion's roar are only cheap imitations. . . .

CHAPTER XXXIII
Lux:
Fatherhood

SCALES LIKE HOT COALS, my breath scalding steam. It feels good to stretch my wings, after so long. My great neck swings from side to side as the vale unfolds below. Why am I here?

Gray shapes by the river, men screaming and dying in the mud, men fleeing or fighting or carrying wounded. Killers hard on their heels. The scent of fear is strong, intoxicating, and for a moment I nearly dive in, eager to splash like a child in all that warm blood.

Bad idea. I pull back, shaking away the notion like a dog shakes off water. *Can't go that way. Can't give in to the rage.* I catch a new scent, not quite human. *Could it be her?*

From this height, the world seems small and far away, like memory. But while the eye is easily distracted, my other senses steer true. I sniff my way through the blood-reek and rotten dust, closer and closer as things become clearer and clearer.

Then I see her—Ava—my daughter. A low groan blasts from my jaws, a joy as sharp as grief. I will go to her now, become a man again, and all will be as it was. But no . . . she is not alone.

There, at the front of the pursuing horde, I see the Obulan captain, an entity of flame and shadow. Amid a press of living bodies—hopes and fears, flesh and chemicals—one thing is clear: this creature does not belong. The way he bends over her, dominating her body and spirit, it is enough to turn even a good father into a killer.

But I am already a killer.

And something rises inside me like lava from the earth. I dive steeply, a feral roar building inside my chest. The demon spots me from afar, his attention drawn away from Ava. Sensing his peril, he immediately changes shape, his armor falls away, and he becomes hard to see, a shadow-thing. My body collides with his nothingness, talons first, and he twists himself around me like a serpent, hissing and spitting as I bear him into the sky.

I am what I am, an old power of earth, in conflict with a darkness older than I, older than matter, intent on consuming me. Higher and higher we climb. I would hurl him into the sun if I could. But my wings grow weak as the shadow spreads across my scales, sinks into the linings of my skin, his power mingling with mine, turning my rage, my only weapon, to chaos.

My body fluctuates between former beings, changing under the influence of the demon. Now a dragon, wreathed in wings of fire. Now a leviathan, wingless, eyes like smoking pits. Now a man with scales, my flesh undulating with peaks and vales like the endless waves on the shores of annihilation.

Finally, I take hold of him, bathing him in dragon fire. After a few seconds, much of his shadow evaporates, leaving only a dense clot of blackness, somehow unharmed by my breath. Then I feel it, a black tendril, worming its way into my mind. First my thoughts, then my memories.

"A sad life," says the demon. "You have given up everything, only to die."

"Get out!" I roar in the dragon speech as the ground

rushes toward us. "You think to frighten me with threats? I came into this world naked, screaming, and soaked in someone else's blood. And that's how I intend to leave it!"

"I do not bleed," he says smoothly. "Powers older and stronger than you have tried to kill me."

"We shall see," I growl as I drive him into the dirt, the ground rippling, then exploding beneath us, a wave of dust rolling out in all directions.

We wrestle and writhe, rolling in the blood-rot of the battlefield, then down to the riverbank, churning up mud, and crushing the wilting reeds. His foulness surrounds me, blinding me, choking me, turning my rage to chaos. The river hisses and boils where we touch it, steam billowing into the sky.

Losing control, I fluctuate between countless forms, fighting with whatever body I take. Some are common, an eagle, a serpent, a mountain lion. Some are rare or long extinct. Others have no names in any language. Just as I am about to lose myself to the chaos, I am a man again.

The demon towers over me, pleasure radiating from him. "I'm disappointed," he says. "I thought you'd be a hard thing to kill."

Reaching into my chest, he lifts me effortlessly, absorbing some of my nature into his own. Thus strengthened, he transforms, becoming a dragon of smoke and shadow. As his form changes, his talons grow, scraping the flesh from my bones.

"Coward! Fight me as I truly am!" I scream and rave until blood clogs my lungs, then merely gurgle, tongue sagging, drool leaking from my mouth.

"I have killed a thousand of your kind," he sneers. "What

are you against me?"

When I am well and truly skewered, he drags me to the shallows, the current tugging at my open wounds. Planting a taloned foot on my chest, he forces me under. Water pours over me, murky and cold. I see the outline of mountains, the sunless sky, then nothing. The breath goes out of me, I begin to drown.

I struggle in vain, feeling the heat of my blood as it is taken by the river. I see the light of the sky through foam and swift water. I reach for it, but a kick drives me deeper into the muck. *As poor a grave as a man could ask for.* My eyes slowly close, but some part of me refuses to die.

"Daddy, Daddy!" I hear Ava calling through my death dream. Then I see her, a child still, hurrying toward me through a field of flowers, a lizard egg in her hand.

Of all the moments I have lived through, this is the most precious to me. I see it in every detail, the moment when Ava called me daddy for the first time.

She learned to speak a week after landing. She read books ravenously and adapted to human speech as if she was born for it. I remember her tiny, elfin hands, her skin, always light no matter how long she worked in the sun, her voice, as high and sweet as the summer wind.

I remember her and I remember me, and as I do, my dragon form returns, and the demon jerks back as if burned. I see him in that moment. I see how he shrouds himself in power but is empty inside. I see that he cannot be killed as the living can, but his influence can be broken and his power banished.

Slowly, like the gray sunrise over a stormy sea, I rise out of the water, breathe deep of the wet, moldering air. My enemy flinches away, gliding and sliding on his belly. Not fast enough. I snatch him up like a lizard, my claws finding a hold in his undead substance, drawing him in.

The river boils for a moment, then rolls around us as I gaze into him, sparks dripping from my lips. I heave his body onto the bank, and bury him in flame. *Burn.* The muck beneath us dries up, cracks and melts away. *Burn.* He tries to squirm out of my grasp, his tail thrashing like smoke on the water. *Burn.*

By the time my fire fades, all that remains is a sickly stain. His essence is in my jaws now. "What are you?" he says, his voice no longer calm, no longer smooth, a choked hiss full of fear.

"I am a father who wants to see his daughter again," I say, and end it.

CHAPTER XXXIV
A Daughter's Blessing

I OPEN MY EYES and stare up at the dreary sky, gray and starless and cold. When I passed out, the prince was crumpled underneath me, bleeding from a dozen wounds. Now he's gone.

"He's dead," says a gentle voice. "I'm sorry. They wanted to take you too, but I wouldn't let them."

"Who?" Glancing around, I see a cloud of dust rising as knights bear Hector's body toward the city. Oberon is sitting cross-legged by my side, watching the procession fade with sad eyes. I find I have no tears left.

"It is over," he says. "I watched it all transpire, helpless as a child. A darkness has passed from this world, power defeated by power."

The Obulans, weakened and pitiful in number, vanish into a dust storm that is building on the edge of the valley. They move quickly in attack, but even faster in retreat. And it wasn't me who made them do it.

"He came back," I whisper shakily, standing with some effort, a dull ache in my side.

Oberon stands behind me. Most of his more serious injuries have healed, I think, but it's hard to tell because there's so much blood covering him, soaking his curly hair. Instinctively, I shift my jerkin slightly, feeling for my own knife wound, only to find it bandaged. "You?" I ask, a raindrop striking my forehead and dripping down my nose.

"It's done," he says, taking a step back. "You'll be fine."

"Thank you," I say, searching the battlefield for a sign of my father. A raincloud passes over, hardly wetting our skin.

"Look," says Oberon, pointing. I follow his gaze toward the river. "Do you see?" Using the back of his hand, he gently turns my chin until I am facing the right direction. "There, by the bank."

At last I see him, my father. Broad wings and iron skin, raising his proud head out of the river, ink-black water dripping from his scales. He takes to the sky, shrugging off a shadow which vanishes like smoke in the wind.

He is still far away, silhouetted, but I can feel his eyes on me like cuts of jade. I smell him in the wind as he dives, his great wings spread wide, his breath hissing steam. It is said a dragonblood who eats raw meat will go mad. But all I smell are the bodies of clouds and devoured wind.

"He's come for me," I whisper, squeezing Oberon's hand. My fingers tremble, not wanting to let go. Finally, eyes still fixed on my father, I step forward to meet him.

He is a dragon, yes. But he is undoubtedly my father, Lux. I see him now, tired from a long day in the fields, a shovel over one shoulder, black soil sprinkling from the blade. I see his sweat dripping in the dust as he unbuttons a shirt for washing. I see him clipping his beard in the reflection of a garden pail. He farmed so many things, all to distract himself from life. I wish he would have told me.

He's close. I feel the heat of him. His hand on mine, showing me how to sharpen a spade. His pride in watching me pull weeds and never missing the roots. His laughter, which was loud and startling enough to faint the goats. His tears, which I have never seen until this moment—like when old waterskins burst on a hot day, the contents splashing down his scales, glistening on his nebula eyes.

We all weep for each other. Even dragons.

Crashing down in the dirt not far off, he coils and squirms, watching me from the corner of one eye. He seems hesitant to come any closer.

I don't want to appear frightened. I don't want him to think less of me, or that I do not love him for what he is. I rush toward him, noticing as I do his many wounds. Oberon, standing nearby, only watches, knowing this is something I have to do on my own.

By the time I reach my father he is human again, lying near a fallen tree, more dirt and blood than man. I know I should be overjoyed, but I feel this transformation as what it is, something final and irreversible.

"Ava," he whispers as I hurl myself down beside him. "My precious daughter."

"Father!" I cry, and bury myself in his neck.

Pulling away, I raise a hand to heal his wounds. I have that power, or I did. But try as I might, I cannot touch the least of them. I begin to weep. "Why can't I heal you?" I ask desperately, trying to dress the gouges on his chest.

"Don't," he says, ignoring the pain. "You cannot heal me because it is not right for me to be healed. My time is over."

"Don't say that, Father, please!" I pull away and look into his eyes. I've lived this moment so many times in my head, but nothing came close to the reality. I don't know what to say.

"You've grown," he says. "I dreamed . . . that you hated me."

"How could I?" I shake my head in confusion. "I've missed you so much."

"I do not deserve your love," he coughs, choking on blood. "What was I but a selfish oaf?"

"You gave me everything you had. You sang to me!"

"Only ballads of war and heroism. Nothing of longing or love in my few songs. What sort of life is that for a little girl?"

"It was enough for me. Now please let me heal you."

"Ava," he breathes as the last flicker of life begins to leave him. "I do not know who I am or what I am. We're alike in that way. I do not know where I came from, but I know why. I know that I love you, and that without your love I am a coward and a waste. Now I am finished. And as I leave the world, remember my failure, and do not let it be yours. Find the truth of your birth."

"I will, Father. I love you, Father. Don't go."

He smiles, his beard torn and bloodied, his teeth as white as moonbeams against his copper skin. Not knowing why, I begin to sing to him, one of the simple melodies he used to hum to me as a child. He harmonizes on the chorus, grinning a little, until a bout of coughing forces him into silence.

"I finally understand," I say, seeing the answer in his pain. "We all feel like orphans. Even those of us who have parents who love us. Because we're looking for another, the one who gives life, to take us home."

"Find the truth," he says. "Find what I never could and live a worthy life. Oh, Ava, I am not worthy to call you my daughter! Not after everything."

I close my eyes, my hand on his chest, a single tear escaping. "If you think your brokenness has won, then you don't know mercy."

"I am not forgivable for the things I've done," he says,

exhaling slowly, his very last sound.

"Let Archeälis decide," I whisper, my cheek to his, my tears covering him. "And be at peace."

CHAPTER XXXV
The Beginning

MY FATHER'S FUNERAL was the most attended event in the history of Vanfell. Everyone came to pay respects to the one who drove the enemy away, and to see what they could of a passing legend, one of the fabled dragon race, perhaps the last of his kind.

They also came I suspect to see Oberon, the Lion of the Desert, but few were bold enough to approach him. They mostly hid their eyes or nodded their respects from afar. It is difficult for humans to encounter the supernatural. They don't know whether to bow with covered heads or run away in terror.

The funeral was held outside of the city on a hill called Mentiron where it is said the world is wounded. The songs they sung spoke of resurrection and eternity, but all I could think about as I watched the flames rise was Father, how he lay at my feet and died in my arms.

I wept for him, especially for the things he said and the despair he held in his heart at the end. But I hope to see him again, in one world or another. Oberon was with me the whole time, Raul and Cora too.

It was good to see them alive and to say goodbye. Raul's shoulder was bandaged from where a scimitar cut him. It was not a grievous wound, but I healed it anyway, drawing out the infection with a kiss.

At the end of all things, I realize that none of us could have saved the city alone. We did it together, for all who love this world. One might even say we defied our fates. When I told that to Cora she laughed mirthlessly and shook her head. "Who believes in oracles anyway?"

With the war over, Oberon seems his former, joyful self, although he is realistic about the future. "A shadow has passed away," he told me the night my father died. We sat together with bandaged wounds beside a great funeral pyre, listening to the flames shifting in the wind. He looked at me as he spoke. "But the greater shadow, the Light Eater, has only retreated. He is biding his time. We have conquered a single Inferno, but there will be more. Your greatest test is yet to come."

The Obulans retreated to their volcanic lair, free for a time of the evil that drove them to kill so many innocent people. But the Light Eater is not finished with them, I fear, not ever.

Already, I feel his powers at work from beyond the world, powers that oppose life and everything I am. Oberon feels it too, and sometimes I catch him staring at the southern horizon, as if the intangible gates of night lie just beyond the ocean's edge. I can only hope that when the time comes we'll be ready.

Hector died a hero, and I still can't think of him without a small smile, remembering the moment I first saw him, when all the images of princes from fairytales came alive for me. I remember the way he cradled me in his arms and carried me across the battlefield. "So lovely you are," he said. "It isn't right that you should die here." I think the same of him.

Sol died within an hour of his son. The funeral was humbling for me. With the war over, everyone was finally able to mourn their fallen kings, and I attended to support Cora. It was strange honoring the death of Sol, the man who caused me so much pain and hardship. But I have forgiven him.

I realize he was just a broken man, tortured by the loss of his wife. He was not a malevolent king, just a wounded one, lost in a world he could not control, worthy of pity, not hate. He had a good son and daughter, and other qualities to redeem him, but he remained a bitter old fool until the end. I pray for him.

Oberon and I stuck around for a few days to say goodbye. I learned that Raul's family survived the attack on Cora's estate. It was a miracle, really. They hid in a secret cellar in their little house until it was all over.

Raul has elected to remain close to his family and to Cora, for now. He plans to enroll in university using a scholarship that Cora is erecting in Hector's name. But he told me that once he masters his academic pursuits: sword craft, classical mechanics, and philosophy, he is going to find his brother, and maybe his father too. Not to atone for them, but to forgive them. I believe in him and I wish him the best. But it will not be an easy road.

Cora took the throne without fanfare, and she is as fine a queen as she is a friend and midnight vigilante. Her first act as queen was to feed her people and help rebuild their homes. She did not demand that the rich and powerful in Westfell go hungry, but instead distributed the royal supplies. Many of the nobles followed her example.

This city has had enough of mourning and death. As soon as the funerals were over, the battlefields cleaned, and the people attended to, there was a celebration—the much overdue coronation of Queen Coraline.

There was a great deal of feasting and storytelling, ancient verses recited and prayers offered to gods no longer worshiped. Whiskey flowed freely into glasses, iced down with the frozen hearts of icebergs from the northern shores of distant islands. Twenty-thousand-year-old ice was chipped apart and left to steam and frost in glasses of colored liquors which swirled and glistened in the night. I watched the colors, even tasted some, but I did not drink.

Cora danced the tear dance with Viktor to honor his bravery in the defense of her estate. Though her official duties required most of her time, she danced with Raul also. They remained close to each other for the rest of the night, talking openly, laughing often. It warmed my heart to see them together.

During the post-dinner celebration, I danced with Oberon for the first time. We swayed under the magical lights of the outdoor court, the stars as our audience. As we turned, I could see the mountains, then the valley, the river bright in the moonlight, seemingly impervious to the suffering that had taken place just days before. Lords and ladies, wizards and merchants, soldiers and peasants, danced under the same sky, but we paid them no heed. In my memory, it is only the two of us.

The first dance he was quiet, watching my eyes, teaching me the simplest steps. He was patient, but I could tell he wanted to say something.

"Ava," he said during the second dance. "I am in love with you."

My heart nearly stopped. I said all the wrong things. "How?" I whispered. "You're immortal. And I . . . I'm just a girl."

He held me still for a moment. "Angels, immortals, stars, girls, what holds us apart but words and names for things we don't understand?" In the pause, he turned me, stepping back into the song to diffuse the energy in the air.

"My heart knows you're right," I said. "But I can feel it trembling all the same. I'm afraid, Oberon."

"Afraid of what, your light?" he said. "Ava, you are beautiful and brilliant, the crowning work of the hands that kindled the stars. You are gifted and mysterious and powerful beyond measure. Profoundly compassionate, infinitely wise— you are a captivating woman."

"I love you so much," I said, finally speaking rightly, drawing closer to him, my eyes searching his. "You call yourself a soul, but I think we have a truer name where I come from. Oberon, I think you're an angel."

He led me into a turn and the stars whirled, mingling with the magical lights, blue and gold, green and violet. He bent lightly and kissed me on the lips.

It felt like I imagined it, except harder to believe, like our bodies really are part of our souls, and the things we do with one can move the other. I returned his kiss, gentle and slow, ignoring the steps of the dance.

"Are you a guardian angel?" I asked suddenly. "You came into the world at the same time as me."

"It was my focus to protect you," he said, drawing away, but still holding me. "But this is not like that. Of course I will guard and guide you, but I want more out of life. I want to love you."

My courage flickered. "Can you?"

His dark eyes shined with longing. But he said nothing.

Not wanting to cry, I stepped into his arms and laid my head on his chest, one hand pressed gently against his shirt. "Thank you for tonight. Thank you for yesterday and tomorrow."

He held me for one perfect moment as the song ended. Then I led him to a balcony on the edge of the palace and we talked into the night, sometimes about the future.

Mostly we cherished the small moments, and the delight of being with each other and not being chased all the time. I noticed his smile, which I would normally describe as pensive or distant, came easily, touching his cheeks and the corners of his eyes with a soft radiance. It was, I thought, the most charming smile in the world.

"There are particular aspects of Archeälis which can only be communicated to sensuous beings, Ava," he said as we reclined together. Most of the guests had already gone home. "Before I was corporeal, I was blind to them. But he reveals his magnificence and beauty in the blue of the sky, as seen by eyes, in the taste of honey on my tongue, in the cool storm wind and the rustling of leaves. The way you feel to me right now, your head on my chest, it's the greatest of them all."

"I wish tonight could last forever," I said.

Oberon just held me, his silence echoing my every desire.

That was last night. I can still feel his skin as I traced the lines of his tattoos and fell asleep beside him. The morning came and the day followed in preparation for travel. We acquired all the proper food and clothing for the journey and even a few tools to help rebuild my home.

And now, too soon, the night fades like a dream. Necessity takes over and we hit the road again. I could use the pulsar shard to speed things along, but I don't want to. I need the walk. And what good is rushing through life?

I need time to think, time to mourn my father, and time to renew my spirit. Through the supple leather of my rucksack, I feel the shape of the star-metal urn I made for my father out of the shell of my cocoon. The weight of his ashes is heavy on me. He deserves a proper burial amid the fields he loved, and I need to visit his sister, Mira, in her forest garden and tell her about how he died so she can mourn him, as is his due.

I stand beside Oberon in the war-torn valley as the sun goes down. The city is behind us. The world ahead. I look out toward the pulsar fields, our destination. I look toward where I know the ruins of my cabin still lie, black and smeared by dust and rain. It has been mere weeks since I last saw it, and I feel I've aged years.

We will go back together to the pulsar fields where we entered the world in fire and silence, in the same moment. I will make a life as the guardian of the fields. I do not own them, as a shepherd never owns the ground beneath her feet, but they are mine to watch over.

I have dreamed these past few nights and even walked the pathways of the universe. But for all my searching, I haven't met the goddess again, my other self. I need to find her and talk to her. I need to know who she is and how she lives in me. Maybe she could offer some insight into where I came from, to help me decide where I go.

I look to my right at the strong young man I've grown to love. There's no logic to it, caring for someone so much, but love has its own rules. The far-off look in his eyes reminds me that I still know so little about him, about who he is. He's been quieter than usual today, lost in prayer and rumination, and I think I know why.

"You really have to go, don't you?" I say.

"My focus is fulfilled." He swallows, the words heavy in his mouth. "When we reach the fields, I will step into them, and only Archeälis knows where I go next."

"You have such a faith," I breathe, trying to understand. "You love so well."

Oberon smiles at me, radiantly young and alive, yet older than the eldest stars, a servant to the Great Spirit who is in everything. How hopeful I was to think I could keep him, that his love for me, though undimmed, would overcome the adoration he feels for his maker, would overcome his duty. His heart is mine, but his soul serves another.

When I first saw Oberon, he looked so young and innocent and out of place in that cold tower. I wanted to cradle him like the child he was. It is not like that now. He is no longer a child, but I still want to hold him, now for different reasons. More than that, I want him to hold me.

"He's out there," Oberon says, his voice featureless. "As the guardian of the fields, eventually you will have to confront the Light Eater."

I nod, trying to mask my heartache with strategy. "I need to know what he wants with the Obulans and how he plans to enter the world. If he intends to use the pulsar fields to do it, then I need to stop him."

Oberon shakes his curly head. "I know his kind. It is not a matter of keeping him out of our world. That's not up to us."

Following a series of switchbacks, we come to a lone tree on a hilltop thick with sagebrush. My eyes trace the river to where it curves east toward the sea. "Us?" I ask, my voice searching.

"I do not know where my next focus will call me," he says, touching the gray bark of the tree with his thumb. "But I know we will meet again." Suddenly, his tranquil demeanor cracks with emotion. "Oh Ava, I would move heaven and earth to see you again."

"You said *us*," I breathe, clinging to that shred of hope. "Did you mean it? Or is this all just pretend?"

"Archeälis has chosen me to oppose the Light Eater. The path I walk may take me far from you, far from the created universe, to places where even you cannot follow. But if his evil threatens you again, I will be there."

"I knew it was too good to be true," I say. "Loving you. Why did you tell me you loved me, only to leave?"

"I . . . had to," he falters. "I'd rather you know that I love you, though I will be far away, than wonder. You are and will always be more to me than a focus."

"Don't, please. Not you, too. It wasn't enough. We didn't have enough time."

"Ava." He seems physically shaken. "Leaving you is the hardest thing I've ever had to do."

I touch his shoulder to ease his anxiety, or to salvage my own fractured heart. But I see, beneath the passion of goodbye, he is tranquil as still water. He is at peace with what he has to do, to leave me. Yet even as his back is turned, I've never felt so loved.

"Life is the light between blinking," he says as if sharing a secret. "And I will see you again ere your eyes shut."

As his words blow through me, I lean back against the old, lonely tree, feeling its branches around me, the life in all its leaves. "Oberon, how do you do something you don't want to?"

"Trust," he says simply. "I know that good is coming to me, even if I must be patient."

"Easy for an immortal to say."

"I know the Great Spirit will improve me, and you, if we are humble and listen, if we have the courage to chase his name in the wind."

Oberon's words make me brave. I feel him on the other side of the tree, and reach my fingers around the trunk to grasp his. He squeezes my palm, hard, and I savor the strength in his hand.

Together we gaze out at the valley unfolding to desert and feel the warm breeze on our skin, sweet with first flowers. There must be a thousand shades of blue in the sky, a thousand more in the place between the blue and the rose-petal fires of dusk.

"At least we have this." I hold the vale in my eyes. "This last walk together."

"If we get lost on the way, we could delay our parting another thousand years," Oberon says with the hint of a smile. "My new focus can wait that long, don't you think?"

Somehow, the joke makes me smile. Then I laugh aloud and hug him, breathing the scent of him, leather and cherry smoke and arid wind, feeling his curls on my cheek.

My God, I will miss him. But I will not be alone. I have the pulsar fields, my brothers and sisters in the dust. I have my memories, questions about my past that need answering, and my hope.

The last mysteries are never easy. And here we are, an angel and a fallen star, lost as we were the day we met, hoping to find our own way home.

The Author

Brian Toups was raised on Florida's emerald coast. When not crafting worlds, he enjoys gymnastics, wakeboarding, and ultimate frisbee. His short stories have been featured in *Zetetic* and *Every Day Fiction*. *Star Kin* is his debut novel. To stay tuned on upcoming novels or to discover more of Brian's writing visit: briantoupswrites.com.

Made in the USA
San Bernardino,
CA